W9-ATK-811

Charmed Wishes

Myra Nour
Anya Bast

ELLORA'S CAVE
ROMANTICA PUBLISHING

An Ellora's Cave Romantica Publication

www.ellorascave.com

Charmed Wishes

ISBN #1419954881
ALL RIGHTS RESERVED.
As You Wish © 2004 Myra Nour
Ordinary Charm © 2004 Anya Bast
Edited by Raelene Gorlinsky and Briana St. James.
Cover art by Syneca

Trade paperback Publication: December 2005

With the exception of quotes used in reviews, this book may not be reproduced or used in whole or in part by any means existing without written permission from the publisher, Ellora's Cave Publishing, Inc.® 1056 Home Avenue, Akron OH 44310-3502.

This book is a work of fiction and any resemblance to persons, living or dead, or places, events or locales is purely coincidental. The characters are productions of the author's imagination and used fictitiously.

Warning:

The following material contains graphic sexual content meant for mature readers. *Charmed Wishes* has been rated *E-rotic* by a minimum of three independent reviewers.

Ellora's Cave Publishing offers three levels of Romantica™ reading entertainment: S (S-ensuous), E (E-rotic), and X (X-treme).

S-*ensuous* love scenes are explicit and leave nothing to the imagination.

E-*rotic* love scenes are explicit, leave nothing to the imagination, and are high in volume per the overall word count. In addition, some E-rated titles might contain fantasy material that some readers find objectionable, such as bondage, submission, same sex encounters, forced seductions, etc. E-rated titles are the most graphic titles we carry; it is common, for instance, for an author to use words such as "fucking", "cock", "pussy", etc., within their work of literature.

X-*treme* titles differ from E-rated titles only in plot premise and storyline execution. Unlike E-rated titles, stories designated with the letter X tend to contain controversial subject matter not for the faint of heart.

~ Contents ~

As You Wish

Myra Nour

&

~ *Acknowledgment* ~

so

Thanks to Raelene, my new editor, for being so helpful and talented.

Prologue

ଇର

Once upon a time, long ago in a land far, far away, there was born a girl of extraordinary beauty. Her parents named her Amira, meaning Queen, because she was so lovely and they hoped her future would shine as brightly as her physical appearance.

Fate was not as kind to the fair maiden as her parents had prayed. Her silken, gold hair, delicate face, and slender form drew the attention of not only those who truly loved her, but the unwanted attention of a powerful, evil sorcerer. The wizard Bakr desired the fair maiden and wooed Amira with words plucked from a dead poet's heart, and the finest silk woven by spiders, creatures created with his magic. His final gift was a breathtakingly beautiful rose carved by trolls from blood-red rubies dug from the Earth's belly.

Alas, the fair maiden was in love with a handsome youth named Omar. Being kind in spirit, Amira turned Bakr down gently, but a scorned sorcerer is not to be reckoned with, and the earth trembled as the wizard's anger spewed forth violently.

Bakr strove to create a unique and cruel punishment for the fair Amira, turning her into one of the djinn. She would not be an ordinary djinn, like those who granted three wishes of a new Master, moving on to a new owner each time they were fulfilled. Amira would be forever condemned to stay with a Master throughout his lifetime, fulfilling his or her deepest, darkest sexual desires.

Every djinn is governed by rules, set forth by the Master djinn, Hadji. A powerful sorcerer may succeed in changing the edicts slightly, as Bakr did, adding one specifically tortuous command. Amira was compelled to watch the fulfillment of her Masters' sexual desires while she was forever denied physical release, unless it came by her own hand.

Throughout the endless centuries, Amira lived alone in her lamp, serving countless self-centered Masters, and long ago sickened by their lustful, selfish fantasies. Oftentimes, sorrow overcame her and she dared to dream of the day a caring Master would release her from eternal imprisonment. The fair maiden wept through the centuries and millennia, her tears sparkling like splintering diamonds dropped from a dragon's eye. Would any Master ever fulfill her wish?

Chapter One

ಐ

Nick finished his java at Starbucks, and then started for his car parked down the block. On the way he passed Anne's Antiques and Collectibles, a tiny shop crammed between a Krispy Kreme and Carl's Comics. It was one of those places piled high with flea market finds, mostly junk, but a few jewels managed to shine amongst the clutter. Wryly, he thought the sign should read Anne's *Junk* and Collectibles. Just as many other pedestrians, Nick paused for a few seconds and stared inside, his eyes sliding with disinterest over the items offered for sale.

Strolling on, he halted after he passed a few storefronts, then returned to examine the "collectibles". He didn't know why he was pulled back, but it seemed an irresistible urge. After peering at the crudely made statues and commonplace glassware jammed against each other on several end tables, his gaze landed on an old sofa behind the tables. Shaking his head at himself, it hit Nick why he'd returned. The worn burgundy velvet settee with heavily carved rosettes on the back looked exactly like the one his grandmother had owned and treasured.

Recognition had drawn him back; curiosity pulled him into the shop. Feeling obligated to look around, he browsed the stacked shelves in a few minutes, finding the old cups, saucers, and plates uninteresting. The knick-knacks were not the fine pieces of artwork his grandmother had collected, but rough knockoffs, made in places like Mexico, Korea, and China. Snorting softly to himself, part in disgust at calling such items antiques and part due to the gritty dust that lay over many items, Nick wandered toward the front. His undirected steps took him back to the sofa. He stood behind it and ran a hand along the tattered velvet, its texture evoking memories of flopping on grandmother's settee, his feet propped up on the arm.

Nana would give him a gentle reprimand, but her chuckling smile always softened her firm words. How he'd loved his nana. Shrugging, he turned to leave. Grandmother Adesso was long gone, and sentimentality had no place in his busy life.

An object sitting on the nearest table caught his eye—it stood out starkly against all the junk surrounding it. An old oil lamp, the kind depicted in the Arabian Nights tales. The one found by Aladdin. His thoughts once again flitted back to summers spent at his nana's, how he loved her reading fairy tales to him at bedtime. One of his all time favorites had been Aladdin's Lamp. This lamp was no less dirty and scuffed looking than the collectibles around it, but it had presence. It looked out of place, a fish out of water. He was compelled to go over and examine it and didn't understand his own actions in doing so.

Picking it up, Nick was impressed by its heaviness; perhaps it was better quality than it looked. Black coloration ran rampant on most of its surface, only a few places gave evidence to its metal origin—brass. Flipping it over, he was pleased to find the underside less tarnished. Strange writing scrolled around the circular bottom, some of it obscured due to age or rubbing.

The writing looked Arabic. He knew this because one of his coworkers was from the Middle East, and a secretary had recently asked him to scribble her name in Arabic so she could see what it looked like. After one person had asked, it became the craze in his office—to have Mohammed write everybody's name in Arabic. He'd not asked, or cared, but his personal secretary had taken it upon herself to do it for him, bringing the slip of paper excitedly to him just last week. She was such a sweet elderly woman and thought she'd done something he'd appreciate, and he didn't want to hurt her feelings by showing complete lack of interest. Taking it with a slight smile, Nick had waited until she left before sticking it in a drawer. It'd been totally forgotten until today.

He was shaken from his thoughts when the only shop employee in the place came up to him, putting on a helpful face as she asked the inevitable question, "Can I help you?" A hopeful gleam shone in her eyes and Nick thought she was probably the owner. He had a friend in the antiques business, and even though he sold fine quality items, it was still a tough business.

"I'll take it."

The woman took the lamp from him, walked briskly to the beautiful old cash register and rang up the purchase. Twenty dollars, plus tax, was a pretty good buy. While she wrote out the ticket, his thoughts idled over the lamp. Why am I buying it? He couldn't answer his own question, other than to figure it was a spontaneous purchase, something he didn't normally indulge in.

His busy life was ordered, scheduled, and pigeonholed—except when it came to women. Only with the opposite sex did he enjoy spontaneity, allowing himself the luxury of making instantaneous decisions to go home with someone he'd just met. Vacations were also centered around this impulsive thinking, or not thinking, so to speak. The rest of his life was taken over by controlled thought processes and major decisions. He enjoyed these breaks from the rigors of his career. True, his two-week vacation was chosen carefully—anything from a cruise to a trip to Europe. But once at his destination, he let instinct and feeling take over instead of planning every detail.

The other few weeks he received as hard-won compensation, for all the overtime and responsibilities of his profession, were completely spontaneous. Either he just jumped in his car and drove to a state he'd never visited before, or hopped a flight to a strange destination. Meeting women from around the country was exciting; each state had its own unique flavor. Tanned beauties along the sandy beaches of east, west, and southwest coastlines; dark-eyed Senoritas from the southwest; aggressive career women of the east coast; soft-spoken southern belles; lovely buxom gals from the mid-west; and the athletic women from northeast America—his list could go on and on.

A throat clearing shook him out of his reverie. The middle-aged shopkeeper was gazing at him strangely. He was probably staring into space with a lascivious look on his face. Just thinking of his conquests made him hot. Thanking her politely, he grinned to himself as he left. If the conservative-looking owner knew the true track of his thoughts, she'd probably be mortified.

Once outside, he walked with brisk steps to his yellow Viper, pitching the bag onto the floorboard of the passenger side. Taking off with a more than normal spurt of speed, he headed the long nose of the car toward home.

* * * * *

Without being aware of it, Nick ignored his purchase, perhaps forgot it. The crumpled bag sat on the car floorboard for weeks, until a date exclaimed when her feet landed on it one night. Scrounging beneath her four-inch heeled shoes, he withdrew the bag and took it upstairs with them.

Nick pitched the bag onto a chair once inside and proceeded to move forward with this night's true purpose, to work lovely Diana out of her clothes and her pretend modesty. A sweaty, pleasant sexual session followed, and he outright lied when he promised to call, as they kissed at the door.

At the click of the lock, Nick's thoughts were already on his next conquest, a sweetmeat of a sexy lady who happened to be a new employee. He barely recalled the departing woman's name. Certainly, he had no intention of calling her; one-night stands were more his style. His answering machine would cover him if she phoned, while his well-versed and experienced secretary took care of stray phone calls from the irate females who bothered to call him at the office.

There were women he had longer relationships with, but none of these women were interested in a commitment and their interactions were solely based on both participants attaining sexual satisfaction.

The beer he'd grabbed from the fridge was downed before he noticed the out-of-place brown bag lying in the middle of his favorite leather chair. Annoyed, he picked up the bag and headed for the kitchen. His foot had punched the lever to open the aluminum trashcan when his fingers started to itch.

Chapter Two

℅

Setting the purchase on the green granite countertop, Nick scratched his fingers furiously, and then picked up the crumpled bag. But, then his palm itched like crazy. Scratching his hand until it reddened, he stated out loud, "Okay, you're not going in the trash."

Chuckling at his idiocy, Nick fished the lamp out of the bag and then threw the bag away. This time his palm remained calm. Sitting on the couch, Nick plopped the old lamp on the coffee table. What was it with this ugly thing? Why did he like it?

Everything in his apartment was modern, from his furniture to his abstract paintings, courtesy of an interior designer he'd fucked one weekend. Luckily, she'd been like-minded and demanded no further "dates". Of course she did demand payment for her services, which he agreed with, until he saw the results.

The clean modern lines were all the rage with his business peers. The modern furniture looked cold to him, the predominant white not adding any warmth. He was convinced, too, that whoever created the pieces didn't keep comfort in mind. Personally, he'd preferred a comfy recliner and a thickly padded couch to lounge on. But as a successful investment broker who often had business dinners to host and frequent women visitors, he was forced to keep up appearances. He had to wear the persona that others expected of him, even in his own apartment.

The paintings that hung on his walls were the worst. Nick never understood the globs of paint that flowed or splashed across abstract artwork. They looked like an angry child had painted them.

Nick knew if he were honest with himself and true to his own personal tastes, his apartment would be furnished with antiques. Not the "fru fru" embellishments of his nana, but elegant pieces, such as Queen Anne style.

Picking up the old lamp, Nick blew out a breath. *Maybe that's why I bought this.* Because he really did like its old world charm. But if he were going to keep it as an *objet d'art*, it was going to have to look presentable. Setting it back down on the counter, it took him a few minutes of rambling through his kitchen drawers to locate the polish he'd purchased to clean the sterling silver frame that held that god-awful abstract above his couch. He hated polishing that frame and it usually turned a dark gray before he tackled it. His weekly maid, Maria, would probably polish the frame if he asked. But for some reason, he felt it was his burden to bear.

He read the jar label. Good, it would work for most types of metal, including brass. Thumping his jaw, he stared at the dirty lamp. He needed something to rub the polishing cream on with. Maria brought her own cleaning supplies, so no dirty rags would be left in his apartment. Going quickly to his bedroom, Nick grabbed one of his neatly folded T-shirts. Soft cotton. An ideal polishing cloth.

First, he squirted out a good dab of polish onto the lamp, then spread it with one corner of the shirt. He stuck two fingers under a folded layer of the material and rubbed vigorously. The scrubbed area came out a dark golden-red. It was the lovely patina of old brass.

As Nick examined the cleaned spot, an eruption of blue smoke suddenly shot from the spout. Startled and confounded, Nick flung the lamp away from him. It landed in the middle of the room, in an upright position. Fumes of blue mist billowed from the spout, gliding swiftly upward and forming a tornado shape. Nick sat stunned and immobile.

Abruptly, a dark shape began to solidify within the smoke. A woman's figure. The mist slowly dissipated, leaving a gorgeous young woman standing in front of him, her hands clasped together in a prayerful attitude. She was dressed in a harem outfit, which reminded him of the costume worn by Barbara Eden in that old TV show.

Even her long, silky gold hair was drawn up in a fashion that imitated the TV genie. Her costume was made of velvet and silk, the color a pale blue with navy trimming the edges. Blue fringes hung just below her bust, swinging gently as she moved. An intricately woven silver belt hung low on her hips, resting at the waistline of the pants. She was breathtaking.

"How may I serve you, Master?"

Nick had sat dumbstruck while the smoke erupted from the lamp. At the softly spoken words, his bottom jaw dropped. Was this…could this be real? Finally, sanity returned and he said, "What's going on here?"

The woman's lovely brow knit slightly. "You have called me from the lamp to serve you." Her sweet smile lit her whole face and she gently added, "I am your genie."

"But…but…that's not possible."

"Am I not here?" She cocked her head at him, looking cute and mischievous.

"Yes."

"Do I not look real?" She ran one hand slowly down her sleek thigh.

Nick's throat went dry and his cock hardened instantly. Those luscious curves certainly looked real.

"Of course you look real…but you can't be. There are no such things as genies."

Her chuckle vibrated through him with its feminine appeal.

"Few mortals think we are real, until faced by our essence."

She strolled over to the couch and Nick found himself scrunching down into its hard back.

"Touch me." She held out a delicately shaped hand.

His momentary fright disappeared. He wanted to touch more than just the proffered hand, but restrained himself. Her skin was warm and soft. She felt real.

Coming out of his fugue state, he said firmly, "Wait a minute, this is a joke." Glancing around his living room, he asked, "Are we on Candid Camera?"

Shaking her head and smiling, she said, "No, and you do not really believe that."

She was right. He didn't. No magic mirrors or special effects could make a gorgeous creature slip out of a small lamp in a plume of smoke. "You are an honest to goodness genie?"

Covering a giggle, she responded, "I am, Master, although not always good. But, yes, I am a genie."

"And what should I call you?" He smiled encouragingly.

"Amira."

"A lovely name." His voice had grown husky and his cock hardened just looking at her. His attention refocused on the fact that he was faced by a genie.

"So...you grant me three wishes?"

"No," she shook her head, sending her silken ponytail swishing back and forth. "I grant your wishes as long as you are my Master."

"Really." Nick rubbed his chin. "This is starting to look up." Staring at her lush curves, his thoughts flew here and there. "All right, I wish for a million dollars." He tapped the palm of one hand. "Right here."

"Oh, I'm sorry, Master. I can only grant certain kinds of wishes."

"Wait a minute, you're setting conditions. I thought I was the Master," he chuckled.

"You are." She executed a graceful bow of her head and upper body. "But I am restricted by rules."

Folding his arms, Nick stared at her. "This sounds fishy, but go ahead, give me the bad news. You're probably going to tell me I can only use my wishes for the good of mankind, or maybe I can't wish for things like material gains."

The genie sighed softly. "I wish that were so, Master. I can only grant your sexual desires."

"My sexual wishes?" Nick stared hard at her. Was she serious?

"Yes." Her lovely face was totally serious.

As he leaned back into the couch, Nick's arms gripped his body tight in a self-hug. Congratulatory. She could grant a life-long dream come true? "You're not kidding, are you?"

She shook her head in the negative.

"Anything I wish sexually?"

"Yes," she whispered.

Man, how many of his hot dreams as a youth had been filled with imagining a genie at his disposal? Lots.

Nick's mind was a whirl of possibilities. Any sexual desire? He had so many. He had already managed to fulfill sexual fantasies many men only dreamed of, but still, there had to be some that were out of even his reach. His thoughts latched onto the potential. Finally, his mind was spinning with so many erotic images he had to take a break.

Shaking himself mentally, Nick zoomed in on the very bizarre reality of a genie standing patiently, awaiting his sexual desires. He realized she was the most beautiful woman he'd ever laid eyes on, and he'd known plenty. Those amber eyes matched perfectly with the golden hair that caressed the slender waist. Even her skin matched, with its golden-brown glow. She was a golden goddess.

Suddenly, he knew what he wanted. He wanted to see his genie naked. See if the curls covering her pussy were as golden as the rest of her. He wanted her.

Going up and down her form with his eyes, he could find no fault with the firm, round breasts that were exposed above the low cut bodice of the pearl-trimmed harem top. Her curving waist flared into womanly hips, and he bet her butt was as inviting as her breasts.

Finally his eyes came up to her golden ones. "My wish is to fuck you."

Chapter Three

∞

She breathed out, a barely discernible sound. "That is not possible."

"Why not?" His jaw clenched. He was inexplicably angry at her refusal.

"It is part of my genie code. I can never make love to a Master." Her eyes seemed sad.

"And if I wish it?" he insisted firmly.

She gave him a thoughtful look. "You can command me, Master, but once you reach your pleasure, I will disappear and my lamp along with me."

"Where would you *disappear* to?" That thought was very disturbing to him.

"Nowhere. I will simply cease to exist."

Her lovely eyes gazed back at him, her expression bland, as if she cared not if he wished her out of existence or not.

Nick rubbed his chin. He didn't want this lovely creature to disappear and be destroyed by his selfish wish. No matter how much he wanted her.

"Then I'll have to wish for someone else." Was that relief he saw wash over her features?

His eyes wandered the room, as if seeking help. He zoomed in on three framed photos on an occasional table. One was of his nana, a second of his mom and dad. The third small frame was the one that drew his attention.

It was a younger Nick who stared back at him, his arm draped around Sharon's shoulder. They'd been high school sweethearts, and he'd been deeply in love. Then Sharon had dumped him abruptly for a handsome college boy.

Nick had been broken-hearted, and it'd taken him a long time to get over Sharon. Ever since then he had not let one woman get so close to his heart again.

He smiled sardonically. That was then—over and done with. But he'd still enjoyed fucking Sharon's sleek cheerleader body. Bringing his eyes back to his genie, who stood quietly watching him, he said, "I'd like that girl." He pointed at the photo.

"As you wish." She nodded slightly. "To begin the wish, you must kiss me."

This was becoming more interesting. Nick took two steps and wrapped both arms around her slim waist. His cock pressed into her belly, but she acted as though she didn't notice it.

"Wait."

She placed one hand against his mouth as he leaned down to kiss those delectable lips.

"You need to know how to end the wish."

"End it? Why would I wish to do that?" He could barely think with the soft flesh of her waist pressing into his arms. Of course he was the one doing the pressing.

"You may not be pleased with it."

Not be pleased with his first love? He grinned, but nodded to please her. "Shoot."

"If you decide to end a wish, clap your hands twice and say Amira."

"That's all?"

She nodded, then her amber eyes flitted to his lips and she looked shy again. A becoming flush rose in those golden cheeks. "As you wish."

Inching toward her, he touched her lush lips with the barest movement, then pushed gently into their softness. Their lips molded together in heated contact. She tasted wonderful, like honey and an exotic perfume all mingled together.

His cock pounded. Oh how he hungered for his first wish to be granted. To bury his cock deep into her golden pussy would be heavenly.

He sucked on her bottom lip, but she pushed against his chest. Perhaps his kiss was more invasive than the rules allowed. But he wanted more. He desired her. Barely conscious of his surroundings, Nick reluctantly withdrew his mouth when she shoved hard against his chest.

Nick watched in amazement as the genie dissolved in front of his eyes. Her disappearing act took some getting used to. He waited in anticipation. Would Sharon really appear?

As the blue mist dissipated, another form took shape and it took a few seconds for the woman to be clearly visible.

She was heavy-set with wide hips. Her hair was short brown. He frowned. Who the heck?

"Nick?"

The woman's voice trembled and she looked like she was going to faint.

"Who are you?" he asked, anger at Amira ripping through his body. What kind of tomfoolery was this?

"It's me, Sharon."

"Sharon?" Nick stared at her chubby face. Had his genie dug up another woman named Sharon?

"Nick, we dated in high school."

His heart plummeted to his feet and he turned to stare at the slim girl in the photo, then back at the stranger who claimed to be Sharon.

His girl had long, glorious blonde hair and a skillfully made up face. This woman had none of these attributes.

Her brilliant green eyes drew his gaze. *They* were familiar. A queasy feeling jumped around his stomach.

"Sharon?"

"Yes," she gave a big sigh of relief. "What's going on? Where am I?"

"Amira." Nick clapped his hands twice. He was relieved when she reappeared instantly as she had promised, and Sharon disappeared.

"You were not pleased with your wish, Master?"

Nick's jaw tightened. She looked so darn innocent when she asked that. He folded his arms. "Hardly."

"Was she not your sweetheart?" Amira looked puzzled.

His hands fisted. "It seems so…but that was not the Sharon I wanted."

"Oh?" A twinkle lit her amber eyes.

Nick sighed. It was his fault—he hadn't been specific enough. "I meant the young Sharon in the photo."

"I see." Glancing at the framed picture, she asked, "Do you wish me to conjure her now?"

He stared at the photo. Somehow, knowing what Sharon looked like now spoiled the illusion for him. "No."

He walked over and picked up the frame, musing over how time could change a person so much. He could have been married to her all this time if things had gone like he'd wanted. Would she have looked the same? Or would her life have been different with him, allowing her to stay unchanged?

Nick chuckled. He was being way too philosophical. Just because he looked much the same as his high school days, except for a more mature appearance, didn't mean most of his schoolmates had. Sharon was probably married with three kids, happy, and content to look like a mother. He knew his attitude was a bit snobby, but he kept in shape and never understood why some people let themselves go just because they were married with kids.

"Tell me, will she remember any of this?" He spoke over his shoulder.

"No."

He was glad to hear that. The thought of Sharon recalling this incident was embarrassing somehow.

"Do you desire a new wish, Master?"

He turned and stared at her. "This is going to take some thought." Waving a hand at her, he said, "You may go back to your lamp, if you wish." She nodded, and the next instant her lush body began to dissolve. That was thoroughly unnerving.

Her upper body was still visible when he asked, "Can I finish cleaning the lamp without disturbing you?"

A small smile escaped her full lips. "Yes, I can see you." In a flash, her body was gone, leaving only a funnel of smoke that was sucked swiftly back inside the tiny opening in the lamp.

Something itched at the back of his mind, and he remembered the sad expression that flitted across her angelic face when he informed her she could return to the lamp. He hadn't meant it as a cruelty, but perhaps it was. Maybe she was tired of being cooped up in that thing. Next time, he'd have to invite her to stay, if she wished.

* * * * *

Amira rematerialized into her home, that which had served as such for centuries. It was furnished very comfortably. She could will into being any material object that would make her existence less monotonous.

Flopping on a heavily cushioned ottoman, she waved one hand, opening up the magic window. It was her eye to the outside world. Frustration made her mood sour. How she'd hoped this new Master would take pity on her, invite her to partake of his world. He seemed as selfish and self-centered as most of her past Masters.

She sighed as she watched him move about the kitchen, preparing supper. Seeing him for the first time after she'd been summoned was most painful. He was very handsome, with short black hair, a nice tanned, muscular body and deep, sexy brown eyes. In fact, he looked so much like Omar—for a second she was startled, and wondered if her love from long ago had been reincarnated. He even sported a neatly trimmed mustache, as had her beloved. But the man had shown no recognition, or any of the kindness that had flowed through her beloved Omar.

She laughed as she thought of Nick's wish gone awry. He had not worded his wishes carefully enough. Was it her fault he was dissatisfied with the Sharon of now?

Amira let out a deep breath. Truly, her new Master seemed no different than other Masters before him, except for his similarity in looks to Omar.

Chapter Four

೮೦

Nick thought long and hard about his wishes. He tossed restlessly all night. Much of that time was spent in convincing himself that he had a real genie at his disposal. And she could fulfill any sexual desire he had. What else could a young bachelor want?

For a fleeting moment, he recalled the hands-off policy of the genie. He was missing out on a jewel. The next instant, he gleefully thought of all the erotic fantasies he could wish for. The genie's rules and her situation fled from his mind.

The next morning was Saturday. He had the whole weekend to play, and knew exactly how he would fill it. Not sure how to approach the genie, he hesitated at rubbing the lamp. Shrugging, Nick lifted the small lid and spoke into the dark interior.

"Hello." He paused. "Good morning, genie."

A small puff of blue smoke seeped from the tip and he backed off. The genie emerged just as beautifully as she had yesterday. Her slender curves materialized slowly within the clasp of misty covering. Today she was dressed in gold satin and looked good enough to eat.

"Good morning, Master." Her voice was smooth as cream and slid over him, exciting his senses.

"Can we dispense with the Master? Call me Nick."

"Yes, Mas—." She stopped and smiled. "Nick."

"See, I didn't change and neither did you. You're just as beautiful as you were yesterday."

She blushed and he was momentarily taken aback by her modesty. It was really too bad about those genie rules.

Folding his arms, he said, "I've chosen my wish…at least for this weekend." At her quiet look that expressed no curiosity whatsoever, he added, "I want a harem. I want to be the sheik, or whatever those guys are called." He thumped his jaw with one finger. "And I don't want to worry about diseases and condoms."

She didn't do an attractive *I Dream of Jeannie* blink, fold her arms, or change expression one bit. Neither did she make a move toward him.

Nick stepped into her personal space, placing his arms about her slim waist. Their kiss today was rather chaste, maybe because he was anxious to get straight to his erotic fantasy. They parted after a mere pressing together of their lips. Amira said, "As you wish."

As soon as he stepped away from her, the room spun in a disorienting fashion and his vision blurred. When it cleared, he was standing in the middle of an enormous room. Arches with marble columns ran the perimeter of the area. Along the edge of each arch were detailed carvings. Between the columns, a two-foot-high, heavily carved stone lattice formed a fence.

His bare feet felt cold. Glancing down, Nick admired the intricate, colorful mosaics of the stones. He definitely wasn't in Kansas anymore.

A shimmer of reflective light caught his eye as it played over an alcove, draped on either side with transparent curtains. Forms stood in the shadow. Feminine forms.

As if sensing his attention like a conductive signal, women stepped as one mass from the covering duskiness.

Nick's eyes ran over one magnificent body after another. He stopped counting after a few dozen. The sexy harem costumes with matching jewelry glittering had been what caught his attention.

The bright colors of their outfits—red, royal blue, deep yellow, dark purple, and dusky rose—in velvet, silk, and satin, overwhelmed the senses. Sapphires, rubies, emeralds, and diamonds fell from elegant necks and draped bountiful bosoms. The material and jewelry still couldn't match the sleek beauty of their varied forms—from dark olive skinned beauties, to glowing skin as pale as an Irish lass'. There were large breasts, with womanly hips to match, slim forms of delicate proportion, and everything in between.

Inky locks, rich auburn, and golden blonde flowing hair adorned a variety of lush bodies.

Nick stood stunned. Even he couldn't have dreamed up such diversity of voluptuous beauties. His genie had outdone herself.

His cock hurt. Glancing down, Nick was surprised by his appearance. Ballooning harem pants covered his legs, and a green velvet vest, trimmed in gold braid, hung on his chest. It was a bit gaudy, more like the cheap outfits you found in a costume shop, and he briefly wondered if Amira had played a mischievous trick on him.

Soft footsteps drew his eyes upward. He was surrounded on all sides by perfumed feminine flesh. Gulping, Nick stared around him, not sure what to do.

"How may we serve you, Master?" An olive-skinned beauty with jet-black hair that fell in a straight sheen to her hips addressed him.

"I want to be pleasured." He folded his arms and tried to look masterful.

A ripple of excited giggles met his words. He felt the ring of eyes around him like a physical force, as if they stripped him merely by looking. Impossibly, his cock became harder.

"Choose she who shall receive your favor." The black eyes of the woman, who seemed to be the leader, probed him. They asked to be chosen.

"Why… all of you, of course." He grinned at their astonished faces. "How could I leave even one delectable bloom among the beautiful garden — untouched."

Soft sighs and a volley of tinkling giggles erupted from his glib answer.

"This way, Master." The dark haired beauty waved toward the alcove. A corridor opened among the rows of succulent flesh.

Nick followed her to the alcove; clearly it was a bedroom. A huge round bed took up the center. It was piled with pillows of every color and fabric, while the sheets were a blood red satin.

The woman nodded at the bed and Nick sat on one edge. The harem beauties surrounded the bed, eyeing him with lust. His cock was throbbing.

The leader gave another nod and all the women began to disrobe. Nick watched a blonde who looked remarkably like Jeannie pull her top off. She stood proudly, allowing his eyes to take in those round globes of flesh with tiny rosebud tips. Then she hooked her fingers in the low-slung waistband and shoved the pants down. Nick's mouth went dry, as sleek, completely denuded pussy lips were uncovered.

A shifting to either side made him realize he was missing the rest of the show. He stared to his right, captivated by the ivory statuesque loveliness of a fair redhead. She looked like strawberry and cream, and he wondered what she'd taste like.

Withdrawing his gaze reluctantly, he watched the dusky leader undress. Her lush curves could have easily graced a girlie magazine in the 1950's. Full hips and large breasts with large, dark brown nipples made his mouth water.

Maybe she was a little overblown according to modern day standards, but Nick thought voluptuous beauty suited her just right. Her olive skin was satiny smooth and seemed to beg for a man's touch. The pouting pussy lips were dark and entreating. Would her cream be as rich and full as her body?

Movement on all sides drew his eyes away. All the women were nude. Nick turned to one side, then the other, and switched his gaze to those kneeling on the bed behind him. He'd died and gone to a man's lustful heaven, for celestial bodies surrounded him.

Chapter Five

 හ

With a collective sigh, the women edged closer, until his body pitched backward. He sank into the soft mattress, groaning as eager hands pulled off his clothes.

Warm, perfumed flesh rubbed against every part of his body. Silken hair flowed over his cock while breasts were pushed gently against his balls. Full lips kissed him for a brief second, then a plump breast was shoved into his waiting mouth.

Hands, everywhere at once, caressing and kneading. His hands were busy as well, squeezing globes of flesh, breasts and butts alike as they neared him. Sighs and giggles ebbed and flowed, as did the bodies around him.

Two tongues licked either side of his cock, while a hot mouth teased the head. He was pulsing, aching to thrust it into receptive womanly flesh. But not yet. His legs spread unconsciously as another tongue lapped his balls.

His face was buried in a pussy, he had no idea which woman it was, and it didn't really matter. She tasted delicious— musky and salty.

"Give us a chance." One woman's strident voice called.

"Yes," a shrill voice erupted. "Move over."

More voices rose in protest and those around him snapped at their sisters. Was there a catfight about to break out? Nick tried to shove aside the wet lips wiggling over his mouth, but she seemed glued to his face.

He felt a flow of flesh shove onto his body, more than had been earlier. The weight of many bodies was suffocating.

It was too much. It felt like he was drowning in flesh.

The woman who had been shoving her pussy at his face spat at another woman, then leapt off him. Nick shoved yielding boobs and buttocks away desperately, clearing enough space to clap and gasp, "Amira."

The room and women disappeared, and he was faced by the genie.

"You were pleased by your harem, Master?"

"Do you watch the fulfillment of my wishes?" he asked gruffly.

A slight flush rose in her cheeks, then she nodded. "It is part of my…duty."

Nick heard the hesitation in her words and wondered what she'd meant to say. "So, you get to watch the action, but a Master can never make love to you. That must be torture." He saw the her eyes flicker with deep emotion before she glanced elsewhere to escape his gaze. Nick knew he'd hit on a deep emotional issue for her. He rubbed his jaw in thought before asking, "So how do you get pleasure?"

Her cheeks blushed again. "I can give myself release, but never can I participate in the pleasure between two people."

Poor Amira, she truly is a tortured soul. Disturbed by his thoughts, he purposely turned his mind back to his wish.

"If you have to watch my wishes, then you know that too much of a good thing can be overwhelming." A quirk of her full lips made him question her motives.

"Exactly how many women did you wish up?" He felt really aggravated with her and wanted to snap at her like the women had done at one another. He calmed himself with a strenuous effort. Deep inside he knew her tale has stirred his emotions and his irritability was but a way to deal with his pity at her condition.

"One hundred."

"One hundred!" he repeated, dumbfounded.

"So many women are too much for my Master's virility?" Her golden eyes definitely had a mischievous light flicker through them.

Normally, Nick would find a slander to his manhood insulting, but these were certainly not ordinary circumstances. "Of course there were too many."

"Would you like to change your wish?"

"First, I need a break." Nick flopped in his chair. He was too wrung out from being nearly drowned by woman flesh to stay aggravated with her. "Would you be a love and bring me a beer from the fridge?"

Amira cocked her head and smiled.

After a few seconds, he snapped his fingers. "Sorry, forgot, you only grant sexual wishes." Getting up with an exaggerated groan that drew a giggle from her, Nick took a beer and flopped down on the chair again.

One swig went down smoothly before he realized Amira was staring at him. Awaiting his orders, he guessed. For some reason it was disconcerting.

Waving the can at her, he said, "Why don't you go in the kitchen and get yourself something to eat."

She shrugged and her plump breasts moved against the velvety fabric. Suddenly, Nick knew what he wished he could have. Her. She would shine like a brilliant diamond among the multicolored beauties of the harem.

Nick sipped the beer and watched Amira as she pulled drawers open and peeked in cabinets. After a moment, he realized she was exploring, not looking for food. She'd stared into the pantry and picked up a few boxes, but then went back to the drawers. Maybe genies didn't eat.

She giggled as she held up a pizza cutter, rolling the ragged, blunt blade along the counter. Tiring of that, the toaster grabbed her attention. She pushed the levers up and down. Her laughter ripped through him, setting his pulse racing. Strange, that her simple actions excited him so.

How long had it been since Amira had been in a kitchen? This made Nick sad. How long, too, had she been cooped up in that tiny lamp?

Shaking off his mood, he called her back into the living room. "I've decided on my new, improved wish."

She strolled back to stand in front of him, her eyes bubbling with mirth. "Perhaps fifty women?"

Amira's lips were quivering and he couldn't fuss at her, she was far too charming. Besides, everyone knew you had to be careful what you wished from a genie. He was going to have to be more specific.

"I think three women will be plenty." He stared at her now serious expression. "To be specific, I'd like the black-haired leader and the blonde who looks like Jeannie."

"Jeannie?" she interrupted him.

"From *I Dream of Jeannie*. Are you familiar with the show?"

That impish smile tugged at her lips again. "How do you think I created her, Master?"

"Nick."

He tried to read her expression, but it was bland. "You mean that you know that I love that show?"

"I know you have desired Jeannie for many years."

"What hot-blooded young male hasn't?" he muttered.

Television lovelies. A world of possibilities opened to him. His thoughts shot to Sam on *Bewitched*, and the leather-clad beauty in *The Avengers*.

"And the other?" Amira asked.

It took him a few seconds to realize what she meant. The third woman he desired to fulfill his wish. "The redhead, the one who looks like an alabaster statue."

That golden head cocked mischievously. "There were twenty-five with red hair."

"The one I watched disrobe, after the blonde." He knew from her earlier admittance, she'd watched him with the harem. His cock sprang to attention, and it wasn't the thought of any of the harem beauties that caused it. The thought of Amira watching his antics with all those women made him horny as hell. It was the swiftest turn-on he'd ever received from a mere thought.

Nick switched to a new track in his head. He was crouched over a female form, his cock plunging into a luscious, wet pussy. Dozens of feminine hands, boobs, and thighs rubbed his body, as well as stroked the beauty beneath him.

The tide of flesh parted, and Amira's sultry face was uncovered. He groaned aloud.

"Master?"

Nick shook himself mentally. Fluid leaked from his cock head just at the thought of fucking his genie? It was a surprising thing.

"Nothing," he mumbled. He jumped up and placed his arms around her for the magic kiss. He needed to move on quickly to this new wish. Desiring the impossible did not make sense.

His cock pushed against Amira hard. This time she definitely noticed. A rosy blush hit her cheeks and her eyes closed just before he kissed her.

It was he who broke the kiss this time. His cock was thrumming painfully, and demanding something he couldn't supply it.

His eyes blurred and he smelled Amira's unique perfume surround him as his disorientation dissolved. He was back on the bed, and three gorgeous goddesses crawled across it toward him.

Chapter Six

Amira knew it was quite wicked for her to play such a trick on her new Master. Not that she hadn't played with her Masters' wishes in the past, or that it was not allowed under the genie rules. The laws were lax in this area, allowing rise to some very nasty tricks djinn played on unsuspecting Masters.

She had tricked Masters in the past—some because she was bored, others to teach them a lesson about their selfish desires. And a few had been done because she was fond of those particular Masters and it was her way of teasing them. There had been pitiful few of these.

Amira analyzed her actions, something she was used to doing after serving a psychiatrist for many years. Now he had been a sexual deviant, but he was not a cruel Master, and had taught her much about herself.

She couldn't say she was fond of Nick yet, she'd not been with him long enough, neither was she bored by him. Was it to teach him a lesson?

The more Amira thought about it, the more she was convinced that was at the core of her trickery. He was self-centered in ways, and seemed bent on his own pleasures. She'd watched him for days while she waited for him to accidentally release her. She'd learned much of Nick and his libidinous ways. He was what the modern age called a playboy. Yet, she sensed more depth lay beneath his charming exterior.

Amira had lived enough centuries that she'd developed almost a sixth sense for how people worked. She liked to call it hunches. She had a feeling Nick could be a much better man than the one he displayed for the world. Perhaps be more sensitive and caring. Maybe he could learn to love and appreciate women.

She shivered and hugged her body. Perhaps what truly lay at the bottom of her interest was her own desire. Her desire for freedom and love.

Amira stared gloomily at the magic window. It was shuttered and dark. Should she open it, peer once again into the harem? With a disgusted snort at herself, she waved it open.

Of course I should see my Master in all his sexual glory, for surely I am fooling myself with wishful thinking.

Although part of Amira's punishment was to watch her Master's wish fulfilled, she'd already watched the first part. She was not required to watch the whole thing. But she wanted to.

Nick was sprawled on his back in the middle of the immense bed. His cock was buried in the dark-skinned woman's pussy, as she rode atop him with a sultry expression on her face.

The blonde crouched over Nick's face and he licked at her pale pink lower lips furiously. The pale redhead knelt by his side, tonguing one male nipple, while her long painted nails gently stroked his balls.

Nick caressed one small breast of the auburn-haired beauty, while his other hand squeezed a butt cheek of the olive woman riding him.

All four groaned and moaned so much it vibrated through Amira, even shielded behind the window. The sight of their beautiful bodies undulating made her desire burst forth. Her pussy was moist and aching.

Without further thought, Amira made her clothes disappear and then blinked a bottle of strawberry scented oil into her palm. If she could not join in their pleasures, she could at least give herself an orgasm. It was all she had, all she was allowed.

Amira poured a good quantity of oil in one palm, and spread it on her breasts. Her nipples hardened beneath her strokes.

As the action on the harem bed continued, she slid a hand down her belly, while the other kneaded one breast.

Nick was now kneeling behind the slim hips of the redhead. His cock rammed into her pink lips. The blonde lay spread-eagled in front of the woman Nick fucked, while the auburn head was buried in the blonde's pussy. Both women moaned.

The dark woman knelt behind Nick, rubbing her breasts over his back, her hands caressing his thighs.

Amira slipped one finger into her folds, stroking herself as she watched. How she wished she were on the receiving end of Nick's large cock.

Pushing her hips forward, she thrust her middle finger inside her wet channel, and then rocked her hips back and forth.

Her breathing increased as she imagined his cock plunging into her softness, instead of her finger.

The foursome seemed to go on and on. The figures switched places frequently. Mouths were licking clits or sucking Nick's cock. Or Nick was alternately fucking and sucking at feminine flesh at the same time.

Amira groaned, her pleasure escalating along with the thrashing bodies. The blonde screamed as Nick's cock plunged into her, and he groaned loudly. The other two women were performing sixty-nine on each other, their lithe bodies writhing as they too climaxed.

As the orgasm rippled through her, Amira imagined Nick's mouth on her pussy. She thrust her hips forward as the imaginary lover thrust his tongue into her folds. The orgasm was strong and beat for several seconds through her clit.

Afterwards, she stretched out on the cushioned couch, drifting off into a half-sleep. Later, noises awoke her and drew her gaze to the bodies on the bed. They were back in action, stroking, fucking, and sucking.

Sighing, Amira waved the window shut. The thought of Nick enjoying the three lovely women again saddened her.

Getting up, she stepped into her bathroom, then into a bubbling tub, soaking for hours, it seemed. After the Jacuzzi, she felt restless. Walking into the lush garden adjacent to her main room, she spent the rest of the day wandering through its fragrant beauty. It soothed her enough that she was able to sleep that night.

Amira's body didn't require sleep, but she found it a pleasant habit left over from her human days. And it helped pass the time. There'd been stretches when she'd slept through centuries, awaiting a new Master.

No matter how wonderful her magic world was within the lamp, she got bored. The genie rules and magic gifted to her allowed her to create any number of rooms to keep herself entertained — gardens, luxurious baths, exotic bedrooms, and so on. She could even conjure up a woodland scene with a babbling brook, if she wanted.

But, she couldn't create human companionship. The one thing she desired above all else. She got tired of rearranging her living room in order to occupy herself. It had been through many changes through the years. Once, she'd been charmed by the Victorian age and surrounded herself with the embellishments of that period.

She went through a long period of being in love with Roman architecture. Marble columns and rich mosaic floors made her abode look like a palace.

Right now, her main room was decorated in Arabic style. She always returned to her origins. It made her feel more in touch with her long-lost human side. Amira flopped onto an ottoman, frittering away the rest of the evening reading romance novels.

The next day, the four people went at each other off and on all day. Amira peeked in on them occasionally, but had lost her intense interest in watching the sexual activities.

In boredom, she flipped on the television and watched old movies and series.

With relief, later that evening, she heard Nick's call. Amira materialized in front of him. Nick was nude. He looked glorious and tired. She averted her eyes from his flaccid cock. Just looking at it started such a hunger in her loins that it was painful.

"Thanks for a wonderful weekend." He grinned, and then headed for the kitchen.

She watched him make a sandwich. She'd made sure there was an assortment of delicious food in the harem, but Nick and the women had probably finished it off today.

He walked stiff-legged toward her, a coke in one hand.

"I'm going to shower, then go to bed." He paused and stared at her. Waving one hand at the room, he added, "You can stay and watch TV if you want."

Amira nodded, but returned to her home after he disappeared into the bedroom. If she watched another program, she'd be ready to pull her hair out. It was not what she wanted.

After settling into the softness of her bed, she realized what she did want. Human company. To talk, laugh, and share stories. She sighed and hugged her pillow.

"He's not Omar," she mumbled. She must quit connecting the two. It made her miss Omar with a fierceness she'd not felt in centuries.

The next few days, Nick returned home from work late and did paperwork at his desk for hours. He completely ignored her lamp, as if he'd forgotten her.

Chapter Seven

∞

On Thursday evening, Nick pitched his briefcase on the coffee table and sank into his favorite chair. He was glad he was done with all the paperwork for a new client. Normally, he wouldn't mind extra work brought home, but he was still tired from the orgy this past weekend.

Even though he worked out at a gym several times a week and played racquetball regularly with friends, those sexual sessions had been exhausting. He grinned. A fellow would have to be Hercules to not be completely wrung out.

Oh, he'd enjoyed every luscious second, but it'd be a while before he indulged his senses that much again. Nick stared at the lamp. He'd dismissed Amira from his thoughts the last few days.

What did she do in that tiny thing for days on end? He strolled over to it, his hand lingering near the handle. Should he call her? Would he be required to make a wish if he did?

The last thing he wanted right now was a sexual circus. He went into the kitchen, fetching chips and coke. He stood in the doorway and contemplated the lamp.

The nagging thought of poor Amira stuck in the lamp made his decision for him. Picking up the top, as he'd done last time, he said, "Amira?"

Backing off quickly, he watched with interest as she appeared. His heart sped up. Why, he didn't have a clue. Certainly, he wasn't afraid of her.

"How may I serve you, Master?"

Was it his imagination, or did his genie look drawn and sad?

"I have no sexual wish, if that's what you mean."

A confused expression overcame her delicate face.

Nick grinned. "I thought you might need to stretch your legs…and I wouldn't mind some company tonight."

Her lovely brow cleared and a slight smile lingered on her lush lips but a second, and then just as quickly disappeared.

Now he was puzzled. Did the *almost* smile mean she was pleased by his invitation? Or did the swift dissolution of that smile mean she did not care to keep him company?

"I was going to cook supper." He paused and waved an arm toward the kitchen. "I thought we could talk while I cook, or you can help—if you wish."

She nodded and followed him into the spacious kitchen. Nick gathered everything he needed to make homemade spaghetti. The kind his nana had taught him.

Amira sat on a bar stool and watched him. Unsure what he should discuss with a magical being, Nick began telling her about his client. A rich old man who was married to a younger woman he couldn't keep up with.

She laughed. "I have had many Masters like that."

"Have you?" Nick glanced at her thoughtfully as he rolled ingredients into meatballs. "How many masters have you had?"

Amira stared at him, her eyes glazing. "Too many." She shook her head. "I cannot remember the number."

"That's all right. It was a rhetorical question anyway." He chuckled.

"What?"

"I meant—it really doesn't matter."

Her squished-up nose was too darn cute. Nick leaned over the counter and dropped a quick peck to it.

Her expression couldn't have been more stunned than if he'd slugged her. Nick was appalled that no Master had apparently ever shown this wonderful woman affection. Take. That's probably all they ever did.

Sexual desires and wishes. Nick almost sliced his finger cutting a tomato. He too was now counted among that number. Would she remember him when their time was over?

"Let me help." She placed a hand over his and pried the knife from him.

Nick set mushrooms and the remaining tomatoes in front of her while he gathered other ingredients. He watched as she smoothly chopped the vegetables.

"You like to cook?"

Her eyes flitted up, twinkling merrily, her lips quirking. "Not really, I usually burned the food when father insisted…that is, before I became djinn." She sliced into a juicy tomato and took a bite. "Delicious." Picking up the remaining piece, she held it out toward him.

Nick hesitated for a second, but he took the tomato from her hand with his mouth, flicking up a drop of juice that ran down her finger. Amira took a sharp breath, her eyes dipping to her work.

Idiot! Hadn't he figured out by now that sexual teasing was torture for his poor genie? To feel, taste, and smell sensual pleasures all around you, but never to partake of them was cruel.

"The guy who cursed you must have been a supreme asshole." His stomach had tightened seconds ago with the sensual tension between them, but now he felt only boiling anger.

Amira's cheeks flushed and her lovely golden eyes came back to his. She didn't say a word, but her eyes spoke volumes. Suddenly, Nick wished he had the bastard right here in front of him. His fists balled as he imagined punching the jerk until he was senseless.

"The sauce smells wonderful."

Her abrupt switch in topics told him she did not wish to discuss it further. Nick turned and stirred the sauce. "Hand those to me, hon." He kept them both busy preparing and cooking dinner.

As he worked, he changed the topic to safe ground—his grandmother. Amira's delighted giggles at shared childhood escapades hit his senses almost as strongly as the erotic tingles that'd erupted when he'd taken the tomato from her hand. How he loved to hear her laugh.

After everything was ready, Amira helped him set the table. She dipped her eyes shyly as he directed her to add another setting. Clearly, she hadn't expected to be invited to dine with him.

Standing by the table, he rubbed his jaw and stared at her satin costume. All pink today. She looked like a tasty confection, waiting to be consumed. "Maybe you'd better change into something more casual…spaghetti sauce has a habit of spotting one's clothes."

She smiled. "One Master showed me the twirling method." She used her hands to make the motions.

"True," he nodded. "But it's not nearly as fun as just diving in and enjoying it." He grinned at her. "That's why I never order spaghetti in restaurants."

With a wave, Amira's harem costume disappeared and new clothes draped her curvaceous body. Nick sucked in his breath. Tight jeans hugged her legs and hips, while a simple red T-shirt clung to her breasts. She looked like an all-American girl and so damn sexy his cock came to attention immediately.

Clearing his throat, Nick pulled out a chair and bowed. "My lady."

Amira's eyes sparkled like amber diamonds as she eased into the chair. Nick piled their plates full, then poured wine for them both.

"You like wine, I hope?"

She nodded, and then ran one hand over the basket-covered bottom of the bottle. "I like it...wine reminds me of older days."

"Me too. Nana never drank anything but wine from her homeland — Tuscany." He held up his glass toward her and they clinked in a toast. "Taste it, the best imported Chianti I can find."

"Mmm. Wonderful."

Nick twirled a loose forkful of spaghetti. "And my cooking?"

Amira leaned over and forked a mouthful. "Mmmm."

He laughed and attacked his food with gusto. Amira followed his example, not worrying when sauce droplets fell on her shirt. By the time they finished the meal, the wine had been polished off as well. Nick was feeling very happy, and Amira giggled more than he would have guessed she would allow herself.

Grabbing her hand, he tugged her into the living room, pulling her down beside him on the couch. Nick flipped the TV on, gratified when he found a Jeannie rerun. Amira sighed in exasperation, but didn't protest when Nick gently pushed her head down onto his shoulder.

She snuggled into a comfortable position and they watched a double rerun special. When a commercial blared, Nick glanced at Amira. She'd been quiet for minutes and he could hear her soft breathing. Tipping her face up, he was not surprised to find her sound asleep.

"Sleep, my angel," he whispered, kissing her lips softly.

Chapter Eight

∞

Amira awoke completely disoriented. It took her several seconds to realize she was clasped in her Master's arms. They must have fallen asleep after drinking the delicious wine. Sometime during the night, they'd fallen flat on the wide couch and readjusted their bodies. Nick's arms were still about her waist, while her head rested on his hard chest.

She could have lain thus for another century. She listened to his strong heartbeat. How nice he'd been to her last night. Treated her like a regular mortal. She sighed. It was but one night. Magical in its own way, but not a real part of her life.

She was djinn. A creature condemned to an eternity of service.

Amira glanced up at his sleeping features. How handsome he was. So much like Omar, it was painful to look at him. Should she stay in his arms? Let him awaken and find her there?

She blinked back tears. Perhaps her Master would feel sorry for her, like he seemed to be indicating with his behavior. He would show her kindness when it suited him. But love? She doubted it. Hadn't she kept hope alive through many centuries that love would bloom between her and a Master?

The thought of love between her and Nick made her chest ache. She was already enthralled with his looks; she couldn't help it. She had tried her best to keep her distance emotionally, to see him only as another selfish Master bent on his own pleasure. But last night had blown that fragile concept.

What could come of such wishes? Amira's mind went back over the Masters who had been promising, those with some kindness in their hearts. When it came down to it, they had chosen to pursue their own delights rather than be tied down to one woman.

She glanced back up Nick's hard chest to his square jaw. He had been a playboy when he called her forth, a man used to pleasures of the flesh. The likelihood of him choosing one woman over many seemed as questionable as wishing dragons still ruled the skies.

Nothing could come of her wishing otherwise. Nothing but a broken heart, torn anew after so much time had partially healed it. Biting her lower lip, Amira blinked, dissolving in Nick's arms.

He mumbled, but did not awaken, as she poured her dematerialized body down the lamp's spout.

* * * * *

Nick was surprised when he awoke sprawled on the couch. He'd never done that before. Running his hand through his hair, he recalled last night. Amira, spaghetti, and too much wine.

He glanced down, half expecting to see her golden head on his chest. Had that been a dream? Picking up a strand of gold hair several feet in length, he realized she had been clasped in his arms. He smiled, remembering how good she'd felt there.

Where was she? He glanced toward the kitchen. Not there. His eyes shot to the lamp. Somehow, he knew that's where she'd fled. Now, where did that thought come from?

Nick sat up and stared at the genie's abode. She'd enjoyed being in his arms; he clearly recalled that now. Then why had she run back to the lamp first thing in the morning?

Because, he answered himself…maybe she's wise enough to know it's not a good thing. This getting so close to a being that shouldn't even be real, but was.

Placing his hands on either side of his temples, he rubbed vigorously. "What's the matter with me, acting like a teenager in love—with my genie!"

This was useless. He had to get his mind on other matters.

Luckily for Nick, he'd taken today off. He needed to get out of the apartment, clear his mind. Exercise would do the trick. He packed his gym bag and grabbed a protein bar on the way out.

Pumping iron and playing a few rounds of strenuous racquetball was good for his mind as well as his body. It seemed easier to think about nothing while he lifted weights. It worked, until a lithe blonde in shorts that teased him with brief views of her tight butt drew his thoughts to sex.

Walking away in disgust, Nick went to the steam room. Sweating in the heated room soon distracted his mind from sensual pleasures.

When he left, he still wasn't ready to go home. Instead, he headed for the Gulf, driving mindlessly for hours, up one street and down another, not really enjoying the tall palm trees and lush vegetation.

It was nightfall by the time he returned. He was tired and grumpy. He'd taken a shower in the gym, so he pitched his bag to the side and fell onto his bed still clothed. Sleep overtook him like a sledgehammer.

The next morning he walked by the lamp several times, staring at it mindlessly. Finally, he stopped in front of it and struck one fist into the other.

"She is mine. My genie, to do with as I wish." Wondering if Amira had heard his rude statement, he felt shame and turned away.

A Victoria's Secret lingerie catalog caught his attention. Left there by his latest conquest, the one before he found Amira. She'd been showing him teddies and trying to get his opinion on which to purchase for their pleasure.

Flipping through the magazine, he found the slim blonde with big boobs that had caught his attention. She was gorgeous. Just what he needed to take his mind off his genie.

"Amira," Nick commanded, standing near the couch.

She materialized. Today, she wore all white, from the velvety fabric to the small seed pearls trimming her top. She looked like the angel he'd called her two nights ago. Her eyes were red-rimmed. Had she been crying? That thought made him very uncomfortable.

"I am ready for a wish." His voice came out rougher than he intended.

"Yes, Master." Her tone was unsure, her expression puzzled.

Flapping the magazine at her, he pointed, "I want this woman for this weekend."

Amira gazed at the photo. "She is most lovely." Her golden eyes came up to meet his stare. "Do you wish the same conditions?"

"Huh?"

"No disease or condoms." Her expression didn't change a bit as she repeated his earlier statement.

"Right. Just tag that onto any wish I give you from now on." He folded his arms, trying to act impatient, even though he really wasn't. What he felt was a desire to stay with her, wrap his arms about her again and feel her snuggle into his body.

"Well?" He'd better get on with this wish, anything to distract him from desiring Amira.

"As you wish," she whispered.

Her eyes dipped down as she approached him for the kiss. Grasping her chin, he brought her face up, noting the long lashes lying against her skin. She was refusing to look at him. Fine. He felt the same way.

Amira's perfume invaded his senses as she dissolved, and a new form materialized. It was Rachel. She was wearing the same white teddy as the magazine ad.

"Oh, hello, you must be Nick."

He was surprised that the supermodel seemed to know him. "Have we met?" How could he have forgotten that?

She giggled. Not Amira's gentle exhalation that set his senses aflame, but a sharp note that grated on his nerves.

"Amira told me about you." She paused and knitted her brow. "I can't remember where I was, but she set up this blind date."

"Doesn't matter," he shrugged. "You're here now." He cleared his throat. "What...do you want to do?" He hadn't expected a date—this was kind of awkward.

Another loud giggle erupted and Rachel ran one long-fingered hand down a sleek thigh, drawing his eyes to her barely covered groin.

"It seems I intended this to be an evening of sex." She ran a hand down her hair, not mussing her shiny tresses a bit. "But, I don't remember leaving the house like this."

Nick walked up to her. "Does it matter how you got here?" He placed one hand on her collarbone and rubbed her neck. "I'm all for a night of hot sex."

Chapter Nine

ꝏ

Her mouth opened and he quickly placed a finger over her full lips to stop any further jarring giggles. Then he replaced his finger with his mouth, shutting off any further comments. He didn't care to hear her thoughts on the matter. He wanted to fuck.

Her arms came up and latched onto his neck like an octopus. Her mouth was hot and sweet, her tongue felt like a snake inside his mouth, slithering over his tongue with forceful thrusts. Nick didn't know where that strange thought came from, but shoved it from his mind, concentrating on her slim curves.

His hands rubbed and kneaded her tiny ass, and then he pulled her hips against his erection. She sighed into his mouth and he was thankful it wasn't a giggle. Untangling her arms, he picked her up and carried her into the bedroom.

As he passed the lamp, a swift thought flashed through him. Would Amira still be able to see him in his bedroom? Probably. That thought made his cock throb even more, but also caused a flash of guilt to run through him. That was really odd and he thrust such a strange emotion from him.

After he placed Rachel on the satin comforter, she stretched like a cat, drawing his eyes to those lush breasts. His hands went to the tiny straps and he pushed them down, none too gently. Both round breasts popped out, barely bouncing.

Even while he grasped a firm breast in each hand, disappointment flashed through him. Implants. Nice looking, even felt almost real. But he preferred natural to *fixed*, even if the woman's breasts were somewhat droopy due to their size.

Ignoring his feelings, Nick leaned down and latched onto one pink nipple, sucking gently. He played with the other nipple, rolling it between two fingers. Rachel groaned loudly and flounced restlessly.

"Oh, yes, baby, fuck me," she screamed.

Nick drew back for a moment, astounded at her fierce arousal. She opened her perfectly made-up eyes and stared at him curiously. Probably because he'd stopped. Why didn't he see lust in her eyes if she was so darned turned on?

"Take it off, baby." He reached for her teddy, but she stopped him and waved at his clothes. Nick grinned and stripped quickly. Then he grabbed at her lingerie, but again she stopped him.

"What's up?" he demanded, getting a little frustrated with her coy behavior.

She blushed deeply. "I...I put on a little weight last week, and I don't want you to see."

Weight? Where? Nick ran his eyes down her frame. He couldn't see an ounce of spare flesh on her except for those enlarged breasts. But, if she was going to be paranoid about it, he could accommodate her wishes.

He concentrated on her breasts again. It took but a few sucks and her stellar breasts were heaving with her arousal. Nick kissed her, and then stared at her face. Make-up still perfect, not even a flush marring those chiseled cheekbones. Strange.

He felt her hand fumbling between them and realized she was shoving the material at her crotch to the side.

"Come on baby, stick it in me."

He didn't find her statement arousing, not one little iota. Shrugging inwardly, he held his cock and positioned it at her opening. Once he eased in, she shoved upward, moaning loudly as he sank inside.

Nick withdrew and rammed into her hard, on purpose. She moaned again, not changing cadence at all. He thrust into her again and again, sometimes gently, sometimes with force.

Her long lashed eyes were closed, her face posed in perfection. She looked like she could be in the middle of a photo shoot instead of being vigorously fucked. But those moans and groans continued unabated.

In frustration at her composure, Nick draped her long legs over his shoulders and shoved into her with the weight of his lower body.

"Oh yes, baby, fuck me," she whispered, her lips set in a perfect pout after she spoke.

Now where had he heard that before? And why was *baby* becoming an irritant instead of an endearment?

Choosing to ignore her perfect persona and exaggerated turned on condition, Nick fucked her. Her pussy was hot and slick. He closed his eyes and concentrated on that wonderful feeling. Amira's lush figure popped into his mind and his cock throbbed as he thrust into the wet woman flesh beneath him.

He raised her ass up in the air, supporting his body with both hands like he was doing push ups. He called this the airborne position. It provided incredible sensations the higher the butt was positioned and resulted in deeper penetration.

His cock rammed into the teddy. Cursing, he jerked it aside, but soon it had slipped in the way again. Fumbling with the joining in the groin, he discovered a snap. Popping it lose, he flung the soaked material to the side and shoved into her.

Rachel stared back at him. He was disappointed. The image of Amira had fled.

For some reason, he didn't wish to look at her face at this particular moment. Without a word, he withdrew and flipped her over.

"What?"

As Nick pulled her small rump upward, he answered the obvious, "Doggie."

"Oh," she giggled, then wiggled her ass in his face.

Ordinarily that would have pleased him, but for some reason, it didn't. Clamping down on his own moodiness, Nick slipped his forefinger into her hot channel. From here, he got a close view of her goodies.

Dark pink lips, slick with juices. And black pubic hair. The blonde hair was just as fake as her tits. Disappointment shot through him. Before he could think any more ridiculous thoughts, he slid into her pussy. Rachel moaned and moved her hips in a round motion.

As he plunged into her, he couldn't help picturing Amira's round ass. His hands kneaded Rachel's buttocks hard. Her hair would be blonde. Real. It would match the hair on her head. Well, it might be a tad darker, but still blonde.

He couldn't hold back any longer. The thought of plunging into his genie's luscious body set his cock on fire. Nick released his sperm with several fierce spurts, moaning slightly. Afterwards, he flopped on top of Rachel, then rolled to the side.

It took him a few minutes to realize the model had been chattering ever since they finished. What about, he had no idea. He glanced at her. She didn't seem to notice he wasn't paying attention to her either. Her hair was sleek, her body posed in a lovely sideways fashion. He realized she knew how good she looked.

Nick nodded occasionally as she continued to talk about mundane things. Complaints about her pay, the high prices of couture apparel, the hassle of waiting for an opening at the Sea Mountain Inn Spa, and so on. Things he guessed would be important to a woman, or at least to a woman whose life was built around maintaining her beauty.

A flash of understanding hit him. Even while fucking, Rachel seemed to focus on keeping her perfect image. Her make-up must not become smeared or her hair mussed. He was convinced her loud reactions during sex were more a show than real emotion. She was maintaining that perfect image. Perfectly lovely. Perfect lover.

After twenty minutes of half-listening to her exclaim over a new fashion designer, he knew only one way to shut her up. Nick fucked her again. She was beautiful, even with her enhanced boobs and mismatching hair colors, so getting hard was no problem. But his irritation with those slight imperfections was making him impatient to be done with her.

He showered after their less than stellar session, afraid for a moment, when he heard her enter the bathroom, that she was about to join him. Oh, he could fuck again, but he had lost the desire to do so. At least, there was no interest at this time and with this woman.

Rachel sang a little ditty. Off-key. Thank goodness she kept it down to a dull roar. Pushing the glass back, she stood two feet away, so the spray wouldn't hit her.

"Do you have a razor?"

"Razor?" he repeated like an idiot.

She ran one hand down her thigh. "I have to shave twice a day. I can't stand stubble. Can you?"

How could he say no without looking like the idiot he felt? "Behind the mirror." Where any intelligent human being would have thought to look. At least she'd asked.

Frustrated, he quickly finished showering. Stepping around Rachel, he dried off, watching her procedure. She wrapped a large towel around her hair carefully, tucking in the ends snugly.

With a thrown kiss in his direction, she stepped into the shower. Her lithe form was outlined in the mist behind the glass. Lovely enough to make a man's cock jump. Glancing down, he grinned at his manhood. Flaccid and uninterested.

The next instant, he grimaced. *What the hell is wrong with me?*

Chapter Ten

~

Amira is wrong with me. He knew that for certain, for as he stared at the swirling mist, his mind went to a more curvaceous body. He mentally replaced Rachel's slim curves with Amira's lush ones. The breasts stayed full and round, but were natural and soft.

The waist curved in more dramatically, making a perfect hourglass figure. Her hips were womanly, her ass rounded globes. His eyes flitted down those imaginary sleek thighs, his mouth watering as he anticipated the pink lips and pale hair he'd discover.

"Baby, do you have any lotion?"

"Wh...what?" Nick felt shaken from a daydream.

"Lotion." Her voice was strident, her lips drawn in a moue of irritation as she leaned out of the shower.

Nick opened the cabinet. Lotion. He didn't use lotion. His eyes searching, he was gratified to indeed find a bottle. He'd forgotten about Jennifer's stash. They fucked infrequently, but she kept a few items handy.

He smiled. Now there was a woman after his heart. Someone who was as mercenary as himself when it came to sex. Fuck. Get out. Look for a new conquest. Keep a great sex partner on tap for those dry spells.

"Here," he shoved the bottle into Rachel's hand.

She took the top off and sniffed. "Hmmm, I don't care much for lavender."

"Sorry, that's all I have."

Rachel sighed loudly, and then shut the shower door firmly.

He could see her smoothing the lotion on her slim body. It would feel ultra soft afterwards and smell heavenly. He liked lavender. But he had no desire to run his hands over her body — just yet.

He went into the bedroom and flopped on the bed, staring at the ceiling.

Later, Rachel sat down on the edge of the bed, running her fingers through his chest hair.

"Are you tired?"

"Yes, I am."

She sighed in an exaggerated way. "Gee, I'm usually awake until two or three in the morning."

He glanced at her smooth face. She must sleep late then. "I've had a long day."

She giggled. Nick cringed. Her fingers tickled his chest. "Did I have anything to do with that?"

"Some." He patted her hand into stillness. "I'm going to get some sleep." He hesitated. "You're welcome to join me."

"Sure," she snuggled against him.

Rachel fell asleep in a few minutes. He wished he could do the same. Thoughts of an ethereal Amira kept running through his mind.

In the middle of the night, a hand stroking his cock awakened Nick. It felt nice, very nice. He groaned as soft lips slipped over the head and a tongue swirled around the tip.

He knew it was Rachel's body he caressed, but in the cover of darkness, it was easier to pretend otherwise. Amira was aroused by his touch. It was her mouth that teased him like a witch. And it was her hot pussy he thrust into repeatedly. Afterward, he fell into a deep sleep.

The next morning, he examined the sleeping beauty beside him before jumping out of bed. She was still lovely, even with her tangled hair and mascara that had smeared. Of course, he doubted she'd believe it.

Taking a refreshing shower, he was gratified to find Rachel awake once he finished. Yawning, she pinched his ass as she passed him on the way to shower.

Nick grabbed clean clothes from his closet.

Rachel walked in some time later, beautiful and nude. He ignored her, continuing to look through some paperwork.

"I...don't have anything to wear."

"Your teddy," he nodded toward the crumpled lingerie on the floor.

"Yuck!" she screeched.

Glancing again at the teddy, Nick couldn't blame her. He was being a thoughtless clod.

"Do you want to borrow something of mine?"

"Men's clothes." Rachel faced him, hands gripping her waist.

She looked magnificent and pissed off. Abruptly, she snapped her fingers. "I know. We can go shopping."

"Shopping?" Nick got a sick, sinking feeling in his gut. God, what did he do to deserve this? Shopping for clothes with a woman was a man's worst nightmare.

"Yes," she almost jumped up and down. "That'll give me a chance to check out Vera Wang's summer fashions."

His stomach stayed queasy. Whatever he felt, he was responsible for her, so to speak. Because he'd wished her here—she had appeared almost nude.

Wish! Nick perked up. He'd forgotten he could get rid of her easily. As he stared at Rachel's cute backside as she dug through his shirts, a flush of guilt shot through him. He'd fucked her and now he was going to shove her off like spoiled food?

He gritted his teeth. *Well, isn't that what you usually do?* No. He wasn't quite that callous. He at least fed the lady of the moment dinner; usually sex was preceded by a date. Maybe dancing or a movie followed dinner.

Rachel was a supermodel for Pete's sake. Nick shrugged, snagged by his own conscience. He glanced through the door at Amira's lamp. Also, there was *her*. If he sent Rachel home early, then he'd have the whole rest of the weekend to spend by himself. It was either a new wish, spend time with Amira, or go looking for a new conquest.

Somehow, the thought of going prowling didn't appeal to him. The thought of spending another evening with his genie made him very uncomfortable. He sighed and watched Rachel push her arms through the sleeves of a shirt. *I guess she's an acceptable choice.*

By the time they got dressed, it was lunchtime. Nick stopped at a nice Italian restaurant, one that made home-cooked meals. By the time they left, he was ready to pitch Rachel from the car.

Cheese was fattening and sauce too rich. Nothing would do for her svelte figure. Of course she'd eaten salad, but then complained of still being hungry, eyeing his chicken parmesan with interest. He'd offered her a bite, but she daintily refused. Only when he'd finished the meal with a slice of cheesecake had she consented to try a bite.

That bite had turned into half his dessert. He didn't mind sharing, but the "I'm so thin and must maintain my weight" act got on his nerves. Damn! Why didn't she just say she wanted some cheesecake?

After lunch, he drove downtown. Rachel dragged him from one shop to another. Intimate little places where a man could hardly find a spot to rest or a corner to hide in. He had to "ooh" and "ah" over each piece she modeled for him. He didn't have a clue as to whether the black cocktail dress looked better than the red, but each time he chose wrong, Rachel reprimanded him gently.

Hell, she was treating him like he was her boyfriend. Nick almost clapped his hands after the last "You're not trying Nick, baby." But the shop was not an ideal place to have a genie materialize in. The shop girls giggled and smiled, keeping a close eye on them both. He fell into a stupor of sorts, agreeing with many of her purchases simply to speed the process.

When the car was jammed with purchases, he was shocked to see six hours had passed. His stomach was growling and his feet ached. Nick gripped the wheel and barely missed hitting a car turning in front of him. He really did feel like throwing Rachel from the car this time.

"I'm hungry," she whined.

"Me too," he snapped.

Rachel rubbed his shoulder. "I love Indian cuisine."

"I hate it."

"Well," she clutched her middle and pouted. "Where did you want to eat?"

"Home."

"Home! I don't cook." Her shrill response hurt his ear.

"I do the cooking in my house."

"Fine." She flounced on the seat. "Maybe you could just drop me off at my place then. I hate home cooking."

"Just what I had in mind." Nick grinned for the first time in hours. Who but Amira knew where she'd whisked in Rachel from? Could have been New York or LA. He very much doubted she lived in Houston. Thankfully, she seemed to be totally unaware she was in unfamiliar surroundings. He'd driven her downtown because that's where the couture shops were located. Maybe Amira's magic worked on Rachel's senses, muddling them somewhat.

"Don't you need the directions?" Her lovely blue eyes were puzzled.

"No, baby, I don't." Nick ignored her fuming glances and screeched into his parking lot.

Chapter Eleven

ഇ

"What now?" She dug her nails into his arm.

Maybe she was afraid he was going to leave her stranded in the parking lot. A lovely thought. But he had a better way to rid himself of her.

"Wait here. I'll take care of everything."

Rachel gave him an unsure stare, but pulled out her lipstick and started redoing her lips. That'd keep her busy a few minutes.

Nick practically ran into the elevator and then into his apartment. When Amira appeared, he barked, "Send that woman back to her home—with all her purchases."

"Purchases?"

"Don't tell me you haven't been watching this whole fiasco today?" He stepped close to her and tried staring her down. It didn't work. Her gaze was innocent.

"I did not watch everything you've done this weekend."

"I thought you had to." Nick said softly.

She shook her head. "Only the first part of the sexual wish."

"I see. You can come and go as you please." He wondered just what she'd been privy to during all the fucking that'd been going on in his bedroom. His cock hardened at the thought.

"More or less."

He wasn't going to get any more information out of her. She was being very secretive about her genie regulations.

"Is she gone?" He interrupted her stare over his shoulder.

"I'm sorry Master, your questions…interrupted me."

Now she stared right at him, her eyes bold and challenging.

He frowned at her.

A few seconds later, she said, "It is done."

"Good. Now, I'm going to fix me some dinner." He hesitated. "Have you eaten?"

"Yes, Master."

"Nick." He used a forceful tone. Somehow, when she said Master it made him feel much less than a master of his domain, especially when she gave him a censoring look.

"You know, you don't have to stay in that lamp all the time." He walked into the kitchen, throwing the words over his shoulder, "You can watch TV, do whatever you want in the apartment."

He glanced at her as he fetched a beer. "Feel free to go anywhere you want. You can even go shopping."

She shook her head. "I cannot."

"Why?" he interjected, impatient with her answer.

She strolled into the kitchen. "I can only go within the bounds of my Master's domain."

"You…mean you can't go outside my apartment?"

She nodded.

"That sucks." Why did that thought make him so darn angry? He started fixing a sandwich, anything for a distraction. It failed. He flung the knife down. "How do you keep from going insane? If I were stuck in this apartment all the time—I would be crazy."

"Oh," she smiled sweetly. "I can conjure almost anything I want to keep myself occupied."

"Like what?" He really was curious about that.

"Books, music. I even have a television."

Her face was pleased, as if she truly enjoyed these items. He was glad.

"TV? Interesting." He frowned. "But still, I'd get bored even with those after a while."

She laughed. It was a beautiful, rich sound, one that made his pulse leap.

"There is much more to keep me entertained." At his quizzical look, she continued, "I have a garden with almost every species of flowering plant known to man. It is several acres. I have an extensive library—with some books so rare, humans would kill to get their hands on them. And I have a bathroom fit for a sheik."

"With a Jacuzzi?" Why did his mind latch onto her last statement? And why did an image of Amira in his arms, her legs wrapped around him while bubbles lapped their bodies, fly into his mind?

"Oh, yes. I also have a large modern shower, and a heated pool twenty feet long. Three sides of the bathroom are surrounded by a glassed-in garden, filled with lush jungle plants." She paused, staring into space. "It is a most pleasant way to spend an evening."

Nick gulped. How he'd love to while away an evening making love to Amira in each water source she'd described. Now, that'd be heaven.

She reached across him and took a cookie from a plate. Her full breasts bumped into his arm, making his cock jump.

Nick didn't usually indulge much in snacks, he was too health conscious, but occasionally he had to have some chocolate chip cookies. Right now, he'd like to indulge his sweet tooth in something earthy and womanly.

"You like cookies?" he asked to distract his wandering thoughts.

She giggled, and licked a dollop of chocolate off her lower lip. So much for distractions. Nick wished he could have licked it for her.

"I love chocolate chip."

"Can you wish any food you want, while in your lamp?" He'd discovered in their short acquaintance that his genie did eat and enjoyed doing so.

"Yes, anything I desire—cookies, lobster, steak, pheasant, kibbee."

"What's kibbee?"

"A Middle Eastern dish. Very delicious. Maybe I'll make it for you one day."

"That'd be great." He smiled into her eyes. Food could be a great comfort for her. It was disconcerting to realize that was important to him.

"What about company?"

Her eyes turned sad. "I can never conjure people or animals into my lamp to keep me company."

"That bastard!"

Amira's eyes flashed surprise, and then she quirked a smile of understanding.

"Have many of your Masters allowed you to stay outside...so you're not alone?" Why did the mere asking of that question make his stomach clench?

"Very few."

There was his answer. He had a feeling it would be negative. Poor Amira.

She smiled softly, her eyes shining. "There was one who made my days as happy as any human's."

What a profound statement. Most people complained about their lives. Most would kill to have Amira's magic ability to conjure things as she did. Most people thought they wanted to live forever. But, those same people would probably die from boredom or loneliness if they had to go through centuries of solitude.

"His name was Ali."

Nick chuckled; he couldn't help it. "That's a well known name."

"Yes," she grinned. "Even in my land it was, but he was an uncommon boy."

"Boy?"

She nodded. "He found me when he was ten years old. My lamp had been buried in a sand dune for a century. Ali was hunting for buried treasure."

She laughed and he did along with her.

"He was very disappointed when he found out I could only fulfill sexual wishes. Of course, at that age, he had none."

"But he grew up." Nick was really interested in this story and hoped it hadn't ended badly for Amira. She seemed very fond of the boy.

"He had a few wishes, once he reached maturity. But Ali fell in love with a neighbor at eighteen." She smiled gently. "After that, he had no further wishes."

"And no further use for your services?"

Amira's smile held. "For a short while he forgot about me, until his bride cleaned my lamp one day."

"What happened?" The possibilities were endless. A woman and young bride. Did she let loose with hidden desires?

She laughed softly. "Oh, Yasmine was in shock. At first she was angry with Ali, mostly because he kept my secret hidden. But she had a kind heart, and she liked me. She invited me to stay with them."

"Huh?"

"Like a family member. I lived in a small room they built for me. I ate with them, and herded the goats. I even helped raise their many children."

"You liked it?" he asked softly, sure by her happy expression that this was so.

"Yes," she whispered, her eyes shining with tears.

"Why are you sad?" He patted one of her hands.

"Because, it was the happiest I've been since I loved Omar." She took a deep breath. "Humans die, as Ali and Yasmine eventually did."

Who was Omar? Only Amira's sadness kept him from asking.

Chapter Twelve

✍

"Did you live with one of their children—after?"

She shook her head to the negative. "They did not wish to tempt their children, in case my secret was ever discovered. Through magic, I made myself look older as Ali and Yasmine aged, so the children and neighbors wouldn't grow suspicious."

Amira paused, staring at the counter. "After Yasmine passed, Ali discussed things with me. We decided that I would say I was going to live with distant relatives. After Yasmine's death, having a single woman living with them would seem improper. Even though long ago Ali had proclaimed I was a distant cousin."

"Poor Ali. It must have been hard, losing you both."

She sighed. "It was, but we both knew his death was near too. Ali had no will to continue without his Yasmine." She glanced up at him, tears slipping unashamedly down her satiny cheeks.

"He took my lamp back to the sand dune in which he'd found me. It was a very hard journey for an old man."

"But he loved you." Nick said softly.

"Yes, he did. The only Master I can truly say—did." She took another cookie, but had a hard time chewing. The crumbs seemed to stick in her throat.

"I watched his passing. He was much loved by his children and friends. He had a grand funeral with much weeping."

He squeezed her hand, not knowing what to say.

Her eyes came back up, the tears had dried on her face. "You are loved by your family, correct?"

He nodded, not sure where she was going with this.

"And, I'm sure you have many friends who are fond of you?"

He shrugged. "A few."

"Who will mourn my passing?" Her eyes had turned hard and introspective.

"But…you live forever, right?"

"Exactly." Her jaw clenched in anger. "I will live past the time of the last man, as long as I stay djinn. No one will miss me, love me, or ever know I existed."

Nick was stunned. She was right. All the Masters she'd ever had would be long gone. No one would be left who knew or remembered her. Men had a legacy in their children, a way of remembering those long gone from this Earth. Amira would never experience such things.

"Did you want a family, before you became a genie?"

Those lovely golden eyes looked molten with emotion as they stared into his. "More than you would ever guess."

Nick took a quick swig of beer. God, what did you say to a person—being—like Amira? How could he or anyone else ever hope to console someone with such a sorrowful future stretching in front of her for an eternity?

"May I retire to my lamp?"

"Sure, do whatever you want." He clenched his fist on the bottle as she turned into a foggy mist.

* * * * *

Why did Nick have to be so kind? It made her sorrow run even deeper. If he had acted callous to her story, she could have turned her anger at him into other feelings. As it was, he had even become upset with her. She wrapped her arms about her bent knees and wept. Cried for Ali and Yasmine as she hadn't done in millennia, then wept furiously for herself as she'd not done in centuries. She could almost hate him for that.

The next day, Nick lifted the lid of her lamp, as had become his habit.

"Good morning, Amira. Please come and go as you wish. I'll be late tonight, I have an important meeting at work."

She appreciated her Master being thoughtful and informing her of his schedule. Otherwise, she might have worried when he didn't return home after work. She did take him up on his offer and spent the day lounging around his apartment. It wasn't especially exciting, but at least it was a change.

Amira had fallen asleep on the couch when she heard his key in the lock. Nick said "hello", then told her he was off to bed. He did look tired. She was disappointed. She enjoyed their conversations.

Choosing to do something really different, she decided to spend the night on the couch. Well, not too different, this had occurred just recently. Of course she'd fallen asleep in Nick's arms, but the memory was so pleasant, she hoped to recapture the essence of it.

The couch was not too comfortable, but was fine after she fetched several soft pillows Nick kept in the closet. Sleep was hard to grasp. Her mind kept returning to her Master's arms holding her. Finally, she waved a sleep spell over herself.

In the morning, Nick seemed shocked to find her relaxing on the couch. He fixed coffee and offered her some, but she refused. She would blink Turkish coffee for herself once she got ready to get up. She felt way too lazy and content, watching Nick prepare a quick breakfast.

"Will you be late tonight?" she asked as he walked toward the door. He looked so handsome in his modern suit.

He hesitated. "Not sure." He slipped out quickly without saying another word.

Nick acted rather strange, but then she still had trouble figuring him out sometimes. Amira shrugged. Perhaps he had impending business matters overtaking his thoughts.

She puttered around the apartment for hours, going through his things and familiarizing herself with each item. That got boring though. Running a hand over a dresser, she found a minute amount of dust. It was an aggravating problem she'd noticed about Texas. Dust seemed to creep over everything. Of course it couldn't compare to the fine granules of sand that blew in her true homeland, but it still made keeping things clean a chore.

Amira smiled. She knew how she'd spend her day. Cleaning. Not really caring if she got her clothes dirty, but realizing they were not optimal for the task ahead, she materialized clothing more suited to the job. Jean shorts would do nicely and a soft cotton top.

She was pleased once she waved her new clothes on, but then there was the problem of cleaning supplies. Searching through Nick's cabinets, she found Mr. Clean and Lemon Pledge. Both would do nicely.

Amira chewed her bottom lip. She had a problem. Nowhere could she find an old rag to use. She pulled out Nick's dresser drawer, but hesitated over his T-shirts. He probably wouldn't like her to riffle through his things and then use whatever she wished.

Sighing, she ran her eyes around the apartment. If only she could blink up a cloth, but that would be out of her jurisdiction to do so. She could conjure a whole harem, including pillows and satin sheets, as long as it was encompassed by her Master's wish. Clothes for her body were okay. Amira fingered the soft material over her chest and smiled.

Chapter Thirteen

Nick was having a hard time concentrating at work. His thoughts sometimes revolved around the luscious women he'd encountered, thanks to his genie. But most of the time, his mind latched onto Amira herself. He admired her beauty, her kindness, the way she handled the sadness in her long life, and the sweetness that seemed to be her fundamental nature.

This morning, he'd found her stretched out on the couch, still in the emerald green harem costume she'd worn the day before. It didn't matter that the material was crinkled, she looked as lovely as the day he'd first seen her. Her face was more relaxed in the morning, and she'd greeted him with the sweetest smile.

How had he acted? Uncommunicative. It was true he had the meeting that night, but even if he hadn't he would have thought up some excuse not to go home on time. Amira was taking up too much of his thoughts. He had to shake off this spell he'd been under since meeting her.

Nick nodded when his co-workers broke up the discussion for a coffee break. He sat in the conference room alone, thinking. Had she put him under a spell? Nick went over everything that'd happened since he met her. No. He really didn't think so.

Amira was a magical being and sometimes the air around her seemed to glow with power, an unseen thing. But he didn't believe she'd cast a spell on him. He'd not been prompted by strange feelings to do things he normally wouldn't have. His wishes had been exactly what he would want.

He smiled. True, she had tricked him a few times, he was sure of that. Creating one hundred women to fuck had to be classified in the trickster handbook. And Rachel. He was sure there was deception involved in that dealing, and he intended to ask Amira the next chance he got.

When he walked in the door that evening, he was totally shocked. Amira stood next to his TV, her back turned to him. Her tight, round backside was barely covered by a pair of shorts. Her legs were long and gorgeous, the thighs sleek, the calves delicately shaped. She was nude from the waist up.

"I'm home."

"Oh!"

Her exclamation told him that she hadn't been expecting him. She turned quickly, a white ball of material in one hand.

His mouth dropped. Her breasts were perfect. At least a size C cup, and their fullness didn't droop a bit. In fact, they were round and pert. Nick gulped, his eyes examining the pale pink areoles. Even as he stared, the nipples hardened, as if in reaction to his gaze. The color tuned darker, a delicate rose.

Nick licked his dry lips. How he wished he could suckle on those beauties.

"Oh," Amira repeated, but with a different intent. She crossed her arms over her breasts. Each globe was held in a hand, the flesh pushed up over her palms.

"I'm sorry, Nick, I didn't know it was so late."

He couldn't take his eyes from her breasts, even though it was impolite and she half-covered them now.

Clearing his throat, he said, "That's all right. What were you doing anyway?"

She laughed. "Cleaning." She waved one hand with the white material. That one breast bounced free, calling to him like a Siren's song.

"Oops." Amira frowned and repositioned one arm so it covered both breasts. "Let me fix that." With a wave of the free hand, a top appeared over her breasts. It was a cropped white cotton shirt and stopped just below her breasts. She hadn't bothered with fashioning a bra.

Her beaded nipples thrust against the thin fabric. It was the sexiest damn outfit he'd seen on her to date. But, he wouldn't have minded if she'd chosen to stay shirtless.

Dragging his eyes from her chest to her face, he asked, "Do you always clean in the nude?"

"I have shorts on." She crinkled her brow.

"Yes…of course, I meant partially nude." That's not really what he meant, he wasn't sure where he was going with this. A sudden image of Amira completely naked flashed through his mind. She was facing the wall, as she'd been when he entered, her lush bottom begging for attention, her ripe breasts swinging as she vigorously dusted the TV. His cock pushed against his pants painfully.

Get a grip!

"You never did answer my question," he pointed toward her. "Why the bare chest for cleaning?"

A giggle shot from her, even though she tried to cover it with one hand. "I could not find a cleaning cloth, so I used my shirt." She shook out the white material. It was a shirt similar to the one she had on now, just a bit longer.

"Um, you know, Maria is going to be pissed."

"Who's Maria?" She swiped at a corner of the television.

"My maid."

"Oh dear," she dropped the cloth, then quickly bent and retrieved it. "I did not mean to take the woman's livelihood from her. I was bored."

"Amira, it's fine. She'll just have less to do when she comes Wednesday."

"Why hasn't she been in?" She walked into the kitchen and he wondered what she was up to.

"Maria's been on vacation, she'll be back tomorrow." Amira came toward him with a beer in hand.

"Thanks, sweetie." He took it from her, staring at her firm abdomen before taking a sip. The fine golden hairs across her stomach drew his attention. How he ached to run his hand along the silken length of her abdomen. He turned and stared at her lamp. "We're going to have to do something with that."

"What?" She came around from behind him and stood beside him.

He smiled at her charming face. "Unless you wish to have a new Master, we'd better hide it or something. Maria has a penchant for polishing metal objects." He knew that his maid ran a dust cloth over the silver frame even though he kept it polished. He'd seen her do it.

Amira's eyes went to her home. "I…could change its appearance."

She hadn't denied wanting a new Master, but offering him a solution answered for her.

"Really? How?"

With a wave of her hand, the lamp was surrounded by a blue mist and out of it appeared a beautiful bottle—one that looked suspiciously like the bottle on *I Dream of Jeannie*. She went over and picked it up.

"See, it will not need polishing."

Nick took the bottle from her. A shiver ran down his back. It was a duplicate of Jeannie's. "What if Maria dusts it?"

Amira shook her head. "It must be polished vigorously to call me forth."

He nodded and placed it carefully back on the TV. "Should work fine." He turned and gazed at her. "Now, for you."

She shrugged, the fabric pulling across those magnificent breasts, outlining their pert shape even more. "I can stay in the lamp."

"No need for that." He grinned broadly. "I'll just say you're a distant cousin." He waved a hand about the room. "That will explain the clean rooms, too."

She clapped her hands happily.

"I've got paperwork to do." He knew his excuse sounded lame, but he had to get away before he really did lay his hands on her. And could he stop himself, once he did? He wasn't sure.

The next day, their ploy worked perfectly on Maria, who didn't seem a bit upset that Amira had cleaned the apartment. At least, that's what Amira reported to him when he got home. Maria always came during the day.

The rest of the week, Nick used work as an excuse to stay bent over his desk and tried to dismiss Amira from his thoughts. It didn't keep him from listening to her twinkling laughter as she watched some program on television—or from seeing her gorgeous body as she moved about the apartment. She even fixed him sandwiches Thursday, when he didn't want to stop and cook dinner.

Thoughts of coming in catching her half-nude were making him insanely horny. He had to keep his distance. He had also decided he must have a grand sexual wish this weekend. Maybe submerging himself in sensuality would drive wanting Amira from his system.

Chapter Fourteen

୧

Nick was totally wrapped up in his paperwork this week. Amira became slightly bored and she was tired of watching TV alone. She sighed and flipped on Animal Planet. She loved animals; they were so guileless.

Was Nick playing a game with her? One of "ignore the genie". It seemed silly when they had just begun to connect in a very human way. She flushed as she recalled the day he'd walked in to find her cleaning. He'd been quite shocked. Was that the problem?

Did he find her undesirable? No. Amira shook her head at herself. That was really silly. She may not have had sex in millennia, but she could still recognize lust in a man's eyes. Was that it then? He desired her?

Amira glanced into the kitchen, where Nick had his desk set up. His head was down and he was writing furiously. If he did want her, then that would explain a lot. He was trying to fight something that had no chance.

She sighed. It was a fight she'd been having internally ever since she met him. They seemed doomed to unfulfilled desire. It was not a pleasant thought. Lounging on his couch, watching him periodically, didn't seem like such a good idea all of a sudden.

Walking to the door, she said softly, "I'm going to my lamp."

He turned, his look guarded. "Okay. See you tomorrow."

She disappeared quickly into her home. He hadn't asked why she wished to leave, a clear message that he didn't want her around either. Tears shimmered in her eyes and Amira swiped them away in frustration. Lying down on her couch, she blinked a sleep spell. She didn't want to think about their situation anymore.

* * * * *

Amira was awakened by Nick's call. She had no idea how much time had passed until she materialized.

"How may I serve you, Master?"

"I want a wish to keep me occupied this weekend." His jaw was clenched, as if he fought for self-control.

It must be Saturday then. He'd not even said good morning. She felt sad. "Yes, Master. And your wish?" He didn't even bother to correct her calling him Master.

"I want a girl that looks like this."

He showed her a magazine, something to do with cars. It didn't seem Nick's usual reading material. A flash of surprise shot through her. The girl he pointed to was wearing a very skimpy bikini, her lush body barely covered. Her blonde hair flowed down to her hips. *She looks so much like me.*

"But I don't want her to be irritating."

"What?"

He waved the magazine. "Like Rachel, only concerned with her looks and what new dress she should buy." He stared hard at her. "I wondered if you conjured up those great qualities on purpose."

Amira held in a giggle, and shook her head. "I did not, Master. She was herself."

"Hmmph. Well, just make sure this one knows how to carry on a decent conversation." He shook a finger at her. "And no genie tricks. I don't want a dog either."

"That is insulting to my art, Master." She did feel insulted.

"Maybe…but I have a feeling you've played some tricks on me."

"As you wish. Are you ready?" She would just ignore his remarks.

He nodded, then stepped toward her. The kiss was short and without any heat. She'd felt awkward in his stiff arms, and thought by his face he felt the same way.

Amira withdrew to her lamp as Marty materialized. She was a duplicate of the woman in the ad. But Amira had chosen to alter Marty's appearance slightly. She had to keep her Master on his toes. And he had no say as to when and where she could choose to use *genie tricks*.

The woman was dressed in a bland beige suit and tiny cat glasses perched on her nose.

"Very funny, Amira," Nick threw toward her lamp.

Laughing heartily, she sprawled back into the ottoman, clutching her middle. After a few minutes she heard moans coming from Nick's living room. That was fast. She sighed and sat up to watch. She must see at least the beginning of his wish.

Nick's chest was bare and the woman's hands ran up and down its hard length. Marty's suit had already been stripped from her. Her full breasts pushed upward from the lacy black bra she wore, and matching panties barely covered her full hips. Nick and Marty were locked in a kiss, and Nick's hand slipped beneath one side of the bra, kneading her flesh.

Amira's breathing increased and without thinking, her hand went to one breast. She stared down at her hand. *No, I do not want this.* She stared back at the couple. She wanted him.

There was a way, but it was dangerous, because it might call Hadji's attention to her. Long ago, she'd met a powerful djinn, one owned by the friend of her Master at the time. He was lucky. He only had to fulfill three wishes for his Master and then move on. But he'd been around for centuries before her. He had gained much knowledge, observed wizards, and read forbidden books.

Ziyad had told her of a spell, one that would draw her into a human's mind. While there, the djinn would know the person's thoughts and feel what they experienced. He'd shared this information with her for two reasons. One, he fancied her and had always been disappointed they could not have sex. Two, he felt deep sorrow for her condition.

But a warning went with the spell. Hadji might sense the powerful magic and come looking for the perpetrator. And who knew what punishment the King of djinn might inflict on one of his subjects. He had the ability to fling a djinn into an infinite void where no life existed. It was a chilling thought. Or he could simply inflict immense pain on the djinn for whatever length of time he chose.

If she ever decided to use the spell, Ziyad suggested it be done sparingly so as not to draw Hadji's eyes down upon her. Until now, Amira had never seriously considered it. No Master had ever won her affection that much, at least in the sexual realm.

Shaking off her worries, she watched Nick's hand slick over the woman's hips. She wanted to be there, with him.

Taking a deep breath, Amira settled herself in the middle of the room. She concentrated her powers, pressing her hands together as she centered her magic into the core of her being.

By the power of wind, let me flow and join.

By the power of air, let me remain unseen and unfelt.

By the power of water, let me feel the life force.

By the power of earth, let me experience the sexual pleasure.

Wind, air, water, earth — let it be so.

Amira into Marty, joined by earth's mystical force.

She was sucked through the air as swiftly as when she materialized. Amira blinked, surprise flashing through her. She hadn't been sure it would work.

Nick faced her, his lips but a breath away. His hands were stroking her bare sides, and then one slipped beneath the bra and pushed the fabric up. Her breath quivered as one hand stroked gently, then palmed the entire breast into his hand, squeezing and kneading. His hand slid around her back and popped the snap, and then he shoved the bra off.

"You're so beautiful." he whispered against her mouth.

"Thank you," Marty whispered back. But to Amira, it was as if the words had left her own mouth.

Finally his lips, those sexy lips she'd ached to kiss for more than just the granting of a wish, descended on her mouth. He tasted like mints and coke, a most pleasant mixture. He sucked her lower lip into his mouth and suckled it for seconds.

Amira groaned and was surprised when Marty groaned aloud. She seemed to have some influence on the woman, or she just happened to feel exactly as Amira did.

Her hands went to his temples, held him there, and then they slipped behind his head, playing with his hair. Their kiss deepened and his tongue sought hers. Amira lapped at his warm tongue, astounded by the arousal it caused.

Her pussy lips thrummed, as if in time to some unseen music. The whole area ached and she felt moisture gathering in the folds.

Nick pressed deeper on her mouth, as if wishing to draw more pleasure from her and it did for her. His hand had left her breast and tangled in her hair, pulling her to him forcefully.

His other hand slipped down her neck, and gathered a breast into his palm. He rotated it, exciting the nipple without even touching it. He withdrew and stared at her.

"Do you know how much I want to taste you?" His eyes ran down her body, and stayed glued to her breast, until the nipple pebbled even more beneath his gaze.

"No, yes," she moaned, thrusting her breast into his hand.

He grasped her neck with one hand and tilted her head back, kissing her fiercely, and worked his way downward. He nipped her neck, seeming to sense the exact spot that was most sensitive.

"Oh, Nick." She dug into his upper arms.

His kisses continued until he popped her nipple into his mouth. His hot tongue swirled around the peak. It felt like she was dying, her body burned so much. But she knew they were just beginning.

Chapter Fifteen

ဆာ

Amira watched Nick's dark hair centered over her breast. It was hard to breath properly. She moaned as sensation rippled through her. His hot tongue licking at her aching nipple, then the pulling of her pebbled flesh into his wet mouth, was ecstasy.

Her hands slid from his arms up to his head, pushing him into her, deeper. She sighed, "Yes, succor me, my love."

Nick's head paused for a moment before he continued. She'd made a big mistake, using an archaic term, one that filtered through Marty's mouth. Nick seemed to notice but then didn't truly question it, or didn't care. But now she knew for sure that she was influencing the woman whose body she shared.

He stood up and lifted her into his arms. She stared into his lovely dark eyes as he carried her to the bed. His bed. Never had she dared to dream of stretching along its coveted length.

He sat her on the edge, standing tall in front of her. Amira ran her hands up his hard chest, squeezing the muscles, and then tweaking his brown nipples. Touching his male flesh excited her. She wanted to rip his clothes from him and to run her hands over his firm body. He grinned and arched his back. This not-so-subtle action shoved his groin into her face.

Sliding her hands down, she quickly unbuttoned then unzipped his pants. Nick was intent on watching her every move. She pushed his pants down, groaning as his covered cock bumped her face. He wore silky loose underclothes. Caressing his muscular thighs after he kicked the pants out of the way, she kept one hand on his upper thigh, rubbing, while her other hand slid to his engorged flesh. She never knew touching a man's cock could bring such pleasure. A new kind of hunger tore at her insides and demanded satisfaction.

Nick's breathing deepened and he closed his eyes, while his hands played in her hair. Her palm caressed his skin through the silk, making her clit throb and him moan.

Part of her wanted to rip into him quickly, make love in a hot, fierce way that would satisfy the fire in her belly with lightning speed. But another part of her desired sex in the slowest fashion imaginable—a marathon of lovemaking. She'd waited so long.

She edged the shorts down slowly. The whole time she stared up at him. Nick was now looking down, watching her undress him. His face was flushed, his eyes hot. Her breath caught at his look. A warmth ran through her body, making her pussy grow hotter and wetter.

The silk shorts reached his cock and hung there for a second before allowing it to spring free. Amira's breath hitched. She kissed the hot flesh, then ran her natural silk—her hair—over his skin, rubbing up and down.

"Oh, fuck, that feels good."

Nick's words reverberated through her. She felt the very same.

Amira had never taken a man's cock into her mouth, but after seeing it done so many times over the centuries, it was something she'd always wanted to try. Watching Nick for all these days, she had come to love every inch of his hard body, and wanted to explore it thoroughly.

Slipping one hand up his thigh, she gathered his scrotum into her hand. She rolled it gently, and then licked the tip of his cock. It bounced. Releasing his sac, she held the base of his staff and tentatively slipped her mouth over the bulging head.

He tasted divine. Amira relaxed her mouth and slid further. Experimentally, she sucked, like an infant suckling at its mother's breast.

"Yes," Nick said huskily, his hands squeezing her scalp.

Imitating the actions of others she'd watched through the years, she moved her head up and down. It was difficult, but she picked up the rhythm quickly. In between her bobbing motions, she popped his cock from her mouth and gave the tip swirling licks of her tongue. She couldn't seem to get enough of him. She wanted more. A pleasurable glow grew in her pussy, one that demanded she suckle him deeper.

"Marty, you know how to make a man as horny as a teenager." His hand pushed her head down harder upon his flesh.

Being called Marty distracted Amira. It also made her realize she had control over the woman's actions. She felt a flash of guilt, but then dismissed it. Marty engaged in sex on a regular basis, this she could pick up from her mind. It wouldn't hurt her to *miss* one session, although Amira had no idea what the woman would think when it was all over.

She slipped his cock out, then stroked his length with her tongue, fondling his balls at the same time. Amira stared up at him in dazed passion.

"Come here," Nick pulled her up into his arms.

"You didn't like?" She placed a pretend pout on her lips.

"Too much," he chuckled. "I want to come inside your pussy."

Strangely, his crude language made her even hotter, even though he was really talking to Marty. Amira wondered for a second if Nick would speak such words to her.

He drew her forward for a forceful kiss, then still maintaining it, leaned into her body. She fell onto the bed.

"Move up to the middle." His eyes lanced over her skin, setting up little tingles just from his look.

"Now, it's my turn." He gripped her knees and pulled them into a bent position. "Open wide."

Amira's legs trembled as she complied. Nick was staring at the core of her womanhood. And even though it really wasn't her pussy, it felt like it was. Moistness wept from her lips as he stared.

He knelt between her thighs and gently opened her. "Beautiful." His breath flowed over her slick flesh, making her clit throb.

When his mouth descended onto her, she reared up. His tongue slid over her clit, slowly, circling. Amira's stomach quivered and her legs felt weak. His tongue slipped into her folds, giving them attention, then returned to her stiffened nub. She cried out and twisted beneath his soft touch. Pleasure built in her, until she felt like a dam ready to burst.

It was heavenly. It was everything she ever dreamed it would be with him.

Without her realizing it was coming, an orgasm ripped through her aching clit. Her hips shoved upward to meet his thrusting tongue.

"Nick, please don't stop."

He chuckled against her throbbing flesh and continued with his onslaught.

Amira felt a pressure in her whole pussy. The orgasm that erupted this time was huge, and lasted for endless seconds. She panted, pushing his face into her harder. Her head thrashed on the sheets and she groaned loudly.

Nick licked at her satiated clit until the last beats of the climax petered out. His experience and knowledge of a woman's response guaranteed he would know the exact moment.

"Hmmm, you tasted good, but I bet your pussy feels even better." Nick edged up her body, resting his large cock at her opening.

She spread her legs wider, inviting him inside.

When Nick slid into her channel, she felt filled completely, her inner walls stretched. She shuddered and clamped her inner muscles tighter. Her arms stroked up and down his back as he started moving inside her. He bent her knees and draped them over his shoulders.

She felt exposed as he plunged deep into her. "Oh," she panted. It felt unbelievably good. She'd forgotten just how wonderful sex did feel.

He leaned down and took her mouth in a deep kiss while shoving into her wet flesh. Amira raked her hands along his back. She wanted to stay like this forever, with Nick embedded deep inside her.

"Yes, make me feel it." Nick said hoarsely.

His movements hit something deep inside her. Perhaps it was the *G spot* that many modern women spoke of. Whatever it was, her pussy seemed to have a mind of its own, stroking his cock with inner movements. She whimpered and arched upward to meet his thrusts forcefully.

She was surprised when another orgasm shot through her. As he continued thrusting into her, more small orgasms beat an erratic rhythm. It felt like her whole body was climaxing.

He repositioned her legs, which had slipped a bit. His eyes were dark with lust, his body moving with fast, furious motions. Nick was enjoying this position as much as she.

Then he came back for more kisses, his tongue working mad magic inside her mouth. When he sucked on her tongue, she felt as if part of her soul went with it. She was his, had been from the moment she first saw him.

Chapter Sixteen

ಐ

Nick eased her legs down, and bent to suckle on one nipple. Heat burned, setting a path between her aching pebbled flesh and her clit. Nick plopped her nipple from his mouth suddenly, flinging his head back.

Amira watched as the orgasm overcame him, his neck stretched taut. At the same time her pussy went into spasms, matching him spurt for spurt. Nick fell forward, supporting his weight with his arms.

His head was buried in her neck and he kissed it, and whispered, "Amira."

Her whole body froze. After a few heartbeats, Nick slid to the side and cuddled her within his arms. He seemed to be unaware he'd spoken her name aloud.

What did this mean? That he wished it was she instead of Marty? That thought sent a thrill of joy through her. Amira caressed his arm, pleased beyond words. His gentle breathing told her he'd slipped into a snooze.

"Habibi," she whispered.

Her eyes were drooping and she yawned. Maybe she should join Nick in a quick nap. The thought of awaking in his arms and making love again made her happy.

A jolt to her system woke her from being sleepy, as if someone had set hot pokers to the soles of her feet.

Hadji, she whispered in her mind. She dare not even say it aloud. His eye was seeking her. She felt it roaming the spaces of their magical realm.

With a shiver, Amira dissolved and fled back to her lamp. Once inside, she reclothed herself in a harem outfit and sank into her ottoman. Clutching a soft pillow to her stomach, she breathed slowly, trying to still any stirrings of her presence.

Hadji's eyes passed over her, but she felt the aftershock like sharp electric jolts along her nerve endings. Never again did she dare use that spell. She shivered violently once the djinn King's essence was completely gone. That was too close.

She lay sunk in the thick padding for hours, unable to move, almost afraid to breath. Noises from the apartment drew her up to stare out the window. Nick and Marty were stroking each other's bodies.

With a shiver, she closed her view to the world. She had no desire to watch any further sexual activities. What she'd experienced with Nick was glorious, but could not be repeated. To watch him and Marty have intercourse would pierce her heart with sadness.

Amira went to her garden and strolled for hours to soothe her restless mind.

Nick was having a blast. Now this was the kind of woman he'd dreamed about. She was so beautiful, so responsive, with no qualms about fucking. Amira had done a bang-up job this time. He had no complaints.

He grinned. He'd played a trick of his own, searching for hours through magazines at the bookstore, until he found a beauty similar in looks to his genie. There had been surprise on Amira's face when he showed her the photo.

Marty was in the bathroom, humming a song. At least she could carry a tune. He couldn't seem to keep his eyes off her lush form, watching as she dried her hair. They'd just taken a shower and engaged in a rousing session of fucking.

Some intrusive thought niggled in his mind. Nick tried to shove it away, but it insisted on being heard. Sighing inwardly, he acknowledged that perhaps wishing up a woman who looked like Amira wasn't just a trick. He wanted to make love to his genie, but since he couldn't, he did the next best thing.

"Aren't you hungry?" Marty walked up to him, pinning her hair atop her head. Not in a sexy, cascading fashion, but a tight bun that pulled her features into firm lines.

"Starved." He jumped up.

What was it with her? Marty was a damn sexy woman, and a tigress in the bedroom. But now, she seemed to be transforming herself back into the no nonsense figure she'd first appeared as.

To cement that image, she slipped the long sleeved blouse back on. She could have stayed nude for all he cared. He had planned on padding naked into his kitchen, but she glanced at his body, a quirky smile on her full lips. Feeling paranoid for some reason, he slipped his undershorts on.

"Do you cook?" he asked with a casual tone, out of curiosity more than anything.

She shrugged. "Sure, I can, but I prefer eating out…or someone else's cooking."

Nick chuckled and grabbed a pan. A nice pasta would be a quick starter. He really didn't like anyone cooking in his kitchen and was happy with her answer. As he gathered the ingredients, he wondered at his own thoughts.

That was not completely true, he hadn't minded when Amira helped him with the spaghetti. Strange, he'd almost forgotten that. She'd helped him with small things too at other times, and even fixed him a sandwich once. And he didn't mind.

Marty leaned over the counter and watched him. He wished he could see her long legs, but from here all that he could see was from the waist up.

"What do you do for a living?" She glanced at him with curiosity.

"I'm an investment banker, and you?"

"Oh."

Nick glanced up. Why did that exclamation sound derogatory? Or was he just paranoid again.

"I'm a genetic scientist."

"Damn!" He threw a handful of salt over the noodles.

"What?" Marty's tone was clearly offended.

"Sorry, I just hate a woman being more brilliant than me." Nick made his statement with a smile and humor in his voice to placate her. He really didn't give a damn if she was smarter.

Amira. She had tricked him again. Whipped up the duplicate to the woman in the magazine, but paired her brain with someone else. He seriously doubted a geneticist would pose for a car magazine.

"You know," he said as he added cheese to his creation, "I've never understood what genetic scientists do?" As soon as that left his mouth, Nick knew he'd made a mistake. Ask a scientist to explain what they do?

Marty actually rubbed her hands together. "My favorite subject." She dipped a finger into his sauce and licked it. "Yum, delish." She stared into space.

"Well, Nick, we work on modifying an organism's own DNA or introducing new DNA to perform desired functions. Presently, I'm working with a company to investigate whether aging can be slowed."

He nodded. "I've heard some talk about that." His stomach rumbled and he realized that pasta was not going to fit the bill. Taking a large T-bone from the fridge, he cut it in half and set it on his stove grill.

"Goody, I'm really hungry."

Nick had hoped Marty would stop at her simple explanation, one he could even understand. But he wasn't that lucky. She delved into her research with glee, naming DNA strands she was experimenting with and giving him statistical numbers.

By the time the steaks were cooked, his brain was ready to explode. Too much information in too short a time. He felt like he was back in college.

All through the meal, she continued with her barrage of information. Afterward, Nick grabbed a beer, offered her one, but she declined. He lounged on the couch, but Marty perched on the edge, still talking excitedly.

Nick glanced sideways at her luscious legs peeking from beneath the blouse. For some reason they didn't look as inviting as when they had entered the kitchen. The longer she chatted, the less attractive she looked to him.

Would she shut up if he fucked her again?

Chapter Seventeen

No. Somehow he knew she was wound up and wouldn't run out of steam for hours.

"Amira." Nick clapped loudly two times.

"Yes, Master."

Nick swallowed hard. God, she was beautiful, dressed in black with gold trim and a dangling gold chain riding low on her hips. Her face looked frail today and he wondered if something bothered her. Had he done something?

Staring at the space where Marty had been last, he realized he had, by wishing for a woman who looked like Amira. Had that insulted her?

"Your wish did not go well?"

Amira's soft question interrupted his thoughts. "Not exactly...well, some of it did."

A confused look shot over her angelic face, then was gone, replaced by the previous one. What was it? Sadness? Regret? Nick received a flash of understanding. Maybe a bit of both. Was that it then? Did Amira wish to make love to him as badly as he wanted her?

Gentling his tone, he said, "She was perfect as a sex partner, but a little too brainy."

A slight smile tugged at Amira's lush lips.

"Did you do that on purpose?" Nick smiled, to let her know he saw the humor in it also.

"Maybe," she shrugged, but then laughed and waved her hands. "I'm sorry, Master, I couldn't help it."

"Oh, I see, because I wanted someone who could carry on a conversation beyond clothes and make-up."

"Yes," she coughed into her hand, covering another belly laugh.

"I guess I deserved that." He stared at her, considering a new wish. "I've still got tonight and tomorrow. I want a new woman, an attractive one, of course."

"Any magazines to show me, Master?" Her brows lifted and her eyes twinkled merrily.

"No, just conjure me up someone beautiful, but no blonde this time." Amira's body jerked slightly, as if he'd slapped her. Nick wished he could take back those words. He hadn't meant to hurt her.

"Is that all?"

"Don't bring me an idiot, but definitely not a brain surgeon…just someone with normal intelligence." He rubbed his jaw. There was something missing with both gorgeous women—Rachel and Marty.

It took a few seconds, but it hit him. Liking. They had both enjoyed fucking him, but neither acted like they particularly cared for him. *Why does this matter to you now?* Nick stared at Amira. It was her. He knew she cared for him. Did he hope to replicate that feeling?

Not liking the direction of his thoughts, he quickly said, "I want this woman to be crazy about me."

Amira seemed startled, but then shrugged, "As you wish." She drew near him, then stopped. He had to walk the last few steps. This close, her frailty seemed even more pronounced. Nick placed one hand along her cheek, running his hand through the silken hair at her temple. Should he stay and keep her company?

He gritted his teeth. No. He'd already made his wish, besides he shouldn't give in to his genie. She already had the upper hand in their *relationship* more than he cared to admit. *Keep in control, ol' man.*

He meant to place a quick peck to her lips, but once he felt the give of her soft lower lip, nothing would do but a full-blown kiss. He licked her lip before flicking his tongue inside her mouth, stroking her tongue with his.

One hand slid to her ribcage and caressed it slowly. Her heart beat rapidly beneath his fingers and her mouth opened wider for his invasion. She was accepting him.

But then she broke the kiss, placing one finger against his lips. "No." Her groan was denial, with need locked up in its agonized tone.

Nick laid his head against her forehead. "Amira, I want you so badly."

She stepped away from his arms, her breasts moved erotically with the heavy breathing of her chest. Amira seemed to be trying to get control of herself.

Damn! He was tired of controlling his lust around her. Damn her curse. Anger flushed through his whole body.

She disappeared in a flash and Nick held one hand toward the mist. "Come back." His whispered words went unheard.

When the mist cleared, a slim, black-haired beauty faced him. She barely reached his chest, whereas Amira was but a half head shorter than him. He stared at the woman, calming his agitation and letting lust take over for him.

Amira had done her job in a spectacular fashion again. The woman was totally different from Marty, but lovely in her own right. She was nude. That was somewhat of a surprise. Rachel had been wearing a teddy, and Marty was fully clothed.

The woman sported a light tan all over. Her face was cute and almost child-like. Average breasts, coupled with a slender form, were enticing. The black hair covering her pussy was neatly trimmed, a mere line over her lips. It was Nick's favorite form of pussy covering. He licked his lips.

"Hi, I'm Jen. Amira sent me." Her voice was low-keyed and pleasant.

"I'm Nick." He didn't question Jen's nonchalance at standing stark naked in front of a stranger. Amira seemed to imbue some kind of magic that worked on the women, so they thought everything was perfectly normal.

Jen walked toward him, a slow sway of her hips drawing his eyes downward again.

"Mmm, you're handsome." Her hands went straight to his shorts and worked them down slowly. She knelt and stared at his cock as it bounced free. "Mmm, even better down here."

Jen stared up at him and ran her tongue along her lower lip. His cock was already hard—her nude appearance had seen to that. But when her long, pink tongue slipped out, his cock jumped, bumping her chin.

She giggled and then caressed it from the balls all the way to the tip. "Yummy."

Jen spent a few minutes tonguing his balls and lapping with that long tongue up and down his cock. He was throbbing by the time she opened her hot mouth wide and drew him inside.

Her head bobbed up and down a few times, then she slid downward, and kept going. Nick gulped. He couldn't believe it. She took his whole length down her throat. He'd dreamed of being deep throated, but never thought for a minute, he would find a woman capable of the deed.

"Argh," he groaned, placing one hand on her head.

That black head kept slipping up and down. Hot wetness slid around his cock as her mouth massaged him in deep strokes. Nick shoved his groin toward her and kept his hands in her hair, in motion with her as she bobbed.

It felt so good, he couldn't hold back. His orgasm shot into her greedy mouth, and Jen kept sucking gently as he pumped. He stared down as she plopped his cock from her mouth. Her long tongue flicked out, lapping at every drop that leaked out.

He breathed raggedly. Damn, but that was sexy. She nudged his half-stiff cock and licked the whole thing, front and back. The woman was insatiable. If he'd not already engaged in sex several times with Marty earlier, he was sure he'd be rock hard again in moments.

"That's enough, baby." Nick shoved her head back gently. He couldn't believe he was pushing a woman away from his cock, but he was beat. "I'm sorry, I won't be able to fuck you tonight."

Jen gazed up at him, a silly, happy expression on her elfin face. "That's all right, I enjoyed sucking you off."

Strange answer. Most women got downright demanding when it came to getting their rocks off as well. None of that chauvinistic "lie there and take it" stuff of the past for the modern woman. Shrugging inwardly, Nick simply accepted her statement. Maybe she was one of those babes who got off on sucking a man's cock.

He walked to the couch and flopped down. He felt boneless. "Can you get me a beer?" He'd asked before thinking that she'd probably refuse, tell him she wasn't his servant or something.

"Sure."

Her cute butt bounced into the kitchen as she literally skipped. As she came toward him, her face was alight. Weird. Maybe she was also one of those women who enjoyed acting submissively. Not that fetching a beer was submissive, but most of the women he was acquainted with would have refused to do it in the first place.

Quit your bitching, he told himself. Maybe she's just nice.

He took the beer, then opened one arm, inviting her to sit. She cuddled on his chest, warm and soft. Nick flipped on the TV, not even aware when he slipped into sleep.

He awoke to something nibbling his cock. Nick sat up, alarmed for a second. Jen's giggle drew his eyes downward. She was nudging his cock with her nose.

"No," he pushed her head off him. "I told you, no sex tonight."

She sighed in an exaggerated way, putting a big pout to her lips. "But I wanted it."

"We can't always have what we want." Nick's voice came out gruffer than he intended. For some reason, his statement made his thoughts flicker to Amira. *What is it with you? She's just one fucking woman.* He ignored the inner voice that started naming off her qualities that set her far and above other women.

"Here," he shoved Jen's head into his lap. "Eat it if you want, just don't make me come again."

Chapter Eighteen

ℰ𝒪

After Jen got his cock good and hard, he tugged her hair. "Come here, beautiful." He pulled on her arm, hiking her body upwards. "Let me eat your pussy."

Her breath caught and her eyes lit with lust as she rose above him. She propped one leg on the back of the couch, the other on the arm and then lowered herself toward him.

Nick stared at the dark pink lips before he slipped his tongue between the folds. He pulled her hips up and down gently, using her body movement to gain deeper access to her wet flesh. She tasted musky and feminine.

Jen groaned loudly as he lapped her slick skin, then flicked her clit swiftly. Her orgasm hit his tongue and he licked every drop.

Afterward, she slid down his body, her pussy very near his rigid cock. Nick kept one hand over it. "I'm going to shower, then go to bed." He stood and held out one hand, pulling her up. In the bedroom he shoved her gently onto the bed, hoping she'd take the hint and stay there.

His shower was refreshing and relaxed his muscles. Nick was fearful Jen would jump in the shower with him, but he found her curled up on the bed. She looked sleepy. Maybe her powerful orgasm had worn her out.

The bed felt wonderful. Jen cuddled up next to him like a kitten, and soon he was drifting off.

He was dreaming, a bizarre one at that. A large snake was crawling up his leg, tickling his thigh hairs. When it nosed his cock, he was scared and turned on at the same time. His cock hardened as the reptile rubbed its chin up and down his hard flesh. When it opened its mouth wide and slid its mouth down his cock, he still stayed rigid.

Nick awoke in a flash. He glanced around, confused. His cock was throbbing. He stared down to assure himself a snake wasn't swallowing him whole.

The room was in semi-gloom, but there was enough light to see a head over his groin. Jen. Nick groaned as her mouth slid all the way down his shaft. He felt a suctioning around his whole cock. It was as if a vacuum had been turned on his dick.

"Argh." The orgasm that gripped his legs was strong. His thighs trembled.

Nick sighed deeply after Jen lapped up his sperm with her tongue. She settled in his arms afterwards and went straight to sleep. What was he going to do with this wildcat? Fuck her, if she'd give him a chance to rest. He was not eighteen anymore, he needed a little time to recoup.

When Nick woke the next morning, his cock was hard, as usual.

"Mmm, you've got it all ready for me." Jen was starting to edge toward his groin.

"Oh no you don't." He placed one hand on her head. "I've got to piss." He spent more than his normal length of time in his morning routine. No way was he going back to bed.

He was picking a pair of undershorts from a drawer when movement caught his attention. Jen was on her knees, crawling toward him. She looked more feline than ever, dangerous, and her eyes were greedily glued to his cock.

He turned, his back shoved against the dresser. When she reached him, she rubbed her hair against his feet like a cat. Her cute butt stuck up in the air.

Nick stood immobile, seemingly unable to move as she licked her way up his leg. By the time he felt wetness stroking his balls, his cock was engorged.

"No," he said, his voice coming out weaker then he intended. "Nooo." Nick's tone turned into a drawn-out exclamation as her warm mouth slipped over his dick.

God, she was good. He shoved his hips toward her, pushing her head down as she moved.

"Suck it, you bitch," he panted.

Nick stopped her just before he climaxed. After she plopped it from her mouth, he said huskily, "Lick it clean." She did, lapping up the fluid shining on the head.

Jen licked her lips after she rocked back on her heels. "Don't you want me to finish you?"

"No. I'm saving my sperm for you. I'm going to fuck your brains out."

"Wonderful," she giggled. She jumped up, ran to the bed and flopped down, spreading her bent legs wide.

With that view, he was tempted to ram into her cunt immediately. But he wanted to eat first. Besides, he wanted to choose the ideal time to fuck her.

"I'm going to eat breakfast first."

"Wait," Jen squealed and ran to the door. "Let me fix it for you."

Nick clenched his jaw. Shrugging, he walked into the living room and flopped on his favorite chair. He watched her.

It irritated him, her presumption of taking over his kitchen. But, if she could cook, maybe it wouldn't be so bad to be waited on.

That led his thoughts to Jen's extreme behavior. What was up with that woman? She was constantly turned on, like a live wire. Nick rubbed his chin. Not completely true. She seemed to be tuned in and turned on by his state of arousal. Her behavior was not what he'd call normal.

Normal? Nick groaned. He was an idiot. Once again he worded his wish in a way that Amira could twist it. He'd asked her for a woman who was crazy about him.

Suddenly the movie *Coming to America* popped in his head. Eddie Murphy as the prince had hated having a woman shoved onto him who only wanted to do what he wanted her to do. That's how he felt right now.

This was the worse case of "too much of a good thing" he had ever experienced. He bet Amira was lounging in her lamp laughing her ass off at him.

Nick stared at Jen, who was popping bread in the toaster. He was pissed off—at Amira for her trickery, and Jen for sucking him dry. Her small, tight ass jiggled as she moved around. His cock responded and Nick touched his hard flesh. He had a little bit more to give.

Striding quickly into the kitchen, he grabbed Jen by the arms, drew her toward the dining table, and flipped her around. Shoving the salt and pepper shakers toward the end of the table, he pushed the surprised woman belly down on the cool surface. It was a perfect height for fucking.

With no words, he rammed into her pussy. She was moist and his passage was easy.

"Oh, Nick. I thought you wanted to eat?" Her breathing was heavy, her tone excited.

"I changed my mind. Now open up that cunt wide for me," he ordered.

Jen moaned and spread her legs wider, pushing her ass up more. He plunged into her with hard, long strokes. She was tight, hot and slick.

He slapped one round cheek, enjoying watching her flesh spring back up. Again, he slapped her, a tad harder.

"Mmm," she groaned, wiggling her hips.

Her pussy clamped tight around his cock as her excitement built.

Nick whacked her ass repeatedly, ramming into her hot pussy each time after he slapped her.

He leaned over, spreading her arms above her head and fucked her deeply as he held her wrists.

Jen whimpered, flinging her head from side to side, and shoving her ass toward him.

"Deeper," she panted.

Nick didn't know how much deeper he could go without puncturing something, but he complied, thrusting into her savagely, throwing his whole body weight behind his strokes.

She screamed with pleasure as his cock hit her cervix.

"You want to be fucked?" Nick felt brutal, like he wanted to tear her soft tissues to pieces.

"Yes," she screamed, undulating her abdomen.

Her pussy stroked his cock inside her hot walls. It felt so good, but he was not even close to coming. He continued to fuck her for a long time, not changing position as he normally would have done. Nick had no desire to look into her face, he only wanted to fuck her cunt.

Jen continued to writhe, moan and occasionally scream beneath his wild thrusts. He knew he was good, but not that good. It was Amira's play on his words. The woman twisting beneath him couldn't help herself—she was turned on by everything he did. For some reason, that thought angered him even more.

"What do you want, bitch?" Nick growled at her.

"For you to fuck me, Master."

Chapter Nineteen

❧

He was stunned for a few seconds, but then realized she was simply playing the submission game. He'd set the tone by spanking her, pinning her arms, and talking crudely.

He plunged into her slick flesh in one long stroke. "What am I?"

"My Master."

"You're damn right."

It helped his arousal, this illusion of mastery. His cock throbbed. Closing his eyes, Nick concentrated. Amira's round, full ass appeared in his mind. He groaned aloud as he fucked her deep, sinking into the hot flesh beneath him.

"You feel so good," he moaned, gripping her hips and pulling her toward him.

A whimper erupted from the woman. Nick's blood boiled, he was on fire. His balls hurt, felt full as if he hadn't fucked in a week.

"I'm coming," he said hoarsely. In his mind Amira moaned in reaction to his statement, her hot pussy massaging him as he climaxed.

He fell on top of the soft body, holding his weight off her. His sperm shot into her slick flesh in bursts as he gently pumped his hips.

Afterward, Nick disentangled himself from Jen. They both jumped in the shower for a quick rinse off. Jen looked at him hungrily, but didn't go down on her knees. She looked sated, for the moment. She offered to soap his back and he accepted gratefully. Her massage felt wonderful.

They both attacked the cold breakfast with gusto. Nick put an action movie in the DVD and managed to get through most of it before Jen touched his cock. He stared at her gamine face as it descended toward his half-hard cock. Neither she nor his cock seemed to have much sense. Enough was enough.

Clapping his hands twice, he shouted, "Amira."

He'd never been so happy to see a woman disappear from his life as the petite Jen. Whether he was glad to see his genie or not, he couldn't say.

"You fooled me again."

"How so?" Amira's face was expressionless.

"You know how." His voice came out angrier than he felt. "That woman sucked me until I felt like a used noodle."

"What a pleasant description." Those amber eyes twinkled.

"Quit laughing at me, genie." Nick was having a difficult time keeping a straight face.

"It was you who desired a woman who was crazy about you," she stated firmly. "Do you have a new wish?" She changed the subject mid-stream.

"No. The weekend's almost over." He started toward his desk. "You can stay or go, it's your choice."

He didn't have to glance back to see she'd disappeared. He'd learned very quickly to recognize the slight tremor of power in the air just before Amira appeared, or just after she left.

Nick was still aggravated at her latest escapade, so felt some satisfaction that she'd chosen to hang out in her lamp.

It was difficult to concentrate on his work, but he managed. Work that could wait until tomorrow, but he wanted to start it tonight. He had a new client with complications due to many children, several ex-wives, and a slew of grandchildren.

The next few days, he stayed late at the office, straightening out the client's problems, and avoiding Amira. He could have saved his energy as far as his genie went. She never popped out of her lamp, nor did he discover her lounging on the couch.

By Thursday, Nick had lost his frustration with Amira's tricks and laughed at the humor of it instead. Also, he missed her charming presence, and he felt guilty.

Chapter Twenty

೮ઝ

Amira decided to stay in her home until Nick called her again. He was really peeved at her, so she'd allow him some time to cool off. A flush of guilt washed through her. She really had pulled a good one on him this time.

She'd watched much of the sexual activities going on. Jen had taken Nick's cock into her mouth, as she desired to do. Of course the woman had acted overzealous, thanks to the magic instilled in the wish.

She giggled. Really, it'd been too much even for the stallion Nick.

Amira had learned one important thing. Her Master didn't seem to know what he really wanted, although through the fulfillment of each wish, he seemed to be getting closer to the truth.

Nick wanted gorgeous women to screw. But would he be satisfied with just one? He wanted someone with intelligence, but not so brainy he would feel stupid in comparison, like with Marty. Neither did he want a woman who couldn't discuss things he was interested in. Hadn't he had some cozy conversations with her about the international economy, politics, and antiques? Very diverse subjects, but ones he was enthused about, and so was she. Her Master seemed surprised and pleased when he found out how much she did know about the subjects.

Was there even the remotest chance Nick would realize she might be the woman for him? She sighed. By Hadji's eyes, she truly doubted it. Nick had everything in his world set up the way he liked it. What could possibly make him wish to change it?

Love.

A tear slid down Amira's cheek. She knew now that she loved her Master. It seemed to be foreordained by his being a twin in looks to her beloved Omar. She had tried her best to deny her attraction, to place distasteful qualities on Nick, and to distance herself further. Nothing worked.

Even her tricks backfired. Nick came out looking better in each instance. He wished for a harem, but realized overindulgence was ridiculous. He wanted a particular woman in Victoria's Secret, but was not satisfied with her due to her personality. Then he wished for a woman to be crazy about him. Many men would have been happy, Amira thought, with a woman who couldn't get enough of them. But not Nick. His dissatisfaction didn't seem to be just with the rabid way in which Jen approached sex and pleasing him. Maybe he saw something deeper that was missing?

Amira laughed. She was being silly, a dreamer. Surely she was attributing qualities to her Master he didn't possess. Maybe he simply wanted to be more in control.

So, she chose to seek solace in her home. Nick would probably have said she was *hiding* in her lamp. She glanced through the window occasionally. Her Master came in late, then spent hours working at his desk. He would have no time for her, even if she wished to be in his apartment.

Distance was good for them both. Nick needed to concentrate on his work and she needed to get control over her growing feelings. The last time, when he'd been with Jen, it had been the most difficult. She wanted to be in the woman's place so badly. The sex was overpowering and Amira brought herself to release more than once as she watched.

But in the end, it was a fruitless pursuit, observing the two. It only deepened her sorrow. Never before, had she found it so difficult to stay within her role as djinn. She wanted to be with

Nick always, to be the woman he turned to with love shining from his dark eyes.

Amira jumped when her Master's voice called her. It was Friday, not the weekend yet. A little early for a sexual wish. Perhaps he wanted some company? She shook her head at herself even as her body materialized in front of him.

"Master, do you have a wish?"

"No." He smiled, his teeth making a sexy contrast to his tanned skin. "It's a holiday and I'm off for three days."

Amira was confused. He had a long weekend and didn't desire a wish?

Nick walked over to her and picked up her hand. "I thought we could spend the time together. I missed you this week."

Her throat was dry and her heartbeat was hammering like mad.

"Do you want to keep me company?" His voice was hesitant.

Oh Hadji. Her stunned silence had made Nick question her interest level. If only he knew.

"Master, I would love to keep you company."

"I know you like to use proper etiquette when a wish is imminent," he grinned, "but can we dispense with the *Master* for the next three days?"

She blushed. "As you wish."

Nick laughed, and then swung their joined hands all the way to his face. He kissed the back of her hand swiftly, then released it.

"You hungry?" He had started for the kitchen.

"A little bit."

"Great. I thought I'd grill burgers. By the time they're done, you should be hungry."

Amira followed Nick into the kitchen, and then watched as he made the hamburgers. Nick had waved away her offer of help.

He glanced up from shaping a patty. "Why don't you change into something more comfortable?"

Amira nodded. Her harem clothes were quite comfy, but she knew Nick considered jeans and T-shirts the best for lounging around. She examined what he wore.

The T-shirt he wore stretched across his broad chest, while the beige shorts showed off his brawny thighs exquisitely.

With a wave, Amira changed into jean shorts and an off the shoulder white Mexican style top that stopped below her breasts.

"You look beautiful," Nick smiled at her.

He waved at her to follow as he walked onto the balcony. It was the first time she'd been outside his apartment. The balcony was rather small, about ten by five feet, but big enough for the two of them to enjoy. A round barbeque sat in one corner.

The Texas heat hit her in waves. Amira flung her head backward, letting the rays wash over her. She sighed happily. It reminded her of home. After a minute, she leaned over the railing, gazing at the city below. Houston was a busy place, with many cars, roads, and impressive buildings.

It was exciting to watch all the activity. She heard the burgers sizzling on the grill, then Nick strolled to lean beside her.

"Something, isn't it?"

She nodded. "Man's modern cities are huge." She breathed deeply of the heavy, moisture-laden air. "What I wouldn't give to see endless sand dunes though."

"Has it been a long time since you were home?"

"Yes," she hesitated in thought. "I've been in America since the turn of the last century. Before that, my Masters ranged the length of Europe."

"How exciting."

"Not really." She gave a sour smile to no one but the empty air. "Remember, I cannot go outside my Masters' domain."

"Oh, I'd forgotten." He touched her shoulder briefly.

She shrugged. "There were a few who took me with them on travels, but most were terrified someone would ferret out my secret, or stumble across my lamp. While they were gone, I was usually kept locked in a secure place."

Nick stared at her, but she looked at the city, not wishing to see the empathy in his eyes.

"That must have been boring."

Finally, she turned and flicked him a quick gaze. Yes, his eyes were sympathetic. "It was, but I put myself in a sleep spell during those times." She pointed, "I think your burgers are burning."

Nick walked quickly to the grill and flipped the meat. He seemed to sense she didn't care for this topic. He knew when to prod and when to retreat.

Switching subjects, he asked her what countries she'd lived in and her favorites. This was a pleasant topic, one she enjoyed sharing with him. They talked through the consumption of the hamburgers, and for hours afterward. He was truly interested in her travels, as he loved going on journeys himself.

They had retired to the living room, continuing their discussion over cokes and popcorn. Amira was interested in hearing about the countries Nick had visited, as well as the different states within the United States. He had gone on tours, a fascinating invention of modern man. Through them, Nick got to really see many majestic buildings, including the ancient structures.

She had lived through the time of the pyramids, but had never seen them. How she'd love to visit these places, ramble through the crumbling edifices, and see the people living as they'd done for hundreds of years.

"You know," Nick interrupted her thoughts. "I have a vacation coming up in a few months. I can take you with me."

"Would you?" A sheen of tears coated her eyes and she blinked fiercely to dispel them. "Where did you plan on traveling to?"

He shrugged. "Hadn't decided." He eyed her. "Maybe I'll let you choose."

Amira's heart beat with joy. He would do that for her? The happiness radiating through her body was almost too much to handle. "Do you want to watch TV?" She grabbed the remote and flipped it on before he answered "Sure."

She could see Nick staring at her out of the corner of her eyes. He seemed perplexed. They spent the rest of the evening in comfortable companionship, laughing at old shows and talking endlessly.

Amira slipped off to her lamp after Nick started yawning. He looked surprised and disappointed when she started dissolving. That was satisfying to her on one level, but disturbing on the other. Was he beginning to enjoy her visits as much as she did? Could this mean anything? She wasn't sure. Her own confusion over her feelings, and doubts about Nick's, led to a very restless sleep that night.

The next morning she was awakened by her Master's cheerful voice.

"Wake up sleepyhead, we have a whole day in front of us."

It didn't take long for Amira to shower and change. This time she decided to materialize in American attire. She blinked on a short white skirt with a red silky shirt. White sandals completed the outfit.

Staring at her reflection in the full-length mirror, she thumped her chin. She needed something. Flipping a lock of hair from her chest, she had it. Her hair. Nick had stared at it yesterday and asked if she ever wore it any way but in a high ponytail. She did and had through the centuries. But when she first appeared to Nick, she came as the fantasy he held closest to his heart—that of the djinn in *I Dream of Jeannie*.

With a wave, she let her hair down into one long braid down her back. She'd favored this style on many occasions. Perhaps Nick would like it also.

Chapter Twenty-One

ରେ

Nick had thoroughly enjoyed spending the day with his genie yesterday. He was glad he'd thought of it. She was delightful company and seemed as enthused about their time together as he was.

Amira was surprisingly easy to talk to. She listened carefully, but was not hesitant in voicing her opinion. And that surprised him the most. She knew a lot about a variety of topics. He didn't know how she kept so informed when she was locked up in that lamp so much, but she did. Then he remembered she had a television and access to books. He loved reading too, although he never seemed to have time anymore. What he wouldn't give to get a look at the ancient texts she'd mentioned.

When she appeared this morning, his breath was taken away. She was such a beauty. She looked like the all-American girl, only much more striking than most.

"I love what you did with your hair."

Amira's eyes dipped shyly and she played with the braid falling over her breast.

"Here," he waved toward the kitchen. "I have breakfast all ready."

"Oh," she strolled in front of him. "It looks delicious."

Nick pulled out a bar stool for each of them. "I thought we could eat here." He started loading his plate with pancakes, knowing Amira wouldn't make a move until he did. That servant thing, he guessed.

Aggravation shot through him at that thought. It wasn't fair that a lovely girl like Amira had to suffer for centuries, waiting on lustful old men. Nick swallowed a gulp of orange juice. He wasn't old, but she still served him. And as much as the idea of her being a servant bothered him, he had to be truthful—he wasn't ready to give up those luscious wishes, even if that meant Amira wouldn't be a servant any longer.

Stabbing a sausage, he plunked it down on her plate. "Try one of these." He watched her daintily taste each item, trying to distract his mind from unpleasant thoughts.

"I thought we could go rambling through this huge flea market today. You never know what antique you might stumble across."

Amira glanced around his apartment. "But all your furniture is modern. I know we discussed your grandmother's antiques…"

He shrugged. "I do like them. It's fun to treasure hunt, even if I don't buy."

She smiled. "It sounds like fun, but I can't go."

"Even if I pack your lamp in my backpack?"

She stared at him. "Only if you ask me for a wish while we're there."

"Oh." He frowned. "That's not what I had in mind." He waved at their plates. "Let's finish, I'll think of something."

Afterward, they took their coffee to the balcony, watching the traffic increase and feeling the day warm up swiftly. "Amira, I was remembering what you said about Ali and how you lived with his family…how you even helped herd goats."

She nodded.

"Well, taking care of goats would fall outside of a sexual wish."

"It was on Ali's land. I was on his domain."

Her eyes were curious, probably wondering where he was going with this.

"I live in an apartment. Technically, the whole building is within my home territory. I can't go into other people's apartments, but there is the lobby, a gym, a clubhouse, and a café."

He placed his cup down and pointed. "Look down there, see that pool? It's within my domain too."

Amira's gaze flicked over the pool and came back to his face. "You are right."

Picking his cup back up, he took a sip. "So, how about spending the day with me exploring my world here?"

She took a deep breath. "I'd love to."

"Great. How do you feel about working out at the gym?"

"Wonderful."

Were those tears in her eyes? Pleasure flushed through him. He was making Amira happy, very happy.

They spent another hour chatting, letting their breakfast settle, then he changed into his gym clothes. Amira had to simply wave one hand to change into black gym tights and a matching top that left her abdomen bare.

Nick swallowed, hard. He was going to have a difficult time concentrating on working out. Amira was hesitant about leaving his apartment, glancing upward like she expected to be struck by lightning. But once out the door, she relaxed.

He'd never thought a hallway would be exciting, but Amira exclaimed over the interesting design of the carpet and the landscape pictures on the walls. She definitely needed to get out more.

The gym was a whole new experience for her. She kept running from machine to machine, so that he didn't really get much of a workout. But that was okay. Although the gym was not crowded, the few guys pumping weights couldn't take their eyes off Amira. He couldn't blame them, but at the same time, stayed by her side to ward off any flirtations. She was his.

After their workout, it was lunchtime and he took her to the café. Amira was delighted with the light entrees and chose a chef salad. She also thought the café interior was charming, with its tiny tables and cute chairs to match. He'd never thought about it, but the café was cozy. He usually was too busy to bother stopping there, but maybe he'd have to make more of an effort. The food wasn't bad and neither were the prices.

When they got back to his apartment, Nick suggested they watch a movie. They selected *You've Got Mail*. He'd already seen it, and in spite of it being a chick flick, he really liked it. But Amira had not, and Tom Hanks was one of her favorite modern actors.

Amira was wiping her eyes at the end scene. Maybe watching this particular movie hadn't been such a good idea. Not because it made her cry, but its romantic theme spoke to the heart. It made him feel a little sad. He and Amira could never get together, working out their differences as had Tom and Meg. Their dissimilarity spanned millennia and took huge culture leaps.

Nick clenched his jaw. *Why am I getting maudlin? It's not like I want to marry her.* Warmth flashed through him at that thought. Nick was worried. He seemed to be getting way too involved for his own good.

He jumped up. Action was good at distracting one from getting too sentimental. "I thought we could go to the pool for the afternoon."

Amira smiled, but then looked worried. "Outside?"

He nodded, "Remember, it's still within my domain. I pay rent here, expensive at that, and use of the pool is part of that payment."

"Okay." She stood, looking uncertain.

He pointed. "I'm going to my bedroom to change." He picked up a magazine and handed it to her. "Why don't you find a bathing suit you like?" Nick wished he'd chosen more carefully as he eyed the slick cover. Victoria's Secret. If he remembered correctly, it was filled with sexy swimsuits.

When he returned, his stomach felt like it sank all the way to his feet. Amira had chosen a black bikini with gold edging.

The tiny triangles barely covered her breasts and the bottom tied at the sides.

"Do you like it?" she asked anxiously.

"The gold matches your eyes," he muttered, trying to recover from his shock. He'd not answered her directly, but she seemed to accept his statement as such.

"You look nice." She smiled sweetly.

Nick had his swim trunks beneath the shorts and shirt he wore. The apartment manager didn't like people traipsing around in bathing suits through the halls. Not that he could blame him, with some of the bodies around here. Of course Amira could give a man a heart attack.

"You need a covering."

Amira didn't question, simply waved and a floor length, see-through black sarong appeared around her hips. Damn. Didn't cover much, but would ward off the manager.

The walk down to the pool seemed much longer than the one to the lobby had been. He tried his best to keep his eyes off his genie's lush figure but he couldn't. He used conversation as his excuse, running his eyes over her curves while they chatted.

She seemed to be oblivious to his attention. Nick smiled. He knew that was because at heart Amira was an innocent. It wasn't that she hadn't experienced physical love. She had told him of her passion for her long dead lover. But she had a freshness to her nature, in spite of her mythical age. A naiveté.

The pool was crowded, as it always was on the weekend. It was one cool spot where you could pass the time pleasantly in the sweltering heat. A buzz of whispers erupted as they entered. Nick knew he created a stir among the females whenever he went to the pool, but he'd never worked up this kind of attention. Necks craned, both men and women, for a look at Amira as they passed by.

Nick was pleased when a couple left a pair of lounging chairs. He flung their towels over them just as the pair was leaving.

"Sit." He waved at her chair, relaxing in his. He stripped the shirt off, and then eased the shorts down.

Amira untied the sarong before sitting down. Beautiful beyond words. Those long legs were curved just right, her abs firm, while her waist dipped in deliciously. Her breasts and hips were womanly and made for a man to ride.

She had piled her hair on top of her head. It gave her a regal air, especially with the long neck that was exposed. How he wished he could kiss that long stretch of flesh.

His cock was rock hard. Glancing around, he saw all eyes were on Amira. Picking up the backpack, he placed it over his lap and fished for the sun tan oil. Next, his sunglasses were found and put on. Then he pulled out the water bottle and offered her a drink.

Amira waved away the bottle, but Nick took a deep swig. He had to distract his thoughts or he'd never be able to come from under the cover of his backpack.

A neighbor, an old fart of a pervert, came to a stop at the end of Amira's chair for the sole purpose of leering at her.

"Nick, who is this lovely young thing?"

"My distant cousin." he snapped. It took some minutes to get rid of the old man. By that time, his cock was flaccid.

Nick spread sun tan oil over his body, then glanced at his companion. She couldn't die, so probably didn't need to worry about cancer. But then, maybe she could burn.

"Here, Amira, you'd better put this on."

She spread it over her face, then her arms. His eyes followed every route. When she palmed it over her legs, his cock came to attention again.

Nick turned away. It was one of the most difficult tasks he'd ever set himself. He stared across the pool at three young women. Denise, Susan, and Teresa. He'd dated all of them. When they noticed his attention, they giggled and waved. He returned the wave.

"Who are they?"

He shrugged. "Just some neighbors I know."

She giggled. "Not like your other neighbor."

Nick groaned. "Thankfully, we don't have too many like him here."

The sun beat down on them unmercifully. It felt too hot to talk. Nick lay back, closing his eyes beneath the glasses, so he wouldn't be tempted to look at Amira. She did the same.

Waking from a half-snooze, he realized they'd been lying there for some time. His skin felt on fire. Damn, it was hot.

"Want to go for a swim?"

Amira nodded. He followed behind her, but her backside was as delicious as her front. Taking a few big steps, he passed her and jumped into the cool water. *Okay, cock, you can do whatever you please now.*

As Amira eased backward down the ladder, he watched the gentle sway of her round hips. His cock did indeed do as it wished—became hard as a rock.

Chapter Twenty-Two

Amira was thoroughly enjoying her time with Nick. Who would have thought a simple day by a pool would be so exciting? Of course any adventure outside her lamp would be thrilling, but still, the cool water and hot sun seemed to fit her needs more than adequately.

Nick was being so attentive, offering her water periodically so she wouldn't dehydrate. Once, he ran to the changing area where a vending machine stood and brought her back a coke, because she mentioned how nice one would be. He was making a point of talking about subjects they both enjoyed, and steering clear of those he knew upset her.

Just the fact that he thought of bringing her poolside showed his consideration. Was he beginning to care for her, or did he feel sorry for her? Normally, she would have seen right through any insincerity, but with her emotions so involved, she was having a hard time being clear about anything.

Amira shrugged. Why question his behavior—she just needed to enjoy the beautiful day and the handsome man who kept her company.

They spent several hours splashing and playing in the water, interspersed with swimming. Nick had a powerful stroke and she had trouble keeping up with him, but it was fun. They raced back and forth across the pool during the break periods when children had to sit out. Her Master seemed reluctant to exit the pool and she knew why.

Nick's arousal had not gone unnoticed by her. His cock had been hard almost the whole time just before they jumped in the pool. If nothing else, he clearly found her attractive. She slid her eyes sideways, noting his broad, muscular chest. They were hanging onto the edge of the pool, chatting, only she couldn't seem to keep her mind on the conversation. His hard masculine body called to her. How she wished she could make hot, passionate love to Nick.

"Hey kids," he waved across the pool, jarring her from steamy thoughts. "Be back in a minute," he said to her quickly.

She watched him swim up to a boy and girl, youngsters about eight years old. Squeals erupted from the children as Nick grabbed each in turn and pitched them in the air. This rough water play went on for long minutes. Amira was glowing inside by the time Nick started back toward her. He loved children.

"Who are they?"

"Neighbors. Sweet kids." He glanced back across the pool "Their mom is super, but she has to work long hours sometimes."

"Don't tell me you babysit?" She couldn't keep the astonishment from her voice.

He chuckled. "No, but those evenings, Becky and Brad spend a lot of time here at the pool." He shrugged nonchalantly. "I try to take a dip after work, when I can. I enjoy playing with them. They're nice kids."

Amira had it now. Nick spent time with the children during those times. "You like children?"

He nodded, turned to her and grinned. "Their mom too."

She snorted and slapped his shoulder lightly. While she was sure Nick did date the mother from his statement, he also wished to change the conversation. She was as sure as Hadji was her King, that Nick loved children. It was a nice quality she wouldn't have thought to attribute to his playboy behavior.

Amira wasn't quite ready to let it go that easily. "Do you want kids one day?"

"Sure, when the right woman comes along."

That was a surprising bit of information. Did that mean Nick was waiting, looking for that special woman?

"What about you?" He turned and watched her face.

"I wanted at least ten."

"Ten!"

At his shocked look, she had to smile. "Remember, people had many children long ago...so many died at birth or at a young age."

"That's true." Nick placed one hand over her hand gripping the poolside and squeezed gently. "I'm sorry."

She stared at his large hand. She looked so frail beneath its strength. Tears threatened to spill and she dipped water with her other hand, washing her face with the cool water.

"Are you ready to get some more sun?" She had to change the subject quickly.

Nick glanced around the pool, then nodded, following behind her as she got out.

Many people had left already, mostly leaving children who were being watched closely by a few lifeguards.

"Where did everyone go?" She stretched out, wiggling her hips to find just the right comfortable spot. Nick's eyes flashed to her upper thighs, his look molten. She hadn't meant to stir his senses, but couldn't say it was such a bad feeling either.

"Getting late." His voice was slightly gruff. "Some have places to go."

"Dates?" She stared sharply at her Master. "Am I keeping you from anything?"

He laughed. "Not anything I wish to do." He purposely turned the heat of his dark eyes upon her, letting her know without words he desired her and being here with her was what he wanted.

Amira flipped to her stomach, unable to take her Master's intense interest. Her pussy was moist just from his look.

"Let me oil up your back." Nick leaned over her, waiting for her to nod.

When he untied the bra top and pushed the strings to the side, her nipples tingled. Those strong hands spread the tanning oil over her back, giving her shoulders a soothing massage before moving lower. She sighed, unable to stop it from escaping.

"Feels good, huh?"

"Yes." That's all the answer she could manage. Nick's touch was stirring up sensations she thought long dead. Of course she could pleasure herself anytime she wished, but it just wasn't the same.

Chapter Twenty-Three

❧

Nick's hands caressed the small of her back, making shivers run all the way up to her neck. They slid, one to each side, smoothing the oil over every little niche. Her breasts ached for his touch.

He paused and her breath hitched as warm oil splattered the length of her legs. Quickly, he spread it up and down before it ran off, then taking his time, began massaging it into her skin. Starting at her heels, he worked his way up, until his hands stroked the flesh at her bikini line.

"Ooh." Amira bit her lip.

"Very nice," he said softly.

Whether Nick meant her feeling or his own, she didn't know and didn't care. She was living the moment.

His fingers teased the edge of her bikini and her clit throbbed. She pictured those long fingers slipping beneath the fabric and sliding along her slick folds. Gripping the towel beneath her, Amira unconsciously clenched her buttocks. A light slap to her ass made her jump and her clit beat erratically.

He efficiently tied her bra straps. "Turn over."

When she flipped over, she kept her eyes closed. Seeing Nick's desire would push her over the edge. His hands touched her cheeks as he smoothed the coconut-scented oil gently on her face, his hand gliding down to cover her neck.

"Smells nice." A nervous quiver thrummed in her voice.

"Hmmm."

Nick continued with his attention, rubbing the oil on her upper chest, his fingers flirting with the bra fabric. Amira held her breath when one finger slipped inside the bra, as if by accident. She didn't say a word when that finger flicked over her nipple, causing it to pebble more. But she had a hard time keeping a groan inside.

As if sensing her tortured state, he picked up her closest hand, rubbing the oil on it, then working his way up her arm. He paused to squeeze more oil on his hands, and then gave her other arm the same treatment.

The hot sun, warm oil, coconut scent, and the strong hands stroking her body, were making her insides go mushy. Her pussy felt like the sun licked it with special attention, setting it on fire. Her clit throbbed and moistness gathered in her folds.

Amira's stomach quivered when Nick's hands glided over her abdomen, sliding around her waist, then up to her ribcage. His caresses slid downward and she held her breath when his fingers plucked at the tiny strings on the side. Those marvelous fingers slipped across her lower abdomen, rubbing a little deeper under the material with each stroke.

Her hips arched slightly upward as his fingers played briefly with her pubic hair. Her hands were clutched tight next to her body, gripping the towel tightly. She let out her breath in one long sigh as his hands slid away from her bikini to her legs.

Like he had when she lay on her stomach, he started with her feet, massaging the oil into them, then sliding up her legs gradually. By the time he reached her thighs, she was panting and her stomach trembled.

It was both frightening and wondrous to be under his control this much. She knew he could make her climax with a few well-placed strokes of his fingers. She was that close.

Amira opened her eyes, startled. She had forgotten the djinn rules in the space of so many minutes. Glorious minutes she didn't regret. But she must stop any further encroachment.

Her head seemed to take forever to turn toward her Master. She was held spellbound for long seconds at the lust in his eyes as he glanced at her. Then his eyes followed the path his hands made as they moved upon her. She swallowed, not able to stop him yet.

One hand stroked her upper thigh, while the other edged under the bikini, caressing so near her lower lips, a mere movement toward him would plunge his fingers into her hot folds. Her clit throbbed madly. Hadji, she was on the verge of orgasm.

Placing her hand desperately over his hand, she cried, "Stop."

Nick's fingers stilled, but he looked at her in confusion. "What?"

"You must stop." Amira bit her bottom lip, shoving his hand into his lap. Her eyelids fluttered down for a second, then she gazed at him. "I cannot be brought to satisfaction by my Master's hand."

Nick's neck flushed red and his eyes turned hard. "Damn your genie rules! Are you sure?"

She nodded. It was too painful to talk.

He lay down on his chair, exhaling a breath laden with frustration. Amira peeked beneath her half-shuttered eyelids. He was staring at the sky, hands behind his head, his cock pointing straight upward.

"I'm glad no one is sitting close to us," she giggled.

Nick turned to her, frowning, completely ignoring his raging erection. "Yes, otherwise you probably wouldn't have let me massage the oil on you so long."

She flushed. Poor Nick, he was frustrated and angry. She couldn't blame him. She had passed anger many centuries ago, but exasperation still sat in her stomach like a sour piece of fruit. How lovely it would have felt if she could have allowed Nick's skilled fingers to bring her to orgasm.

"I'm sorry." She offered what she could, her words.

He turned on his side, then let out a long breath. "No, it's me who should be apologizing. I never start anything I can't finish." A large grin flashed across his face.

She knew he was trying to turn the situation humorous. He knew it was not her fault.

"Hey, are you getting hungry?"

She nodded, glad Nick had come to grip with his frustrated senses.

"Let's rinse off in the changing area, then go grab a bite at the café. Is that okay?" He jumped up and held out one hand.

"That would be wonderful."

It didn't take long for them to get clean and change. Amira blinked up shorts and a shirt. Nick wore what he came to the pool in. Dinner was fun, especially interjected with the silly jokes he kept telling her. She knew her Master was trying to lighten the mood, and it worked.

By the time they returned to his apartment, they both were in high spirits, and nothing would suffice except a comedy movie. After that, they watched a campy horror movie that had them laughing more than the funny one. Popcorn was scattered on the floor and coke cans littered the coffee table by the time they called it quits.

Amira quickly made the mess disappear. When she glanced at Nick, he looked content and tired. Her eyes were drooping too. He held out one arm and she sat down tentatively, then shrugging, cuddled against his chest.

Chapter Twenty-Four

ೕ

Nick stroked Amira's hair gently, listening to her breathing. She had fallen asleep but moments ago. He would never forget their day together. It had been one of the most wondrous and most frustrating in his memory. He smiled softly. That's the way his genie made him feel half the time—horny as hell and not able to do a thing about it, and charmed by her very presence at the same time.

What am I going to do with you? Keep her, his mind replied.

What else? Nick tried to shove that thought aside, but it kept edging back, demanding attention. Finally, he quit trying to fight his growing feelings. He stared at the magical woman resting on his chest. *Do I love her?*

His chest felt tight at that thought. He had the same joyful emotions he'd experienced as a youth around Sharon. And that scared him.

He stroked her hair slowly. Would anything come of pursuing such a wondrous being? He didn't know, but every feeling he'd buried as a youth fought for life. Nick wanted to love again, to be immersed in those crazy, drunken sensations.

Could Amira ever have a normal life? Would she ever be able to make love...to him? His hand tightened unconsciously on her shoulder. She mumbled in her sleep and he lightened his grip. He'd never been one to turn down a challenge or tuck his tail in defeat.

Nick smiled grimly. So, he had thrown down the gauntlet. Impish thoughts kept invading his warm feelings and he became frustrated at his warring mind. If he did figure out a way for

Amira to be normal, then that meant losing her genie abilities, which meant no more sexual wishes.

The selfish thoughts were shoved to the back of his mind. In his head, he pictured pushing a little man dressed in a red devil suit into a closet and slamming the door.

Shaking his head at himself, Nick didn't know how effective his method would be, but at least it was a start. If he was going to figure out how to help Amira and ultimately himself, he had to control the id side of his nature that wanted everything for itself.

In spite of his disturbing thoughts, he was drowsy. The sun zapped the strength right out of you. He felt like a big lazy cat, with no desire but to rest.

When Amira had settled into his arms, Nick thought to spend the rest of the evening in relaxation. This evening had been pure fun.

But when she wiggled in her sleep, readjusting against his chest, his wayward mind latched onto the sensual experience they'd exchanged poolside. His breathing increased as he recalled the velvety softness of her skin beneath his fingers. Remembered how Amira had responded. In fact, as his fingers had edged near her bikini bottom, she'd looked ready to explode.

His cock rose beneath his shorts. Amira chose that moment to awaken and stretch her arms wide, and then turned toward the television. He hoped she wouldn't notice his arousal. He didn't want her to think him some randy young man who couldn't control his urges for one night.

He stroked her arm gently. Nick knew he was closer to that uncontrollable, horny image than he cared to admit. Amira's soft laugh thrummed through his chest. She was watching TV while he couldn't take his eyes off her.

Her long legs were visible in this position, plus one breast and the top of her head. But that was more than enough to kindle his interest further.

It'd been those beautiful legs that he'd stroked earlier, his oil slicked hands easing slowly toward her groin. Nick groaned and shifted his body slightly.

"Are you all right?" Amira sat up and turned toward him.

Nick stared at her angelic face and sinfully lovely body. "Yes—no."

Her brow creased, then she grinned. "Which is it?"

Letting out a deep exhalation, he ran one hand down the side of her head, and then grasped her chin. "I'm fine. I had a wonderful day. Yet, I'm in agony."

"Agony?" She flicked her eyes over his face. "Can I help?"

"Yes," he whispered huskily. "More than you could ever know."

With that statement, he leaned over her and placed the merest kiss to her full lips. Bending her backwards, so she was sprawled across his lap, he stroked her lower lip with his tongue.

Amira remained close-mouthed, her brilliant golden eyes staring at him in alarm.

"Master?" she whispered against his mouth.

"Open for me." He kissed the corner of her mouth, and then latched onto her lips. His cock throbbed as Amira's sweet lips parted.

Their kiss was lingering, their tongues engaging in a dance as elaborate as any he'd performed on a dance floor. He gently caressed the delicate skin on her neck while they kissed, then slid down, palming one breast. He wanted to feel her heart beat while they kissed, to gauge the extent of her feelings. Her rapid heartbeat pleased him.

Amira withdrew and said, "Nick."

"Shhh." He placed one finger over her lips. "It is enough—for now."

Turning her body, he settled onto the couch, pulling Amira deeper into his arms. It took a bit, but finally his cock calmed down and he relaxed with Amira snuggled against his chest.

* * * * *

The next morning he awoke to lovely Amira curled in his arms. He was so happy it didn't seem real. *Do I deserve this? Do I deserve her?* Nick snorted at his silly thoughts. Amira stretched and gazed up at him sleepily. Those amber eyes could draw a man in, to get lost in their beauty.

"You hungry?" he asked to cover the shakiness inside.

"Mmm." She yawned widely, then covered her mouth quickly. "First, I'd like to shower."

Nick jumped up and pulled her to stand beside him. "Can I join you?" His voice went deep with lust as an image of them soaping each other shot into his mind.

Amira looked startled, but then her face shuttered down and became expressionless. "I can't…it would be dangerous."

He gripped her face gently and placed a quick kiss to her full lips. "That's okay." It really wasn't okay with him, but it wasn't her fault. It was those damn genie rules. "You go first then, and I'll gather the breakfast items."

She disappeared in a super flash of blue energy. Nick stretched one arm out, but it was too late to stop her. He had meant for her to use his shower. For some reason that seemed important.

As he prepared the ingredients for an omelet, he analyzed his own mind. Did he want Amira using his shower…marking her territory, laying claim to his male domain? He smiled. That thought had a warm, fuzzy feeling attached to it.

Images of a gloriously nude Amira showering entered his mind. Strolling to the bathroom, Nick managed to clear his mind and calm his cock to half-staff. He showered quickly, thrusting away intrusive thoughts of rubbing a slick, wet Amira. He heard her moving about the living room, and finished his morning routine super fast.

"You look lovely." He was pleased with the simple white sundress she wore. It made her look more innocent than ever. He walked over and tugged one braid. "Cute." She had a long braid hanging over each breast, lending more to the naive image.

He took a deep breath in, she smelled as delicious as she looked. "What is that fragrance?"

"Jasmine."

Smiling, he took her hand and seated her at the bar. "How do you like your omelets?"

"Surprise me."

Nick whistled happily as he whipped up their breakfast. They finished their last cup of coffee outside, enjoying the morning air and each other's company.

"I'm sorry Amira, but I've got some paperwork to do—a new client tomorrow."

"You don't have to apologize, I have loved every minute of our weekend."

Her words made his stomach warm. She'd used the word our, but he was sure it was unconsciously done. Amira always seemed to hold herself from him. Could he blame her? After so many centuries and Masters, what hope did she have of gaining normalcy?

"It's not over yet."

Chapter Twenty-Five

એ

She cocked her head at his statement, but then strolled into the living room and picked up a magazine.

By lunchtime, Nick had his work in order. Amira fixed them sandwiches and he told her about his client as they ate.

"You've got a little mayonnaise on your mouth." He dabbed at the corner of her lip.

Her tongue came out to lick the spot he'd just cleaned. His cock jumped at the sight of her pink flesh. Jumping up he headed for the living room. "I've got to run to the store." He received a nod and sweet smile from Amira.

It took him some time to find all the items he wanted. His genie was lounging on the couch, reading a romance book, when he returned. It would be hours to dinnertime, and Nick knew how he wanted to fill them.

"Have you ever played Monopoly?"

She shook her head. "What is it?"

"A game." Nick took down the box from the closet, then spread everything on the coffee table.

"I would never have guessed you like to play children's games." Amira giggled.

He grinned. "My niece and nephew got me hooked on it."

"Where are they?" She picked up the tiny dog, then each piece in turn.

"Dallas. They visit several times a year, and they usually beat the pants off me in Monopoly."

"How delightful." She smiled at him, her eyes brilliant yellow diamonds. "You love them."

"Yes, yes I do." He nodded, arranging the cards. Amira was a quick study, and it didn't take but a few games before he was struggling to keep ahead of her. He could tell by her smiling face she loved the game. He was surprised when glancing at the clock later. It was getting close to dinnertime.

Slapping the table lightly, he said, "I've got to fix dinner. Why don't you finish that book?"

"Need any help?"

"No. This is my treat for you." He didn't want to share that he was preparing her a gourmet meal, not until she set eyes on his masterpiece.

Amira strolled to the archway between the living room and kitchen periodically, watching him prepare, then returning to the living room. He was glad — her presence would have been distracting while he was cooking.

After everything was ready, he set the table, using his good china, then lit the tall candles resting in the two brass candlesticks. Everything looked perfect.

"Damn," he muttered. He was still dressed casually. Running into the bedroom, he got changed in record time, putting on a pair of slacks, shirt, and dinner jacket. Coming back into the living room, he met Amira's curious eyes.

"I want tonight to be special." He ran one hand down a lapel. "Could you change into something that you'd wear to a romantic dinner?"

Amira jumped up, her gold eyes aflame with excitement. With a wave, her appearance changed dramatically. A simple black dress molded to her curves, set off with a string of pearls. Her hair was swept up, leaving her elegant neck exposed. Tiny pearl earrings in her earlobes matched the necklace. She was gorgeous, everything he could have wished or desired.

"Dinner is served." Nick held out an elbow and Amira slid her hand through his arm.

Nick looked so handsome and was so gallant, she was overwhelmed for a few seconds. When Amira saw the lovely china and candlelit table, she knew she was in for a romantic evening. Her stomach fluttered in excitement.

After pulling her seat out, Nick placed two oysters on each of their plates.

"Our appetizer, smoked oysters." He poured wine into their glasses. "And this is Chardonnay." He glanced at her. "Ever tried it?"

She shook her head and took a sip. "Mmm, wonderful." Following Nick's example, she let the oyster slide down her throat. She hadn't wanted to tell him she'd never tried the shellfish either. The oyster's appearance had always kept her from tasting it. But she didn't want to hurt Nick's feelings after he went to so much trouble. It didn't taste bad, but neither was she crazy about it.

"Good?"

"Delish." She took another sip of wine. Finishing off the other oyster wasn't that bad, especially after more wine.

Jumping up, Nick cleared the small plates and bowl that had held the oysters. He set a fresh salad in front of her, then sat and dug his fork into his bowl.

"I love salad," Amira stabbed a large mouthful of lettuce and tomato.

"Me too. But save room, there's lots more."

When they finished, Nick brought over a pot and spooned a wonderful smelling meat mixture onto their plates.

"Beef bourguignon."

Then he set a large bowl between them and served them both portions. "Angel hair pasta with gingered beef flavoring."

To her surprise, he poured a different kind of wine into another wine glass. "Burgundy."

"Oh, Nick, you're going to spoil me."

"Don't say that until you've sampled." He grinned and pointed to her plate.

Amira rolled her eyes dramatically after taking a big bite of the beef, then again after tasting the pasta.

Laughing, he dug into his food with gusto. After they started slowing down, she rubbed her stomach. "You should have been a chef."

Nick paused midway to his mouth with a forkful of beef. "I thought about it."

She was so full she didn't think she could take another bite. Amira was fearful Nick was bringing on another entrée when he got up, but he returned with a delicious looking dessert. Mousse. One of her favorites.

"You shouldn't have." She moaned in exaggeration.

"I told you to save room," he chuckled, picking up her dessert spoon and placing it in her hand.

She placed the luscious chocolate in her mouth and closed her eyes. It was to-die-for delicious.

When the last spoonful was consumed, Nick pulled her chair back and escorted her to the couch. He brought a bottle of champagne with him.

"What are we celebrating?" Was this part of the gourmet meal?

"Us." He kissed the end of her nose. "Life." He placed a deeper kiss to her mouth.

Chapter Twenty-Six

&

Amira was dumbstruck. Just what was Nick up to? He strolled into the kitchen and returned with two tall, slim wine glasses. After he popped the cork, he poured the glasses full and handed her one.

"Are you trying to get me drunk?" she teased, already halfway there.

"Maybe." His dark eyes bored into hers over the glass rim, unclothing her with his look.

Nick proposed a toast and they clinked glasses. By the time she'd sipped her way through the champagne, she was giggling a lot and feeling very pleasant.

"Come here, beautiful." He set his glass down and placed one hand around the back of her neck, bringing her forward. She half fell onto his chest, propping herself above his face.

"Kiss me." His eyes demanded more than he was saying.

"Why?" She couldn't still the giggle that escaped.

"Because I wish it." Nick's voice was gruff and she knew he no longer played a game.

She should have slipped out of his arms and sat on the end of the couch—out of reach. But she didn't want to. She wanted to kiss him too. Leaning down, she brought her mouth to his. He tasted of champagne and chocolate.

Opening her mouth, she had no other thought than to taste more of his hot mouth. His tongue stroked hers with little flicks, inviting her to do the same. Her heart seemed to be running away, it beat so swiftly.

Nick slipped one hand to the pins in her hair and slid them out. Her hair fell around her shoulders, and he gently smoothed down the mass.

Amira licked Nick's lower lip, then sucked it into her mouth. His hand ran up through her hair and he pulled her mouth forward for deeper contact. They were one. One breath, one life. His strong heart beneath her hand and she circled her fingers on his muscular chest.

Nick left her mouth and licked her earlobe. Her pussy lips were moist and craved something. It took a second to realize she wanted his touch, a dangerous wish.

"Amira," he whispered in her ear, his tone throaty.

Her neck felt weak, her body boneless. His kiss dipped down and she felt his warm tongue on her throat. Her breath hitched as he hit a particularly sensitive spot.

"Oh," she groaned.

His hands slipped to the tiny straps of the dress, pushing them down until the material barely clung to her breasts. She arched backward as Nick palmed each breast, kneading gently. His lips continued kissing her overheated flesh as he went downward.

Her chest quivered when she felt his lips softly kiss her cleavage. She pressed her head back into the couch and kept her eyes closed. A sharp gasp escaped her when wet warmth stroked across her breasts, a mere inch above her nipples.

She had to look. When she saw Nick lapping at her skin, it made her clit throb as if he caressed it instead. Pushing her breasts up with both hands, he moved his mouth over her beaded nipples, rubbing his closed mouth back and forth across the material. Her hands moved up his arms to his head and she twined her fingers in his hair, wanting to push him into her flesh, but not daring to be so bold.

Amira moaned when he opened his mouth and sucked on her nipple through the silky cloth. Releasing her flesh, he brought his face level with hers and stared into her eyes. He wanted her to see the lust in his eyes, and something else, a depth of emotion she had thought never to see again.

A shiver ran through her body. She had to be either mistaken or mad. That could not be love she saw. Nick's hands squeezed her breasts gently, and then he worked her dress lower, caressing her exposed nipples with his thumbs.

"Stop!" She shoved his fingers off her breasts.

Nick sat back, his look surprised and confused. "What happened? Did I hurt you?"

"No…please, we have to stop. It is forbidden." She sniffed back a tear. In reality, what she thought she saw reflected in his eyes hurt more than any physical pain he could choose to inflict on her.

Nick folded his arms, his jaw clenched. "You know, I'm really sick of those stupid genie rules of yours."

Amira sat up straight, pulling her dress back up. "They're not my rules," she spat.

He sighed and ran one hand through his hair. "I'm sorry. It's not your fault."

"That's right, Master." She made her voice sarcastic but firm. "No one can give me satisfaction. You might as well get that through your head."

"Uh, you forgot to add *thick* head." Nick chuckled.

She took a deep breath. While she normally appreciated his humor, now was not the time. She suddenly felt so sad and defeated. "May I go?"

He stared at her for a few seconds, then nodded.

She dared a last glance at Nick as she dissolved. He looked frustrated, but thoughtful.

* * * * *

Nick called to her the next morning. He was going to work late that night, and the next evening he had a business meeting. Of course he told her to come and go as she pleased.

Amira chose to stay inside her lamp while he was at work. Memories of last night haunted her throughout the day. Her breathing increased each time she recalled their heated kisses and Nick's sensual stroking of her breasts. Finally, in frustration, she'd brought herself to an orgasm. She'd thought of their embrace as she caressed her clit, and was surprised by the power of her climax.

Fortunately, her Master came in so late—he didn't call to her. He walked quietly, as if trying not to disturb her. The next day she spent in his living room, watching TV and flipping through every magazine in his rack. He came in at bedtime and seemed pleased to see her. They talked for a few minutes, and then he excused himself for the night.

Amira watched his broad back disappear through the bedroom door. Restless and lonely, she watched old horror movies until after midnight. The thought of being by herself in her lamp did not appeal to her, so she cuddled up on Nick's couch.

He was surprised to see her sprawled on the couch the next morning, but gave her a quick kiss on the way out. Better than that, he told her he'd be home straight after work. Amira hugged a pillow to her chest. That was special.

In spite of the sexual wishes he chose to use on weekends, Nick still liked to go out on Wednesday nights. He had told her he went to bars or nightclubs to meet women. Tonight he'd chosen to forgo his regular night out—he was staying at home with her.

* * * * *

The dinner date with Amira had gone spectacularly, until she became fearful as he kissed her. Nick was determined to break down her reluctance. He knew he couldn't make love to her, but he could push it to the limit of her rules and he intended to do just that. What that would accomplish besides leaving him extremely frustrated, he didn't know — but something inside him whispered he must pursue not only Amira's character but also her lustful side. Push her to her boundaries as well.

Was there a secret to breaking her genie bondage? Nick didn't have a clue, but being with her felt right. Maybe he could get her to tell him more about the conditions, help him figure out a way to work around the rules — that is, if she wanted to make love as badly as he did.

And did he really want to break the curse that held Amira to him in servitude? He stared at the busy street. He'd stopped for a cup of coffee and to think before he returned home. People bustled back and forth, busy with their lives. One couple strolled by, arms draped around each other's waist. They were young and it was very apparent they were in love — the way they gazed at one another.

Is that what I want? Yes, a tiny voice whispered in the deepest recesses of his heart. Another couple walking by grabbed his attention. They were at least in their sixties, and held hands like newlyweds. The couple paused to stare into the window of a shop next to his table, and Nick got a good look at them. They talked like old friends and the look in their eyes, while not lust-filled like the young people, was brimming with love that came from a lifetime of living together.

That's what he wanted — what both couples had. The lust and physical attraction that came with newfound love, and then the deep, committed love that came from living with your loved one for years.

He swirled the cold coffee in his cup and held it up for the waitress to refill.

That was it then. To allow his love for Amira to blossom, and hopefully hers in return, the genie bonds would somehow have to be broken. No more sexual wishes. Nick grinned. Why did that thought bring such joy to him? *Because you're in love*, he answered himself.

But did Amira love him? Taking a sip, he went over her behavior with him and the way her eyes softened when they were together. He'd had plenty of women who gazed at him with lust, even one with an obsessive love, but none with true committed love. Bringing Sharon's image to mind, he thought about how her eyes had looked and how she'd acted, before she fell out of love with him. It was very similar to the look in Amira's eyes.

A shiver ran down his back. Was that true love then? If Sharon could fall out of love so easily, would Amira too? Would she leave him if he found a way to free her?

Chapter Twenty-Seven

&

Anger lanced through his fear. No. Amira was not like that. Amira wasn't Sharon. Besides, he would give her no reason to leave him, but so many splendid ones to stay.

Nick stared at a fancy shop across the street. It was filled with expensive clothes and the accessories women loved. Amira could wish up anything in that shop. She could live a lifestyle many people would envy. Except for her freedom, she had so many wondrous things at her command.

Would she give all that up for him? In frustration, he slammed his cup down, sloshing the coffee onto the table. Mopping the spill up with a napkin, he crumbled the paper in his hand.

An image of Amira's sweet face floated before him. How could he forget the look of sadness, lust, and disappointment on her face when she conjured his wishes? She might be pleased with her ability to wish up anything she desired, but she was not happy having to watch her Master's fulfilled sexual wishes, while she remained chaste. She certainly hadn't been happy watching him.

He took a calming breath of relief. He knew women. And he knew as sure as he had an Italian name, Amira was saddened by the parade of women he wished up. She *did* have feelings for him. It was also clear that she did not like the servitude and lack of freedom the curse placed upon her. Her story about Ali had made it crystal clear what her feelings were on the matter.

Nick jumped up, ready now to face his genie and his destiny. Somehow, he had to convince her they belonged together.

When he got home, the sight of Amira fixing supper for him pleasantly surprised him. He always hated anyone else messing around his kitchen. But not Amira. Nick had enjoyed teaching her how to make a few dishes and right now she was putting the finishing touches on pasta and marinated chicken. She looked so right in his home.

They chatted throughout the meal, their conversation flowing easily, which was nice since the night before had ended on an uncomfortable note. Afterwards, they followed what was quickly becoming a nightly routine — popcorn and watching a movie.

Sleeping With The Enemy was on and though they'd both seen it, Nick watched it again with interest. He had concentrated before on the more chilling elements, but now he watched the developing relationship between the hero and heroine with interest.

"I'd do that for you." he stated out of the blue.

Amira turned and eyed him quizzically. "What?"

"Fight for you." He stroked her hair gently.

"Why?"

"Because a man in love will do anything for his girl." His pulse leaped in his neck. Would Amira believe him?

"Wha...what are you saying, Nick?" Her look had shifted from curious to frightened.

"That I'm madly, completely head-over-heels in love with you." He took her face between his hands so she had to gaze into his eyes.

"Are you?" she whispered. Those amber orbs glowed and shimmered with held-in tears.

Drawing her toward him, he kissed her, urging her mouth open with his tongue. Somewhere in the back of his mind a niggling thought fought for attention. And it burst upon him as their kiss deepened and changed what started as a chaste kiss into burning lust. He had thought that perhaps proclaiming his love would end her curse. But no magic had ripped through the room, and Amira seemed the same.

Nick pushed her gently back and examined her face. She looked flushed and happy. "Do you feel any different?"

"What do you mean?" She stared at his lips, clearly wishing to continue.

"I thought if I said I loved you, it would put an end to your genie days."

Her eyes dipped downward, then returned to his, sadness now flushing through their depths. "No," she whispered. "That is not the key."

"Then, what is?" He hated the way his voice came out so demanding, but he couldn't stop himself.

Amira shook her head. "Remember...I cannot tell you. It would negate the result."

"So—I have to keep trying until I hit it correctly?"

She nodded, staring at him uncertainly. Did she think he'd give up?

"I've always gotten what I set my heart on." He gave her a reassuring stare, the kind he used with clients during meetings. He wanted her to believe in him.

A tear slipped down one satiny cheek, and he wiped it gently away.

"And you? How do you feel about me, Amira?" His voice caught in his throat. He felt like a kid in the throes of a first crush.

"Oh, Nick," she sighed. "I loved the way you looked when I first saw you. How could I not?"

"Omar." He clenched his jaw.

"Yes. But you are not he." She laid one hand along the side of his face. "You are your own man. Unique. You are intelligent, sweet, funny, and caring."

"Me?" He couldn't keep a chuckle from erupting. He'd never thought of himself in those terms, except maybe for the intelligence.

"Yes, you." She smiled sweetly, her eyes glowing. "I admit, at first it was hard to see many of those qualities beneath your playboy exterior."

Nick swallowed hard. That was a mouthful. How close had he come to losing her, or never gaining her love in the first place?

"But, gradually your good qualities shone through. I…wasn't sure if you loved me until you declared it just now. I did feel you cared for me, what I think, how I feel about things. That you worried about my imprisonment as a djinn." She gazed into his eyes. "How could I not love you?"

"Cara," he kissed her softly. "Well, I do love you. You are sweet, kind, smart, a fine conversationalist, and we share many of the same interests."

"That's quite a list." Her eyes looked worried. " But, we cannot make love."

"Not for now, but there are other things we can do. Besides, we're going to get rid of that damn genie curse."

She cocked her head. "What other things?"

He placed one hand over her left breast and gently circled her nipple through the cloth covering it. "Touching, kissing, licking."

Her eyes closed as he rubbed her beaded flesh. She reopened them and stared at him, her look tortured. "But these things will only cause us…discomfort. We cannot consummate our physical love."

"You know, I've been wondering about some of those genie rules. What exactly do they say about climaxing?"

Amira blushed. "That I cannot be brought to fulfillment by a Master, nor he be brought to pleasure by his djinn."

"How long has it been since you've read these edicts?" He removed his hand from her breast and massaged her neck, hoping to relax her.

Her brow wrinkled in thought. "I...I don't remember reading them since I was first cursed."

"It's been centuries!" Nick sure couldn't rely on his memory if it'd been that long.

"Try millennia," she frowned.

"We need to take a look at these rules. Might be some loopholes we can use."

"Loopholes?" She looked confused.

"A lawyer term. Meaning, we might find a way around those laws."

When Amira continued to stare at him, uncertainty stamped on her face, he urged gently, "Can we see those rules?"

Chapter Twenty-Eight

Nodding, she snapped her fingers and a beige-yellow roll of parchment appeared in one hand. She unrolled it carefully, ignoring the faint crackling of its weathered texture.

"Read it aloud."

"*Kul djinn ismaou hazehee alkalimat aldiniyah allazena koutebou beyad Hadji alkawee.*"

Nick chuckled. "No, in English."

"Oh, sorry," Amira flashed him a quick glance. Her eyes were focused as if her attention was centered on something faraway — which it was.

Clearing her throat, she read, "All djinn heed these sacred words, those set down by the all-powerful Hadji."

Nick listened for a minute then touched her arm. "Cut to the good stuff."

"Huh?" Amira's porcelain skin was pale, her thoughts clearly elsewhere.

"The part that pertains to you not being able to satisfy a Master or reach orgasm with him."

Amira nodded absentmindedly, and then ran one finger down the scroll. Taking a deep breath, she read, "The djinn known as Amira shall never gain sexual release by *iro*."

"What is that?"

Blushing, she said, "Her Master's cock."

"Continue," he waved toward the ancient paper.

"Nor shall a Master's cock enter into the djinn Amira to give her ultimate pleasure. Nor shall a Master's hand or tongue be used to give Amira release. Neither shall Amira bring a Master to sexual release by *kittah*...the djinn's vagina, her tongue, or her hands. All these acts are forbidden."

"Anything else?"

"What do you mean?" Amira gave him a puzzled look.

"Anything about kissing, fondling, or licking?" He stroked her hair. "You know...foreplay."

Her eyes widened and she stared down at the scroll clutched in her hands. "Nothing." Her voice was a mere whisper.

"Then, we can play all we wish—as long as my cock doesn't make you climax, or my tongue and hands. And the same applies to you—not bringing me to orgasm by using your tongue, hands, or vagina."

"Is it true?" Amira looked scared.

Nick tapped the paper with one finger. "It's spelled out in Hadji's own words."

She let out a deep breath.

Nick took the scroll from her stiff hands and laid it on the coffee table, and then placed his arms around her waist.

"I'm frightened."

Kissing her gently, he soothed her. "I know. But it'll be all right." He kissed her cheek. "Do you trust me?"

"Yes." Her voice quivered slightly.

"Come with me." He held out one hand, pulling her up beside him.

Amira followed Nick into his bedroom. Once they reached the bed, he drew her into his arms, looking at her for long seconds before capturing her lips. She knew he was trying to reassure her, and his confidence had helped, yet her stomach fluttered nervously.

As with every time he kissed her, Amira grew weak-kneed and her pussy grew moist. Nick's kiss was more possessive than ever before and demanded her complete surrender. Her stomach was in knots and her body felt as if liquid fire raced through her blood. Her legs trembled and she would have collapsed if not for his hard arms holding her up.

His lips slid to her cheek and then around to her earlobe. Nick licked her lobe, wetting it, and then blowing on it gently. A shiver ran down her neck, raising the hair at her nape.

A moan sighed from her as he laved her whole ear, circling his marvelous tongue around it, finally pulling her earlobe into his mouth. He nipped and sucked it for long seconds, until Amira was panting, digging her hands into his soft shirt and stroking the firm chest beneath.

"Oh, let me," she groaned, moving back. Amira stroked his jaw, and then turned his face, bringing his ear to her mouth. Reciprocating, she stroked her tongue around the swirls, and then sucked on his earlobe.

"That feels great," Nick whispered huskily.

Amira's clit jumped in response to his words. It was a powerful feeling, turning him on so much by simply fondling his ear.

"I want you," he spoke softly into her ear as she licked his earlobe. Pushing her back slightly, he asked, "Are you hot?"

"Yes. I can barely breathe, such warmth is running through my veins." Amira pulled her shirt from her body and flapped it a few times.

"Let me help you with that." His hands slid to the bottom of the short T-shirt, edging it upward and pulling it off her.

Amira's legs went wobbly with the turmoil of her emotions when he went down on his knees. She stood breathless in anticipation as he undid the button on her jean shorts, then the zipper. Her lower lips were swollen and begged for his touch. Would he stroke her pussy? Her clit throbbed, desperate for fulfillment.

Her breath expelled in one great gush as Nick slowly slid her shorts down. His hands caressed her thighs. He flung her shorts to the side and kissed each thigh.

When he stood back up, Amira placed her hands on either side of his buttoned shirt. "My turn." She jerked the fabric, popping the buttons off.

Nick's chest heaved and his eyes devoured her. He stood like a statue as she slipped the shirt down his arms and caressed his flesh. How she'd longed to touch his muscular chest. Now he was hers, to fondle at her leisure.

Going to her knees, she swallowed hard as she drew the zipper on his pants down. The slacks fell in a puddle around his ankles. His magnificent cock pushed against the silky undershorts, demanding attention and freedom.

Glancing upward, Amira was mesmerized by the fiery look in his brown eyes as he stepped out of the pants and kicked them to the side.

Imitating his earlier actions, she kissed each thigh, so near his staff it nudged her cheek. Flushing with excitement, she kissed her way back up to his chest.

Nick slid one hand behind her neck and arched her backward, so she had to look at him. "I'm going to kiss every inch of you, woman."

Amira's abdomen quivered at his words. Woman. She knew he meant *his woman.* And kiss every inch of her body…that was a fantasy about to come true.

With one swift, hard pull, he brought her to him, melding their lips in a soul-searing kiss. Her breasts were squashed against his rigid chest, her mouth conquered by his. Nick's cock nudged her lower belly. Stretching to her tiptoes, she slid her lower lips up and down his hardness. Moisture leaked through the panties.

Bending, he picked her up, and then laid her gently in the middle of the bed. Then, just as gently, he turned her onto her stomach. Amira crossed her arms under her head and waited for whatever he had in store for her.

After flipping her hair to the side, Nick massaged her shoulders, then kissed the back of her neck. Amira's buttocks clenched. It felt so good. His hands slid down to her bra, unsnapped it, and then pulled it off her. It was a flashback moment to the tender treatment she'd received at the pool. Anticipation flushed through her. Exactly what was Nick planning to do to her?

Those strong hands kneaded the middle of her back, working their way to the small of her back. She moaned.

"Your skin is so soft, cara." Nick's voice was husky.

"What does cara mean?"

"My love."

Chapter Twenty-Nine

෩

Nick's lips grazed her back, placing gentle, warm pecks all along its length. His hands slid to the sides of her breasts. Amira sucked in her breath. She groaned as his wet tongue laved her flesh. Her nipples ached, wanted his tongue to soothe their pain.

His tongue continued downward, licking her sides, and then moving over, to the small of her back. Strong hands kneaded her buttocks and she shoved upward to meet his strokes without being aware of it.

"Oh," she sighed.

Nick nipped her flesh above her panties, then using his lips and teeth, pulled them down. Her pussy throbbed.

His hands slipped the panties the rest of the way down, skimming her flesh as he pushed them off. Now her whole backside was bare to his eyes. It made her feel vulnerable, yet a part of her wanted to expose even more to him.

When his hands caressed her derriere and his tongue followed with wet strokes, she thought she'd jump off the bed.

"Nick," she sighed.

A hot, wet tongue slid down the crevice of her buttocks, and her vagina tightened in reaction. His hands slid down her legs, all the way to her feet, massaging her insoles.

"Mmm," she moaned.

Amira jumped when his tongue licked the bottom of her foot—it tickled. Nick's hands glided up her calves, his lips following each caress. A nibble here, a kiss there, and licks thrown in between, drove her insane.

Wiggling, she pushed her mons into the satin sheets. She was so hot from his foreplay, she felt ready to burst.

When his lips paused at the juncture of her thighs and ass, she held her breath. Would he dip his tongue into her womanly center?

She moaned loudly when Nick's warm tongue slid along the bottom of one buttock, rimming the roundness at the bottom. His wet tongue lavished the other cheek with long strokes as well. Wetness pooled between her lower lips. She wanted his touch so desperately, it was almost painful.

Nick slipped his tongue into her slit, plunging it several times into her slick folds. She jumped forward a few inches, out of his reach.

"What?" Nick muttered against one cheek.

"You must stop that...I almost climaxed." Sanity returned and Amira whipped her eyes in a panic around the room. Everything looked normal — no hint of Hadji's presence.

He kissed each globe. "Okay." He sighed, sounding frustrated. "Turn over, sweetheart."

After settling into a new position, Amira went weak just looking at Nick. He was kneeling, his large cock hard and pointing right at her. An erotic hunger burned through her nerve endings.

"Open your legs." Nick moved between her thighs again when she complied. "Wider."

His voice pulsated through her body, heightening her excitement. His eyes devoured her, seeming to sear her pussy with heat. Or maybe it was simply her own response to his orders. Her nerves tingled, while her nipples stabbed the air — begging to be sucked. And her lower lips were swollen with need, while her clit beat madly.

She desired his touch all over, and Amira knew she was going to get that wish fulfilled. The thought was delicious and her stomach quivered in anticipation.

Nick leaned down and gave her a wet, open-mouthed kiss that left her breathless. He moved down, kissed her chin while his hands caressed her collarbones. Then his lips rubbed against her neck, laving it with long strokes of his tongue.

Tiny shivers ran down her back, while her nipples puckered even more. Amira moaned softly when Nick took each breast into his hands.

She closed her eyes, arching off the bed and thrusting her breast into his mouth when his hot tongue flicked one nub. Grabbing his head, she ran her hands through his soft hair and pulled him closer.

"Yes, suck them."

Nick complied, latching onto her with hard pulls of his lips.

Amira panted. She flounced restlessly when he kissed his way to her other breast, then licked around the areola. He nipped the pebbled flesh and she whimpered.

"Oh, harder." She didn't mean for him to bite harder but Nick seemed to sense her need for more force. Her nipple was tugged into his mouth like a vacuum, satisfying the aching need.

Nick released her and gave the nipple a last flick, looking up at her. "You're so beautiful."

"And you."

He smiled and then his head dipped down. His lips started below her breasts, trailed down the ribcage, sucking before moving on. He licked and kissed his way down her body to one thigh as his hands led the way with massaging caresses.

Amira watched as Nick's black hair melded with the gold of her pubic hair. She shuddered as a wet, warm lave of his tongue washed the area between her thigh and groin.

Looking up, Nick grinned, and then continued his torturous path down her leg, all the way to her feet.

Her clit continued to beat erratically, even though Nick was no longer close to it. She jumped when he took her left big toe into his hot mouth and sucked on it. It felt funny but also made a flush of heat run through her blood.

"Mmm, even your toe tastes good." Nick's eyes twinkled.

She laughed, a deep throaty eruption, intertwined with desire and need. Amira's stomach quivered when Nick started kissing her legs, working his way slowly back up her limbs. His head stopped again just below her groin.

"Put your knees up, cara." His eyes changed, the brown color deepening to almost black as he stared at her pussy. "Wider," he said huskily.

Her legs trembled as she spread them open more. She was completely exposed to his view. It made her feel helpless, but also powerful. A strange combination.

Placing his hands on either side of her lower lips, Nick pulled them apart.

"Lovely."

His breath wafted over her slick flesh, making her shiver. She couldn't take her eyes off him as he edged closer. Nick's eyes locked with hers as he slowly stroked her slit with his tongue.

"Argh." A gurgling moan pushed past her lips.

Again, his tongue dipped into her folds and rimmed the edges, but not touching her clit. Tiny rippling tingles gripped her pussy.

"Stop!" She pushed one hand against his head.

He withdrew. "You're close?"

She nodded and bit her bottom lip. "Nick," she sighed. "How I wish you could bring me to pleasure."

"One day." He placed his hands along her inner thighs. "For now, close your eyes and imagine my tongue licking you."

Chapter Thirty

❧

Amira did as he asked and jumped when his tongue wet a path near the juncture of her thighs. His artful tongue swirled across her flesh, and then he sucked the skin into his mouth.

She groaned loudly. Nick's tongue went wild, flicking her thigh swiftly. In her mind, he was laving her clit, and her sensitive organ responded. Panting breaths escaped her as her pussy convulsed and several small orgasms shuddered through her.

After her last climax flowed through her, Nick stretched out beside her, cuddling her into his arms. Suddenly, she remembered the djinn King. Trembling, she searched for Hadji's eyes, but could not sense his omniscient presence anywhere. Relief sighed through her.

The springy hair on Nick's muscular chest drew her attention. She pulled several strands of the curly hair upward, but then her eyes wandered downward, to his cock. It was half hard, but as she played with his chest, it began stiffening.

Rising up on one elbow, she said, "Now it's your turn." Her other hand slid down his belly and her fingers wrapped around his engorged flesh.

Nick thrust his cock deeper into her hand, while he stroked her hair.

Amira's body still sang with unleashed sensation, heated tingles shot through her as she played with his staff. Stretching upward, she plunged her tongue into his mouth, demanding his kiss.

She was satisfied when he sucked her tongue, then licked her bottom lip. Amira ended their kiss abruptly, kissing down his jaw, and then all the way to his right nipple.

Nick's breath caught as her tongue flicked his male nub. Her hand stroked his cock as she gently sucked his nipple.

His hips thrust upward and he moaned.

Giving his nipple a last flick, she kissed down his rippled abdomen, then spent a few seconds swishing her hair gently back and forth across his cock.

"Oh, God, that feels so good," he groaned.

She felt his hands moving restlessly in her hair. Amira adjusted her hold on his hard flesh, bringing it to an upright position. She licked her lips. She'd dreamed of tasting him so many times, and now the opportunity faced her.

Closing her eyes so she could concentrate on taste and touch, she slid her tongue across the sensitive head of his cock. Soft. Nick's hands stilled in her hair as she ran her tongue over the tip again and again, getting the texture and flavor of him.

She loved the yielding hardness beneath her tongue. A small bead of liquid leaked from the tiny hole. Breathless with anticipation, she licked it up.

Wetting her lips, she slid her mouth over his cock, gliding her lips down. She gagged and popped him out. "Sorry," she blushed.

Nick ruffled her hair. "It's okay sweetheart. You have to find your limit. Not too many women can take all of a cock." He stroked her cheek. "It still felt wonderful."

Taking a breath of relief because Nick wasn't disappointed in her, Amira slid her mouth back onto his engorged flesh.

Her gut tightened with excitement. Having his cock in her own mouth felt so much more real than when she'd been inside Marty's body. She moaned and her mouth went lax for a few seconds as hot desire sank into her limbs, making them weak.

Nick stopped her a few times when her teeth accidentally grazed his skin. But after that she learned how to adjust her lips to cover her teeth. She tried different techniques she'd seen women do to her Masters over the centuries—swift and slow sucks, licking of his whole cock, and flicks of the head. She hesitantly sucked one of his balls into her mouth. She knew this part of Nick was very sensitive and she did not wish to hurt him.

The whole time she explored how to suck a cock, her body thrummed with sensation and need. Her nipples were hard peaks and ached, while her pussy was swollen and throbbed unmercifully. It surprised her that pleasuring Nick could make her so hot.

"Stop, baby." He tapped her head to get her attention.

Amira plopped his cock from her mouth. He was close to climaxing. She stared with greedy eyes at his dark beige-pink cock, its purplish head swollen, with a drop of moisture shining at the tip.

She wanted to suckle it more, but knew she must restrain her urges. Glancing up at Nick, whose breathing had calmed a bit, she bent and licked up the droplet.

He moaned. "Come here." His hands wrapped around her upper arms and he pulled her into his embrace. Nick kissed her, searing her lips with his heat and her heart with his love.

Their kiss lasted for long, lust-filled moments. Amira returned his demanding kisses with an abandon she hadn't felt since making love to Omar long ago.

"Are you ready?" he asked.

Her heart thudded heavily in her chest. Nick was going to consummate their love—plunge his beautiful cock into her aching pussy, yet deny both of them fulfillment.

Flipping her over, he adjusted her body so she was beneath him. Without him asking, she spread her legs. Amira stared into Nick's dark eyes as she felt his cock at her opening, and then held her breath as he slid inside.

"Tell me when you feel close to climaxing."

She nodded and arched upward when he filled her completely. Amira just hoped she would perceive her body's response in time. Although she was very familiar with the building pressure that signaled an orgasm by masturbation, she wasn't too sure about lovemaking. It'd been so long—would she recognize it? *You better*, her mind whispered back.

Amira thrust the worries from her and circled her arms around Nick, running her nails lightly over his back. Bursts of erotic sensation shot from her vagina, gushing through her veins like magic.

Nick drew back, then pushed into her inch by inch. Closing her eyes, she concentrated on that luscious sensation. Her slick juices coated them both, making it easy for him to thrust into the deepest part of her channel.

"You feel wonderful." He kissed her, plunging his tongue inside her mouth at the same time he rammed his cock in one hard stroke.

Her lower lips tingled and pleasure was building between their joined flesh.

"Nick, get out," Amira cried shrilly, alarmed at how close she was to climaxing.

He withdrew swiftly, his eyes worried. "Are we okay?"

Taking a deep, calming breath, she nodded.

Stretching out atop her, Nick gave her sweet, sultry kisses that stimulated her, but not overly much.

"Ready to try again?" he asked after a few minutes.

Amira couldn't keep tears back. "I'm afraid. It was so wonderful...and I almost..."

"Shhh," he placed one finger over her lips. "It's all right." He smiled lovingly. "Once you get used to a man's cock and tongue again—it shouldn't make you come right away. And you'll be able to control it better."

One hand reached between them and he tweaked her left breast. "Which means, we'll have to practice a lot."

"Practice? But you already know how, and—" She stopped when she saw the laughter in his eyes.

"I meant practice restraint."

Amira blushed, but then laughed with him.

"Now, let's take care of your little problem."

He got on his knees, positioning himself between her thighs.

"What about you?"

"The two can be dealt with at the same time."

She wasn't sure what Nick had in mind. But if it was like what he'd done earlier when he licked her thigh, she was all for it. In fact, her clit jumped just at the thought.

Nick stayed on his knees, one hand gliding up and down his cock, while the other stroked her leg.

Chapter Thirty-One

ঝ

"Open your sexy lips with your hands and show me your forbidden treasure."

Amira's cheeks flushed with heat, but she complied and spread the delicate folds. She looked at him, awaiting his wishes.

"Rub around the outside of your inner lips."

Her eyes closed as she smoothed her slick flesh with one finger.

Nick's stomach tightened at the sight and he pumped his cock harder. Those pink lips were swollen and had darkened to a deep rose. The fragrance of her feminine arousal drove a shard of pleasure through his dick. A tiny drop of semen flowed from the tip.

He spread the fluid over the head and positioned his hand in a circle.

Amira was getting into the mutual masturbation, her eyes now following his hand movements as she swirled her finger in her vulva.

"Stick your finger in your pussy and imagine it's my cock fucking you."

She moaned gently when her finger slipped inside. His cock was rock hard. How he wished it was his cock instead of her finger plunging into that soft flesh.

"Amira, play with your clit."

Using the juices on her finger, she started gently stroking the hidden nub. Her back arched and her hips moved upward. "Nick, I'm close."

"Good cara, so am I." His balls felt ready to explode and the blood was pounding strongly through his rigid cock.

"Rub it harder, baby. That's my tongue eating you."

She groaned, her finger moving in a rapid rhythm. When the orgasm gripped her, he could see her vagina convulsing.

"Come for me, Amira." Nick fucked his hand, imagining thrusting into her pussy. His sperm shot out and he pumped his hips, rubbing her upper thigh wildly as she thrashed in the grip of a strong orgasm.

Only when her body totally relaxed, did he release his cock and move forward to stretch out beside her. Staring at the wet spot on the sheet, Nick mumbled, "I better clean that up after a while, or Maria will kill me."

Amira giggled and snuggled in his arms.

"Satisfied?" He kissed the top of her head.

She took a deep breath. "It was very nice. I just wish…" Her words halted — there really was no need to complete them — they both felt the same way.

He hugged her to his chest. "Soon, cara."

* * * * *

The rest of the week went so well Nick kept wondering when disaster would strike. That superstition was courtesy of his nana, who always became fearful when life went along too smoothly.

He and Amira talked and talked, getting to know each other in an intimate fashion he'd never experienced with any other woman — including Sharon.

Their sexual encounters were so wild and hot, he often felt like a schoolboy during them. Even though they couldn't fully consummate their love, exploring all the ways they could please each other was priceless.

Amira had a natural sensuality that was ripening day by day under his tutelage. Her unskilled fellatio had quickly changed into a level as good as Jen. She couldn't swallow all his cock, but was working diligently to achieve that goal. Not that he insisted on it—Amira wished to do it for him. And she also truly loved sucking him.

On the other hand, his cara loved getting her pussy eaten. Although they'd worked hard to stretch out the length of foreplay before she climaxed, the excitement was still too much for her. Of course they also finished with some type of mutual masturbation to push them over the edge.

* * * * *

Nick sipped his coffee. He'd stopped at the outdoor café, where he liked to think while drinking. His thoughts went to the most important part of their relationship—their love.

He hadn't felt this happy, almost giddy, since first falling in love with Sharon. Sometimes he wondered if he deserved someone as wonderful as Amira. But he usually shook such thoughts off quickly. After all, he was Amira's salvation from a life of servitude.

Even though he hadn't broken her genie curse, he was confident he would. Certainly, he hadn't demanded she serve him in any manner, especially in the wish department.

Nick's logical side came out and he considered those wishes with a critical eye. Did he truly want to give them up? Being honest, he knew that was a painful choice. When mentally picturing Amira on one side and all the things she brought with her—including love and happiness—the wishes didn't weigh as heavy in his favor.

The multitude of luscious beauties and wild fantasies he could wish up were awesome. But deep in his heart, he knew what he wanted. A relationship like his grandmother and grandfather had.

While his parents fought constantly and eventually divorced, his grandparents had been the steadying influence he needed. He wanted what they had.

Glancing toward the window where he'd seen an older couple window shopping last time he was here, it hit him why he envied their closeness. It reminded him of nana and nonno.

Although people could often fool you, he was convinced his grandparents had never cheated on each other. They were a totally devoted couple. Searching his innermost feelings, Nick knew he would not be happy with himself unless he was involved in a faithful relationship. As far as Amira, he had no worries in that department.

Commitment. Now there was a new concept for him. It didn't make him squirm as it had in the past when a few women tried to tie him down.

Thoughts of staying with Amira for the rest of his life brought nothing but a warm, fuzzy feeling. It was something he wanted with all his heart.

Chapter Thirty-Two

❧

Amira hugged herself. She was so happy. Finally, after so many centuries, she had fallen in love again. And Nick loved her back.

Their relationship still seemed a miracle to her. A djinn and a playboy? Certainly she never would have thought love would hit her from that direction.

Omar had lived near her and their families both raised camels. It had been almost natural that they'd fallen in love.

Nick was different. A modern man from the technological age. A leader among men, and one who was used to getting his way, especially with women. Now he wanted her. And he was determined to break the curse that bound her to serving Masters as a djinn.

She sighed while thinking of his dark good looks. Although he looked remarkably like Omar, he was very different. Certainly Nick was superior in the lovemaking department.

A warm flush ran through her body as Amira thought back over the last week. They'd explored ways of mutual excitement—ones she'd only been privy to by watching her Masters. Now she was experiencing sexual pleasure in all its many facets. Nick had such an inventive mind.

As if she'd conjured him by her thoughts, he walked in at that moment. Taking her by the hand, he headed for the bedroom. They couldn't get enough of each other and often ate supper after engaging in extensive foreplay.

He quickly stripped the bed and then, going to the closet, returned with two sets of cotton sheets. With efficient moves, Nick remade the bed, laying the top cover over the fitted.

"What's up?" she asked with curiosity.

"Don't want to mess up my good sheets." Nick grinned. Picking up a bag he'd brought in with him, he withdrew a bottle of scented oil.

"Lie down in the middle of the bed — on your back," he commanded.

She followed his order, her nipples beading with anticipation. What did he have in store for her?

Nick massaged the oil into her skin, all the way from her feet up her torso, and then along each arm. At first, she thought he was going to give her an all-body massage. That thought made her nipples tingle. His slick hands smoothing her flesh was sensual. Her nerve endings came alive beneath his strokes and her skin quivered wherever he touched. When his hands swirled over her breasts, her nipples tightened to even smaller buds.

Nick slid those skilled hands down to her thighs, rubbing the crease where they joined her body. Amira gasped. Using his thumbs, he stroked the line along her pubic hair, just shy of her lips. Ecstasy swirled through her mind and ran in steamy rivulets through her blood. While she awaited his next move, her stomach trembled in anticipation. Pouring more oil onto his palms, Nick's fingers slipped inside her lips, coating her whole pussy with the liquid. Her inner fluid seeped out to meet his touch, melding with the scented oil.

"Nick," she moaned, her neck arching backward, grinding into the soft mattress, as blazing sensation ran through her pussy like liquid fire.

"Delicious." He took a deep breath, watching her.

When he finished with her lips, he stood up and handed her the bottle. His erection stabbed the air, calling to her.

"Now, you oil me."

Getting to her knees, she poured the oil onto her palms, then spread it over his hard chest. She enjoyed the texture of his muscles as she massaged his torso. Tweaking his nipples, she was rewarded by his sharp, indrawn breath.

Her hands slid down his six-pack abdomen, playing for long seconds with the springy hair trailing below his belly button. His cock jerked.

Wishing to torture him as he had done to her, Amira slid her hands past his cock. Taking a deep breath, she was excited by his musky scent. How she longed to take his long length and soothe it with her tongue. But Nick had a new game in mind and she was more than willing to play along.

"Don't forget my back."

Amira didn't understand this part of the game, but grabbed his waist and turned him. Then she oiled his back, going around his cute ass and stroking the liquid on his legs.

Nick moaned when her hands finally slipped up his brawny thighs, and then kneaded each cheek of his buttocks.

"Turn," she ordered.

His cock jutted in her face when he did. The veins stood out, the large head was shiny and swollen with desire. When she slowly slid a hand on each side of his staff, he groaned. Her hands glided up and over, repeatedly. The whole time, her swollen pussy lips cried for his touch.

"Stop," he said huskily. "Now, lie on your stomach."

Nick quickly spread the oil over her back and legs, leaving her butt until last. When his hands slipped over her cheeks, she arched upward. Massaging gently, his fingers glided to her pussy. He slid his oily fingers over the lips, making sure they were soaked, even though he'd rubbed them earlier from the front.

She groaned. Moistness leaked from her stimulated vulva, mixing with the oil.

After Nick finished spreading the liquid, she felt him edge over her body. Their slippery flesh melded as if they were one skin. The smell of the orange-scented oil and the sensation of his body over hers were sinfully delicious.

It felt rich and lusty. Her skin soaked up stimulation as Nick began sliding up and down. His oil-drenched body hair tickled as it rubbed against her, and Amira giggled. The whole act suddenly felt carefree, full of childish abandonment.

But then Nick's cock slipped between her cheeks, rimming her crevice with his hardness. Breathing was more difficult as her heart galloped madly.

When his cock slid into her lips, her breath hitched. He slipped up and down, teasing her folds until her clit began beating erratically.

"Nick."

His movements halted and cool air hit her overheated skin as he got up.

"Turn over," he whispered.

Once facing him, she glued her eyes to his rigid cock. She almost came just looking at him.

Nick stretched out atop her, caressing her face with his fingertips before catching her lips in a demanding kiss. He withdrew and teased her with chaste little pecks.

Aggressively, Amira brought his head forward with one hand. She bit his lower lip for punishment, then shoved her tongue into his mouth.

He moaned, and then parried her thrusts with his tongue.

"Give me your tongue," she whispered into his mouth. When she sucked on it, Nick took her mouth possessively.

His head moved down and her body thrummed with sensation as Nick sucked her breast. He gave her nipple a last wet lick. "You're going to make me come just from kissing."

Amira smiled, but it turned into a sigh as Nick stroked her breast.

"I'm going to caress you all over." He grinned, then started moving his body. His hands rubbed her arms and then slid to her breasts, while his legs moved along her lower body. It was sensual and exciting in a whole new, tingly level.

As when he'd rubbed her backside, her senses sprang to life. Parts of her skin felt alive as they'd never been before, sensitive to his least little movement. Her flesh tingled, as if tiny electric sparks leapt through her nerve endings. Her lower lips became swollen until she ached for him to relieve the pressure.

Using his torso, Nick moved up and down her length. Having every inch of her body stroked with slick oil by a hard masculine form was exotic and mind blowing. Her nipples puckered with excitement and some of those electric-like tingles radiated outward, sending shards of pleasure through her pussy.

"You like my treat?" Nick bent for a scorching kiss.

"Heavenly," she sighed.

Catching her lips in another searing kiss, he slid his oil-drenched cock inside her.

Amira gasped and gripped his biceps. "Oh."

It took only a few long strokes of his hard length before she stopped him.

Nick got off, then switched positions. He knelt over her face, so that he was staring down at her pubic hair. The sixty-nine position made her stomach quiver. How she longed to suck his engorged cock. If it were not for her juices mixing with the oil on his staff, she would have. She'd seen some women do just that over the years, but she couldn't handle the thought of tasting her own fluid.

She knew what he wanted—they were going to help each other achieve orgasm by mutual masturbation. Amira placed one hand on his thigh, and then slid her other between her lower lips.

"That's it, baby."

Nick's husky voice made her more excited. Her clit responded to her gentle strokes and an aching pressure built between her lips. Watching her lover pump his cock was driving her to the edge. And sliding her hands up and down his thighs added to her excitement.

"Come for me, cara."

His breath wafted over her heated flesh, while his hands caressed her inner thighs.

Amira shoved upward as the orgasm ripped through her. She gazed on with hot satisfaction as Nick erupted into a climax. His sperm shot onto the bed, but a few drops fell on her chin. Gliding one finger across her skin, she licked his seed off her finger. Her other hand rubbed wildly between her lower lips, even as she watched Nick's sperm gush out.

The sight of his pulsating cock and the taste of his liquid on her finger threw her into yet another spasm as she came again.

Chapter Thirty-Three

๛

After their torrid masturbation lovemaking, they cuddled for a long time, then had a leisurely supper. Sleep that night overtook Amira as if someone had knocked her out.

The next morning was Saturday. She was surprised when immediately after breakfast Nick said he had an errand to run.

She felt bereft after he left and flipped aimlessly through his magazines. They'd been spending so much time together—she really missed him.

Amira snorted. She was being silly. Nick did have a life outside this apartment. But what could he be doing?

She was in the middle of watching a terribly boring movie when he strolled in two hours later. Nick had a strange look on his face. Amira jumped up and kissed him. "Is everything all right?"

He cleared his throat. "Sure. I just have something to ask you."

Amira realized he was nervous. A chill ran down her spine. Nick nervous?

"Here, sit down." He directed her to his favorite chair, while he perched at the end of the couch.

"Amira, since you came into my life, my world has been turned upside down."

That chill in her spine crawled around to her stomach. Now he was making her nervous.

Taking her hands, he continued, "You showed me there is magic in this world. You made it possible for me to fulfill exotic fantasies." He stared over her head.

What was up? Did Nick no longer want her?

Returning his gaze to her, he said softly, "But the greatest gift you brought me was love."

Amira's knotted stomach plunged to her feet.

"While I loved having you as my genie and all the luscious wishes you gave me — I want something different now."

Nick fumbled in his pocket and brought forth a tiny box. He scooted off the couch and onto his knees in front of her.

Her heart was doing flips and the blood rushed out of her face.

"Amira, you're not going to faint, are you?" Nick grasped her hands tightly, his eyes worried.

Taking a few trembling breaths, she shook her head. "I'm okay now — please continue."

He stared at her, as if to reassure himself. "I want you to marry me. I want you to be mine forever."

She sat stunned, unable to move, her body overwhelmed by a cascade of emotion.

"Amira…Amira."

She shook herself. Nick's sweet eyes were staring at her, almost in a panic. Did he think she would refuse him? Before the final step, she had to discover the limits of his love.

"What about the curse? What if it can't be broken?"

Nick's lower jaw stiffened and his grip tightened unconsciously. "I believe in me and I am determined to find the answer. But, if not, then we'll just be the hottest couple on the block…who never officially consummate their marriage."

Her heart thudded. He loved her deeply and truly. Nick was willing to give up the ultimate pleasure for her.

Placing both hands on his face, she said softly, "I would love to be your wife."

They were suddenly thrown apart by an electric charge. Amira slumped into the chair. It was as if a bolt of lightning had run through her body. She glanced up. Nick was bent over and gripping his stomach with his arms.

"Amira, what just happened?" He moved slowly, painfully, and grasped her hands again.

A flash of brilliant white light erupted between them, throwing their bodies apart again. It was so powerful Amira was blinded for several seconds. Blinking back tears, she sucked in a breath when her vision cleared. A tall, imposing figure seemed to fill the room. It was Hadji.

She had only seen him once—when she was cursed into an eternity as a djinn. That one time was more than enough for her. Being in the King's presence was terrifying.

"Amira," the soul-jolting voice boomed. He pointed toward her. The force of his magic crackled in his fingertips. "My daughter," he hesitated, then sighed. "No more."

Not knowing what to say, she slid to her knees and awaited Hadji's words. Did he mean that the curse had been lifted or that he was about to banish her into a netherworld?

"Is this what you wish, my child?"

For a few seconds, she was stunned by his question. He was talking about the djinn curse. What creature in their right mind would chose to remain a servant for eternity? Then she recognized that it was but a ritualistic question. Taking a deep, quivering breath, she realized she was not being condemned into nothingness, but about to be given her freedom.

"Yes, with all my heart, great Hadji."

The powerful djinn simply nodded, then clapped his hands twice. Amira's ears rang with the force of his claps as the bright light flashed once more. The King of the djinn disappeared as quickly and magnificently as he had appeared.

She shivered, slid shakily back up into her chair, and then sat upright and glanced at Nick. He had sat in shock and silence while Hadji appeared. Probably that was for the best. The djinn King would not look kindly on being questioned by a mortal.

"Are you all right?" At his nod, she smiled—a smile that lit up the room, so great was her happiness. "You have done it, my love—broken the curse."

He shuddered and seemed to come out of the bemused state he had been in. "No," he stated in disbelief, his eyes traveling her body up and down. They came back to her face. "Yes, it's true...I don't feel the shimmer of power that always seemed to surround you."

She nodded, her body still numb with shock.

His eyes went to the spot where the great djinn had materialized. "That was Hadji?"

"Yes," her voice trembled.

"You are no longer a genie," he stated, waiting for her nod. "You are mine alone."

Nick stood up and pulled her up with him. Grabbing her in his arms, he spun around several times.

"I'm getting dizzy."

He laughed and halted the whirling dance. "You've kept me dizzy from the moment I set eyes on you." Nick captured her mouth in a deep, warm kiss.

Pulling back, he exclaimed, "I forgot." Bending over, he retrieved the box which had fallen to the floor. Opening it, he held it out toward her.

Amira held her breath. It was spectacular—a brilliant, round solitaire diamond ring.

"It's two carats. I hope it's big enough."

She chuckled and held out her left hand. "Plenty big enough."

Nick slipped the ring on her finger. She stared at it, mesmerized by its flawless beauty and overwhelmed by the change in her life within just a few moments of time.

"What now?" she asked uncertainly.

He pulled her into his arms again. "Oh, we'll discuss wedding plans and such later. But right now I want to make love to the woman who stole my heart."

She blushed. Nick was talking about consummating their lovemaking.

He tugged at her T-shirt feverishly, almost ripping it as he helped her pull it off. She undid her jeans while he flung his shirt off, then pushed his pants down. They were both stripped nude in record time.

When she started for the bedroom, he grabbed her arm.

"No time for niceties." Nick captured her lips in a searing kiss and pulled her down to the floor with him. He was atop her and nudged her knees open.

He broke the kiss. "We've had plenty of foreplay this week — wouldn't you agree?"

She nodded, watching the fiery lust flash through his eyes. Amira spread her legs wider as his cock sought her entrance. When he plunged in one long, hard stroke, sheathing himself to the hilt, she moaned.

As he moved, deep in her pussy a heat began to build. She arched her body toward him, seeking more contact, more of his hard cock pounding into her.

Nick breathed raggedly, then kissed her possessively.

Amira rotated her hips, circling her inner walls around his staff.

"You're so hot, cara," he groaned.

Her nails raked his back as electrifying sensation ripped through her nerve endings.

"Amira," he cried hoarsely.

His cock seemed to grow even bigger inside her. He was close. Her body writhed as the pressure increased between her lower lips. Amira's arms and legs clung to him in need, as her swollen lips clasped his cock, demanding more.

A rippling wave of orgasms made her pussy spasm and she screamed aloud.

Flinging his head back, Nick gave a guttural cry. Her vagina grasped his cock, greedily milking all his fluid as it convulsed around his hard flesh.

After her panting breaths calmed, she gazed up into Nick's loving eyes. "Were…you satisfied?"

He chuckled. "Honey, that was the best damn orgasm I've ever had."

She blushed. Probably he was being romantic and overstating his feelings, but she could accept it at face value.

"What about you?" He caressed the hair over one temple.

Taking a deep breath, she released it. "It was magical."

Nick laughed, a deep, hearty burst of joy. Amira joined him.

Chapter Thirty-Four

෨

After they made love two more times, they cuddled on the couch.

"Now that you're mortal, have you thought about what you want to do with your life?"

"Beside spending it with you?"

Her quip pleased him.

"This may sound silly…but I've always wanted to go to school."

Nick hesitated before answering. He didn't want to hurt her feelings, but he just couldn't see her in a room surrounded by kids. "Did you have any schooling before you were made into a genie?"

"No, but I have studied through the years. I thought perhaps I'd take the GED."

"Amira, that's a wonderful idea." He'd forgotten about her extensive library.

"And then I'd like to go to college."

He stared at her. College? "Don't you think that'd be a bit much?"

"Why? Wasn't your President Lincoln a self-taught man?"

"Yes he was." He examined her sweet face. She was quite serious. He shrugged. "It's fine by me, if that's what you wish to do." He stroked her cheek. "But, as my wife, you know you won't have to work—unless you want to."

She smiled. "I don't desire to work. I've done that for centuries." She stopped when he chuckled. "An education is just something I've longed for, dreamed of. Can you understand?"

"Yes, of course I can." He gave her a quick kiss. "And after college?'

Her golden eyes stared into space. "I want to travel, see the world."

He hugged her. "We can certainly do that. I have plenty of money and a great vacation package." Nick nibbled her lips. "I might even start my own business, something I've dreamed of doing. That way, I can take off anytime I wish."

"Oh, Nick, it sounds heavenly." She hesitated for a few seconds. "And we'll have many children, too?"

"Anything you wish, my love," he chuckled.

She stared into space, while twirling the hair on his chest. "Nick, will we be like so many other couples?"

"Of course we're not—we're special." He pulled her into his arms.

"No, I meant…so many people divorce."

He turned her face upward and kissed her tenderly. "Never. I'll love you forever."

"Forever!"

Amira's fear shot through his heart. What an idiot. He kissed her again. "I meant, I will love you all the days that we have to live."

She sighed. "That sounds lovely."

"It does at that." He squeezed her gently to his chest. "You may not believe this, but you've brought magic into my life in a way I never expected. And I'm not talking about your genie powers."

She sighed deeply, moved by his romantic statement. He kissed her thoroughly, seeking to drive all worries from her sweet mind.

When Nick kissed her, Amira realized he filled her with love and magic too, giving her all the things that made life worth living.

The End

About the Author

∞

Myra Nour grew up reading s/f, fantasy, and romance, so she was really thrilled when these elements were combined in Futuristic Romances. She enjoys writing paranormals, whether the hero is a handsome man from another planet, or a shapeshifting werewolf.

Myra's background is in counseling, and she likes using her knowledge to create believable characters. She also enjoys lively dialogue and, of course, using her imagination to create other worlds with lots of action/adventure, as well as romance. She uses her handsome husband as inspiration for her heroes—he is a body builder, a soldier, and has a black belt in Tae Kwon Do.

Myra welcomes mail from readers. You can write to her c/o Ellora's Cave Publishing at 1056 Home Ave. Akron, Oh. 44310-3502

Also by Myra Nour

80

Future Lost: A Mermaid's Longing
Mystic Visions *(Anthology)*
Sex Kittens *(Anthology)*
Shifter's Desire: Vampire Fangs and Venom

Ordinary Charm

Anya Bast

෪

Chapter One

&

Serena fought back a hard twinge of loneliness as she pushed aside a branch and stepped into the grove of oak trees that grew in the exact center of her thousand-acre property. The trees had been planted in clusters of three over 150 years ago — when her family had first purchased the land. The natural power within the very earth here, augmented and reinforced by the magick of her own bloodline, thrummed beneath her feet. It made her stop for a moment and close her eyes before continuing to the flat rock in the center of the clearing that was polished smooth from over a century of use, from over a century of her ancestors kneeling on it to perform rituals or connect with the ones who had passed on before them.

The oaks were symbols of strength and wisdom and Serena could feel that heavy, old knowledge within them, as well as the Dyads, the small OtherKin who lived within each tree, protecting them.

Sometimes Serena came here because she had some specific question to ask, some help she needed. A kind of energetic record of her entire maternal line, all the witches who'd come before her, resided here. It was like accessing an infinite *Encyclopedia Mystica*.

But today she was here only because she was feeling alone.

Her jeans protected her knees as she knelt on the stone and closed her eyes. The energy in the place swirled around her for a moment, nearly knocking her over, then settled down. Her consciousness expanded and deepened into the Otherworld, the space superimposed over waking reality. The Otherworld was only accessible through deep commitment, raised awareness and intense concentration.

She murmured the words needed to open the energetic doorway, "By oaken pillars, three by three. Reveal to me my family tree."

First came the most powerful memories of her maternal line, the ones that had caused the deepest grooves in her family's time and space. They were the energies closest to the surface of the Elder's memories of their lives, the ones that had made the most profound impact. Absolute terror tended to make deep grooves in a person's psyche.

Serena winced as the voices pounded into her mind.

Are you a witch?

Why do you torment these God-fearing people?

Thou shalt not suffer a witch to live. We will not suffer you to live.

How long have you been in the snare of the devil?

How can you expect to have a clear conscience without a clear confession?

Confess!

Confess!

Most of the women accused of witchcraft over the centuries had not been witches at all. They'd just been caught up in climate of paranoid hysteria, or they'd been strong women that someone had wanted to get rid of. Some had been women who had owned property that another had coveted.

But some of the women who had been accused really had been OtherKin witches...and many of those women had been her ancestors.

People that weren't OtherKin could feel the ones that were without true understanding of what it was they felt. Perhaps they couldn't figure out exactly what was "off" about an individual who was OtherKin, but they knew somehow that they were different. It frightened them into reacting, into destroying That Which Was Not Like Them. That's how it had been since the beginning of time. That's how things remained to this day.

She fidgeted, causing her glasses to slip down the bridge of her nose. With a forceful mental thrust, she pushed as quickly as she could through that layer of pain and despair. There was beauty past it — beauty, knowledge, sisterhood, hope and, most of all, love.

Past that barrier was the knowledge of her family line — the Elders.

Finally the energy evened out and colors swirled through her mind's eye. Mental images of her great-grandmother Margaret and grandmother Mary floated through her consciousness. They smiled at her. She felt an energetic hug around her shoulders and heard her great-aunt Agatha whisper in her ear, *"Take heart. We're never far."* Then her image wavered and Agatha looked to the right. *"Someone's coming!"* she whispered. She disappeared. They *all* disappeared. The level of deep consciousness to which Serena had descended collapsed, pushing her up and up fast and hard.

Jolted from the deep level of concentration she'd had to attain, Serena opened her eyes. She tried to stand, but was so dizzy and light-headed, she lost her balance and fell. She landed right on the tube of banana-flavored lip balm in her pocket and winced at the sudden pain in her hip. Her glasses flew from her face, leaving her seeing only blurry shapes. Blinking in surprise at her abrupt fall from tranquility, she groped in the grass for her glasses.

Hoof beats on the soft forest ground filled the air and she stilled. Anger flared. Who he hell had dared trespass on her land? This was *her* place and hers alone.

And where the *hell* were her glasses?

The hoof beats grew closer. "Who's there?" she called to the blurry grove.

No response. The only sound was of hoof beats slowing and growing closer. Finally, she found her glasses and put them on. The world came into focus once more.

A huge stag stood over her as she lay there sprawled in the grass. She gasped at the rack of antlers this very old beast displayed on his head. His dark brown eyes, flecked oddly with green, blinked. For several moments, they regarded each other in silence. Serena's heart beat out a frantic tattoo in her chest. His flanks and body were rippled with sleek, strong muscle. He seemed the very essence of power.

Neither of them moved for long moments.

Serena wondered what a stag would do if he felt threatened. Those antlers looked damn sharp. But…was he even a truly a stag? Serena had heard tales of shapeshifting OtherKin. Serena had never really given them much thought. But Agatha had said some*one* was coming.

Without taking her gaze from his, she reached out with her consciousness and touched him minutely.

Raw strength poured into her, and base sexuality. This was an animal of sensuality, of spirituality, of the forests. This was the Lady's consort, himself.

Serena breathed heavy and placed a hand carefully to her chest, where heart pattered out a fast rhythm. She'd touched him mentally for only a second and her entire body hummed with sexual awareness. Her breasts felt heavy and her nipples were hard. Her body was excited as though it had been primed by foreplay.

She tipped her head back and whimpered. Her state of arousal was so intense that it almost hurt. A soft whuffle filled her ears and she felt a velvet nose against her shoulder. Teeth gently grazed then bit her shoulder.

She *should* have been alarmed. By all expectations, she *should* have screamed or *something*, but instead all she felt was peaceful. The stag bit with enough pressure to pinch a little, but not to really hurt. Stunned, Serena allowed the contact.

With speed and agility that made her gasp, the creature released her and sprang to the side. Muscles working gracefully and his short brown coat shimmering in the dappled afternoon sunlight, the stag bounded past the line of oaks and into the forest beyond.

She lay panting and sprawled on the grass in shocked wonder. Her mind stuttered and tripped as she took the time she needed to process the event. After a few minutes, she reached up and touched her shoulder where the stag had bitten her. A deep, yet painless, indentation of two rows of teeth remained in her flesh.

* * * * *

Wiggle, the fattest and friendliest of her silky black cats, rubbed against her calf. Serena scooped him up and buried her face in his fur, then walked out onto the front porch and deposited him on the white porch rail of her rambling farmhouse. She supposed it was a bit clichéd for a witch like her to have seven cats…especially since three of those cats were *black*. But she couldn't help the fact that they kept showing up and needing homes, and she didn't have the heart to turn them away.

She leaned against the rail and stared out across the darkening, tree-spotted land. Somewhere in the distance, an owl hooted. It was a beautiful place where she lived, though sometimes lonely. The thought made her think of her ex-husband, and made her stomach twist in a sickening way. Any thought of Brian produced that reaction in her. Even five years afterward, what he'd done still affected her.

The screen door opened on a whine and her sister, Rowan, peeked her head out. "I made rosehip tea. Want some?"

"Sure."

A minute later, Rowan backed through the doorway with two steaming cups in her hands. Serena took one and sank into one of the wicker chairs on the porch. Rowan sat down in another one opposite. A bite of autumn flavored the evening air and the breeze smelled of leaves and wood smoke. Autumn was Serena's favorite season.

She glanced at Rowan. "When are you leaving?"

Rowan took a careful sip of her tea. "Tonight. Probably right after I finish this."

"So soon? You just got here." Serena tried to keep the patheticness out of her voice. She and her sister were like day and night and often didn't see eye to eye, but Rowan was still her sister and her closest living relative. When their mother had died in a car crash eight years ago, Serena had been twenty and Rowan had been eighteen. They had inherited the large family house and the huge amount of forested land that went with it. But Rowan had wanted to live in Newville, instead of out here in the country. So, using the advance from the sale of her first book along with some of her share of the life insurance money, Serena had purchased Rowan's half of the property. Rowan had moved into Newville. Serena had stayed out here, with the trees and the ghosts.

Rowan looked at her apologetically. "I have to get back to the city. I have to meet a man." She looked down and took a quick sip of the tea.

Serena snorted. "What's so special about a date? You have those all the time." A twinge of jealousy ran through her despite her flippant tone.

Rowan was tall, slim and beautiful with long black hair and large blue eyes. She was a goddess and men fell at her feet in worship. Serena, on the other hand, was short, overweight, and plain. She had the same blue eyes as Rowan, and the same glossy black hair bequeathed to them through a long line of blue-eyed, black-haired women. But nothing beyond the color of their eyes and the color and texture of their hair marked them as related. Serena had not inherited the body or face Rowan had—

not by a long shot. The only other thing they shared was their magick.

All through their lives, Rowan had been more popular, had fit in better with others, had had more dates, and more friends. Serena had been the dumpy older sister that only got to go places because Rowan had insisted she be included. It rankled Serena to this day that it had been that way. Still, Rowan's heart had been in the right place.

Rowan glanced away and took a minute to answer. "This one is special. I have to go."

Serena snorted again. "Lots of them are special. I swear, Rowan. You date these men a couple times, and then dump them. How many males have you gone through since you started dating?"

Rowan looked up at her with those big blue eyes that had melted countless hearts weaker than hers. "I haven't kept count."

"Lots, Rowan. There have been lots. Who are you looking for, Mr. Right?"

Rowan's perfect lip curled up and one of her sculpted eyebrows rose. "Nah. Mr. Right-for-Tonight."

Serena laughed and took a sip of her tea. "You're hopeless." *And wild.* Rowan had grown up wild and rebellious and had never outgrown it. To the unschooled eye, she looked sweet and innocent. A modern-day sleeping beauty with long dark hair, straight from a fairy tale. Serena knew *that* was just a clever disguise. Rowan was a sexual predator, willing and able to use men for sex…and only for sex. Serena sighed and relented. "Well, if it's for a really good lay, I suppose I can let you go. Although you get good lays all the time."

"What about you, sis? When's the last time you got laid?"

Before she knew she was even doing it, Serena touched her shoulder where the bite marks from her encounter in the forest a few days ago had faintly scarred her. She supposed erotic experiences with the local fauna…or whatever that creature had been, didn't count. "Uh, it's been a while," she said softly. About five years, to be exact.

Rowan winked. "Come in to the city with me. I'm sure we can rustle up a man for you."

Serena winced. That brought too many memories of growing up together with Rowan and accepting her charity and social castoffs. She shook her head. "No. I'm happy enough here by myself. Men are way too much trouble, even when you can cut them loose in the morning."

Rowan leaned forward. "I understand that what happened was traumatizing, Serena. But Brian is in jail now and will be for a very, very long time. You can't allow your life to come to halt because of that asshole. It's not right. If you do that, he wins."

Serena shook her head. "It's not that complicated," she lied. "It doesn't have anything to do with him." It *was* that complicated and it *did* have to do with Brian. "I simply don't want to get involved with another man." At least the last part wasn't a lie.

The crunch of gravel under tires met their ears. Headlights flashed through the trees that lined the two-mile long driveway leading to the house. Serena stood. "Who could that be?"

Rowan set her teacup down and stood beside her. "Feels like—"

"Morgan," Serena finished for her. Morgan was their first cousin who lived several states over. "What the hell is she doing here?"

Morgan's green sedan pulled into the small parking area beside the house and she climbed out. The middle-aged, dark-haired woman waved a cheery hello at them both, then hurried over to the passenger side and opened the door.

Out climbed a *god* of a man.

Beside her, Rowan took in a sharp breath of appreciation. That's when Serena knew she'd been right in her initial reaction. After all, Rowan was a discerning expert in the man area.

He was about six-foot-four, muscled nicely pretty much everywhere the eye could see. His hair was longish and tangled, a dark brown streaked with shades of blond. He wore a pair of tight blue jeans that showed off a fine ass as they rounded the car and walked toward the porch. A dark blue T-shirt that allowed his defined muscles to show covered his torso. Serena cocked her head to the side, letting her gaze slide down his strong-looking arms. That's when she realized something very important.

The man was *handcuffed*.

"Looks like you may be getting a man whether you want one or not, Serena," said Rowan softly.

Morgan prodded and poked the man up the stairs until they stood at the top. "Hi Serena, Rowan. Nice to see you," she greeted as though nothing were amiss.

"Uh, nice to see you, too, Morgan," answered Serena.

Morgan gestured toward the man. "This is Cole. Say hi, Cole."

Cole grunted out a hello.

Serena tipped her head to the side and examined the man's hewn-from-stone visage. He seemed sort of familiar to her in a way, but that had to be just her mind playing tricks on her. She'd never met him before. There'd be no way she'd have forgotten him if she ever had.

"Serena, I really need to talk to you. Got a minute?" Morgan asked.

"Since you drove all the way from Massachusetts and didn't tell us you'd be bringing a…uh…*friend*, I guess I do," Serena answered with a tight smile.

Morgan shook her head. "I didn't come here from home. We were in the area. Sarah and I were in the state visiting a coven. We were going to stop over and say hi. Anyway, maybe Cole and Rowan could chat in the living room, and you and I could discuss something in private?"

Serena stared at Cole, who stared back at her from the fall of hair across his face. He didn't really look like the *chatting* type. "Is he safe?"

Morgan waved her hand. "Completely. He's a kitten."

Cole gave a disturbing caveman-like growl.

Apparently she meant a *feral* kitten. "Uh, and the handcuffs would be because…?"

"That's one of the things I wanted to talk to you about."

"What do you think, Rowan?" Serena asked uncertainly.

"I think I'm curious as hell." She walked toward the door, turned, winked and crooked a finger. "Come on, big boy. Let's see if you have a working vocabulary."

That was so like fearless Rowan.

Cole hesitated for only a moment before following Rowan through the door. Serena picked up her teacup and followed, keeping a careful eye on the man. One false move toward Rowan and she'd call up a spell and zap him one between the eyes.

She entered the living room, which was decorated comfortably in shades of blues and greens and scattered throughout with old overstuffed chairs and sofas. A merry fire burned in the fireplace and candles lit the mantel. Morgan grabbed her arm and yanked her toward the kitchen, nearly causing Serena to slosh tea over the rim of her cup.

Once in the kitchen, Serena whirled on Morgan. "What's with you? You're acting even battier than usual and you're scaring the daylights out of me."

"Lower your voice," Morgan said.

Serena glanced at the doorway and spoke softer. "Where's Sarah, anyway? You two are never apart." Sarah was Morgan's live-in love. Serena set an arm akimbo. "Tell me what the hell is going on!"

"Fine," said Morgan, drawing a breath. "Here it goes." Then she fell silent.

Serena sipped her tea and stared at her as though she had all the time in the world. "So...anytime, dear."

"Okay! Okay!" Morgan turned, walked and then paced back. Her long green skirt swirled around her legs with her movements. "He called himself Cole when we picked him up, but his real name is Cernunnos."

Chapter Two

✣

She choked on her tea and started coughing. Morgan pounded her on the back.

"Cernunnos?" Serena finally gasped. "*Cernunnos?* You're joking, right? Come on. He's a thought form created by OtherKin and humans. If he even exists at all, Cernunnos resides somewhere far from this—"

"I'm surprised to find you so skeptical, Serena. You, after all, are OtherKin, yourself. Most non-OtherKin would believe *you* are fiction, and if you told them you were not, they'd lock you away in an institution. In the past, they would've burned you at the stake."

She set her cup down on the small, round kitchen table. "They still might," she muttered.

"Cernunnos," Morgan confirmed, "otherwise know as Herne the Hunter, or the Great God Pan, is now in your living room."

"The Horned One, the god of fertility, life, animals, wealth, and the Underworld is now handcuffed and sitting on my living room sofa?" Apparently, she hadn't been too far off base when she'd thought of Cole as being a *god of a man*. He truly was a god.

Morgan nodded solemnly. "The Lord of the Hunt, himself."

"Sweet Lady." She walked to the kitchen doorway and half peered into the living room where he sat glowering at Rowan.

"Mmm-hmm. That's what I said when he attacked the high priestess of the Three Ash Coven. That's why he's cuffed in cold iron."

Her head whipped around in Morgan's direction. *"What?"* she screeched. Then she said in a softer voice. "He's sitting out there...*with my sister*. Are you crazy?"

"*He* might be a little crazy." Morgan shrugged. "But we don't know why he did it. Maybe he had cause. Alana is such a manipulative bitch sometimes."

She stared openmouthed. "I don't understand," she said finally.

Morgan shrugged again. "We don't either. Sarah and I found him at the edge of the woods the other night on the way back to our hotel. He was naked and disoriented. At first, we thought he was just some guy who'd had a bad night, been on a hunting trip and gotten drunk, whatever. But when we touched him, it was clear to us that he was powerful OtherKin. He asked to see Alana, so we brought him to her, and he instantly went at her."

"How do you *know* he's Cernunnos?"

"Alana told us, but when we pressed her to tell *how* she knew, she clammed up. To verify what she said, we did an origination spell on him and found out he's really, *really* old, yet young at the same time. We have no idea what that means." Morgan stood and stretched. "Anyway, it's your job to figure all this stuff out, not ours."

"Excuse me?"

"The Elders said you're supposed to keep him."

"Excuse me?"

"That's what they said. They were very clear about it."

"But-but I just talked with the Elders the other day and they didn't mention anything about—"

"Well, I talked to them yesterday and they did mention it."

Rage, disbelief and fear battled within Serena and threatened to explode. "Morgan," she said in a deceptively quiet voice. "You do remember what happened to me just five years ago, don't you? How can you expect me to handle a man like this? How could the *Elders* do this to me? I'm not strong enough to keep a man like him! He'll punch straight through me, even bound with cold iron. He'll escape and probably kill me in the process."

Morgan held up her hands, palms out. "I don't go against what the Elders want, Serena, and they want you to play babysitter. I do know that if they thought he'd hurt you, there's no way he'd be here right now. You're safe, Serena. No matter what you might think. No matter what you may believe, or any of the fears from your past that may be raising their ugly heads right now. The Elders *always* know best." Morgan snapped her fingers and disappeared.

"Morgan!" She whirled around. "Morgan, don't you dare!"

Silence.

Serena stood there for long moment looking into the space that Morgan had recently occupied. "I really hate it when you do that!" she cried. Morgan was extremely strong at invisibility illusion. Serena couldn't conjure that to save her life.

Outside, Morgan's car started up. Soon the spray of gravel as Morgan hightailed it away from the house reached Serena's ears. "Yeah, you better run," she muttered.

With a sigh, she turned and went into the living room. Cole and Rowan sat across from each other talking in low voices. Rowan tilted her head back and gave a ringing laugh. What? The caveman could actually speak? The caveman could make someone *laugh*?

Impossible.

Rowan sobered when she spotted Serena crossing the room toward them. She glanced at her watch, set her teacup down and stood.

"Oh, no. You are not leaving me here alone with him, Rowan."

Rowan gave her an apologetic look. "I was serious when I said I had to go meet a man, Serena."

She pointed at Cole. "You can't leave me here alone with a serial killer just to go on some stupid date! It's practically siblingicide or whatever they call murdering your sister."

Rowan opened her mouth, closed it and looked away. "You assumed it was a date, Serena. It's not."

Cold fear washed through her. Not only was Rowan beautiful and wild, she also had a quite a knack at endangering herself. "Then what it is?"

She looked away. "I can't say."

"Rowan," Serena said in her best I'm-your-older-sister-and-you-better-obey-me voice.

Rowan looked back at her and narrowed her eyes. "I. Can't. Say." she repeated in a voice like steel.

Now Serena wanted to keep Rowan here for more reasons than just Cole. "You lied to me," she accused, folding her arms over her chest.

Rowan stared at her, storms flickering in the depths of her blue eyes. "I didn't *lie*. I simply didn't correct your misconception. It's-it's really important that I meet this man, Serena. Like life or death important."

Serena glanced at Cole. "This may be life or death, too," she whispered angrily.

"I'm not going to hurt you," drawled out Cole from the couch. "Don't get your panties in a bunch." His voice was low, deep and smooth like black silk. Serena couldn't suppress a shiver. "Let your sister go. I have no quarrel with you. You'll be safe enough." He raised his wrists and rattled the cold iron cuffs that bound them. "Anyway, I've been defanged."

Rowan cast her a look of triumph. "See!"

Serena sighed in exasperation. "Has everyone gone insane? We're trusting murderers in handcuffs to tell the truth now?"

"I wasn't going to kill Alana," Cole said calmly. "Never had any intention of that. I'm not a murderer." He smiled and it was cold, feral. His teeth flashed for an instant and then were hidden behind his sensual, curved lips. "It was a just a gut reaction to a person who'd done me a mighty hard wrong turn, but I never meant to hurt her."

While Cole spoke, Rowan had gathered her coat and purse and was headed for the door.

"Excuse me," Serena shot at Cole. "I'm trying to have a conversation with my sister here." She didn't wait for his response. She turned on her heel and rushed out of the house after Rowan.

She caught Rowan's sleeve before her sister had a chance to run down the porch steps. "Stop."

Rowan turned to look at her, stuffing her hands deep into her pockets. "I really have to go."

Serena released her. "I know. I just wish you'd tell me what was going on."

"I can't. Not right now." She turned and walked down the stairs.

Serena sighed. When her sister got like this pushing her only made her more stubborn. "Be careful. I love you, sis."

"Love you back." Rowan glanced at her before climbing into her car. "And you be careful, too."

Serena watched Rowan start her red sports car and drive away, then turned and headed back into the house. Cole sat on the couch staring at her with interest in his eyes.

What the hell was she going to do with this guy?

"You don't have to look so worried," he drawled lazily.

"Oh, really? And why should I believe you?"

"I feel no rage directed at you. You didn't have a part in what happened, whatever it was. I can feel it."

Feel no rage directed at… Her mind stuttered over his words. "Huh? *Rage?* Oh, that's *so* reassuring. I'd prefer if you didn't use words like that, please. What the hell is your deal, anyway?"

He shifted on the coach. "If you bring me something to eat and drink, I'll tell you all I know."

"You're hungry?"

He nodded. "I haven't eaten in over twenty-four hours."

What was wrong with Morgan? How could she be so cruel? For the first time since she'd seen him, Serena viewed him as a person with basic needs. Anyway, letting him starve would incur the wrath of an ancient god, she supposed. Still, she wasn't going to go out of her way for him.

Of course, maybe he was playing her, too. Trying to get her close to him so he could snap her neck with his elbows or something. She drew up a spell in her mind and stored it, ready to cast it at him if she needed to. As long as he was in cold iron, the spell would be powerful enough to knock him unconscious.

"I'll be right back." She turned and went into her kitchen, grabbed a plate of cold vegan tofu chicken out of the refrigerator, a fork and a can of soda.

When she returned, she deposited the plate and can on the end table beside him. "Sorry, I don't have a lot in the house. I need to go grocery shopping."

He raised his hands and jingled the cuffs. "How am I supposed to eat?"

"I don't know." She shrugged. "But I'm not taking your pretty little bracelets off, bub, and I'm not getting any closer to you than I have to."

He settled back into the cushions and flicked aside a hank of hair that had fallen across his eye with a jerk of his head. He gave her a slow smile. This time his smile was anything but cold. In fact, the look in his eyes was so warm that it played havoc with her stomach. Butterflies abounded. The man seemed to ooze sexuality. He was stunningly beautiful for a deranged demigod. "How about you feed me then?" he suggested with the lift of a brow.

Her stomach did a somersault imagining those perfectly sculpted lips so close to her fingers because that made her think of his lips close to *other* body parts. His tongue all warm and... Great Lady! What was *wrong* with her?

"Oh, no way." She shook her head vigorously, making her chin-length black hair fly. Her glasses slid down her nose and she pushed them back up with a finger. "You have to be kidding me. I am *not* feeding you by hand. You'll crack me in the head with your elbow and eat my spleen or something."

"I mean you no harm, I said." He sighed. "Looks like it's either feed me or watch me starve, beautiful."

Beautiful? Great. Now the asshole was making fun of her. She crossed her arms over her chest and flopped down on a nearby chair. "You can starve for all I care."

His sensual mouth curved into a smile. "Hmmm…beautiful *and* cruel," he murmured. "An intriguing combination."

"*Stop* calling me beautiful. I swear to the Lady, I'll toss you out on your ear, *with* the damn cold iron binding your hands so you're nice and helpless, if you keep making fun of me. I'll-I'll turn you into a toad before I do it!" she sputtered without logic. No way could she ever do that. "I don't care *what* the Elders want. I won't be verbally abused in my own home."

The room went silent. Finally, Cole leaned forward, and held her gaze with his. It was intent and dark, fathomless. Her lips parted and her eyes widened as she saw the color of that warm, direct gaze—brown with flecks of green. The strange combination of colors reminded her of…

It couldn't be.

Of their own volition, her fingers found the faint scar marking her shoulder from her recent encounter in the forest with the stag.

"You let me free," he drawled out in a voice that sounded like hot, melted chocolate, "and I'll show you just how beautiful I think you are. It's been a very long time since I had a woman, and you're the prettiest I've ever seen."

She snorted. "You must be desperate if you think flattery and tender little lies are going compel me to free you. Do you think I'm stupid? My sister was just here."

He leaned back. "Your sister? I'm not following."

"My sister is like three *million* times prettier than I am. In fact, we don't even rank together on the same scale."

He looked thoughtful, then shrugged. "She's pretty enough, but she's not my type."

She snorted. "What... *Gorgeous* isn't your type?" she shot back in sarcasm.

He gave her a pointed look. "No. I just like a few more curves to go *with* the gorgeous. I've been watching your curves ever since I got here."

She rolled her eyes. "What a bunch of bullshit." She directed her gaze at the plate. "Go on, eat. Stuff your mouth so you can't speak anymore."

He sighed. "How about this, beautiful, go find some rope and tie my ankles and arms to something. That way I'm completely helpless and you can feed me."

That was an option. She stood. "If only to shut you up," she muttered. She found some rope in her hall closet and bound his ankles, making him wince. Then she looped lengths of rope around his elbows and tied each of them to opposite ends of couch. No way could he move now. She pulled up a chair in front of him and sat down with the plate on her lap. His body heat and the spicy, masculine scent of him rolled off and hit her. Suddenly uncomfortable, she squirmed away from him a little.

He leaned in closer, as close to her as the ropes would allow.

Sighing, she stabbed a piece of tofu chicken with the fork and held up to his lips. He held her gaze with his oddly colored bedroom eyes as he wrapped his lips around it and pulled it off. She noticed that his lower lip was just a little fuller than the upper. The sight made Serena flush with imaginings of *other* ways he could use that mouth.

As soon as he started chewing, he went white. He swallowed hard and started coughing. "What-what the hell is that?" he asked in a horrified voice.

She glanced down at the plate and shrugged. "Tofu chicken."

"Tofu?" He coughed again. "Don't you have any *real* food?"

She gave him a withering look. "If you mean poor, defenseless little animals that have been slaughtered and roasted, no. I'm a vegetarian." A *fat* vegetarian. The Universe simply was not kind. They'd been especially unkind when they'd been passing out the metabolism genes to her.

He grimaced. "That's terrible. I've been dreaming of eggs and sausage."

She grimaced right back at him. "I'd think you'd be less down with the whole carnivorous thing since you're, you know…who you are."

He raised a brow. "Who am I?"

"Uh—" Was she supposed to be talking about this? Damn Morgan for running out so fast! "You know…Cernunnos." She glanced away. That sounded so crazy. "Herne the Hunter. The Forest Lord."

"Right." He expelled a breath and settled back against the couch. "So I was told."

She rested the plate on her knee. "You don't know?"

"I can't remember much before a few days ago. I know my name is Cole. I know I'm OtherKin and when these cold iron cuffs aren't binding my hands I have some truly vicious magick. Therefore, I know I'm a mage. I know I really wanted to find Alana, the high priestess of the Three Ash Coven, but I don't know why." He gave her a pointed look. "I know I'm *not* a vegetarian."

"So you have some kind of…amnesia?"

"I guess."

"Is that all you know?"

"I know one more thing." He paused and looked at her, stared straight into her eyes with that soulful gaze. "You're in deep danger having me in your house, darlin', though that danger doesn't come from me. You shouldn't be anywhere near me. Your association with me could get you killed, but I don't know why."

She shuddered. She would've accused him of trying to play her, trying to scare her into setting him free, if she hadn't felt the truth of his words with her own sixth sense. This was a dangerous man…in many ways. She held tight to Morgan's words. "The Elders would never put me in danger, and they said I was supposed to keep you here."

He didn't say anything for a full heartbeat. He only stared into her eyes. Like a deer caught in headlights, she stared back. "I hope you're right," he finally answered. He broke the gaze and glanced at the plate. "Do you have *anything* else to eat?"

"Uh…I have some Doritos."

"They'll beat tofu chicken any time."

She stood, grateful for the diversion after that intense conversation, and got the bag of chips. She didn't think twice as she fed him with her fingers, no less. Suddenly her mind was awhirl with other thoughts and intuitions. Why were the Elders doing this to her? They must have a reason.

She felt a hot tongue caress her finger and she jerked her hand away as though he'd burned her. "Hey! You licked me!"

He smiled slowly, like a predator. "Mmmm…I was imagining licking somewhere other than your finger."

She stared in shock. Damn if he didn't sound like he meant it. Considering him, she nervously reached into the bag, drew out a chip and ate before she even realized what she'd done. This was a complex man. She reached into the bag again. "Look, I don't get intimate with half-crazed mages who describe their magick as *vicious* and have amnesia. It's kind of a thing with me," she said between crunches.

He shrugged. "I'm very attracted to you. I sense you are also attracted to me. We could indulge that mutual attraction if you wanted. No strings attached. Just you and me, sharing a bit of lust. It's been a long time, Serena." He waggled his eyebrows. "You can even keep me tied up, if you're into that."

She stilled with her hand midway to her mouth at the sound of her name on his lips. How could this god of a man be attracted to her? Then she remembered the shackles. He was just trying to play her again, the bastard. "I thought your memory only began a few days ago."

"Okay, it *feels* like it's been a very, very long time."

"Well, it's going to be a while longer because I won't fall for your little act of *flatter the fat girl*." She plopped the bag down on the couch and stood. "Look, memory boy, it's late and I want to go to sleep. I'm going to get you a blanket, a pillow, and tie you in a sleeping position on the couch, and then I'm going to bed. We'll figure what to do with you in the morning."

* * * * *

"You better hope your nine lives haven't all been used up, cat," Cole muttered at the twenty-pound black feline that had taken up residence on his upper chest. He'd swallowed about an ounce of fur since the creature had decided his chest was a great place to sleep. Five times he'd rocked his body hard enough to dislodge the cat and make it get off him. Five times the damn thing had jumped back up. Cole knew he'd been defeated and had given up. Plus, he couldn't take the fat cat jumping back up onto this chest even one more time.

Cole lay in the dark of the night staring up at the living room ceiling, enduring the warm animal that had a purr like an outboard motor on his chest. The ceiling was painted with small glow-in-the-dark stars. If he concentrated hard enough, he could almost convince himself he was in the forest.

He'd feel so much better if he were in the forest.

These walls made him feel itchy, suffocated, trapped. They were even worse than the bastard cuffs binding his hands and the ropes Serena used to tie his ankles to the legs of the couch. That was one more thing he knew. He'd take forest over manmade structure anytime.

Maybe he really was Cernunnos.

He moved his legs and the rope around his ankles chafed his skin. He grimaced. God, he'd love to get his hands on Serena. He really, really *would*.

In more ways than one.

She was intensely alluring to him. In fact, she had no idea the kind of power she wielded over him. For that matter, she seemed to have no idea how gorgeous she was. He'd instantly been entranced by her beautiful heart-shaped face. Her complexion was lovely—a fair peaches-in-cream with that charming blush to her cheeks. Her blue eyes sparkled with wit and intelligence. Her hair was that exquisite corn silk texture and blacker than the heart of midnight.

Her body was full and curvaceous and the thought of undressing her and exploring it made his cock get hard. Her breasts were large and heavy. How would they feel in his hands? How would her nipples taste against his tongue? How would she feel when he slipped his cock into her? What kind of little noises would she make when he brought her climax?

Oh, he really wanted to know the answers to those questions. If he had anything to say about it, he'd get them.

She was incredibly attractive, that was true enough, but it was her essential energy that drew him to her so hard. There was something about her, something related to him. He let a breath whistle past his lips. It was another of those things he *knew*, but didn't understand.

He *knew* Serena was *his*. Whatever the hell that meant.

He didn't think him ending up in her house tonight was by chance. That spark of deep familiarity and that sense of possession had been there as soon as he'd caught her sweet scent on the air as he'd approached the porch stairs. Now all he had to do was convince Serena she was his. He had a burning desire to do just that.

What he didn't want to do was endanger her. And there was no doubt in his mind, he was endangering her by being in her home right now. He needed to find out what the hell was going on with him. Three days ago he'd awoken at the edge of a forest, naked, and filled with a sense of rage that made the magick within him spark fire into the nearby trees. It had been a supreme act of strength for him to hold back from charring all the living things around him for a three-mile radius.

Someone or something had done him wrong, had turned his life upside down…and he'd been really pissed about it. He'd leashed his rage when Morgan and her girlfriend, Sarah, had found him, sensing they were OtherKin and meant to help. When they'd asked him where he'd wanted to go, one name had been forefront in his mind. Alana Parker.

He'd started with her, and he'd have to go back to her. She was his only lead. Next time he met her he wouldn't instantly attack her, though. That had definitely not gotten him the information he'd gone there to collect. All that had gotten him was a dose of strong magick in the solar plexus from Morgan and Sarah and pretty new pair of cold iron bracelets. Cold iron was the one substance that could sublimate the magick of an OtherKin.

He hadn't told Serena everything he knew. Or, at least, not everything he remembered. He recalled snippets of his past lives. He remembered being a sea captain, in command of everything and everyone on his ship. He remembered being a knight during the Crusades. He remembered being a Viking. A Gladiator. A Celt warrior painted with woad for battle.

Snippets of these lives played through his head like a movie from time to time. He'd smell something that would put him back on the prow of his ship, or walking through a meadow clutching a spear, alert and watching for his enemies. At times, his head swam with the tactile impressions from what he could only assume were his past life incarnations.

He needed to find out what was going on…and soon.

A faint magickal tremor went through his body. Every hair on his body stood up in response. He turned his head in the direction it was coming from. Across the room, the drapes moved. The window opened just a crack, and a thin, wispy white tendril slipped within.

What the fuck?

Serena was no lightweight witch. She'd constructed an intricate golden warding net around her home, a magickal barrier to keep unwanted people and magicks out. A kind of energetic security system. He'd felt it when he'd walked up the porch beside Morgan. It'd felt like walking through thick cobwebs. The only reason he'd been able to get through at all was because Morgan had access and had been at his side and touching his arm. So how could this magick be currently snaking its way across the room toward him?

The more pressing question was *what did it want*?

As the tendril drew near, he struggled against the tight knots that Serena had tied around his ankles. The cat recognized the curl of power approaching them, yowled low and shot off his chest to run and hide. Cole's jaw clenched and he struggled against his bonds to no avail. Serena tied great knots, apparently.

He *really* wanted to get his hands on her…

The wisp of magick reached him and twined around his ankles and wrists. And suddenly…he was free. The magick disappeared. The window closed with a little thud.

"What the bastard hell?" he asked the ceiling.

Maybe he had a friend out there somewhere? Maybe…but there was no time to examine the possibility. He pushed the blanket away and sprung up from the couch. This was his chance to figure out what was happening to him.

He drew a deep breath and flexed his magickal muscles. It was nice to have full use of his powers back.

After a moment of reveling in his newfound freedom, he slipped into the hallway and searched for her bedroom. He had excellent night vision—like a cat or some wild nocturnal animal. He had an excellent sense of smell, as well. Cole peeked into the bathroom and saw the counter was strewn with all kinds of different types of lip gloss, in many different shapes, sizes and flavors.

Finally, he found her sleeping in a king-size four-poster bed in the bedroom at the end of the corridor. It was decorated just as comfortably as the rest of the house. A chair piled with clothes dominated a corner, next to a large rosewood dresser that was also strewn with lip balm containers of all shapes. What was the deal with that? She had a large collection of ceramic fairies displayed on shelves along one wall. He smiled. Definitely not the bedroom of a seductress.

Gentle breathing drew him to her bedside. Her black hair was spread across her pillow and the moonlight streamed in through the nearby window, limning her face in silver. The pale light illuminated the thin strap of her nightgown and the curve of one peaches-in-cream shoulder. He lifted a brow in speculation.

Cole reached out and passed his hand over her face. At the same time, he used a light magick to deepen her sleep and give her sweet dreams. She sighed and parted her lips.

Unable to resist the lure of that lush mouth, he dipped his head and kissed her. "I wasn't lying when I said I thought you were beautiful, Serena," he murmured just above her rosy lips. "We'll meet again, and when we do, I'll make you mine."

He picked up a tendril of her hair between his fingers and rubbed its silkiness. What was it about this woman that made him want her so much? He wanted to *keep* her. The soldier, sea captain, Viking, gladiator and knight in him all pounded their chests and declared this woman *mine*.

And so he would make her.

Letting her hair slip between his fingers, he passed his hand down her body, holding it palm down about an inch above her. He wanted to peel back those blankets and touch her skin-to-skin, but this would have to do for now. His phantom touch slid down her luscious body and cupped her breasts. In her sleep, Serena tossed her head and moaned softly.

His cock hardened and he gritted his teeth. This was pure torture. He wanted to be the one touching her, not his magick, but it didn't seem right to do that without her consent. This way, she could push his magick away if it was unwanted. Even in her sleep, she could do that with her subconscious. As it was, he felt no resistance, which pleased him. It meant that on some level she wanted him, too. Even if she didn't realize it.

Cole slipped his hand down over her stomach and hips, straight to the honey pot. Serena squirmed on the mattress and moaned again.

When he finally took her for real, skin-to-skin and sex-to-sex, he'd strip every bit of material from her sweet body and drag his tongue over every square inch of her. He'd spread her out on her back, cover her body with his and declare Serena his for the taking. First, he'd kiss her lips soft and gently. Treat her like the precious woman she was. Then he'd take her mouth with his and show her just how much she haunted him, tormented him. He'd nip and suck and bite at her mouth and her breasts with such passion that she would writhe beneath him — beg him to enter her. He'd spread her legs then and taste her sex. Tease her clit against his tongue and sip from the very heart of her. He'd lick her slowly from anus to clit until…

"Come for me, beautiful," he murmured.

She whimpered and then softly cried out as his magick possessed her. He'd tipped her straight into climax. She tossed her head and gripped the blankets as the gentle orgasm racked her. After the tremors had eased, she rolled onto her side with a slight smile on her face.

He wanted to slide into the bed beside her, hold her close and bury his nose in her hair to smell the scent of her shampoo and run his hands over her silky smooth skin. He wanted to hold her all night long, protect her from anything that wanted to hurt her. Cole wanted tell her she was beautiful, and *show* her with his body just how gorgeous he thought she was…over and over until the morning light broke through the window.

He wanted to spend all day tomorrow talking with her, extracting every bit of trivia she had to tell him about herself, her life. He wanted to immerse himself in everything she was.

But he couldn't do that, nor would she welcome it if he could.

So, instead, with one last long look at her, his cock harder than the iron in the cuffs that had bound him, he backed into the shadows.

Chapter Three

ଉ

Serena awoke to the morning light streaming in through her window and the happy sound of birds in the trees outside. She stretched and flipped the blankets back. Boy, she was in a good mood this morning. She wondered why, and then remembered.

Oh, yeah. The *dream*.

She sat on the edge of the bed as it came rushing back at her. She'd dreamt that Cole had come into her room the previous night and had told her he hadn't lied when he'd said he thought she was beautiful. He'd also told her they'd meet again and when they did, *she'd be his*.

Whatever that meant.

Then she'd dreamt he slipped into her bed and had proceeded to… Her cheeks blazed with the memory. She really *did* need to get laid…and soon. Her subconscious had driven that point home by taking the first available man at hand and using him to let her know.

Shaking her head, she stood, found her bathrobe and donned it. Then she walked out into the living room to check on her prisoner.

And stopped cold in her tracks.

The blanket she'd placed over Cole was rumpled on the floor by the side of the couch. The ropes and the cuffs lay on the seat. Cole himself was nowhere to be seen.

She grabbed a heavy candleholder on the mantel and brandished it. "Cole?" she called warily to the empty room. How silly, she thought. He was long gone by now.

217

She sat down in a nearby chair, letting the candleholder hit the floor with a *thunk*, and stared at the cuffs. How the hell had he gotten them off? Not that it mattered. Obviously, he'd managed it. And, luckily, he hadn't killed her while she'd been sleeping.

No, he hadn't killed her…but had he given her *a little death*?

She shook her head. No way. *That* had only been a dream. Cole had found a way to free himself and had disappeared immediately, taking all his silly lies and platitudes with him. She should be happy to be rid of him.

So why did she feel sad?

She stood and went into the kitchen to brew some coffee. Maybe she was far lonelier than she'd realized. Spartacus, one of her cats, wound his way around her ankles and meowed up at her. She set a saucer of milk down for him. All the other cats in the house came running at the familiar noises of cabinet door and refrigerator opening, milk pouring, and saucer set on linoleum. Soon the entire kitchen was awash in the pleasant sound of *purr*.

Serena leaned back against the counter and sipped her coffee. She loved her cats, but she didn't want to be one of those old spinster witches who only had felines for company, either.

Looked like that was the direction her life was taking, however.

Even though she should be happy to be so fortunate, she wanted things in her life that she would never have. Here she was, lucky enough to own property and beautiful home, all free and clear. She had her writing career that was bringing in a pretty penny with the publication of her books on witchcraft. She'd just turned in her fifth book to her editor at SacredWish Publishing and was mulling over possibilities for her sixth.

Still…she wished for…*more*.

She shook her head, not allowing herself to finish the thought. That was selfish. She needed to be happy with and thankful for what she had.

Later, she would visit the Elders and have a little chat. For now, she'd allow herself to wallow in just the slightest bit of self-pity.

* * * * *

"Slipped your leash, did you? Should've known *Serena* wouldn't be able to keep you," spat Alana.

The tone Alana used when she said Serena's name made Cole dislike the blonde witch in front of him even more, if that was possible. He had a violent, gut-level reaction to the woman every time he was in her presence. Cole watched Alana eye him warily as she rounded her dining room table, keeping the heavy piece of furniture firmly between them. Her hand, Cole noted, was loosely fisted. Likely she had a spell at the ready if he went unexpectedly psycho like he had before.

He felt the rage he'd felt the last time he was in her presence. That was true enough. His magic boiled and bubbled in his mind. He tamped it down, kept it under control with a superior act of willpower. It was torture. Releasing that energy would be better than sex, and a dark part of him would revel in the chaos it would cause. A part of him really wanted that darkness realized…and it was a strong part. The other part of him wanted to ensure he harmed no one. He gritted his teeth and closed his eyes for a moment, tamping the urge down.

He didn't want to harm anyone. Not even Alana, for whom he felt a large amount of animosity for some unknown reason.

He opened his eyes and smiled slowly, in a deliberately non-threatening way. "C'mere, darlin', I'm not going to hurt you. I only want to ask you a few questions."

Alana's light blue eyes widened with fear. Apparently, he didn't look and sound as friendly as he was trying for. Her long golden hair whipped around as she turned and fled.

He ran around the table and followed her into her kitchen. Cole caught her right before she opened the back door. He slammed it shut with the flat of his palm. Taking her by the arm, he swung her around to face him. "Calm down, lady," he ground out. "I said I wouldn't hurt you."

A hysterical laugh bubbled up from her throat. "And I-I'm supposed to just believe you?" She narrowed her eyes at him. "You lunged at me the first time I met you. You actually got your hands around my throat."

His eyes flicked down to her neck. "Must not have been too bad. I don't see any marks."

She laughed again. "You're a piece of work. You try to kill me, then you break into my house and demand I be civil."

"Your front door was open." He released her and she backed away until she was flush up against the counter behind her. "Anyway, I don't care if you're civil to me or not. I just want some answers. And, see…I'm pretty sure I had a reason to lunge at you. I'm certain I had a *damn* good reason to be angry. You want to tell me what it is?"

She stared up at him, her mouth twisting in a cruel half-smile. Her eyes were cold and hard. Some men might think she was beautiful. Fuckable, at the very least. But Cole didn't like the look in her baby blues. Didn't like the sticky, slimy feel she seemed to have in her psychic energy pattern. She felt nothing like clear, honest Serena, or silky, sensual Rowan.

She pushed past him, running a hand through her long tresses. "Fine, then," she shot back over her shoulder at him. "I want to be done with you. Come into my parlor."

"Said the spider to the fly," Cole muttered as he followed in her sauntering wake.

The *parlor* was Alana's living room. It was decorated in a sun and moon theme, done in deep blues and golds. It should've been soothing, but everything about this woman seemed to set his teeth on edge.

She plopped into a recliner, picked up a pack of smokes from the end table and lit one. She took a drag and exhaled like she was having an orgasm, then leveled her gaze at him. "Look, big guy, you weren't even supposed to remember who I am."

He sat down on the sofa, absorbing her words. Rage built within him. Games *really* weren't what he wanted right now. He took a breath and steadied himself. "You better get to the point, Alana, and fast."

She held her hands up. "Okay, okay. I'm just saying…you shouldn't even be here. You shouldn't have even remembered my name. The invocation must have been slightly off. Something went amiss."

His hand that rested on the couch's armrest clenched. "What invocation?" he asked with forced measured calm.

"The one that triggered the realization of Cernunnos within you."

"So, I *am* Cernunnos? If I'm Cernunnos, who the hell is Cole?"

She sighed at him and rolled her eyes like he should be in the corner with a dunce cap on. "You're both Cernunnos *and* Cole. You were born Colin Peter Striker. But Colin was just the human front for the energy of Cernunnos. *Cole* is the physical vessel for that ancient energy."

"Uh-huh. Have you been smoking crack?"

She rolled her eyes again and leaned forward. "Cernunnos incarnates over and over in human bodies, but most of the time that human incarnation retains no real awareness of that ancient energy within. The incarnations are usually always OtherKin— like a witch, a mage or a shapeshifter. In your case, you're both a mage *and* a shapeshifter."

"Uhm…huh?"

"Think of it as a person with an invisible thread of energy hanging off his back. That thread is connected to an ancient power source that exists somewhere else." She took a drag on her cigarette and glanced away. "The Three Ash coven called forth the slumbering Cernunnos energy within you. It came through the thread that hung off the back of Cole and now resides within him…*you*."

Cole went still and quiet. His fists clenched at her words. The rage built. He pushed it down with effort. Maybe Cernunnos hadn't liked being called forth? "So why can't I remember anything before waking up naked at the edge of the forest a few days ago?"

"The energies are warring inside you right now. It knocked your memory out. Once the energies find a balance, you'll get it back. When that happens, you won't be Cole, not anymore. Not really. You'll be your true self which is a mixture of both Cole and Cernunnos."

"I don't think Cernunnos appreciates what you did," he stated in a low voice that thrummed with an almost otherworldly power. "I think he was happy where he was."

Fear flickered in her eyes. "Yes." She glanced away. "I know that. You shifted when we did the invocation. First you shifted to a wolf and scared the crap out of everyone, then to the stag form of Cernunnos. You ran free for days. We were afraid some hunter would take you before you shifted back to human form. It was like you were trying to escape being trapped in human flesh."

His hands clenched again. "So, here's the obvious question, the one you haven't answered yet… *Why did you do it?*"

Alana stared at something to his left for a moment, then shot out of her chair. She paced to the window and back, taking an occasional agitated puff on her cigarette, until she'd smoked it down to the filter. She stubbed it out in an ashtray.

"Well," Cole finally drawled.

"You were the only one within a four-state radius that was a vessel for an energy as powerful as Cernunnos…and Cernunnos is tough enough to take out the thing we accidentally raised."

"Uh, what? What *thing*? Specifics, please."

She stood in front of him, letting her arms hang limp at her sides. Before she spoke, she lowered her eyes. "The coven accidentally raised a demon," she said softly. "A very intelligent and sadistic one." She raised her gaze. "That's a bad combination."

"What exactly do you mean by *demon*?"

"I mean an entity that means humankind harm. As OtherKin, you understand that everything that we fear or believe, dream, or think—it all manifests as reality in the astral realm. Angels, demons, gods, they're all real and they *all* exist somewhere. We were trying to contact the disincarnate father of one of the members. Somehow, we opened a portal from another dimension—one more commonly known as *hell*—to this plane of existence. This demon, Ashmodai, came through."

"Nice job."

"Don't joke." She turned, walked to the window and looked out. "He's one bad motherfucker."

Shock ripped through him as the demon's name registered in a rush. He *knew* that name. "Ashmodai. He goes by many names. The oldest of them is Aeshma Daeva. He's believed to be the child of the incest between Cain and his sister Naafrfah, and is one of the seven archdemons of Persian mythology. He was assumed to have been among the Seraphim at one time. Medieval scholars of demonology associated him with playful aggression and lust. He is often represented as having three heads—those of a bull, of a man, and of a ram—as well as a serpent's tail and webbed feet. He likes to play games, this demon." He stilled. "How the hell do I know all that?" he asked in shock.

She glanced back at him, giving him a rueful smile. "You, Cole, are big into the study of demons and the supernatural. You have a whole library of books on ancient pagan religions, myth, and legends."

Man, not knowing himself was disturbing. *Nosce te ipsum.* Know thyself. He didn't.

She pulled open a drawer and fished out a wallet and a key chain. "In fact, everything you'd ever want to know about Ashmodai is in your apartment. Most likely there's a ton of information in your library and your computer. Everything you'll need to know about how to defeat him is probably there." She tossed him the wallet and keys. "Have Serena help you. If there's one thing that witch is good for, it's research."

He stared down at the objects—his possessions—in his hand. "So, did you know me before? Before you invoked Cernunnos?"

"I only made your acquaintance in order to get a strand of your hair for the invocation."

"How'd you do that?"

She smiled slowly in a manner that was likely supposed to be seductive, but fell waaay short in Cole's opinion. "We slept together."

He shot up from his chair and pushed a hand through his hair, suddenly feeling nauseous.

"Of course, I could've gotten the hair without actually seducing you. That was just for fun." She gave him a sultry smile. "It was really good, Cole. You're one of the best pieces of ass I've had in a long time." The smile faded. "Too bad you tried to kill me, or I'd invite you into my bedroom right now."

"Sorry about that. I really am." He was sorry about *all* of it. "Like I said, I think Cernunnos wasn't very happy about what you did. I think both Cole and Cernunnos liked things just fine the way they were before."

"Yeah, well, get used to your new self," she shot back. "I didn't do anything that goes against your nature. Cernunnos has always been a part of you."

"When were you going to tell me all this? You didn't seem to be very forthcoming the other night."

Anger flashed through her eyes. "You tried to kill me as soon as you saw me. That didn't exactly make me feel *chatty*. Anyway, Ashmodai will be looking for you. You're the only source of energy around who can foil his play. He's going to sense that and want to take you out. I knew you'd figure it all out pretty quick."

Great.

"We invoked Cernunnos so you can take *him* out. You're the only one with enough magic and raw strength to do it." She fixed him with a sad smile. "You're our only hope, now." She gestured at his hand that held his wallet and keys. "That might help bring some of your memory back, but there's no *going* back. Your memory should return by tomorrow morning. Good luck. The black SUV out there on the street is yours." She jerked her head at the door. "Now get out. Last thing I need is that damn demon here looking for you."

"I have one last question."

She sighed and crossed her arms over her chest. "Shoot."

"Did you use magick to free me last night?"

She frowned. "No."

He stared at her with dark animosity in his eyes. "Why'd you let them cuff me and keep me in the first place? If I'm supposed to be your weapon against some badass demon, wouldn't you want me free so I can fight?"

She smiled and winked. "You are free, big guy. I knew you could do it. Anyway, like Cernunnos, Ashmodai needed some time to adjust to this reality. He shouldn't be cooking yet, but he will be soon…cooking with gas."

"Looking forward to it."

"Yeah, I'll just bet."

He looked down at the set of keys in his hand, feeling a familiarity with them. They were *his* car and house keys. The image of an apartment living room flashed in his mind and he flipped open his wallet, found his ID and examined the address printed on it. Without a glance at Alana, he went out the door.

* * * * *

Serena stomped around the corner of Rowan's apartment building and started toward her car. She was so mad that it literally felt like steam was coming out of her ears. Damn her stubborn sister!

She'd come into town to see if Rowan was all right and to share with her the strange message the Elders had given her that morning after she'd found Cole missing. She'd gone to the oak grove to ask about the mage and, man, had she gotten an earful. But when she'd arrived at her sister's apartment, all that had ceased to be important. Rowan had a huge bruise on her cheek and her eye was almost swollen shut.

After a bad argument, she'd finally persuaded Rowan to go to the doctor to make sure there were no more serious wounds than some bruising. Rowan had steadfastly refused to tell Serena or the doctor how she'd received the injuries. Since she was a protective older sister, Serena had pressed once they'd returned to the apartment...and Rowan had become belligerent and had asked her to leave. Actually, *ordered*, would be more accurate.

"So much for sisterly love," she muttered as she fished in her pocket for her car keys.

There had been fear in Rowan's eyes and that fear had ripped through Serena like a thousand icy daggers. Her little sister was in trouble, *bad trouble*, and she felt helpless to protect her.

That, coupled with what the Elders had said about Cole, had caused the day to turn out pretty shitty. All she wanted was to go home, have dinner, and take a nice, long bubble bath. She'd badger Rowan again tomorrow. No way was her little sis going to give her the brush off on this one.

Deep in thought, she approached her tan sedan and fished in her coat pocket for her car keys.

"Hey, beautiful."

Her steps faltered. She looked to her right, in the direction the voice like melted chocolate over shortbread had come from. Decadent, irresistible…and really bad for you. Cole, gorgeous and beguiling, leaned up against a storefront, watching her with his forest-colored bedroom eyes. "Cole," she said in surprise.

"I thought I recognized your car. Kinda hard to miss the vanity plate *hdg wtch*." He took a step toward her. "You consider yourself a hedge witch since you don't belong to a coven, don't you, darlin'? Be glad you're not a part of the Three Ash." He clenched a fist loosely at his side. "They're on a certain…*list* of mine, at the moment."

What the hell was he doing waiting around for her, or calling her beautiful while he did it? Had she slipped into a *Twilight Zone* where good-looking men paid attention to her? "How'd you get free last night? What are you doing here?" She walked toward him, shaking her head. "Never mind, we have to talk. I have important things to tell you. I contacted the Elders today and found out all kinds of stuff." She babbled on. "Not all of it makes sense, but—"

He reached out as she came near, hooked his finger in the pocket of her jean skirt and pulled her toward him. The action stopped her words…stopped her breath. He frowned, reached further into her pocket and pulled out a tube of cherry-flavored lip balm.

He quirked a brow and looked at her questioningly. "What's up with you and the lip balm?"

"Uh. I kind of have an addict—"

Warm hands grasped her shoulders and then slid around to her back, stealing the rest of her sentence. A hard, hot body pressed up against her. "Let's see if all that lip balm has paid off," he murmured. "Are your lips as soft as they look?"

She completely lost her train of thought as Cole pulled her up toward his face. Her gaze locked on his eyes for a precarious moment that seemed to last forever. The ending of the word "addiction" was still poised on her tongue. He smiled that slow, sexy, confident smile that sent butterflies straight to her stomach and then lowered his mouth to hers.

Shock stole almost all her motor skills and definitely all her cognitive ability. For a moment, she almost pushed him away. Then something gave within her and said...*why not*? She relaxed into his body.

His lips worked over her mouth, slowly sipping and tasting her. His hands trailed down and stopped on her waist. She ran her hands up his arms, feeling the bunch of luscious tendon and muscle as he moved.

Rapture. Utter and complete.

His lips slid across her mouth like silk, rubbing sensually. The action tightened her stomach, made it flutter, and affected areas of her body just south. He nipped at her bottom lip and gave it a slow lick, then pulled it into his hot mouth. Her knees almost gave out. With a sexy little growl in his throat, he enveloped her in his arms, tilted his head to the side and slanted his mouth over hers. His tongue feathered across her lips and she opened for him. He swept inside.

Oh...

The man could kiss. There was no doubt about it. He tasted like coffee and smelled like whatever soap he used when he'd showered, kind of clean and manly. His stubble rubbed her soft skin. She noted the sensation, but hardly minded it. On the contrary, for a kiss like this, she'd endure a little beard burn...or five o'clock shadow burn, or *whatever* it was called.

Dear God, she couldn't *think*!

His tongue rubbed up against hers and his lips worked over her mouth, tasting, nipping, devouring. The entire street fell away. The whole city just disappeared, as far she was concerned. She felt like she was floating in space. He caught her lower lip between his teeth and tugged gently. Then he slanted his mouth across hers once more and plundered again.

Finally he set her away from him. Her knees felt weak. Her lips were swollen and achy. Her mouth felt empty.

How would it be to sleep with this man if that was just a kiss?

"Sorry," he said. "I couldn't resist."

Sobering, she stepped away from him and searched for something cutting to say. She came up completely empty. "S-sorry?" She swallowed hard. "N-no, that's okay," she stammered. It was soooo beyond okay.

He gave her that slow, confident smile again. "But I did notice you kissed me back, beautiful, and really...*enthusiastically*, too." He handed the tube of lip balm back to her and she stuffed into her pocket with a trembling hand.

Well, *that* was like cold water in her face. How arrogant could he be?

Even if it *was* true.

Her spine straightened. Again she searched for something cutting to say. This time she came up with something feeble, but it was *something*. Her mind was starting to thaw out. Yay her. "Well, yeah. Someone grabs me out of nowhere and kisses me, I'm going to kiss back. It's, uh, reflex." She tried to sound flip, but failed.

He rubbed his hand over his stubbled chin. "Huh. Funny. I would've thought that screaming and pushing me away would've been reflex."

She sighed and played with her car keys. "Uh-huh. Listen, I wasn't joking. I don't know what possessed you to do that just now, but it doesn't matter at this exact moment. I have things to tell you. So..."

He took her hand. "Come with me. We'll talk." He pulled her behind him.

"Where are we going?"

He turned and gave her a devilish smile. "My place."

"You have a place?"

He jingled a set of keys in his hand. "Yes. I even have a car."

"Did you get your memory back?"

He gave his head a sharp shake. "I went to see Alana. My car was parked outside her house." He sounded really pissed. Serena glanced up at him. A muscle in his jaw worked as he clenched it. "Apparently, she lured me to her place, then put the whammy on me, so my car was still over there."

"Whammy?"

"I'll explain when we get to my apartment. I was on the way to my place when I passed your car on the street. Alana said there are books and computer files in my apartment on Ashmodai. She also told me you're a crack researcher. I was hoping you'd help me."

He knew about Ashmodai? Go to his place? Her head spun for a moment. She jerked her wrist away from him and stopped. "Wait a minute!"

"What's wrong?"

"I can't just *go* to your apartment. You showed up at my house handcuffed after attacking Alana. For all I know, you just finished her off. I can't even use magick on you if you get rowdy because you're not bound by cold iron anymore, and I can sense your magic is *much* stronger than mine."

"Serena..." He trailed off and stood there looking at her. Finally, he took a step toward her, closing the distance between them. Serena couldn't make herself back away from him. His brown and green-flecked eyes softened as he reached out and cupped her chin. "I can't convince you that I mean you no harm, and the last thing I want to see reflected in your eyes when you look at me is fear. I do mean you no harm, but I'll understand if you choose not to come with me, beautiful." He let his hand fall and he glanced away. "You probably shouldn't be anywhere around me, anyway. I'm not safe. It's probably better you keep your distance."

He turned and walked away from her. She watched as he strode to a large black SUV and put the key in the lock. Why did she feel so compelled to be with this man? He opened the door, climbed in and started it up. He looked so alone.

"Wait," she called. "I'm coming." She ran to the passenger side and climbed in.

"Are you sure, Serena?" he asked.

"Yes. Hell, anyone would want to attack Alana," she shot at him. "For your information, I *turned down* inclusion in the Three Ash Coven," she added primly. "Alana hates me for rejecting her precious circle."

"Ah. That explains the animosity between you two."

She eyed the fancy dashboard of the brand-new gas-guzzling, ozone-depleting SUV and its state-of-the-art CD player. "Guess you aren't an environmentalist, huh?" she commented half under her breath.

He checked a street map and pulled away from the curb. "Guess not. Strange. You'd think the physical vessel for Cernunnos would be."

"So you know?"

He glanced and nodded at her. "Alana told me."

"The Elders told me you'd be getting your memory back soon."

"That's good."

"They also said a really vicious demon named Ashmodai would be sniffing you out because you're the only one around that has the power to match him. He'll want to take you out so he can have some fun."

"Yeeeah, that's less good. Alana told me that, too."

She paused and played with the edge of her shirt. "So…what are you going to do?"

He glanced at her. "Who, me? I don't even know who I am yet. Give me half a second to figure things out."

"I can give you half a second. I only hope Ashmodai will."

They pulled into the driveway of some fancy, old high-rise condos. "I do, too," he murmured. "I do, too, beautiful."

He guided the SUV around the building to a driveway that led to underground parking ramp and reached up to the visor and pressed a small button. The gate to the underground garage opened. "I remember this," he said under his breath. "All this is familiar."

He drove past the gate and found a parking space. Serena and Cole both got out and walked to the nearby elevator. Cole used the remote locking device on the key chain to secure the vehicle. The vehicle blurp-beeped twice as they walked away.

As they approached the elevator, Serena noticed a lanky man in his late thirties leaning against the wall. Instantly, she went on alert, and then chided herself for paranoia. She was jumping at shadows since her conversation with the Elders and the disturbing news of the disincarnate demon that was floating around just waiting for something to do to entertain himself.

The man studied her from head to toe as she walked toward the elevator. "Heeey, princess, aren't you fine?" the man purred at her as they approached.

A greasy feeling of negative intent curled through her stomach. It was her sixth sense kicking in. It wasn't something she ever ignored. She backed away from the man.

"Hey, buddy, back off, okay?" Cole growled as he pressed the up button for the elevator. "She's with me, and I don't like other men shooting come-ons at my lady friends."

A tremor of shocked pleasure went through Serena at Cole's words. Then she remembered that he was simply trying to dissuade Greasy Guy.

Greasy Guy held up his hands as if in surrender. "All right, man. It's cool. I was just dreaming of meeting a pretty woman like her today."

The elevator doors popped open and Serena hurried inside. She didn't like the feel of that man. All she wanted was to be away from him.

"Yeah? Well, keep dreaming," Cole said as he stepped into the elevator and punched the seventh floor.

Just as the elevator door was almost closed, Greasy Guy reached in and held it open with one grimy hand. He narrowed mud-colored eyes at them. "You better watch yourself, boy," he snarled. Then he let the door close.

"Okaaay," breathed Serena. "What the hell was that about?"

He reached out and rubbed his hand on her upper arm. His touch was warm and comforting. "Just some freak. It's all right, Serena. I promise."

A shiver of unease went through her. She really hoped he was right about that. Though she did feel amazingly safe with him. In spite of everything, she felt that security like a warm blanket deep in the heart of her.

She could feel Cole's magick and it was nothing to be trifled with. Cole was the most powerful OtherKin she'd ever met. Plus, he was a big, muscled guy that no one in his or her right mind would ever mess with. But her feeling of security went further than magick and muscle. The point of origination remained unclear, but was there nonetheless.

Cole had said she should stay away from him because he was unsafe. She assumed he meant because of Ashmodai, but if Ashmodai ever came to call, she didn't want to be anywhere but at Cole's side. *That's* where she would feel the safest.

They walked down the wide, opulent corridor that was decorated in creams and blues and stood in front of a large oak door. Cole fumbled for a moment, trying to find the right key. Finally the lock clicked open and they entered a large foyer. The walls were done in a neutral putty color and hung with colorful abstract art. The floor of the foyer was marble, but beyond that was thick tan carpet. They passed through the foyer into the living room.

Serena looked around, taking the place in. His apartment was the ultimate bachelor's pad...a very well-off bachelor.

"Hello?" Cole called. There was no answer.

A perverse part of her had worried that they'd find a wife or girlfriend at his place, a fashion model type with worry just faintly lining her million-dollar face. Perfect hair just slightly mussed in her fretting over where her beloved had gone. Already tiny waistline a tad smaller because she *just hadn't* been able to eat anything these last few days. But no almost perfectly coiffed wife or artfully tearstained girlfriend met them at the door.

After Serena had ascertained the absence of a mate—and found herself disturbingly happy about that fact, too—she padded over the plush tan carpeting calling, "Here kitty, kitty."

Cole stood by an expensive-looking brown sectional in the living room watching her walk around stooped over, looking around corners and calling for a cat that probably didn't exist. "What are you doing?" he asked.

She straightened. "I've been worried maybe you had a pet that's been slowly starving to death."

He frowned. "The good news is I don't think I do." He glanced at the big screen TV and the console beside it that contained a DVD player, a kick-ass stereo system and just about every gaming system ever created. There had to be close to a hundred grand along that wall alone. "Yeeeah." He pushed a hand through his hair and gave her a look that screamed chagrin. "The bad news is I may be a drug dealer."

Serena wandered over to the kitchen. It was state-of-the-art, with brand new shiny appliances, a wine rack, and lots of copper pots and pans hanging over the stove. "Uh…maybe you're a world-class chef?" she asked him hopefully.

"Doubtful. Did you see an answering machine anywhere?"

She walked back to the entryway where she'd seen a table with a phone. "It's here." The message light blinked five messages. Cole came to stand beside her. She hit play.

A sultry, breathy female voice filled the foyer. "Darling, this is Monique. Call me. I'm missing you." Pause. "Darren is out of town on business this weekend. Come see me. *Please*."

Serena rolled her eyes. The woman sounded like she needed a fix. Maybe Cole *was* a drug dealer…of the carnal variety.

Beep.

A perky cheerleaderesque voice was up next. "Hey, Cole, baby. This is Cynthia. I had a fantastic day with you last Saturday." Pause. Her voice lowered, got huskier when she spoke next. "Saturday night was even better. Wanna repeat? Call me back."

Beep.

"Yeeeech." Serena turned away and walked toward the living. She couldn't take any more. It was nauseating.

"I guess I have a few women," Cole said, sounding mightily pleased with himself.

Was it any surprise? The man was stunning. Serena looked back in time to see him push a hand through his hair. The action defined his biceps perfectly and made hunger twist through her body. She looked away. "Yeah. Guess it hasn't really been a long time, like you said."

He frowned. "Guess not. Sure feels like it, though."

There were two hang-ups. Blessedly, the next message was not from a woman. Instead, it was an older-sounding man. Serena wandered back to the answering machine.

"Hey, Cole, just wanted to let you know that we received *Fire of the Ancients*. We love it and only want a couple changes. You did a fantastic job on this game. You're the king of adventure games, man. We'll be getting back to you with more details, but you've done it again. This'll be a hit!"

"Well." He slanted her an unsure look. "I'm the king of adventure computer games, I guess."

"Apparently, that's not all you're the king of," Serena muttered.

He appeared to not have heard her. "So," he said to almost himself. "I design computer games. That explains all the equipment in the living room." He frowned and glanced at her. "Designing computer games is kind of geeky. Do I seem like a geek to you?"

"What?" She turned toward him. "First of all, there's nothing wrong with geeks. I happen to be one myself. Second of all—" She took him in from the top his head to his feet, every luscious well-defined muscle in between, and tried not to swallow her tongue. "No, you don't look like one." Suddenly uncomfortable, she turned away. "Anyway, what the hell does a geek look like?" she finished, irritably.

"Let's explore the rest of the apartment." He turned and walked into the living room.

"Don't you want to call *Monique* and *Cynthia* back?" She mimicked their voices when she said their names. It was childish, but she couldn't help herself.

He turned back toward and fixed her with suddenly hooded and heated gaze. It was the calculating and measured gaze of a predator. Like shark that had just scented blood in the water, or a lion on an African plain that had spotted a wounded zebra.

Shit.

She took a step back involuntarily and bumped into the telephone table. "Are you jealous, beautiful?" he purred as he came closer.

"Uh." Oh, *that* was an intelligent response. Mentally, she smacked her forehead with her open palm.

"Because you sound jealous," he murmured. He reached her and cupped her cheek in his hand. "Maybe I should kiss you again and reassert the fact that I desperately want you in my bed, Serena. It was *you* that balked, remember?"

"I-I'm not jealous," she replied, tipping her chin up a little. "I just don't like to see women make idiots of themselves over a man." *Just like she was doing.* "I just don't...shit—"

His mouth came down on hers, completely stealing the rest of her thought. He seduced her lips to part and kissed her deep.

All the while he rubbed his thumb back and forth over her cheek. He broke the kiss and set his forehead to hers. After making a little purring sound in the back of his throat, he closed his eyes and clenched his jaw. "Your skin's so soft," he murmured thickly. "I can't help but wonder if you're as soft all over."

Serena's breath caught. She used the table behind her to take some of her weight because her knees weren't doing a very good job of it.

He set his hands on either side of her, resting them on the table, and gazed into her wide eyes. "You need to leave, Serena. I mean it. You're not safe around me…for so many different reasons. I want to lead you to my bed, lay you out and take you over and over until the morning light breaks the night. I want to strip you, beautiful. I want to sink myself inside you."

A whimpering sound reached her ears and it took her a second to realize it was coming from her.

He pushed away from the table and turned. "If you don't want any of that, you should leave now. Because you're tempting me something awful."

Serena glanced at the door and back at Cole. He stood with his back to her. Suddenly, he shot a hand out toward the door and it opened.

She stared at the open door, her ticket out of here, out of this whole dangerous mess. If she left now, she'd be free of the whole Ashmodai thing, presumably.

But she couldn't seem to move.

She did want Cole. Of course, she did. She was just surprised, and more than a little wary about the fact that *he* wanted *her*. In her mind, she was still the fat girl in school all the boys ignored. It was hard for her to wrap her mind around the fact that this perfect, beautiful specimen of manhood—this man who could have any woman he wanted—found her attractive. No. Not even that. Cole professed to find her *irresistible*.

How could that be?

She wanted to find out if it was true, however, so instead of walking to the door and out of it like she *should*, she stood staring at Cole's broad shoulders, his tight ass and the back of his head. She *liked* this man as well as found him attractive. He was compelling, mysterious and more than a little dangerous. She found *him* irresistible.

But…what would happen when he got her clothes off and he discovered her overweight body naked? Would the fire in his eyes dim? Serena shuddered. That was something she *didn't* want to find out.

Something Brian had told her once came back in a rush. *You'd be so pretty if you just lost some weight.*

She glanced at the door, then back at Cole. She *should* leave. It would save them both some pain and anguish. She moved to take a step toward it.

He flicked his wrist. The door slammed shut.

Crap.

Suddenly, her mind was awhirl. What kind of bra and underwear had she put on this morning? She flushed as she remembered donning the serviceable blue briefs that sported tiny pink flowers and the boring white cotton bra. Not exactly alluring lingerie.

She just hadn't expected to be seduced today.

A wild laugh rose up in her throat, but it was choked into submission by the look on Cole's face as he turned toward her. A dark, predatory light graced his brown and green-flecked eyes. "You're mine now, beautiful," he murmured.

Chapter Four

ઈઝ

Cole watched Serena's eyes widen and her small pink tongue steal out to lick her lips. She looked uncertain, maybe even a little regretful that she hadn't dashed for the door when she'd had the chance.

There was no way she'd escape him now. She was his until the first morning's light...and beyond. He'd make sure she didn't regret not exiting when he'd presented her with the opportunity.

He took in her curves as he approached her. Well, the curves he could see, anyway. He couldn't wait to remove the jean skirt and frumpy green button-down shirt that she was wearing. Cole had noticed she dressed to conceal her body, hide those wonderfully large breasts he so wanted to touch and taste. He wanted to savor every square inch of her. The hunger of Cernunnos rose within him at the thought. Heat skittered out from his cock to envelop his whole body.

Serena's eyes widened. Her silky black hair swung as she glanced at the door again. Her mouth tightened.

He wanted to see that stunning face relaxed, wanted to see that glossy black hair shimmer in the light and feel its corn-silk texture brush his upper thighs as those luscious lips wrapped around his cock. He suppressed a growl of pure *want* at the images flitting through his mind.

Serena was a nice woman, respectable. He suspected she was no virgin, but neither had she been with many men. No, Serena was a good girl. Still, he sensed in her a wild wantonness. He sensed that whoever the man she granted her sexual favor to, she would allow him all the pleasures of the flesh that he wished. In fact, Cole suspected that she'd yearn for those pleasures.

He wanted to be the man.

He possessed a dominant and aggressive sexual personality. He might not know a lot about himself, but he knew that much. Her sweet submissiveness and innate wantonness he suspected lay within her called out to the dominant in him with a siren's song. They would make the perfect match between the sheets. Cole was sure of it.

He walked toward her. "C'mere, beautiful," he purred. "Shall we find the bedroom?"

"Uh—" her gaze flicked away from his and then back. "Shouldn't we find the library instead? The one where we can find the information about Ashmodai?"

He shook his head slowly. "Serena, I'll have my memory back fully by morning. That's what Alana said. It'd be much more time efficient to wait until I can remember where everything is, don't you think?"

"I guess that's logical. It's just that Ashmodai is loose right now and we're doing nothing to stop him."

"Yes, and he's been out there for the past week while I cavorted in the forest and spent some time in cold iron cuffs with no memory. I hardly think a few more hours while we wait for my memory to come back is going to matter. Not to mention the fact that Alana told me that Ashmodai needed some adjustment time, just like I did, and wouldn't be kicking for a while. So, my question remains…*bedroom*, Serena, my sweet?"

She stiffened. Her face twisted in an expression of confusion. "Cole, how could you want me?"

He stopped in front of her. Ah, so that was the problem, her self-deprecation again. "Darlin', I think the better question is how could I *not* want you?" He stopped in front her, reached out and fingered a tendril of her hair. "You don't need worry about that. Not at all. My question is do you want me?"

She looked up at him. "So much."

He took her hand and dragged her further into his apartment before she'd even finished uttering the words. Where the hell would his bedroom be? He could've just taken her right on the floor of the foyer, or up against the wall, but Serena deserved better than that for her first coupling with him. He wanted to see her naked amid a soft comforter and pillows. He wanted to wrap her in his embrace in complete comfort.

They walked through the hallway, passing an office crammed to bursting with state-of-the-art computer equipment. Bookshelves absolutely overloaded with thick volumes lined all the walls. Cole made a mental note as they passed. That was undoubtedly the library. They passed large bathroom, and, *finally*, the master bedroom. He barely noticed the ponderous dresser along one wall, the entertainment center containing a TV and other electronic equipment. His awareness instantly centered on the brass four-poster bed with the fluffy navy-blue down comforter and pillows that dominated the middle of the room.

The only thing beyond the bed that drew his attention was the line of mirrored closets along one wall, in perfect relation to the bed for— "Damn. I'm a kinky bastard, I guess," he mused.

Serena looked at the mirrors and then the bed. "No doubt."

He led her to the bed, took off her glasses and set them on the bedside table. "Can you see without them?"

She nodded. "I have astigmatism. I can see, but everything is blurry."

"That's okay. Mostly, you'll just be feeling." He pulled her into his arms. "Ah, Serena. I can't wait to have you," he breathed as he lowered his lips to hers.

She stiffened against the dominant possession of his mouth, and then relaxed. Her hands came up, fluttering against his upper arms, over his shoulders, to finally twine through the hair that curled at his nape. She sighed against his mouth and parted her lips for him.

Christ. His cock couldn't get any harder.

He reached under her shirt and ran his fingers along her soft skin to cup a breast through her bra. Her swift intake of breath and the hardening of her nipple through the material told her she enjoyed his touch.

He smiled against her mouth. "Like that, do you, beautiful?" he murmured.

"Ah, yes," she hissed.

"Want more?"

She bit her bottom lip and nodded slightly. "I want to touch you."

He stepped back and spread his arms. "I'm yours for the taking."

She bit her lip in concentration. Lust shadowed her dark blue pupils, dilating them, letting him know just how aroused she was. He was glad to see that her desires had eclipsed her fears. She stepped toward him and began unbuttoning his shirt. With every button she freed, she kissed the exposed skin of his chest. Lower and lower she went.

The sensation of her sweet lips on his flesh, her fingertips and nails raking over his skin nearly made him insane. Cole's breath hissed through his teeth and he wound his hands through her hair in an effort to prevent himself from pushing her back onto the mattress and mounting her like some frenzied beast.

She laid a line of slow, deliberate kisses from his belly button to the top of his jeans, and finally his shirt was completely open. He shrugged it the rest of the way off and let it fall to the floor as she began unbuttoning his pants.

She purred somewhere deep in her throat as she pushed his jeans just far enough down to free his erect cock to the air. Soft fingers stroked it tentatively.

He couldn't take it anymore. "*Enough,*" he growled. He pulled her to her feet and pushed her back onto the mattress. His fingers itched to get those clothes off her, but he didn't know if he could manage the task without imploding first. He felt such an urgency to be inside her.

* * * * *

Oh, she'd wanted to taste him. She'd been about to do just that when he'd pulled her up. He was outrageously beautiful everywhere. His cock was long and wide. *Delectable.* Her pussy was swollen and aching for him and her own sense of urgency was reflected in his eyes and actions. She wanted, needed, him inside her right this very minute. He appeared to need to be inside her just as much.

Brian had receded to the farthest corner of her mind. He was still present—the pain he'd inflicted on her would always scar her emotions, her self-image. The hurt he'd caused had been irreparable to some extent…but Cole burned a large part of it away in his lust for her.

He came down between her thighs. Settling his hips against hers, he kissed her hard and possessively. Serena arched her back and moaned when he unbuttoned the top buttons of her shirt and unhooked her bra. When he wrapped his beautiful lips around one of her nipples, she tipped her head back and thanked the universe she'd worn her front-hooking bra today. He laved and sucked each nipple to a hard, rosy tip, all the while making noises deep in throat like he was starving and her nipples were delectable morsels.

He slipped a hand down to smooth up her thigh, dragging his fingertips up her skin toward her pussy and pushing her skirt up as he went. Finally, his hand curled around the edge of her sensible underwear and she felt the tickle of magick shimmy along her skin. "Off," he rasped through clenched teeth. Her underwear rent easily at the seams in response to the small spell and he threw them to the carpet.

Now there was nothing between her and his cock.

He ran his fingertips up her swollen, wet pussy, flicking at her clit gently until she moaned and tightened her hands in his hair. "Ahh, you feel perfect, Serena. I knew you would," he murmured right before he kissed her.

"Please," she gasped. The thought of his shaft inside her consumed her every thought. It was all she wanted right now.

His cock. Her pussy. *Now.*

She tipped her head up and caught his darkened gaze. "Cole, *please.*"

He didn't hesitate to comply with the erotic demand in her eyes and her voice. He pushed her skirt up to her waist, his gaze hungrily taking in her spread thighs and her sex. "Ah, you look perfect, too," he purred. "More lovely than I'd imagined."

He came down on her, fastening his mouth over hers, even as he shifted his pelvis in place and set the head of his cock to the entrance of her slick, waiting pussy.

Yes, she breathed in her mind.

Abruptly, he looked stricken and pulled back. Fear rushed through her. Had he finally realized his mistake?

"Condom," he rasped.

She eased. He was only worried about having unprotected sex. It wasn't that she suddenly disgusted him. "I'm clean and on the pill, Cole," she said.

"I'm not worried about you. I'm worried about me. Didn't you hear the messages?"

She bit her lip. It was true he got around a bit and since he had no memory... "True," she answered.

He rifled through the bedside table and immediately came up with a whole box of condoms—extra-large, ribbed for her pleasure. He grabbed one and ripped the wrapper off. Then he fumbled, trying to roll it on in haste.

Serena stifled the wild laugh bubbling up in her throat. This gorgeous man was all worried and impatient for her? How absurd. She sat up, took the condom from him and stroked her fingers down his length. "Let me," she said.

He tipped his head back at her touch, and his Adam's apple worked as he groaned. "God, Serena, I want you so much that you're going to make me come just by putting the condom on."

Carefully, she rolled it down his cock, taking a moment to hold his lovely set of balls in her hand. In an impatient gesture, he pushed her onto her back, spread her legs and set his cock to the entrance of her pussy.

She settled back, feeling the large crown of his shaft breach her. "Oh," she breathed as her muscles stretched with the invasion. She hadn't had sex in so long. Five whole years. Sure, she'd used a vibrator once in awhile, but Cole was *far* larger than any toy she owned. Could she even take Cole into her body? Her whole body tensed.

"Shh, Serena. Relax for me, baby. Come on. It's okay." He scattered kisses across her cheek and mouth and caressed his hand up and down her thigh. "I want you so bad. I'll be honest, I want to just push myself inside you and feel all that tight, hot flesh wrap around my cock, but I'm not going to hurt you, okay? We'll take this one inch at a time."

She bit her bottom lip and nodded.

He eased himself in a little more, up to just past the crown. Serena gasped and wiggled her hips. God, he felt good. She felt spread and full and…possessed. And he wasn't even completely within her yet.

Another inch wrung a long moan from her.

Another and another.

Cole bit his bottom lip, curled his fingers into the bedding and groaned. "Serena, you're so damn tight. You feel so good. You don't know hard this is, baby." He pushed in another inch. "So hard to go slow," he bit off on the tail of another low groan.

She no longer wanted him to be careful with her, to go slow. Right now, all she wanted was him filling her up. She grabbed his ass and thrust her hips toward him. The rest of him slid inside until he was seated to the base of his shaft.

"Ah, baby," Cole rasped. "Awww, fuck, *yes*."

Serena gasped at the sensation of being completely impaled. No other man she'd ever been with had been large enough to give her this sensation. Serena threw her head back into the pillows, dug her nails into Cole's shoulders and hissed, "Yes." It felt exquisite to be so stretched, so filled and so possessed by this man.

He shafted her slow at first then faster and faster. She wrapped her legs around his waist and enjoyed the way he pressed her into the mattress with every thrust. Her climax came fast and hard, overwhelming her—both in mind and body.

"Serena," Cole breathed above her. His big body stiffened and he thrust as far as possible within her as he let loose.

Breathing heavily, they collapsed in a tangle of limbs and clothes. Damn, they hadn't even managed to get fully undressed. She glanced at Cole. He lay beside her with his hair covering his face.

She pushed her exposed breasts back into her shirt and sat up with the intention of getting dressed. "I don't normally do this kind of thing," she stammered. *Good God*, she'd just slept with some man she didn't even know! Rowan was rubbing off on her. Serena never behaved this way. Not even once in her life had she ever been so impulsive and careless. What strange spell had possessed her?

Oh, yeah. Colin Peter Striker. Better known these days as the physical vessel for Cernunnos. That's what had possessed her.

Cole's hand snaked out and caught her wrist as she straightened her shirt. "The clothes should be coming *off*, not going on, beautiful."

"Cole—"

He sat up and pushed gently onto her back. "You're mine 'til daybreak, Serena."

She raised an eyebrow. "Do I get a say in this?"

A wicked, sexy smile curved his mouth. "I'd have a mind to tie you to the bed if you denied me, but, yes, you have a say. 'Course you do."

As he spoke, he rubbed her collarbone lazily with the pad of his thumb. Back and forth, back and forth, back and... A moan caught in her throat. The man was a *menace*. Even the look of heat in his eyes made her breath hitch.

"I'll admit that was a bit intense," he continued. "It was fast and intense like that because I've been dreaming of having you since I first saw you. I had to be inside you. Now I want to get these clothes off you and take it slower. Real slow and easy. I want to take my time with you. I want to make love to you 'til dawn, Serena."

Ack. She couldn't form words again. He undid the buttons she'd done up and pulled off her shirt.

"What do you say?" he purred in her ear as he unhooked her bra. "Say *stay*," he whispered. "Stay with me, baby."

"I-I guess I can stay."

"Ah, good." He smiled that wicked, heart-stopping smile again. The one that made her stomach flutter and her clit pulse. "Can I still tie you to the bed?"

She shivered...hard. He could do just about anything he wanted to her.

"Mmmm. I heard that." He pulled her bra off, leaving her nude from the waist up. "I'll remember it, too."

"Wha-what?"

He pushed her back and fastened his luscious lips around one nipple. His smooth, hard chest rubbed against her stomach. The sensation had her closing her eyes in ecstasy. "Your thought," he said around a mouthful. "You said you'd let me do anything to you."

Oh. She nearly forgot she'd asked a question. He licked her nipple into a taut point and she tried desperately to hang onto to her train of thought. "You're telepathic?" she gasped.

"Appears so. That's the first time I've heard a thought from you, though." He smiled and glanced up at her with dark, hooded eyes. "Must've been particularly loud."

Man, she was in trouble.

He eased her shoes off and her skirt down her legs, leaving her completely bare to his gaze and touch. He took her in from head to toe like she was a work of art. She cringed and curled her fingers into the blankets, fighting the urge to roll the comforter around her body, to hide herself from him.

He took her hand in his, wrenching her grip free from the blankets. "Get up," he said. He helped her up off the bed and guided her to the mirror-lined wall of closets.

"We need to get around this right now, Serena," he murmured in her ear. Pushing her hair to the side so he could kiss her neck, he stood behind her and put his hands on her hips. She looked at her reflection and blushed. There was her size fourteen body bared to his gaze and her own. No clothing to hide her, no blankets. Nothing at all.

He rubbed his hands over her hips, stroking his fingertips through the patch of hair at the apex of her thighs. Then he brought his hands up over the plump of her belly to her breasts. Serena watched his large hands work her breasts. He rolled the nipples between his index fingers and thumbs, causing her pussy to quicken and heat.

As if he could feel the ache in her sex, he let one hand drift down and rubbed her clit. Her breath hissed out of her hard and fast.

"Look at me," he whispered.

She glanced up into his eyes and saw his thoughts reflected there. He truly did think she was beautiful. By some glorious miracle, he thought she was gorgeous and alluring, and he wanted her...*badly.*

He laid a kiss to her neck, and licked her skin. The action shot a bolt of want straight to her pussy. He circled her clit around and around with deliberate slowness. "Do you comprehend what I mean, beautiful?" he murmured.

She wet her lips. "Yes." He'd made his point abundantly clear without uttering a word. *She* was the one thinking she wasn't fit for him, not Cole. Unlike Brian, Cole thought she was alluring and attractive. A measure of healing licked through her—a balm for her injured psyche.

"Good." He increased the pressure at her clit, deepening and increasing the pace of his touch. She watched his hand working at her sex with excited interest. At the same time, he kissed and sucked on her earlobe. "Then come for me, beautiful," he whispered. He parted her thighs, inserted two fingers into her pussy and ground his palm on her clit.

Her climax tore through her as if on his command. The pleasure rippled through her as the muscles of her pussy convulsed around his thrusting fingers.

"Oh," she breathed. Her knees felt weak.

He pulled free from her body and drew a wet finger up her stomach to trail around one of her hard nipples. She watched his gaze follow the path of his hand. His gaze was dark, taut, and hungry. He wanted her again.

A flicker of confidence curled through her stomach. *He wanted her.* She turned, twined her fingers into the waistband of his jeans and drew him toward her. He'd pulled his pants up, but not buttoned them, so she could see a bit of his dark pubic hair and the jut of one lean hip. Her gaze roved his six-pack abs and the dappling of dark hair across his chest. It still awed her that this man would even look in her direction. "Let's see all of *you* now." She flicked her gaze at his jeans. "I didn't really get to, you know, *see* it before."

He smiled and kept his gaze locked with hers as he toed his boots off, then pushed his jeans and boxers past his hips to pool around his ankles.

She glanced down at his cock, which stood hard and erect from a bed of curly coarse dark hair. Twining her fingers around its length, she raised an eyebrow. "Not bad." It took effort to sound cool, since every part of him made her breathless. It was hard to sound cool when you couldn't breathe. Seeing him fully unclothed nearly stopped her heart.

He playfully swatted her butt, and then gave her a look of sexual intention that was so intense it made her train of thought have a wreck. "Been wondering what you taste like, Serena," he murmured. "I have a mind to take a taste and satisfy my curiosity." He dropped down, wound his hands to cup her buttocks and pulled her pussy to his mouth.

Serena let out a pent-up breath as his skillful tongue darted out to lick her inner thigh, then her clit. Almost involuntarily, she spread her thighs for him. After making a sound of satisfaction in his throat, he parted her folds with his thumbs, and then settled in to devour her sex.

"Ah," was all she could manage.

His tongue flicked out to toy with her sensitive clit and she felt it plump under his ministrations. Her fingers curled into the flesh of his shoulders as his tongue rasped over her. He groaned deep in his throat and yanked her closer to his mouth, as though he couldn't get enough. "Mmmm, Serena. I just knew you'd be syrupy sweet. A man could get addicted." He licked up the length of her pussy and sucked at her clit.

He rubbed her clit back and forth with his tongue while he planed up her inner thigh with his palm and slid a finger within her. Then two. "Oh, Cole," she gasped as he thrust slowly in and out. He found her G-spot, or at least what had to be to her G-spot, and toyed with it.

Serena broke apart. Sweet, pleasurable convulsions made the muscles of her pussy contract around his broad fingers. She keened out Cole's name as her body shook from her climax. Cole helped her to ease down to the floor before her knees gave out. He scattered kisses over her face. "Are you all right, Serena?" he asked.

"*Bla*," she responded intelligently.

He rolled over on his back and blew out a breath. Carelessly, he stroked his huge cock with one hand. Serena watched…with high interest. "You taste good, just as I thought you would. Near irresistible." He turned and looked at her. "I want you again."

And he could have her…

"Get into bed, Serena. I'm going to get us something to eat." He slanted her a wicked grin. "Then I'm going to take you again." He winked. "And then again."

She watched him get up and leave the room, her eyes on every movement of his gorgeously formed male posterior.

Eventually, she stopped doing an impression of a bone-melted mass of goop on the floor, picked herself up and went to the bed. After collecting all the stray bits of clothing from the bed and laying them on a nearby chair, she turned back the comforter and top sheet, crawled in and settled herself back against the mountain of pillows.

Presently, Cole returned bearing a plate of cut apples and some cheese. He stopped in the doorway and stared at her. "Mmmm, now that's a nice sight. You in my bed."

She felt her cheeks heat and she glanced away.

He walked around the king-size bed, set the plate on the bedside table and crawled in the other side. "It was hard finding something in my kitchen that would suit a vegetarian, but I did it." He moved closer to her and balanced the plate of food on his lap.

His body just touched hers and his heat rolled off and sank into her skin. The length of his leg kissed hers. Cole placed a thin slice of cheese on an apple slice and raised it to her lips. She allowed him to feed her the treat. The salty and sugary combination spread over her tongue. She closed her eyes in ecstasy.

The whole situation—being in his bed, under the covers and having him feed her—was so erotic and intimate. She sighed. It felt so good, so *right*, for some reason. Quiet euphoria filled her. She hadn't been this happy in a long, long time. Although, her joy was tempered with the knowledge that this was a one-time thing. She'd better enjoy it while it lasted.

He leaned forward as she chewed the delicious tidbit and kissed her lips. "Do you like it?" he asked.

"Mmmm." She swallowed. "Yes. Interesting combination of tart and sweet."

"Describing yourself? Tell me more about yourself, Serena. I feel comforted knowing at least one of us knows themselves." He bit into a slice of apple and cheese.

She shrugged. "Not much to tell, really. I write books for a publishing house, nonfiction about witches, Wicca, witchcraft and pagan studies. I inherited that land and the house you were at from my mother who died about ten years ago."

"Where's your father?"

"Rowan and I are half-sisters. We actually don't know our fathers. Our mother was a bit...wild. Rowan inherited that wildness. I didn't." She gave him a smile. "Maybe I take after my dad, whoever he is."

"I beg to differ. I think you're both wild and sweet."

She shrugged again. "Believe me, normally I'm as tame as they come and not always sweet."

He set the plate aside, and cupped one of her exposed breasts against his warm palm. She sucked in a breath. "Tell me more. Tell me about the excessive amount of lip balm and the ceramic fairies in your bedroom."

She glanced up at him. "Were you in my bedroom last night?"

He slanted a grin at her. "Uh...yeah."

"Uhmm...did you—?" *Give me an incredible orgasm while I slept?*

"I hope you're not mad." He lowered his mouth to her breast and laved his tongue across her nipple. Her clit started to throb as blood rushed to her sex in sudden arousal. "I knew if you didn't want me in your mind, you'd push me away of your own volition," he said around a mouthful. He grinned up at her. "You didn't."

Breathless from the way he sucked on her nipple and from the sensation of one of his hands under the blanket, working its up her outer thigh, she could barely respond. "I-I should be mad," she shot at him, though there was precious little heat behind the words. "That was an invasion." The words came out in a kind of helpless little moan as he nipped lightly at her nipple. God, she was a wimp.

The slow snake of his hand finally came to a halt at her hip. He pulled her down, so she lay flat on her back and he loomed over her. His gaze ate up her breasts and lips. "I'd like to invade you again. I promise you you'll like it. Spread those gorgeous thighs for me."

Mesmerized by the needful look in his eyes, she did it without question.

He shifted so he leaned over her, bracing himself on one hand, and placed his mouth once again to her breast. He flicked his tongue over her nipple as he stroked her pussy with his other hand. After circling her clit and making her moan, he thrust two fingers in and out of her. "Ah, yes, you taste and feel so good," he groaned. "I can't get enough."

She rubbed her hands over his shoulders, where his muscles bunched and flexed with his movement, then slid them up and curled her fingers into his hair. The energy of her climax slowly built within her. She bit her lower lip and arched her spine as his thrusts grew in pace and intensity. The man was pure sin encased in flesh. No wonder all those women wanted him.

She grimaced. Thinking about other women in Cole's bed wasn't good. She put that nasty notion from her mind.

His finger found her anus and circled it, teasing the nerve endings there. That pushed *all* other thought from her with a jolt. She sucked in a surprised breath and jerked.

"Hush, beautiful. Easy now. I want to feel you *everywhere*. Take you *everywhere*. But if you don't want it, I won't do it, all right? Simple as that. You tell me to stop if it becomes too intense."

She bit her lip harder, nearly drawing blood, and nodded.

"Ah, that's a good girl," he purred in pleasure. He scooped up a bit of the moisture from her pussy and slicked it over her nether entrance, then slipped a finger within very slowly. Her hands tightened on his shoulders as he thrust in and out, gently and at a slow pace. The sensation was odd...indescribable. She'd never realized that part of her body was an erogenous zone. "Mmmm. So sweet. So pretty and tight," he said thickly. "I want to take you here, but it's not the time. You're not ready for this. We're moving too fast."

He pulled free of her body and moved down, pushing the blankets away as he went. Her back arched again as he spread her thighs as far as they could go and held them there. "Another taste," he murmured. He lowered his mouth to her pussy once more and licked up her sex from her anus to her clit in long, mind-numbing strokes.

Her hips bucked at the first lash of his tongue and she let out a long, low moan. "Cole," she said. "I don't know how much of this I can take. I want you."

"Mmmm." He nibbled and sucked at her pussy lips, moving up to her clit. She writhed at the feel of his hot, slick tongue exploring her sex. "And you'll have me, beautiful. When I'm done tasting you." He pushed his tongue inside her and fucked her with it, drawing a low moan from her throat.

She tossed her head back and forth. "Please," she pleaded with him. "Please, Cole."

"You want me inside you, beautiful?" he asked. "You want me fucking you?"

"Yes!"

She felt him shift. He grabbed a condom, tore the wrapper open and rolled it on. Then, finally, *blessedly*, she felt the head of his shaft press against her. She moved her hips against him and he grabbed her wrists, pinning them to the mattress on either side of her.

She was highly aroused so all her muscles were relaxed. He sank himself inside her easily.

She tipped her head back and hissed, "Yes. That's what I wanted."

Releasing her wrists, he came down on her throat, nibbling and sucking at the sensitive skin as his thick cock glided in and out her.

Serena wrapped her legs around his waist and massaged the muscles of his back, working lower and lower until she cupped the cheeks of his gorgeous ass, urging him to thrust harder and faster.

He picked up the pace of his thrusts—the broad, ridged length of him pistoning in and out of her. He levered himself above her, hands flat on the mattress on either side of her head. Every once in a while, he'd drop his head and take her mouth in one of his devastating kisses.

Her climax rose hard and fast, overwhelming her body and mind. "Cole," she breathed as it shattered over her. He kissed her hard, stroking his tongue into her mouth as if consuming the very essence of her pleasure.

Instead of sating her the way a climax usually did, it only made her hungrier for him. She made small noises of encouragement as he continued the punishing pace.

She felt the tickle of magic skitter over her skin. Her mind's eyes flooded with the images of how they looked from behind. She saw the muscles of his finely shaped ass flex as he sank into her pussy over and over between her spread thighs. She saw her hands cupping him as he slammed himself into her again and again.

He let out a groan and shifted the angle of hips. "Ah, fuck, Serena, you feel so good around me. I'm coming," he growled.

Another climax engulfed her body. The muscles of her vagina pulsed and clenched around his shaft. He threw his head back and came with a low, sexy groan that only served to intensify her own orgasm.

When they both calmed, he withdrew from her body. She regretted it. It was then she knew she was growing dangerously attached to a man who would never be more than a fling.

He went into the bathroom to dispose of the condom and she watched every movement of his rear as he walked. She rolled onto her side toward the window and saw that evening had descended outside without her even knowing it.

She felt strong warmth at her back as Cole climbed into bed at her back and enveloped her in his arms. "You're lovely, Serena," he breathed against the nape of her neck. He laid a kiss. "Beyond my wildest dreams."

Serena closed her eyes against the ridiculous tears that filled them.

* * * * *

Cole opened his eyes to pale morning light streaming in past the gauzy curtains of his bedroom window. In a flash, he realized...

Nosce te ipsum.

He knew himself.

Chapter Five

Memories of his life as Cole filled his mind. He'd been born in Glasgow, Scotland and had lived there until he'd been about five years old. He and his parents had moved to the U.S. and he'd grown up here. He was now thirty-five and had been a citizen of the United States for a long time.

He loved all things historical, mythical, mystical, and paranormal. As a result, Cole had taken a strange path at college, studying philosophy and ancient history, as well as computer programming, and had obtained his master's degree. Post-grad school, he'd started developing computer games on his own for a small company, but things hadn't gone very well there. After that, he moved to a larger company and had worked for many years with a team of developers. But Cole was independent-minded and had not been completely happy in that environment. Eventually, he'd moved out on his own. It had been a risk, but he'd succeeded. Now he was a solo developer for *Tago Game Systems* and made a very nice life for himself doing it.

When Alana had put the whammy on him, he'd changed. She'd been right about that. He wasn't "Cole" anymore. He was different. The added energy Cernunnos brought to him had changed him...and it had greatly intensified the power of his magick and his physical strength.

He'd been born OtherKin to one hundred percent, completely human parents. They'd never understood or accepted his "otherness". He'd always had magick, but he'd hidden it since he'd been small after seeing the terror it wrought in his mother's eyes. Even though his parents hadn't known what the OtherKin were, and neither had he for many years, his differentness had caused a rift between them early on. His mother and father had moved back to Scotland a few years ago to enjoy their retirement, and Cole had little contact with them these days.

He'd felt alone his whole life because he'd had no OtherKin with whom to share his experiences. *Hell*, before Alana had put the whammy on him, he hadn't even known what the OtherKin *were* or that he was one. That aloneness and sense of not belonging was what fueled his interest in historical legend and myth. He'd been forever searching for answers to explain himself. It was what had driven him into the arms of all those women. They'd all been empty relationships. He'd just been searching for a connection.

He'd been so unbelievably lonely.

He rolled over, searching out Serena. All he wanted was to pull her into his arms and inhale the sweet scent of her skin and hair. He wanted to tell her he had his memory back.

But the bed was empty.

Disappointed, Cole rose and found a pair of boxers in the top drawer of his dresser. Odd how pleased it made him that he knew where his underwear was. On bare feet, he walked down the hallway, looking for Serena. As he went, he scratched his head and reminded himself to change all his decorations...and furniture. He hated all of it. Actually, he needed to just sell it all off and move out to the country—somewhere quiet and heavily forested.

At the thought of a forest, he dropped to his knees, the memory of the incantation filling his mind. After they had sex, Alana had drugged him with a potent elixir she'd slipped into a beer. The coven had stood around the bed as he lay nude and incapacitated and performed the ritual.

The rage.

Cernunnos had *not* wanted to be called forth. He'd scratched and hissed and fought within him as the words of the witches had called the ancient god and sealed him within Cole's body. It had hurt on a soul level to be fully merged with that primordial, powerful and latent energy within him.

His back arched and he dug his fingers into the carpet as he felt the first tickle of the change coming over him. It was triggered by the rage, just as his first transformation had been. Before he'd changed to a wolf and had stood in the center of the bed snarling and snapping. The witches had run from him. All of them save Alana who'd stared at him with wide eyes. Then he'd shifted to stag form and leapt off the bed and through a window. He hadn't stopped running until he'd been far from the city and had felt the reassuring forest ground beneath his hooves.

The magical tickle skittering over Cole's skin intensified and he felt his body start to morph. *Ah, God!* It hurt every single time. He cried out as his muscles began to stretch and twist. His cry turned into a roar as he shifted.

Through the eyes of a mountain lion, he watched Serena emerge from the office and spot him. "Cole?" she breathed.

He let a trickling growl escape his feline lips. He was pleased to see she had her hand loosely fisted at her side, ready with a spell in case he lunged at her.

Last time he'd been in animal form, he had retained only a sliver of awareness of his human otherness. He did remember his encounter with Serena in the forest and how he'd marked her, but it was like he hadn't really done it. Most likely, he'd been nearly all Cernunnos then, and only a tiny bit Cole. This time he retained almost all of Cole. He wouldn't lunge at Serena, at least not in anger and bloodlust, but maybe in another type of lust. He swished his tail and eyed her speculatively.

She'd donned one of his dark blue T-shirts and a pair of his light blue boxers. She looked delectable. He padded over and sat down by her, so she would know he meant her no harm. He had no idea how long it would take for him to change back. With his large tongue, he licked her hand.

She slithered down the wall and wrapped her arms around his neck. "Did you just change like this without any warning?" she asked in wonder. "Without even trying? Right in the middle of the hallway?"

Yes, and it bothered him. This transformational thing was something he'd have to learn to control. He laid a deliberate lick to the mark on her shoulder in an effort to reassure her.

A moment later, he felt his body contort again. Pain lanced through him as his form shifted. He ended up nude, in human form, clutching Serena as the incredible discomfort receded. She hadn't let go of him, even when he'd been changing.

"Ah, fuck, I need a drink—good strong shot of whiskey," he said.

She laughed, sought his mouth and kissed him. He curled his arms even tighter around her and pulled her down to lay with him. "Are you all right?" she murmured against his mouth.

He twined a hand through her hand, rolled her beneath him and slanted his mouth across hers for a deep kiss. God, she tasted good. "I am now," he said when he finally pulled away. "I remember everything, Serena. I woke up with my memory intact." He traced the mark on her shoulder. "I remember doing this."

She touched the faint scar and their fingers bumped. "I figured that was you."

"It was mostly Cernunnos, but I definitely approve of his choice."

Serena looked stricken for a moment and struggled to sit up. He let her. "So, remembering...is that a good thing?"

"Everything is good save for the fact that when I woke up this morning, you weren't in my bed."

A worried look graced her beautiful blue eyes. She stood. "I've been studying your books since early this morning. I hope that's okay. Come see what I've found."

He stood and followed her into the office. His ancient tomes and delicate-looking manuscripts and journals were spread with care on his large computer desk. He scanned the texts, seeing the books were all opened to the pages detailing Ashmodai.

Leaning over, he punched the on button for his computer. "Did you find how out he'll manifest? Does he stay incorporeal, or can he possess people?" He knew a lot about their adversary, but not everything. Every demon—and there were hundreds—was a little different, worked under a different set of rules.

"Unfortunately, he possesses people. Not only that, he burns up the human bodies of those he takes. They age rapidly while he's within them because they can't handle the level of magick he brings into them."

His computer screen popped up and Cole sat down in the office chair to begin the process of decrypting some of his more obscure files on demons. "Can he possess OtherKin?"

She shook her head. "No. According to what I read, OtherKin magic doesn't mesh with his. The magicks repel each other."

"That's one bit of good news then."

"Yes. But there's a lot of bad news. This is a playful demon, Cole. Demons and playful?" She gave her head a sharp shake. "Not an especially good combo."

"I know about the *playfulness*. His specialty is lust. So he'll be searching out women, probably," Cole said.

"Yeah, I read he's got a tendency toward brutal sexual acts. He's going to be pretty happy to be made flesh."

"Unfortunately...yes. He'll be like a kid in a candy store." Cole pulled up the file he'd been looking for. It was written in Sanskrit. "This isn't the first time Ashmodai has run amok in our dimension. It happened once before to my knowledge. I have this record of it. Hopefully it describes how they put him back where he belongs. To find that out, we need to have this text translated." He looked up at her hopefully. "You don't happen to know Sanskrit, do you?"

She laughed. "Uh, no, sorry."

He pulled a CD-R from a drawer and popped it into his computer to save the file. "Well, we have to find someone who can. The university, maybe. We can take it down there and ask around. I know a professor that might be able to help us."

"Good."

He nodded. "That's a starting point. Next we'll have to find a spell of some sort that will help locate Ashmodai. We need to regain control of this situation. To do that, we need to know where he is. "

"Well, if you go to the university, I can take care of the spell." She moved toward the door. "I'll get dressed."

He grabbed her wrist and pulled her down into his lap. She gave a squeal of surprise. "Understand me, Serena. Listen to me now and listen well. You're not leaving my side. Not with this thing out there possibly searching out unwary women. He might not be able to possess the OtherKin, but I'll make a bet he can hurt them."

"But—"

He put his hand to her nape and pressed her mouth to his to cut her sentence off with a possessive kiss. Her lips were stiff beneath his at first, and then went gentle and yielding. After he'd drunk his fill of her, after his cock had hardened for her, he pulled away with a sigh of regret. All he wanted was to drag her back to bed, but they couldn't indulge themselves now. "No, Serena. You were in danger from the time your cousin brought me to your house. The mark of me is on you. Ashmodai will smell it ten miles away. You stay where I can protect you."

"What about my sister? She was near you, too. What about Morgan and Sarah?"

"Morgan and Sarah went back home, right? So they're far from here now."

She nodded.

"Good. Call your sister and tell her to leave town for a little while. Does she have somewhere to go? Somewhere far from Newville?"

Serena nodded. "Sure. We have relatives all over."

He bit his lip. "You need to go with her, darlin'."

She made an angry noise and pushed up from his lap. "No way. The Elders said I'm supposed to keep you...and keep you *I will*. They said I'm not supposed to leave you alone."

Cole stood and stared her down with a lazy, dangerous gaze. She took a step back from him, so it must have made an impression. *Good.* "If I think leaving town is the safest thing for you to do, you'll go."

"Don't pull that macho crap with me. You have no hold over me, no say!"

"I want you safe. That's all. Safe. The last thing I want to see is you hurt."

"Me too, Cole! Remember, I do have some magickal ability. Have you forgotten? I'm not *unarmed*, so to so speak. Anyway, I'm safest here, where you can watch over me."

As he stared at her, a muscle locked in his jaw. She was a stubborn woman...but she'd gambled and said the right thing. He did think she was safer where he could watch over her, since he didn't trust Ashmodai not to follow her wherever she went. "All right, Serena. But if things get too hot, or if I get hurt and I'm unable to defend you...you run and run hard. You *leave. Promise me.*"

"I promise."

He nodded once. "Go call your sister. I'll take a shower and get dressed. We can stop by your place and get some clothes for you before we head to the university. You'll be staying here until this blows over. Looks like *I'm* keeping *you* instead of the other way around."

* * * * *

Serena stared out the window of Cole's SUV and watched the first fat raindrops of an incoming storm plop on the windshield. The clouds had grown ominously dark overhead. In her fevered mind, it was a portent to the coming battle against Ashmodai.

Rowan had been less than pleased with the news. She'd fought her on it, telling Serena she couldn't leave now, too much was going on. When Serena had pressed Rowan to tell her exactly *what* was going on, Rowan wouldn't tell her. They'd ended up in a screaming match over the phone at one point, but finally Rowan had relented.

Serena had explained that anyone who'd come into contact with Cole since Alana had whammied him was in danger. Morgan and Sarah had gone back home, so they were safe. She and Rowan, they were the ones who'd be flickering the hardest on Ashmodai's radar.

Rowan had a 1:30 p.m. flight out of the Newville airport to Alaska and their aunt's house, and Serena was now breathing easier. Not only would Rowan be safer from this mess, she'd be away from whatever situation she wouldn't tell Serena about.

They'd gone back to Serena's place and she'd packed a bag, made sure the kitty door was opening and closing properly and set out enough dry food and water for her cats. They'd be fine for a while on their own and she'd come back to check on them when she could. Her car was still over at her sister's place and would have to stay there for a bit. Luckily, she'd parked on a side street, where her car wouldn't be towed. It was safe for now. Her own safety, well, that was another issue.

Serena drummed her fingers on the car's armrest as they passed through Old Newville, a wealthy section of town near the university where there were a lot of old, restored homes. The keeper of the Embraced, Gabriel Letourneau, lived in this part of town. "Keeper" was just another way of saying *master vampire*, really. He led the Embraced in this region of the United States. The Embraced were vampires who, unlike the OtherKin, had not been able to conceal their existence to the human world.

The OtherKin had been very good at keeping themselves a secret. In fact, not even the Embraced knew of their existence. The OtherKin were of one mind on this issue—having humans aware of them only brought trouble. The Embraced continually had to fight fear and prejudice. The OtherKin simply didn't want that kind of hassle.

The OtherKin were the stuff of fairy tales and myth. They were the Tuatha Dé Danann and the Y Tylwyth Teg—the sidhe, the fey. They were the shapeshifters, the elves, the dyads, the brownies and the sprites. They were everything that humans made up stories about, but didn't believe were real.

Witches and mages were interbred fey and human. The level of their magick varied individually and by family line. The magick in Serena's maternal line was strong, much stronger than an average witch. It was much stronger than Alana's power, for example. That had threatened the high priestess of the Three Ash. It was one of many reasons Serena had declined membership in the coven. Alana resented Serena's power.

By the time they pulled into the university parking lot, and found a space, the storm was raging.

Cole pointed to a large brown building on the left that sat nestled in a grove of mature trees. Newville University was older and very picturesque. Serena had gone here to take a few classes but had never pursued a degree. "That's where the ancient language professors have their offices," he said.

"Do you know this university?" she asked.

He nodded. "I'm an alumnus." He glanced out the windshield toward the building. "Ready to get wet?"

"I guess."

They got out of the SUV and made run for the building. By the time they reached it, they were both soaked. Serena watched as Cole gave his head a shake, letting water droplets spray from his long brown and blond-streaked hair. His white shirt clung to his chest and Serena tried not to swallow her tongue. "Follow me," he said.

They went through a long open area where students sat on chairs talking or on the floor reading or studying. Serena assumed they were waiting for classes to start. They traveled up a short flight of stairs to a corridor with many small offices off either side. He led her to one and knocked on the door.

"Enter," a masculine voice called.

Cole pushed the door open and a good-looking man in his mid-forties stood up from a desk and greeted them with a warm smile and handshake. "Haven't seen you in a long time, Cole," he said.

"I know. It has been a while. Professor Hardy, this is Serena."

The professor shook her hand. "Nice to meet you."

"Likewise," answered Serena with a smile. The man felt open and friendly to her psychic senses.

"She and I have come to ask you for a favor. It's something only you can do," said Cole.

Professor Hardy laughed. "You always have something particular to ask me. What do you have for me this time? Another piece of research for one of your games?"

Cole fished the CD jewel case from his pocket and handed it over. "I need this translated, Professor. It's in Sanskrit and it's of extreme importance. There's about a page of data there. Think you can do it?"

Professor Hardy studied the disk. "I can try. When do you need it?"

"I need it as *soon* as possible."

The professor nodded. "I have your cell phone number. As usual, I'm very intrigued. I'll get started on it as soon as I can and I'll call you when it's finished."

"Thank you, Professor," Serena said. "We appreciate this very much."

"My pleasure, really. Cole always has such fascinating texts." He laid the jewel case containing the CD on his desk and turned to Cole. "You seem different. Did you cut your hair or something?"

Cole grinned. "You wouldn't believe me if I told you what has changed about me, Professor."

They exited the professor's office and headed back downstairs. The storm still raged outside. On their way toward the double doors, a chattering TV in the corner of the lobby caught Serena's attention. The urgent news bulletin music that preceded a local breaking story blared. Something twisted in her gut. Every tiny part of her sixth sense told her to stay and watch.

She stood still, staring up at the flickering TV screen and listening to every word the broadcaster uttered. With every passing syllable, she felt a little more blood drain from her face. "Ashmodai has my sister," she gasped.

Chapter Six

&

"What?"

Cole settled his gaze on the object of Serena's attention and watched the news broadcast, quickly understanding why she looked and sounded so stricken.

The anchorwoman told of an eyewitness account of an abduction that had occurred in broad daylight in front of the apartment building where Serena's sister lived. The person had reported that a kicking and screaming woman with long black hair had been muscled into a car by a large man with dark hair. In her struggle, the woman had left her luggage on the street. The luggage tags had revealed she was Rowan Archer.

When the broadcast ended, Serena walked to the doors of the building and hugged herself. Cole walked up behind her and put his hands on her shoulders.

"What are we going to do?" she whispered brokenly. "He has Rowan."

"It'll be okay," he said. "We're going to get her back unharmed."

She rounded on him. "How can you say that? A *demon* has my sister!" She whirled and ran out into the rain.

Cole went after her. Thunder crashed overhead as he searched the darkening gloom. Finally, he spotted her beneath a tree, soaking wet. He went to her and pulled her into his arms. She was stiff against him at first, but then she just melted.

"My whole life I've tried to protect her, but I never can," she cried hoarsely as she wept.

All Cole could do was hold her, stroke her hair in the pouring rain and coo little meaningless nothings at her. At that moment, he felt he would do anything for her—anything to make her happy. He wondered why. He'd only known her for about forty-eight hours. His mind returned to that sense of having known her for so much longer than that—for centuries—over many, many lifetimes. Maybe it was true. Maybe that's why he'd marked her in the forest that day. Maybe that was why all he wanted was to be with her. Love wouldn't need a long time to develop if they'd shared centuries together.

Finally, she looked up at him. A look of strong resolve and determination had replaced the panicked grief. "Let's go get the spell, Cole. It's her only chance."

* * * * *

"You need some bait…hmmm…demon bait."

Serena watched Millicent, a witch whose knowledge of spell casting was unsurpassed in Serena's opinion, rifle through a bunch of vials on a shelf. Serena employed her from to time when she couldn't find exactly the right ingredients for a spell she needed. Right now Serena could barely think, let alone cast a spell. She needed expert help.

Millicent was an old hedge witch who'd lived alone her whole life and, as Serena tripped over a large Persian cat in Millicent's storage room, she could see herself as Millicent redux in about fifty years or so.

"Ah! Some hair from a virgin female," muttered Millicent happily as she reached for a jar. "That should work nicely for this particular demon."

Serena swallowed hard. Ashmodai definitely wouldn't have a virgin in her sister. She fought back a sob. If anything happened to Rowan, she'd curl up and die.

But she wasn't ready to do that yet.

They would figure out how to call and bind the demon. It would get Ashmodai away from Rowan at the very least. Sending Ashmodai back to the dimension he lived in was a different matter altogether. For that they needed the translation of the text Cole had given the professor. They had to hope the answer was in there. They also had to hope the professor would come up with a translation fast.

Right now all Serena was concerned with was getting the demon far from her sister. In the short term, that's what mattered.

Before they had decided on this course of action, she and Millicent had tried a locating spell to find Rowan, but Ashmodai must have masked her location with a more powerful magick, because they'd come up empty.

"Let's see, now we need something to bind the creature with. A link from a length of heavy chain! That should do the trick." She reached up, grabbed a bit of chain from a shelf and turned to Serena, her arms laden with various items for the ritual. Millicent's happy smile faded as she saw Serena's morose expression. "There, there, dear, this will work. You'll see."

She drew a breath. "Let's do it and find out."

Twenty minutes later all the materials they'd selected to serve as symbols for the spell were piled in the center of a white circle drawn on the floor of Millicent's large, candle-lit, spell-protected casting room. She, Cole and Millicent stood around the pile, hands clasped, eyes closed.

Magick skittered over Serena's skin as they began to chant the words of the demon-bringing spell together. Normally, they would've needed a coven to gather the kind of power needed for this trick, but they had Cole. He had more magick within him than a whole gaggle of witches. His voice thrummed soft and low through her body, sinking deeper and deeper into her mind until it permeated her every pore. She felt her consciousness separate from her body a little and float over her head as the power in the room gathered and expanded.

Finally, they sent that combined magickal intent out past the walls of the room, searching out the energy they wanted to bring in and bind.

It didn't take long.

Serena's palms began to sweat when she heard the shrieking begin. First it came from far off, but as she, Millicent, and Cole raised their voices and injected more power into the spell, it grew louder as if getting closer and closer, until finally it sounded like it was in the room with them.

Serena's eyes flickered open. When she caught her first glimpse of the beast in front of her, she stumbled backward with a gasp, breaking the circle. No matter. The thing was caught in the middle of the room, struggling to get free, but to no avail.

Ashmodai was about seven feet tall and hovered in the air about four feet from the floor. Good thing the ceiling in this room was high. He didn't have three heads, like the ancient texts said, but the one he had was frightening enough. His face was angular and his head bald. Red eyes glowed from his viciously sharp-boned skull. His chin was pointed almost to the point of caricature. His lips were thin and white. Ashmodai's body was human looking for the most part, though it was inhumanly muscular. His large lizard's tail swished angrily as he ceased his struggle against the magickal bonds their spell had forged and became aware of his captors. Serena stood openmouthed, thinking he couldn't be any more horrific.

Then Ashmodai looked at her and smiled.

Her heart rammed in her chest as she glimpsed his teeth — they were all long and pointed, like a series of tiny daggers in his mouth.

Rowan was somewhere in this thing's clutches…

Rage replaced her fear. She closed her mouth and straightened her spine. "You hurt my sister, I'll slice you thirteen different ways before I send you back the dimension you came from, Ashmodai."

Silence suddenly fell. Realization struck. Had she just threatened a demon with physical violence?

Ashmodai stared at her, and then flicked a long, forked tongue out to slowly lick his thin lips. "You can call me Ash, *princess.*"

She took a step backward and blinked. His voice was the same as the man's who'd hassled them at Cole's apartment building the day before. That man had also called her *princess.* So, he'd been playing with them. Wonderful. Her mind did a little dance as she wondered what had happened to that man he'd possessed. Had the demon burned him up? Was he dead now?

Ashmodai floated forward until the magickal chain that wrapped him stopped his progress with a jerk. "You're the one the Cernunnos marked." He flicked a glance at Cole.

Serena's hand flew to her shoulder, where the stag's teeth impressions still remained. *Marked?* That meant she'd been marked?

"The Cernunnos marked you," continued Ashmodai. "That means you mean something to the Cernunnos. It's *you* I want, not your sisssster," he hissed.

Did that mean he didn't have Rowan? If he didn't...*who did*?

Cole looked at her and Serena gasped. Every muscle in his body was tense and he'd seemed to gain a couple inches and had gained bulk on his already muscular frame. His clothing was stretched to the limit. But it was his eyes that took her aback. They were completely dark, without a speck of white. She couldn't tell if they were the dark brown of his regular eye color, or black, but slashes of green fire flickered through them like lightning on a storm-racked night.

Was Cole still anywhere in there, or was that all Cernunnos?

"Yes, I marked her," Cole/Cernunnos murmured, watching her face. "Marked her as mine." His voice had a strange deep resonance to it that seemed to penetrate the center of her bones. He turned to spear Ashmodai with a piercing stare. "And you will not touch her!" he roared. "You don't belong here, *Aeshma Daeva*. We will cast you back to where you do belong."

Ashmodai laughed again. "The Cernunnos doesn't belong here, either," he sneered. "Trapped in human flesh." He said the word *human* like he talked about a cockroach.

Every cell in Cole/Cernunnos' body seemed to quiver. Ashmodai had hit a nerve with that comment.

Ashmodai laughed. "I freed the Cernunnos from the binding cuffs the other night so he could come play with the Ashmodai. Does the Cernunnos want to play?"

Cole/Cernunnos smiled a bone-chillingly cold smile. "Sure. Let's play."

Without warning, Ashmodai surged violently upward. In Serena's mind, she felt a click and a release of the magickal bonds she'd forged with Cole and Millicent to keep the demon.

Ashmodai was free.

Holy shit.

Millicent had retreated to the edge of the room. Now she surged forward and grabbed Serena's arm just as Ashmodai lunged for her. Serena felt the brush of his claw-like hand and the rotting meat scent of his breath as he missed her, thanks to Millicent.

Serena hit the concrete floor just in time to avoid getting snatched.

An inhuman roar filled the room. Serena watched in horror as Cole/Cernunnos slammed full force into Ashmodai, hurling him back in a kind of ancient god smackdown. They hit the floor and rolled together in a big tangle, smashing into one of the long tables that lined the sides of the room.

Serena struggled to her feet, trying to force her sputtering mind into *drive*. Did she have any magick to counter a ferocious brawl between a demon and a god? If she did, would it be strong enough to have any kind of an impact on them?

Cole/Cernunnos and Ashmodai stood, still pummeling each other. They seemed evenly matched, but her heart squeezed painfully with every injury Cole/Cernunnos seemed to sustain.

She had to try *something* to break this up. Focusing inward, she pulled every bit of her power from deep within her and focused it with clear, crystalline intent. When she was satisfied she'd gained enough strength, she opened her hand in the direction of the battling couple and propelled that magickally laced intent outward toward her target.

Cole/Cernunnos and Ashmodai flew apart like they were two negatively charged particles. Ashmodai hit the far wall with a thump and then landed face-first on the floor.

Cole/Cernunnos rolled toward her and stood up shakily. He raised his hand and chanted something in some language Serena couldn't understand.

Ashmodai rose from the ground and hovered there for a moment. He struggled, which let Serena know that whatever it was that was happening, Ashmodai wasn't in control of it.

Cole/Cernunnos pushed his palm forward and Ashmodai kind of squished back into the concrete wall behind him. The wall itself seemed to be made almost of rubber. Back and back Ashmodai was pushed, further away from them. The wall stretched backward with him until it looked like it was stressed to the point of breaking. Ashmodai roared his displeasure and clawed at the wall, making it crumble.

Serena took a couple steps forward. "Do you have her? Do you have my sister?" she asked wildly.

He clawed at the stone wall, his long fingernails grooving it deeply and making sparks as Cole/Cernunnos pushed him back. "I don't have your sister, witch," he growled.

The wall seemed to swallow him whole and he was gone. The wall bounced back in place without a mark on it.

Serena stared at the wall wide-eyed, a bazillion questions swirling through her mind. Finally, she swallowed hard and glanced at Cole/Cernunnos. He stood staring at her, looking strong and intent…on her. His eyes had returned partially to normal, though they were still an unnatural green and lightning still seemed to crackle through them from time to time. He also seemed to have lost his additional size. His clothes were torn in places. Apparently Cernunnos had left the building, or at least the bulk of Cernunnos' energy, anyway.

Serena blinked. "Are you all right?"

"I'm…okay," he ground out. He didn't *sound* okay.

She walked to him, needing to check him for wounds with her own hands. He had some scratches on his cheek and upper arm. His shirt was ripped at the shoulder and up one pant leg. She reached out to touch his face and he had her wrist in a flash, startling her. "Bad idea, Serena. Don't touch me right now," he said through gritted teeth.

She lowered her hand warily and stepped back. "Okay." She had several questions on her tongue, but they all died at the look in Cole's eyes. It was lust—raw, simple, and very strong. He looked like he'd die if couldn't take her right this very second.

Despite everything that had just happened, Serena's body answered that silent call. Suddenly aware of Cole on a very sexual level, her breasts felt heavy and her nipples hard. Her pussy plumped and began to grow damp. She swallowed hard and met his gaze.

Millicent came bustling up to them, breaking the spell. "I can't believe I just saw that," she breathed. She sounded almost…*jazzed.*

"But Ashmodai isn't gone, is he?" Serena asked. "I mean, you didn't send him back, did you Cole?" She couldn't keep the note of hopefulness from her voice. That would make everything so much easier.

He shook his head. "I don't yet have the key to unlock that passageway. I just sent him away. I threw enough magick at him to put him out of commission until tomorrow at least. I bought us some time, that's all."

Serena tore her gaze from Cole's with effort and glanced at the broken table at the side of the room. "I'm sorry about that. We'll have it repaired, Millie."

She waved a hand. "Never mind. I needed a new one anyway."

"I think I need to get Cole home now. He's looking a little, er, stressed," Serena said. Cole hadn't taken his eyes from her once.

"Of course, dear. You go on. That was incredible. Never seen anything like that in all my days. If you need any more help, please don't hesitate to call on me."

"Uh. We *will* need you. Millicent, do you think you can research a spell that's stronger than the one we just used? Something that will actually hold the demon?"

She bit her lip. "Come back in the morning. I'll see what I can come up with."

* * * * *

Cole didn't say a word on the ride home. He didn't say a word as they entered his apartment, or as he stripped off his clothes and took a shower. His eyes had mostly returned to normal, although they still flashed, from time to time, with rippling green fire. Serena let him be silent, though she was concerned for him.

She was also concerned for Rowan. As soon as they got to Cole's place, she called the police department and discovered there were no new developments in her sister's case. She gave them Cole's phone number as an alternate to call if anything changed. Serena's throat clamped up and she choked down a sob as she hung up the phone.

Where was Rowan tonight? Who was she with? Was she even still alive?

And if Ashmodai didn't have her that meant another OtherKin did. Only another OtherKin could've concealed Rowan's location from the locality spell she and Millicent had performed earlier.

She picked up her bag from the couch and took it into the bedroom. Steam rolled into the room from Cole's shower. The sound of the faucets shutting off reached her ears. Hopefully a nice hot shower had fully restored Cole to his former self. She had to talk to him and she had so many questions. After a minute, Cole emerged from the bathroom, wearing only a towel wrapped around his lean hips. Water droplets glistened across the hard expanse of his chest. His hair was slicked back from a face that wore a determined expression. He stalked toward Serena with that fire in his eyes and she knew she was in trouble.

As soon as he reached her, he buried his hands in her hair and pulled her up to him for a kiss. His tongue penetrated her mouth and swept within sensually. Grabbing his forearms, she gave into the pleasure of his embrace. He was strong enough to support them both and she badly needed support right now. Seeking solace for her jumbled mind and her raw emotions, she folded herself into his arms.

She felt tears well up in her eyes and fall down her cheeks. Cole pulled away a little and ran his thumb down her skin, gathering one of her teardrops.

"My sister," she said brokenly.

He gathered her against him and led her to a chair. He sat down, drawing her down on his lap. "I know."

"I feel so helpless. There's nothing I can do to help her. Not a damn thing."

He soothingly pushed her hair away from her face. "I'd do anything to see you happy, beautiful. If there was something I could now to help your sister, I'd do it." He rubbed his thumb over her cheek and a muscle jumped in his jaw as though he was gritting his teeth. That strange green fire arced through his eyes again.

"Your eyes. What's wrong with you?"

"It's the part of me that's Cernunnos. It's strong and wild and insatiable. The battle with Ashmodai nearly overwhelmed the part of me that's Cole. I had to fight to stay in balance."

"Insatiable? Insatiable for what?" she asked, already suspecting she knew the answer.

His eyes flickered completely dark green for a moment. "My mate."

"Huh?" That wasn't the answer she'd been expecting.

"The wildness in me needs something to ground it. I need to lay with my mate. I need a release for some of this energy within me. I can find that by immersing myself in her."

She swallowed hard. "Who's your mate?"

He smiled a little in an unnerving way, pushed her hair back and rubbed the marks on her shoulder. "Who do you think, Serena? I marked you."

She pushed up from his lap and stumbled back. "You could have asked me! What if—what if I don't want to be your mate? What if I didn't want to be *marked*? What is this, the damned Middle Ages? Women have free will now, you know. We can vote now and everything."

"You always have a choice, beautiful. I won't force you into anything."

She crossed her arms over her chest.

Cole stood. The green fire in his gaze intensified. "Ah, come on now. I know you feel what I feel."

She narrowed her eyes at him. "What do you *think* I feel?"

He took a step forward. "That you and I have known each other a very long time. Much longer than just a few days. It's true. I can sense it. I can *feel* it."

Her jaw went slack. "What do you mean?"

"I can remember bits and pieces of all these other lives I've had, Serena. All these other incarnations. You're in them all. In one capacity or another, we've known each other a very, *very* long time."

She couldn't deny that she felt it, too. The first time she'd seen him, she'd recognized him on some level.

He took another step toward her, his eyes darkening a noticeable degree. "I'm holding myself back right now because you're understandably upset about your sister. If you weren't, you'd be sheathed around my cock right now." Her stomach quivered at his words, at the tone of base sexuality in them. His hands were loosely fisted at his sides, as if he fought the impulse to lunge toward her.

She let her gaze travel up his body—from his strong feet to the top of his head—and she licked her lips. Maybe she should let him. She needed something to distract her from her disturbing thoughts and emotions. Cole had the ability to push every last one from her mind, at least for a little while. She could sacrifice herself to the fire that was Cole. He could take all her worries away.

So, she looked up at him and let heat show in her gaze.

He was there in a flash, burying his hands in her hair and kissing her deep. He almost knocked her right off her feet, but he held her up as he plundered her mouth. He broke away and brushed his lips across her cheekbone. "Let me have you, Serena." His voice was strained and beseeching.

"You can have me any way you want me, Cole."

His eyes flared brilliantly for a moment. "Strip and get on the bed, beautiful," he told her in a barely controlled voice.

She slipped her glasses off and set them on a nearby table. Serena held his gaze as she toed off her shoes and dropped her jeans and underwear to the floor. He watched every movement with aroused fascination. Stepping back, out the puddle of her recently discarded clothing, she pulled her shirt up over her head. Now she was clad in nothing but her silky white bra. She reached around and unhooked it and let it fall to the floor.

Cole's hungry gaze roved her flesh. His considerable cock tented the towel that covered him. He alone had the capacity of make her feel gorgeous, beloved and desired. The look in his eyes right now made her wet, made her clit plump with anticipation for whatever it was he had in store for her.

He looked up at her. "Bed," he said hoarsely.

She crawled onto the bed and watched as he gathered four white silken ties from his dresser drawer. "Uh, Cole?"

"Don't you trust me?"

"I do. It's just that I've never—"

"You did say *anything*, darlin'." He strode toward her with them in his hands. "I want you bound and at my mercy." Not waiting for her answer, he grasped her wrist, pulled it to the side and tied it to the bedpost. Without a word, he did the same to the other. He set the last two ties on the bedside table. Then he stood back, taking in the sight of her spread out and vulnerable to his whims.

She laughed a little nervously. "Do this often, do you? Got the ties all ready and everything."

"I like to tie my women up. I like to dominate them in bed. I like to tease their bodies until they're screaming for my cock. I like to take them in the ass. I like to talk dirty to them. I like all kinds of things." He shed his towel and crawled onto the bed toward her. "It's true I slept with many women before, beautiful, but now you're the only one I want."

Swallowing hard, she realized that she was this man's *mate*...if she wanted to be. If she wanted to go down that road once more. *If.*

"I remember now that I'm clean, Serena. I had tests for STDs on a regular basis in the past. Unless you want to use protection, we don't have to."

All she could do was shake her head. Her pussy swelled with a rush of blood and heat at the thought of having no barrier separating them.

Cole parted her legs and knelt between them. His cock was huge and hard, so ready to impale her. He leaned forward and kissed her long and deep. "Ah, Serena," he murmured. "I'm coming to be very attached to you."

She shivered at the emotion in his voice, but couldn't respond.

He ran his hands soothingly down her body, running his fingers over her breasts, sides and stomach. His gaze trailed his touch, leaving fire behind. "I won't be able to be gentle with you. I can't go slow right now. Are you sure you're ready for me?"

Rendered mute by the needful look in his eyes, she could only nod.

He grasped the back of her knees and pushed up and out, so she was completely bared to his view. A gasp escaped her throat. She felt aroused and deliciously vulnerable.

"It's so pretty," Cole murmured. He slipped his hands under her to cup her buttocks. "Like ripe fruit. I'm going pull those pretty pink pussy lips apart, baby, open you up and eat you out. I'm going to suck on your clit until you scream." He lowered his mouth to it as though starving.

Serena grasped the ties on either side of her, arched her back and cried out at the unexpected onslaught. There was no seduction this time, no soft kisses or caresses. This was full-out pussy eating.

She groaned. And it was *good*, too.

He licked up the length of her sex, stopping to pull her labia into his mouth and tease the entrance of her pussy. Then he moved up, circling her clit with the tip of his tongue and flicking at it. Pleasure rolled out from that point of her body, tingling through her. He made noises like she was the most wonderful woman he'd ever tasted, like he couldn't get enough.

"Cole," she gasped.

Her toes curled as he lifted her up from the bed and attacked her with renewed fervor. He slid his tongue into her pussy and thrust in and out just like how she wanted his cock. Her hips bucked involuntarily.

"You made so much luscious cream for me, Serena. Are you excited, baby?" he queried from between her spread thighs.

"You-you know I am," she gasped.

"You like my mouth on your pussy, Serena? What do you like best, hmmm? This?" He flicked the tip of his tongue around her clit and circled it until every muscle in her body went taut and she moaned. "Or do you like this better?" He dropped down and sucked her labia into his mouth, then slid his skillful tongue into her pussy and fucked her with it.

The reflection in the wall of mirrors showed her face slack with ecstasy, her wrists bound and Cole's head between her thighs. His powerful back muscles rippled as he moved. An orgasm flirted hard with her body. Watching him eat her out was more erotic than she ever imagined it could be. All she could do was tip her head back on a helpless moan.

"I think you like both. I know I do," said Cole.

He let her ass settle back on the bed and moved his hands to her inner knees. With gentle exertion, he pushed down, bracing and pinning her legs to the bed. In this position, he had her completely at his mercy and spread wide. He lowered his mouth to her clit and sucked relentlessly at the aroused bit of flesh.

"Cole!" she cried out as her climax steamrolled over her.

He didn't stop even when her body shuddered and bucked beneath his. Letting up a little on the pressure of his tongue on her clit, he gentled and cajoled her body straight into another state of high arousal.

"I have to have you around my cock," he said, rising over her. He pushed her knees up and took the other two ties from the bedside table. Each one he wound around her ankle and tied to the headboard near her wrists. She was now spread out completely to his gaze and touch. Her thighs were parted as far as they could go. Her sex was offered up to him as if on a platter.

Now she really felt vulnerable.

He made a purring sound deep in his throat and his eyes flashed green. He reached out and ran a finger though through her pubic hair, trailing lightly down over her plumped clit, to her pussy, and pushed in. "Ah, baby, you're so warm, so tight. Silky." He added a second thick finger to the first and fucked her with them.

Considering her position, with her knees pretty much level with her chin, the thrusting motion was almost straight up and down. She could see his fingers sink in and pull out of her glistening, wet pussy. Her sex made a slick sound every time he pulled out as though it didn't want to give up those thick digits.

All she could do was make a whimpering noise. She wanted his cock.

"Mmmm, that's so good," he murmured, "isn't it? Tell me. Do you like it when I do this to you?"

She bit her lip and let it go. "God, yes," she breathed. She felt drugged from the pleasure.

"I need more from you," he growled.

Yes, *more*…

He pulled his fingers free from her body and rubbed her moisture over her sex. Swirling his wet finger around her clit made her hips jerk involuntarily. "You're killing me," she moaned.

"You so eager for my cock, beautiful?"

"Yes."

He rose up on his knees and set his cock to the entrance of her pussy. "Then take me," he said as he thrust down, burying the thick length of his shaft within her. "Take *all* of me." He drove into her, burying himself to the root of his cock within her hungry pussy.

Serena sucked in a breath as the muscles of her sex closed around him tight as a fist. Her whole body tingled from having him connected to her so intimately, filling her…virtually an extension of her.

Cole stilled, thrust within her to the hilt and grasped the headboard above her. His low, sexy groan filled the air. "Ah, Serena, you feel so good. God, so sweet."

He started to shaft her.

Serena bit her bottom lip as she watched his cock glide in and out of her at a mind-blowingly slow pace. He seemed far too huge to be able to fit in her, but, oh, she was glad he could. He filled her so perfectly, stretched the muscles of her sex exquisitely far. At this angle, he sank into her much deeper than he had before.

Serena looked up at him. His chest was starting to shine with perspiration and his muscles rippled and bunched with exertion as he labored above her. She closed her eyes as a wave of pure, unadulterated pleasure swept over her.

"Oh, yeah, baby. God, that's so good," Cole groaned over her. "You feel so good around me." He picked up the pace of his thrusts. "You're creaming hard for me now. So wet. Watch me fuck you, beautiful."

She stared as the long, thick length of his shaft plunged into her faster and faster, stretching her pussy wide with every deep, hammering downward thrust. Her climax built, threatening to explode over her. "Oh, God…Cole!" she cried as it shattered through her body.

He kept up the relentless piston-like pace as the muscles of her pussy convulsed around him. She grabbed onto the ties that bound her as her body was racked with a delicious wave of ecstasy.

Then she felt his hands on her bonds he freed her ankles, then her wrists. "Hold me, baby," he murmured. "Touch me. Please. I need to feel your arms around me."

She wrapped her legs around his waist, put her hands on his back and massaged her way over the flexing and bunching muscles.

He lowered his mouth to hers and took her in a possessive kiss. They bumped teeth, both trying to get further into the other's mouth. Cole slammed into her pussy over and over, driving her ass into the mattress with every penetrating thrust, and then snapping his hips in a way that exerted pressure over her clit.

He nipped her shoulder where he'd marked her in stag form, then bit gently. Serena felt his cock jump inside her as his own climax crashed into him. She cried out as another orgasm hit her full-force. She dug her fingernails into his back as she came. His come filled her pussy, mixing with her own cream.

"Ah, baby, *baby*," he groaned as he collapsed and then rolled to the side. "My God. You just feel better and better to me every single time."

Serena closed her eyes, breathing heavy. Cole had given her what she'd wanted — to be fucked senseless. To have all her worries thrust out of her as sure his cock thrust into her. But now that it was over, her concerns rushed back at her. Tears rolled down her face.

"Hey," said Cole softly. He drew her into his arms. "Hey, it's okay," he soothed.

Meaningless platitudes. It was not okay.

He held her against him and let her sob out all her fear and frustration until she finally cried herself to sleep.

Sometime in the night, she awoke to darkness. She stilled, trying to figure out what it was that had pulled her from her slumber.

The phone rang.

Serena pulled herself free of the tangle of Cole's embrace and lunged across the bed to grab the phone. "Hello?"

"Serena?"

"*Rowan?* Where are you? What happened? Ohmygodareyouokay?"

"I'm fine. I'm fine. Calm down, sis. I'm at home. I got this number from the police. Where are you anyway?"

Why the hell did she sound like everything was perfectly normal? "*What happened?*" Serena shrieked into the phone.

Silence on the other end.

"Rowan?" Serena asked, calming down. "Are you still there?"

"I'm here."

Cole sat up and drew closer to Serena. He ran his hand down her back and the touch comforted her. "Don't pull this secretive crap with me, Rowan. Tell me what happened."

Rowan sighed. "I've been in a little trouble lately, okay? Someone, a man, was trying to protect me. He forced me to go with him because he believed I was in danger. I was fine the whole time, Rowan. He probably saved my life."

"You didn't have a freaking phone where you were? I've been out of my mind with worry!"

"No. There was no phone. I swear. He forgot his cell phone and we were way out...at a cabin. No electricity. No phone. I called the cops as soon as I got home, told them I'd gone of my own free will. Told them to call off the search party, or whatever. Honestly, I really didn't think you'd even know what happened. I didn't think *anyone* would know and then I came back and saw the local news—"

"Who is this man who was protecting you and what kind of trouble are you in, exactly?"

Silence.

"Goddamn it, Rowan!"

"It's for your own good that I don't tell you," Rowan said softly. "You've protected me my whole life, now it's my turn."

Click.

Serena stared at the phone. "She hung up on me," she exclaimed in disbelief. "I can't believe it."

Cole took the phone from her and set it back in its cradle. "Is she okay?"

"Yes." She sighed in relief. "She's fine." *Hopefully*.

"Good. Worry about the fact she hung up on you and that she's withholding information later. Enjoy her well-being now." He leaned back into the pillows and pulled her against him.

She settled the crown of her head under his chin and relaxed into his chest. Ahhh…she could get used—

"I could get used to having a mate," Cole said.

She stiffened.

He rubbed his hand up and down her back "Why does the word 'mate' seem to strike terror in your soul, beautiful?"

"Uh." She swallowed hard. "I-I was married before."

The movement of his hand stilled.

"We divorced about five years ago. Right after he, uh, tried to kill me."

He sat up. "What?"

She rested on an elbow and looked up at him. "It was for the insurance money. He'd taken up with this woman he worked with, you see. They were having an affair, but I didn't know it. One weekend they were supposed to attend a conference in a nearby city. That's where I thought he was. Instead, he broke into the house like he was a burglar with the intention of ransacking the place and killing me."

Cole was quiet for a long moment. Green fire jumped once through his eyes. "He wanted to make it look like you'd caught a burglar in the act and the burglar murdered you." It was more statement than question and was uttered in a low, angry voice.

She looked down and swallowed hard. "His girlfriend was going to give him an alibi. Tell the cops she'd seen him at the conference. Once he collected the insurance money, they were going to start a faux courtship so it didn't look too suspicious and eventually get married. That's, uh, that's what he told the court, anyway. He ended up confessing to everything."

"I see," said Cole, in a strange, quiet voice. Serena was starting to understand that when Cole went quiet, it meant he was very riled up in some way and was trying to control it.

"But I caught him in the act that night and, well, he was OtherKin, but my magick had always been a lot stronger than his, so I knocked him unconscious and called the cops." She picked at the blanket with her thumb and forefinger.

Those memories still made her nauseous. Brian had kissed her before he'd "left" for the conference. When he'd broken into her home, he'd been an entirely different person. He'd been someone she'd never known. She stopped picking at the blanket and looked up at Cole. "He's going to be in jail for a long, long time," she finished.

Cole was quiet for a long time, his gaze searching her face. "You do know that if I ever meet him, I'm pounding the crap out of him." He sounded fierce and protective. A man protecting his mate. A thrill of pleasure went through her.

She laughed.

* * * * *

In the morning hour that lay just shy of dawn, the phone rang again. Cole roused, pulling himself from under Serena's sleeping weight and picked up the phone. "Hello?"

Silence.

Cole sat up a little more. "*Hello?*"

"The Cernunnos should keep his eyes open today. It's time to play."

Click.

Chapter Seven

൸

Serena turned over and asked sleepily, "Who was that?"

"We need to get up, beautiful. I think Ashmodai wasn't as crippled as I thought he'd be by the force of magick I threw at him."

She pushed the covers away and stood. Cole tried not to swallow his tongue at the sight of her standing there swathed only by the silver moonlight coming through his bedroom window. All he wanted to do was to press her back onto the mattress and make love to her slowly, show her everything he couldn't say to her yet. He wanted to make love to her without Cernunnos riding him so hard, pushing him to extremes. Although, from the way she'd screamed the night before, he had a feeling Serena kind of enjoyed the extremes.

"Who was that on the phone?" she asked.

"The demon himself."

"Shit."

Cole stood and pushed a hand through his hair. "Pretty much my sentiment. We need to get back to the university and see if the prof's got our translation." He moved toward the bathroom to take a shower.

"We need to get working on another spell, too. One that will call and hold the demon, but it's got to be better than the last."

"Come on, Serena," Cole said when he reached the bathroom doorway. "Come take a shower with me."

"Cole," she said patiently. "We have other things we need get accomplished."

"Serena," he said patiently right back. "You're not going out of my sight for two seconds today. Not even long enough for you or I to take a shower. Not after what Ashmodai said yesterday. *C'mere.*"

She followed him into the bathroom and they took a fast shower. How he wished they had more time. Cole vowed that once this was over, he'd take a long, hot shower with her…and take her up against the tiled wall while the hot water pounded against them. As it was, he could only allow himself one little groan at the feel of their bodies pressed together under the hot spray. He let his hands roam her soap-slicked body and tangle in her shampooed hair. He could do this for the rest of his life. Every single morning. They'd save money that way. Conserve water.

He truly did feel *mated.*

After they were dressed and had slammed down a bagel slathered with cream cheese apiece, they headed downstairs to go find out if the professor had made any headway on the translation and to go to Millicent's to see if she'd made any headway on a stronger spell. They needed something that would hold Ashmodai for certain this time.

They reached the university, parked in the ramp and trekked across campus to the ancient languages building. When they got there, it was to find the prof's door ajar.

Serena grabbed his wrist when he raised his hand to knock. "Why do I have a bad feeling about this?"

He lowered his hand and raised an eyebrow. "Because there's a demon on the loose that can possess people? I think that'd be enough to give anyone the heebie-jeebies. We still have to knock on the door, though."

"Yes. You're right." She drew a breath. "Okay, fine, go ahead."

He knocked, but there was no response. He pushed the door open and it squeaked on rusty hinges.

"*Oh my god,*" Serena breathed beside him and clutched his upper arm. "This is just like every damn horror movie I ever saw."

"Professor?" called Cole.

The office appeared empty. The computer screen flickered and dust motes floated through the air, illuminated by the beams of morning sunlight coming through the window.

"Wow," Serena muttered as they entered. "Worse and worse—"

"Cole?"

Serena screamed and jumped toward the doorway, the direction from which the voice had come.

Cole turned, recognizing the prof's voice. "Professor Hardy."

"I didn't mean to scare you, Serena," said the professor.

"I'm sorry," answered Serena. "I'm a little jumpy this morning." She extracted a tube of lip balm from her pocket and used it.

"You're both up bright and early. You caught me right before a class." He walked into the room, set a plastic coffee container on the desk and sat down.

Cole relaxed. Professor Hardy seemed fine. Psychically, he felt fine, too. "We just stopped to see if you'd made any progress on that translation."

Professor Hardy smiled, then turned around to his computer and pulled up a file. "I did. It kept me up all night. As usual, it was a very interesting text." He hit print and handed the hard copy to Cole. "I saved the file to a disk for you, too." He picked up a jewel case containing a CD that lay on his desk and gave it to Cole.

Cole scanned the paper. It appeared the information they wanted was there. Relief flooded through him. "Thank you so much, Professor Hardy. You don't know how grateful I am for this."

"It was my pleasure. But allow me to ask one question?"

"Shoot."

Professor Hardy slid his hands behind his head and grinned. "What have you got against this Ashmodai creature that you're going to do all those horrible things to it?" He paused. "In the context of the game you're developing, I mean."

"It's just a game, Prof, just a game. Every player needs an opponent. Every hero needs a villain."

The professor nodded. "Well, good luck on the design."

"Thanks."

They said their goodbyes and then got the hell out of there. They needed to find a way to hold the demon while they performed the ritual outlined in the text the professor had translated. Cole anticipated an attack by Ashmodai at any time and was suspicious at the reason why there hadn't been one already. A quiet Ashmodai was a dangerous Ashmodai. He wasn't going to waste time. This had to end before anyone else got hurt.

He squeezed Serena's hand as they approached the car. He hadn't forgotten Ashmodai's threat against her. No way would he allow her to be harmed.

"Let's head to Millicent's," said Serena when they climbed into the car. "She said she would research ways to improve the containment spell."

"Sounds like a plan." Cole headed the SUV toward Millicent's house.

On the passenger side, Serena crossed her legs and drew his eye. Her movements made her short black skirt ride high on her tanned thighs. *Fuck.* He wished they had the whole day to themselves. He wished he could just pin her to the bed, take her over and over all damn day long until neither of them could walk straight. Just imagining a day spent like that made his cock get hard.

He put that on his list of things to do if they made it through this.

He slid a hand across the seat and rested it on her upper thigh. "When this is over, you're mine for an entire day, Serena. No goddamn demons to fight. No telephones. Nothing but you, me, and the bed. We'll order in food and just stay naked all day long."

She groaned. "That sounds so incredibly good." Serena shot him a sexy sidelong glance. "So…are you going to let *me* tie *you* up next time?"

He pushed his hand up on her thigh, until his fingers brushed her silky underwear. "If we get through this, you can do any damn thing you want to me, baby. I'll be yours." He rubbed her clit through the material of her panties and drew a low moan from her throat.

They reached Millicent's and Cole parked the car. When Serena tried to get out he reached across her, pulled the door closed and kissed her. She gave a little sigh that made his cock even harder and wound her arms around his neck.

Just five minutes. He just wanted five little minutes with her. Was that so much to ask?

He slipped his hand between her thighs, pushed aside her panties and slid two fingers into her. "Cole!" she gasped softly against his lips.

He groaned at the feel of her pussy walls gripping his fingers, imagining it was his cock. She was slick, wet and ready for a good, hard fucking. One he so wanted to give her. "Damn, you feel so good, baby." He thrust his fingers in and out of her and teased her clit with his thumb. She spread her legs to better accommodate his movements. The movement pushed her skirt up past her hips. He could see his fingers sliding in and out of her sweet pussy.

She tipped her head back and bit her lip. He seized the opportunity to bite the sensitive expansive of throat she'd presented and hold her gently with his teeth, lightly biting her.

"If you don't stop," she panted. "You're going to make me come."

He kissed the place just under her earlobe and smiled. "That's the plan, beautiful. I want you to come for me. I want to hear you cry my name. I want to feel all those muscles way deep inside you convulse and contract. I want feel all your luscious cream spread over my fingers so I can lick it off." He groaned at the thought. "Ah, baby, *come for me.*"

Her body shuddered and she let out a whimper. Sensing she was drawing very close, he bit the place where her neck and shoulder met and intensified his thrusting. Lightly, he teased her engorged clit through the slick material of her underwear. Her fingers bit into his upper arms as she lost herself to him.

"Oh, Cole," she moaned softly as her muscles tensed.

"That's it, baby, drench my hand."

She climaxed and he kissed intense and deep as he greedily thrust into her, wanting her orgasm to be as powerful and as long as possible.

Finally she quieted and he withdrew from her body and licked his fingers. He wanted to spread her legs and lap at her right now, but he couldn't. All he could do was enjoy the scent and taste of her and anticipate taking her later.

"Oh. My. God." she breathed. "You're going to kill me."

He put her hand on his hard cock. "No, baby, I'm going to fuck you repeatedly. You've got me hotter than an adolescent boy in the middle of a girl's locker room after gym class. Do you know that?"

She rubbed his shaft and he groaned and closed his eyes. "It's Cernunnos," she said. "It's an effect of having Cernunnos inside you, is all. It's not me."

"No. It's you, Serena." He leaned over and kissed her. "It's all you. Cernunnos might be affecting my libido. We *know* he is. But all my desire is for you...no other. Just you."

Her eyes went shiny and she bit her lower lip. She pulled her hand away from his crotch with a look of regret. "You better cool down, Cole. You'll scare Millicent going into her house with a raging hard-on like that."

He waggled his eyebrows. "All the better to fuck you with, my dear."

"I'm serious."

"Okay, okay." He closed his eyes and concentrated on mundane things like tuning his car up and cleaning out the closet. It was difficult with the lusty, musky scent of Serena's sex still in the vehicle, but finally he was able to control his wild member. "Let's go in."

They got out and walked up the path to Millicent's large stone house. Flowers bloomed in profusion everywhere in her yard and cats roamed in between the trees, stalking prey.

Millicent opened the door when she saw them walking toward the house. "Come in, come in," she said, ushering them over the threshold. "I've been researching spells for you," she said excitedly. "I think I found just the one."

She led them further into her brightly decorated living room. It was filled to bursting with antiques and dark wood furniture. Pillows of every color lined her yellow, overstuffed coach. A clock on the wall audibly ticked off minutes.

Millicent opened a drawer of her coffee table and extracted a long, thin bottle. She handed it to Cole. It was a murky color, near black. A piece of paper, inscribed with a spell, was attached to the top with a thin red ribbon.

"What's in there?" he asked.

"It's the combined essences of everything Ashmodai loves about being incarnate and in this dimension. If anything will keep him bound in one place, it will be his attachments. There's some blood of a young female virgin, the adrenaline of a holy man, the pure tears of a child, plus a few other things. There's a lot of ground up cold iron to help keep him in one place, too. That last isn't an essence of any of the demon's joys, of course."

Grimacing at all of Ashmodai's pleasures, Cole read all the ingredients on the vial's label, and then looked up. "This must have been expensive to make."

She nodded. "It was, but worth the money, I think. Just don't let any of it get on you. Call the demon forth with the spell, and then throw the potion on him. It should trap him in one place and diminish his powers. You have to do it when he's in his own form, though. Don't do it if he's in anyone else or the demon will be trapped in the one he has possessed and it will kill them. Hopefully it'll buy you enough time to send him back to the dimension he came from. One more thing, do it at midnight tonight. In our dimension and in this time zone, that's the witching hour. Witches have the most power in the half an hour before midnight and the half an hour after. At the apex, that's the power peak. The spell has the best chance to work then."

He palmed the vial. "Thanks, Millicent."

"Anything to get scum like Ashmodai out of my reality."

"The Ashmodai takes exception to that," said Serena from behind them.

Cole swung around to face her, wondering about her comment and the strange tone of her voice.

Serena stood with a butcher's knife to her own throat.

Millicent sucked in a surprised breath and Cole almost dropped the vial. Quickly, he pocketed it. "Serena?" he asked.

"Try again," she snarled. "The Cernunnos is wrong. The Serena isn't home right now."

Cold fear rushed through him. "I thought he couldn't possess the OtherKin," he said to Millicent.

"If she has even a drop of fully human blood in her ancestry, he can. Of course, witches do since we're interbred human and OtherKin."

"Fuck."

Serena/Ashmodai pressed the blade to her throat and drop of blood welled. Cole's heart lodged somewhere near his Adam's apple. "Give the Ashmodai the car keys or I'll kill the Serena."

Cole didn't even think. He just tossed the keys.

Serena/Ashmodai dropped the knife and ran for the door. "The Cernunnos can't catch the Ashmodai." She laughed.

Double fuck. Ashmodai wanted to fucking *play.* He wanted to play some twisted goddamn game.

With *his* Serena as the prize.

"Millicent," he said hoarsely.

She tossed him her car keys.

He raced out the door.

Chapter Eight

❧

With tires squealing and about thirty traffic laws broken, Cole slammed Millicent's sedan to a stop in front of an abandoned building outside Newville. Ashmodai occupying Serena's body had led him on a merry fucking chase through town. Cole's heart had been in his throat the whole time, worried that the demon would deliberately crash the car and Cole would have to extract Serena's broken body from the wreck. He wouldn't be able to take that. He'd die himself before that ever happened.

He didn't bother to even close the car door as he ran toward the entrance of the building, hot on Serena/Ashmodai's heels.

Rage, pure, sweet and intense had filled every part of his being. It overwhelmed his thoughts and brought Cernunnos bubbling to the surface, nearly overpowering all that was left of Cole. He felt his body shift even as he stalked through the doorway, as it had when they'd called Ashmodai forth.

Even as Cernunnos filled him, the Cole part of himself fought the eclipse of his personality. The war raged within him, just as it had when this had happened the last time. Power battled will, shredding his mind at the edges. The Cole part of himself worried what would happen if he allowed Cernunnos complete and utter control.

Magic prickled and tickled over his skin. The intense buildup of energy almost hurt. He needed to release it.

He just needed a target.

Cole had every intention of getting Ashmodai out of Serena's body. Exactly *how* he was going to do that remained elusive. A flash of black skirt drew his gaze as it disappeared around a corner. The building had been a factory at one time. The floor was concrete, and large rusted metal hunks of machinery stood around the huge room. Cole followed the flash of skirt and found a flight of metal stairs. He ascended, hearing the *clank, clank* of each step under his pounding feet.

At the top was a large, open room. The perimeter was lined with long worktables strewn with old clutter. Serena stood in the middle of the room. "The Cernunnos came to play."

Cole took a step forward, rage bubbling through his body. "Let her go," he said evenly. "Let her go before I—"

Serena/Ashmodai laughed. "The Cernunnos shouldn't make threats he can't back up. That is silly."

Almost involuntarily, Cole's hand shot out and a litany of foreign, ancient words that he didn't know he knew poured from his mouth.

Serena screamed and Cole's hand and words faltered and ceased. Was he hurting Serena, or was that Ashmodai's shriek?

Serena/Ashmodai smiled coldly, then laughed.

It had been a trick.

Cole released the magick once more and the words of the ancient spell poured from his mouth again.

Serena/Ashmodai whirled and ran toward a huge window, where the glass had been completely shattered. Cole watched with growing dread as Serena/Ashmodai jumped out.

"No!" Cole yelled. He ran to the window and looked out, his heart thumping hard in his chest. The last thing in this world he wanted to see was Serena's body crumbled and broken on the pavement below. Cold fear choked him.

But when Cole reached the window and curled his fingers around the sill, he saw nothing. *Nothing.* Relief surged through him, tempered by a question. Where had Cernunnos taken her?

The wind gusted, blowing his hair as Cole looked out into empty space. His eyes narrowed when the air below him seemed to shimmer. Perhaps the space wasn't as empty as it seemed.

Jump.

The word entered his mind and Cole knew he hadn't thought it. It was Cernunnos within him, trying desperately to take him over.

Jump.

The word came again, more insistently.

Jump!

Cole climbed onto the sill and jumped.

Chapter Nine

ಐ

Awareness pulled Serena from the silky dark dreamspace she'd been cavorting in. She gasped as the shock of leaving that place grabbed her consciousness and shook it. The last thing she remembered was walking into Millicent's house. What the hell was she doing sprawled face-first on a cold stone floor?

Her head pounded. Gingerly, she pushed up and looked around her. The walls here were white and they seemed to pulse as if breathing. They didn't look solid. At the corners and edges, mist swirled in air currents she couldn't feel against her skin.

She frowned. If it hadn't been for her near migraine of a headache, she would've assumed she was having a lucid dream. Although, who was to say you couldn't have a migraine headache in a lucid dream?

"The Serena is awake. The Ashmodai is pleased."

Serena scrambled to sit up and turn to face the direction the voice had come from. Ashmodai stood a few feet from her. His feet and massive, unnaturally muscled chest were bare. He wore only a loose-fitting pair of pants.

Okaaaay, she definitely wasn't dreaming.

The demon smiled, showing all those dagger-like teeth. Serena's heart thumped in her chest. Inwardly, she groped to gather all her magickal reserve, knowing that whatever she came up with, it probably wouldn't be enough.

Ashmodai took a step forward. The action sent Serena skittering backward on her hands and knees like a crab. She hit the wall behind her and heard a little sucking sound. *Oh, shit.* The damned wall had adhered itself to her back.

301

She was trapped like a fly on flypaper.

Ashmodai let out a booming laugh. "I have the Cernunnos' beloved. She is a good plaything for me."

Serena had the movement of her arms from the elbows down. She gathered her power, along with a specific intent, and held them together in her hand. The magick lay there, tickling the skin of her palm. "Yeah, well, Cernunnos' beloved doesn't want to be played with." It looked damned hilarious, most likely, but she hardly cared. Leaning to the side, she flicked her wrist in Ashmodai's direction, sending the ball of magick straight at him.

The demon roared and staggered back. A flash of bright light illuminated the room and the scent of burning demon flesh made Serena gag. Bile rose in her throat.

When the smoke cleared, Ashmodai stood looking down at his charred chest. He raised his gaze to hers and smiled. "Ah, the Serena is good at demon foreplay. She knows just how to excite the Ashmodai."

What? "F-foreplay?" she stammered, her eyes widening. She dropped her gaze and saw that the demon's pants were now tented by the erection of a huge, monstrous, way-too-big-to-fit-in-anything-but-a-horse demon cock.

Ashmodai waved a hand and his pants disappeared.

And it had little, tiny daggers up and down it that matched his teeth.

Serena opened her mouth and screamed.

Cole crash-landed in front of her. Seemingly, he'd come from the ceiling. He pushed up and went to her.

"Don't get close to the wall!" she said. "It's sticky and will trap you."

"Are you okay?"

She shook her head and looked toward Ashmodai.

Cole's gaze followed hers. "Oh, fuck," he breathed.

"Yeah, that's what he wants to do," Serena said with wide eyes.

Green fire jumped through Cole's eyes. She watched with fascination as his pupils seemed to explode and expand, swallowing the whites of his eyes. Emitting a little snarl, Cole stood. He was taller and bulkier again. His clothes showed the strain of the transformation.

Cernunnos was very much present.

"The Ashmodai played hide-and-seek, but the Cernunnos found the Ashmodai. Too soon for the Ashmodai to have extra playtime with the Cernunnos' beloved, though. That is disappointing."

Cole didn't respond, he just thrust his hand forward, palm out. A stream of blinding golden light shot out and hit Ashmodai square in the face. The sticky, white wall behind her trembled. The stone floor beneath her moved.

Foreign words spoken in a deep, otherworldly voice poured from Cole's mouth. The more he spoke, the more the walls and floor moved. It felt like an earthquake. Desperately, Serena tried to detach herself, but it was as though she were made of the wall behind her.

Ashmodai began to shriek and Cole's chant grew louder and louder.

Finally, the walls and floor started to shake apart and everything went dark.

Ashmodai's form flickered in the half-light. The demon wailed as if in pain. "The Cernunnos won this time, but not next time." He vanished.

Serena suddenly found herself lying on the floor of what looked like a factory. She blinked, letting the world come into focus once more. A little ways from her, Cole lay on his back.

She forced herself up on her hands and knees and crawled over to him. His clothes were shredded in places. She touched his cheek. "Cole?"

Cole allowed Serena's voice and touch to pull him back from the dark wasteland he'd fallen into. He opened his eyes and saw her concerned face. "Serena?"

"God, I thought you were dead," she said. Tears filled her blue eyes.

He pushed up into a sitting position and drew her to him. "I'm fine," he murmured as he stroked her hair. "I have a damned huge headache, but I'm fine." He held her face in his hands. "Are you okay?" She nodded.

"What happened? I was walking into Millicent's and then, *bam*, there I was in this little white room with the demon, then you showed up." She looked at him, bewildered. "What the hell happened at Millicent's, Cole?"

"Well, first, Ashmodai possessed you. Then he led me all over town on a merry chase. We ended up here."

She shuddered. "Oh, my God!" Her eyes widened and she sat up. "Did he age me?"

He leaned forward and kissed her. Arousal instantly tightened his body in a vise. Cernunnos was still riding him hard. He pushed his lust away.

Now was *not* the time for that, goddamn it.

Still, it battered at him. He stood and walked away from her, though it pained him to do it. He couldn't even bear to touch her, be anywhere close to her. Cole turned toward her, but didn't let her see his eyes. He knew they'd betray what he wanted from her. "No. You're young and beautiful, as always. I suspect your OtherKin blood protected you from that. Are you all right?"

She nodded and seemed to practically shake with rage. "Bastard!" she cried. "I thought he wasn't supposed to be able to possess the OtherKin."

He glanced at her, instantly noticing her lips, and the way her short glossy black hair swung with her movements. The scent of her skin teased him. The way her full breasts rose and fell with her breathing almost made him insane.

No. He wasn't going to do this. *Not now.*

He walked further away from her. "It's pure OtherKin he can't possess, the Sidhe and the shifters. He can possess witches and mages because of the diluted blood."

Serena stood and brushed her skirt off. "How'd we end up, um, wherever it was we ended up? That white room?"

Cole stopped in the middle of the floor and looked at her. "I don't know. I think Ashmodai created some kind of fold in the fabric of reality."

She looked at him and gasped. "Cole...your eyes. They're solid black and there's little bolts of green energy crackling through them."

He bit the inside of his bottom lip until he tasted blood and closed his eyes for a moment before he answered her. "I expended a huge amount of magic separating Ashmodai from you," he carefully. "There's pressure in me now that needs release."

"So...what do you need to ease it?" she asked in a soft voice.

He fixed her with a heavy-lidded gaze. "What do you think, darlin'? I want you. Fuck, I *need* you. But now is not the time nor place for that. Especially not for the thoughts I've got running through my head. You were just stuck in a fold of reality with a demon who had every intention of raping you with a dick that would've ripped you in two. The last thing you need from me is lust." She had his love, too, but he didn't think she was ready to hear that part yet.

She took a step toward him and he fought the urge to step back. Serena didn't know how uncontrolled he felt right now. If she touched him, that might be it. He didn't trust himself not to lay her out on the floor and take her right here.

"Yeah," she said. "But he didn't rape me, Cole, and I'm a lot stronger than you think."

"Hell, baby, I know you're strong. But if you knew the things I want to do to you right now..." he trailed off and groaned as the images of everything he wanted from her flashed through his mind. He was going to combust if he couldn't bury himself in her soon.

She licked her lips. "How bad is it?"

"How bad? Bad enough for me to imagine me pinning you to this filthy floor right now and stripping every bit of clothing from you. Bad enough for me to want to press you down face-first, spread those pretty rear cheeks of yours and take you in the ass. Bad enough for me to want to tie you up and take you over and over until you lose consciousness. I want you more than I ever have. But I'm not giving in to it. I won't take you here, right now. I'm not an animal."

"Cole—"

"*I am not an animal.*" He gritted his teeth. "I can control this. I can control Cernunnos." He turned on his heel. "Come on, let's go."

* * * * *

Serena wasn't so sure he truly could control the ancient god within him. Cole's eyes sparked and shimmered black and green. Every muscle in his body seemed tense. His gaze was hot and focused clearly and intently on her. He worried she was traumatized by her recent experience and a part of her loved him for it. By all rights, she should've been traumatized, but aside from being *really* pissed that Ashmodai had taken her body for a damn joyride, she felt okay.

She felt scared, too. She couldn't deny that. Having an evil entity take over your person wasn't exactly a reassuring experience. Hell, having a demon try to rape you didn't exactly make you feel warm and fuzzy, either.

"We're closer to my house than yours," she said. "Let's go there. We can work from there. It's far more private than your condo anyway, and I think calling a demon forth requires a bit of that."

He nodded, reached out to touch her, but then withdrew his hand. "I can't touch you right now. Not in any way." Cole looked like he was on the edge and would snap at any moment.

"Okay. It's okay, Cole. Let's just relax, all right? Do you want me to drive?"

His nostrils flared. "No. Maybe it will help me focus my attention on something other than you. Anyway, I have Millicent's car. You should drive that one."

She almost opened her mouth to say she really didn't mind his attention being focused on her, but she knew he was fighting this. He needed to prove to himself that he was not a slave to Cernunnos, and that he was in control of his body and his responses. Personally, she thought he should get used to the fact that Cernunnos was a part of him now. Cernunnos would be a part of him forever, but he needed to come to that understanding on his own.

And, *damn*, she could handle anything he threw at her. Not only that, she'd be more than happy to do it.

They left the factory, and he followed her to her house.

They pulled up the long driveway and Serena could see flashes of her home through the trees. It was such a welcoming, comforting sight. Feeling relieved, she parked Millicent's sedan and walked up the porch stairs. Cole was right behind her.

Her cats were all fine. She did a headcount as soon as they arrived and refreshed their water containers. After she was done filling the last one—with seven cats, you had to have more than just one—she turned to find Cole leaning up against the kitchen doorway, his still solid black gaze on her.

He looked like he was holding himself back with effort. His eyes were heavy-lidded and his body tense. If she hadn't known better, she would have said he looked drugged. Every single thing he wanted to do to her seemed to blaze in those eerily lighted black eyes. Her body responded with a shudder of pleasurable anticipation.

She drew a breath and her courage with it and looked him straight in the eye. "You know, you don't have to fight this. I'm not fragile. I can take anything you can dish out, Cole." She canted her hip and tilted her head at him. "Not only that, I want to do it."

His whole body tensed. "You don't even know what I'm thinking about right now, darlin'."

She narrowed her eyes and walked toward him. "Why don't you *show* me?"

Green sparks flickered through his eyes at her invitation. "You don't know what you're—"

She grabbed his jeans and undid the button roughly. "Take them off."

"Serena."

"Do it."

"I don't want to hurt you."

"You won't. What? Do you think I'm freaking made of china or something? I'm not going to break."

A crackle of green flickered through his eyes and then seemed to explode outward. She watched as the green consumed the black. In spite of herself, she took a step backward. With a growl-like sound in his throat, he went for her.

As soon as his hands fisted in her hair and his mouth came down on hers—consuming her gasp of surprise—heat erupted throughout her body. Literal *heat*. He was so hot he was burning up.

But the heat he kindled within her was *all sexual*.

He pulled away and tipped her head up so he could stare into her eyes. "Baby, you don't understand what you just invited," he rasped.

She didn't blink. She only put her hand over the pulsing bulge in his jeans. "Yes, I do."

"Ah, fuck, Serena." He pulled her shirt up and off up at the same time he pushed her back against the kitchen table. "You had to do it. You had to go and touch me."

"It's all I want to do, Cole. Haven't you figured that out yet?" Somehow, she got her glasses off and set them on the table. Then there was just a mess of *hands*. Serena struggled to pull his jeans down at the same time he struggled to get her panties off. Finally, she managed to free him to her touch.

She stroked her fingers up and down his length, a low groan of desire bubbling up from the back of her throat. Pre-come had beaded on the wide, plum-shaped tip. She spread it over the crown of his shaft, enjoying the slickness of it. At the same time, she nuzzled his throat, reveling in the scent of him and the feel of his stubble against her skin.

Serena slid down his body and went to her knees. It was time for her to taste him. She licked the head of his cock and his hips thrust forward.

Cole twined his fingers through her hair and ground out her name in a low, guttural voice. He sounded desperate. On the edge.

With her tongue, she explored the mushroom-shaped crown of his cock, tasting the bit of come that beaded on the top. He tasted musky, delicious. She wanted more of him. Widening her mouth, she sucked in the head of his shaft and cupped his balls in her hand.

Cole groaned and fisted his hands in her hair. "Ah, baby, I can't take much of this."

She slid as much of his length into her mouth as she could and twirled her tongue over his silken steel skin. Serena closed her eyes as she started to draw back and push forward. Every time she drew him back into her mouth, the head of his cock hit her tonsils. She wished she knew how to do that porn star trick of deep-throating a man, but she'd didn't. She had to be content with laving over as much of him as she could stuff into her mouth.

When she'd been with Brian, she'd never wanted to do this to him. She'd never wanted to feel him climax in her mouth the way she did with Cole. She'd never wanted to feel Brian's come hit her throat the way she dreamed of feeling Cole's. All she wanted was to taste Cole, feel him shudder under her hands and lips and know that she'd done it all by giving him this long, deep kiss.

But she wasn't going to get it. At least not this time.

"Get down on the floor, Serena," he rasped. He pulled her away from his cock and pushed her down to the linoleum. Cole followed, kneeling down beside her. His hands went to the edge of her skirt. It ended up bunched around her waist. They both went for her bra at the same time, bumping hands. He unclasped it and slipped it off her. As if he couldn't resist, he palmed her breasts, toying with the sensitized nipples. Serena bit her lip. His hands on her made her pussy throb.

She tugged at his shirt and he pulled it off. When he lowered his mouth to her breast, she felt the hard brush of that lovely expanse of muscle against her stomach. She twined her hands in his hair as he sucked a nipple into his mouth.

He groaned in the back of his throat as he teased the hardened nipple back and forth. At the same time, he parted her thighs and pressed a finger into her. "I'm going to fuck this sweet pussy so damn hard you're not going to be able to walk for a week," he rasped.

She gasped as he added a second finger and twisted them until he brushed his fingertips against her G-spot. His thumb teased her clit.

"Tell me how bad you want me to fuck you, Serena. Tell me."

"I-I want you to fuck me, Cole. God...I do." She shuddered as he continued to stroke her. His pinky strayed down to her anus and caressed all the little nerves there, making them jump to life.

"I'm gonna take you here, too, baby. Right here." He pushed the tip of his pinky into her nether hole. "You ready for that?"

"Anything," she groaned. "Cole, I just want you to take me." Her pussy was dripping, she was so excited. "I don't care where. I don't care how. I just want to feel you inside me."

He pulled his hand back and pushed forward, creating friction in both her pussy and anus at the same time. Her eyes nearly rolled back in her head at the delicious sensation of both places being stimulated in tandem. She gasped.

"Do you like that?" he purred.

"Uh-huh," she managed to push out.

"Has a man ever taken you from behind?" he asked as he thrust in and out of both her orifices.

She shook her head. "No."

"Are you afraid?"

She tipped her head up so she could stare into his eyes. "Never with you."

Cole pulled free of her and came down over her body, one hand on either side her head and took her mouth fast and hard in a near bruising kiss.

He pulled away and set his forehead to hers. "Serena, Serena," he repeated. "I wanted this to go slow. I wanted the next time we were together to be filled with what I feel for you. Ah, baby. I wanted us to make love."

Pleasure that had nothing to do with the erotic act they were performing suffused her. She put a hand to his cheek. "Anytime we're together it's making love, Cole."

He kissed her again. His tongue speared in, tangling savagely with hers as they fought each other, dueling for who could get their tongue deepest into the other's mouth. She felt the press of his cock against the slick folds of her pussy, asking for entrance. Whimpering into his mouth in her need, she parted her thighs as far as she could in welcome.

Come on, she chanted in her mind. "Fill me up, Cole," she murmured against his lips. "Make me feel alive and fully in my body again."

He surged into her, seating himself inside her to the base of his cock. Her spine arched as she came hard. Being sheathed around that thick, long member had pushed her over the edge. Her body trembled and shook from the force of her sudden climax.

Cole stayed thrust up deep within her as she convulsed around his length. He buried his face in the crook of her neck and groaned, long and low. Then he reached down, grabbed her ass in his big hands and started to shaft her. Pleasure filled up every tiny bit of her world.

She bit his shoulder and dug her fingers into his upper arms as the long, hard length of him slid in and out of her. He did it so devastatingly slow. She'd expected it hard and fast, not this mind-blowing, leisurely pace. She could practically feel every damn vein of his iron-hard cock rubbing against the walls of her pussy as he thrust in and out.

He pulled up, grabbed her wrists and pinned them to the floor on either side of her head. "Oh, baby, fuck, you feel so good," he groaned. "So damn sweet, so tight around my cock." His base, erotic words and the rasping, needful tone of voice he said them in made every muscle in her body tense to come again. He lowered his mouth to her nipple and rasped his teeth over it. The tiny bit of pain coupled with all the pleasure made her lose herself to him again. She cried out. This time when pleasure overwhelmed her, it almost brought unconsciousness along with it. Darkness spotted her vision as Cole pulled yet another climax from her body.

He pulled free of her and sat back, rubbing his hand over his cock that was glistening wet with her juices. He stared at her with hooded eyes. "Turn over, baby. Turn over for me. I want that sweet ass of yours."

She didn't move, mesmerized by the look of possession in his gaze. A touch of apprehension flitted through her. Serena swallowed hard.

His eyes flashed dangerously. "Don't fight me, love. That would be a bad move right now. Just give me what I want."

She turned over and he grabbed the waistband of her skirt that was bunched up around her waist and yanked it down and off. He urged her to her knees and she put her head down, offering herself to him in the most intimate of ways.

He groaned and rubbed his hand over one of her rear cheeks. "So beautiful. Part those pretty thighs as far as they'll go," he ordered.

She did it and felt so open, so exposed, so unalterably and completely *his*. That alone was nearly enough to make her come.

"God, you're dripping for me. So wet," he rasped. She felt his fingers sink into her pussy. "You're so hot here, Serena. I wish you could feel what I feel. All those silken muscles rippling around my fingers." He thrust in and out.

Serena closed her eyes and moaned.

"All those little noises you make that let me know I'm making you feel good," he murmured. "It's so gorgeous, baby. You're so unbelievably perfect."

"Cole, please, I want your cock."

She felt his fingers slip free of her and the head of his cock press against the opening of her pussy. "You want this, baby?"

"Yes," she breathed. "I can't get enough of it."

He pushed into her and came down over her back. She felt the hard, perspiration-slicked expanse of his chest against her spine. He buried his face in her throat as he pumped his rigid shaft into her. His breathing was harsh in her ear.

"I'm not going to come this way. Are you going to be ready for what I want next from you, baby?" he asked.

"Anything you dish out, I can take, Cole," she said in a shaky voice. "I told you."

He rose up and dug his fingers into her hips, driving his cock fast and hard into her wet, suctioning flesh. Every stroke reverberated through her body. She lay her hands flat down on the tile of the kitchen floor and pushed back at him, driving him further into her body with every stroke.

He dipped his fingers down, coating them in her slippery juices, and then rubbed them over the tight entrance of her ass.

Her hips bucked and a jolt of uncertainty went through her. It felt so unbelievably good, but was there enough lubricant to ease the way? She didn't know a lot about anal sex, but she knew enough to know you needed a lot of lube to keep it from hurting. They were in the kitchen. It wasn't like there was anything to use within reach. Maybe some butter? Strawberry jam? "Uh, Cole?"

He shushed her. "I'm not going to hurt you, baby. It's the last thing I want to do. Trust me." He slid his other hand down her front, catching and teasing a breast before disappearing between her spread thighs to rub and caress her clit. At the same time, he pressed a finger straight into her nether hole.

Serena instantly forgot what she'd been concerned about.

His finger speared in and out of her as his other hand worked her clit from the front. She moaned, consumed by the foreign sensations assaulting her body, from the utter possession he had over her. It was as if her body wasn't hers any longer. It was all Cole's to command now. She didn't mind giving it over to him, either.

Adding an additional finger into her rear, he worked to widen her muscles back there enough for her to take him. Intense pleasure mixed with just a little bit of pain had her eyes rolling back in her head. Cole slipped his other hand to her clit and played with swollen and sensitized bit of flesh. Serena gasped at the sensual onslaught.

He coupled ecstasy with just the slightest bit of pain until she couldn't tell the difference between the two—until the two were one and she couldn't get enough of the troubling, exciting sensation. His cock remained thrust up within her and she felt it jump. "Ah, baby. Do you like it when I finger-fuck you this way?"

"Y-yes," she panted.

"I can't wait to take you back here," he groaned. "You're going to be so hot and tight around my cock. You're not afraid, are you?"

"No," she moaned. Pleasure had narrowed her world down to only his cock, hands and voice. Nothing else mattered right now except Cole and the way he played her body, made it sing.

He put a hand on her hip and began to shaft her again with those long, mind-numbing strokes. At the same time, he continued to thrust those long, thick digits in and out of her ass. "I can feel my fingers against my cock, beautiful. You're so filled up with me right now, baby. So filled up. Every inch of you back here has me in it."

She wanted to sob she was so turned on. She wanted to beg him to take her in the rear at this point. His thrusts pounded her pussy with powerful pleasure. One of her hands slipped on the tile and she reached out in front of her, bracing herself against the cabinet.

"You like it?" he growled, withdrawing and plunging his fingers in tandem with his pounding cock.

"Yes," she cried out, pumping her hips back against him, driving him deeper.

"You ready for the rest of me? You ready to take me into this sweet little ass of yours, baby?"

"Yes!" she sobbed. "Come-come inside me, Cole. Take me all the way."

He trembled against her. She felt his slick skin drag across hers and as he leaned over and brushed his lips across the nape her neck. He pumped into her hard once, twice, the muscled expanse of his chest slipping against her back with delicious friction. Then he pulled free of her body.

Serena tensed, knowing what came next. She anticipated it, welcomed it—wanted it. Still, Cole's cock was wide, thick and long. She could barely take it into her pussy. How would it fit where he now meant for it to go? Even though Cole had prepared her body, had tried to stretch her muscles back there wide enough for him to fit, would she able to take him?

Cole slid his fingers from her and she took a deep breath, trying to relax her body. He pressed the head of his cock into her, and she bucked involuntarily.

He grabbed her hips, holding her in place. "Hush darlin', you can take me. I promise. It'll feel so good. I'll fill you up so full. It'll hurt a little. It'll hurt a little and be a whole lot of pleasure. You won't know if you want me to pull out of you, or for me to push harder and deeper inside. I know you, Serena. I know you like just a little bit of pain with your ecstasy. Just a little counterpoint to make the pleasure all the more intense. Are you ready?"

She drew a careful breath. "I'm ready."

He brushed the head of his cock across her opening and she felt her muscles relax for him. "That's it, baby, your body is begging me for this. Begging for me to take you back here."

Cole put one of his hands on her shoulder and placed the other on her hip. The head of his cock pressed into her, breaching the tight ring of muscles of her anus. She inhaled at the sharp mixture of pleasure and pain. It was exactly as he said. The sweet sensation of him possessing her there, stimulating all those tiny little nerve endings was enough to make her come, but there was a pain, too. A delicious ache of having those muscles stretched that far by the thick, silky head of his cock.

"Oh, Cole," she breathed, and then panted out once. "More," she gasped.

He groaned and slapped both hands to her hips, easing her back against him and slowly thrusting the shaft of him deeper into her. "This is going make me raw, beautiful. You're so damn tight." The thick width of his cock pressed into her slowly until he was seated all the way.

A fevered rush of ecstasy filled Serena at the feeling of him completely filling her back there. "Ah, Cole," she moaned and hit the floor with the flat of her palm. "Oh." Her muscles clamped down on his cock hard and she gritted her teeth at the painful pleasure, wanting him to shaft her and at the same wanting him to stop.

Then he started to move.

What little control she'd had evaporated and she gave a guttural, bone-deep groan. His hips pulled back and thrust forward as he set up an easy, yet relentless rhythm. With every thrust, he sank further inside her. With every thrust the penetration grew easier.

"I can't hold back," he groaned as he picked up speed, pushing her harder with each piston-like movement. "I can't take it slow."

She couldn't respond. All she could do was hang on as he thrust into her body over and over. He slid his hand around her front, dragging his fingers through her pubic hair to thrust two fingers into her weeping pussy.

Serena cried out as he ground his palm into her clit and finger-fucked her pussy even as he took her from behind. Her climax exploded over her body, overwhelming her and driving every bit of thought from her mind. He'd made her helpless and consumed by him, a slave to the ecstasy he'd exerted over her body.

Only *this* existed for her now—only Cole. Only his cock and her body.

"I want more from you," he ground out near her ear in a guttural, rasping voice. "Give me *more*." He withdrew his fingers from her pussy and slicked her juices over her clit as he worked the sensitized bud between two fingers, working it into another frenzy of need. "Whose are you, Serena? Are you mine? Tell me you are."

"Oh, God, Cole. I'm yours. I'm yours," she sobbed and chanted as he pushed her straight into another climax. The muscles of her body tensed and shuddered as another wave of pleasure racked her. The kitchen dimmed as she almost lost consciousness.

Behind her, she heard Cole's deep groan as he exploded within her. She felt him fill her up, his cock jumping and his body shuddering against hers.

He came down on her. Their bodies slid together slickly in the perspiration sheen of their exertion and he pulled free. He kissed her neck over and over, murmuring, "God, Serena. I love you, baby. I love you so goddamn much. You're mine, beautiful, *mine*. All mine."

Serena collapsed to the floor and Cole rolled to the side, gathered her up against him and kissed her over and over, telling her how beautiful she was, how much he loved her, how she was *his*. They were a mess, sticky and wet. None of it mattered.

Shuddering and trembling and half crying from the intense experience and the emotions that clawed and jumped through her, Serena let Cole enfold her in his embrace.

"I do love you, Serena," he murmured into her hair. "I'm not letting you go, baby. Not ever. I'm never letting anyone hurt you. Not ever again."

Serena's half sob turned to a full-out cry at his words. All the pain, all the anguish from what Brian had done to her—everything she'd been holding in for the last five years—came out in a cathartic rush. She held out onto Cole as though she'd drown in the flood of those emotions and he was her life preserver. He held her tight, rocking her back and forth until she sobbed herself quiet and still. They stayed that way for a long time, silent and spooning in the middle of the kitchen floor.

* * * * *

Serena walked into the living room and glanced at the clock. It was almost time. Millicent told them to do it at midnight.

They'd eventually collected themselves from the kitchen floor and had taken a shower together. Cole really wouldn't let her out of his sight. He'd berated himself aloud several times already for taking her eyes off of her at Millicent's house.

As if there'd been absolutely anything he could've done to prevent Ashmodai from possessing her. There wasn't anything she could've done either. One minute, she'd been there. The next second she'd been just...*gone*... Then she'd "come to" sprawled on the floor of that freaky little white room. The lack of control she'd had was more terrifying than the actual possession. The lack of impact her magick had had on Ashmodai was frightening, too. She shivered violently at the memory.

Cole sat on the couch staring at the rolled-up spell, the vial filled with the potion, and the translated text on the coffee table. He'd been staring at that stuff for the better part of the day. Since, mostly, they'd spent the entire day waiting and staring at the clock over the mantel. They were both tense.

She'd convinced him to sit with her out on the porch for a while, though the autumn chill was especially chilly and had driven them inside before too long. She'd gone to the store and made a vegetarian stew after that. Cole had even eaten some it and managed not to spit it out on the floor. In fact, he'd complimented her on it. Surprisingly, he'd also had a cup of the green tea she'd made.

They'd talked for hours, shared every last detail of their pasts. She'd told him about how she'd thought Brian had really loved her and how surprised she'd been that night, how devastated. She'd cried again and he'd held her and let her do it—cry it all out. It was something she really hadn't been able to do before. Hell, she hadn't even been able to cry when she'd been on the stand at Brian's trial. The prosecuting attorney had been furious with her for that. He'd wanted her to be all emotionally devastated for the jury. They'd convicted the bastard without her tears, in the end.

Cole had talked about how his parents were really concerned with the kind of house they lived in and the kind of car they drove. They cared more about their possessions and making money than they cared about being happy. He told her that they'd always thought he was a little strange and that had caused a rift between them.

Most "normal" people could sense the OtherKin in a person, but not understand it. They usually just ended up labeling them "eccentric" or "odd".

There must have been some OtherKin in Cole's family tree, but it was like hair color or eye color, it could skip a generation. Obviously, it had passed his parents by.

Serena felt bad for Cole that he grew up in that kind of environment, and counted herself lucky. OtherKin-ness hadn't ever skipped a female member of her family as far as she knew. They were all witches.

That evening, she'd called Rowan, but her sister had been as tight-lipped as always. Serena had kept the conversation light and hadn't told her anything about the demon than what Rowan already knew. Better she not know the extent of what was going on, since it was clear Rowan had problems of her own at the moment.

"Come here, beautiful."

Cole's voice shook her from her intense stare at the clock. *It was almost time*. She walked to him and he pulled her down on his lap. When he brushed his lips against her cheek, she closed her eyes at the spicy, manly scent of him. She'd fallen hard for this guy and it was so damned scary.

So fast. So hard. So scary.

"Are you going to be ready to perform this ritual?" he asked.

She opened her eyes and glanced at the rolled-up piece of paper. "I'm as ready as I'm ever going to be. I'll get him here.

You throw the potion on him. Together we'll perform the ritual to open the doorway and force him back through it."

Cole sighed. "Sounds way too simple. Ashmodai has something planned. No way is he going to allow this."

"Is it just me, or does Ashmodai seem alarmingly childlike? He always wants to play."

"Uh-huh and his play usually means death, beautiful. If I hadn't blasted that power at him this afternoon, it could've been your death. Let's face it, it probably *would've* been yours. I surprised him...and myself. I didn't even know I knew that spell I threw at him." He laughed. "I guess I didn't. It was Cernunnos who knew it."

The clock on the mantel chimed midnight.

Shit.

"Time's up," she breathed.

They were both motionless and quiet for a long moment.

"Let's go," said Cole.

Serena stood and took the rolled-up spell from the table. Cole took the rest of the items and they walked outside. They'd drawn a circle in the grass by the side of the house, in the center of a patch of trees that had been specially planted for coven circles. They'd stuck a multitude of lawn torches in the ground to light the area. Above them the moon was full. The sky was bright and clear and sparkling with stars.

Their breath showed in the air as they walked to the center of the circle. It was a cold night and it matched how she suddenly felt inside.

They bowed to the four directions—north, south, east and west. They'd already cleared the circle with a white-sage smudge stick. Serena had already memorized the words to the summoning spell.

She just had to stand in the center of the circle, say them aloud and infuse them with a little bit of her own magical soul.

Cole grabbed her hand and squeezed. In his other hand, he held the vial. "Go on, baby."

She closed her eyes and concentrated inward, drawing on the center of herself where all her power resided. She felt herself go woozy and get a bit lighter physically as that power uncoiled like a snake and curled up her spine. Energy trickled through her body, starting at the tips of her toes and rising upward. Slowly it rose, taking her fear and pushing it out as it went, obliterating her doubts.

The power hit her throat, her vocal chords and rose further. Serena opened her mouth and sighed out pure energy, pure OtherKin power. She chanted the ancient words of the spell. Before, when she'd memorized them, she hadn't known what they meant. Now, she still couldn't translate them to English, but she knew the meaning each syllable conveyed. Come to me. Come to me.

Come to me.

There was a pop and crackle of energy to her left. An enraged roar rent the gentle night air. A powerful, evil feeling presence filled the circle. Ashmodai had arrived.

Still, Serena kept her eyes closed, the power focused. *Come to me...*

Beside her, Cole extricated his hand from hers. She heard him pop the top of the vial. Heard a splash of liquid. Heard another roar of rage. The pull on her power lessened. The potion had done its job. It had picked up the thread of the magick she and Cole exerted over the demon and given them a little room to move.

Serena opened her eyes and saw Ashmodai suspended in midair in the center of the circle. This time he didn't pull on an invisible magical chain. This time he only remained motionless, as though frozen in the air. The nervous darting of his red eyes was the only clue she had that the demon was even aware of what was happening around him.

Cole grabbed her hands and pulled her down to the grass to sit cross-legged in front of him. She locked gazes with him.

Together, their power kissed and rolled through the air, swooping and swirling around their bodies, darting through their chakras and out. In spite of the seriousness of what they did now, the feeling of their energy…*making love*…as it did, made her feel giddy and lightheaded. It almost felt like a drug. One she didn't want to come down from.

Cole blinked and said, "Focus."

She wasn't sure if he was talking to her or to himself. Still, it was good advice. She focused on Cole's eyes and started the chant to open the doorway to the dimension Ashmodai had come from, to send the demon back to his own hellish reality.

The ancient words poured forth and Serena actually saw their power come out of their mouths with the spell. Her magick was a light rose color, alternating with purple. It puffed out with every syllable she uttered. Wisps of a green so dark it was almost black swirled forth with Cole's utterances. At the same time, knowing without verbal communication what to do and when to do it, they pitched their voices higher.

A wind started up. It grew stronger and more turbulent, began to whip her hair around her face and become a near deafening sound in her ears.

A slit of white light opened to the right of Ashmodai. It grew longer and longer and wider and wider with every word that poured forth from their mouths. A screaming noise started in Serena's mind. Was it the wind? She wanted to slap her hands over her ears, even though she knew it had no physical origin. It was in her head. Instead, she squeezed her eyes shut. She felt an odd tug from Cole on her hands, as though he were being pulled away. Her eyes flew open.

Something was wrong.

Cole was tugged backward again. He tried to let go of her and she grabbed on tighter.

Another vicious tug.

"Let me go," he yelled over the wind. "You'll be pulled along with me."

"No!" she grabbed on tighter and yelled back. "You're not going to be taken anywhere! You're not leaving me!"

Barely before her sentence was out of her mouth, Cole's hands were ripped away from hers and he flew backward into the opening doorway of the hell dimension as if sucked by some powerful force.

"*Nooooo!*" she screamed as the doorway slammed shut.

$$\mathcal{C}hapter\ \mathcal{T}en$$

80

Silence.

Shock.

The wind died and Serena stared in complete and utter numb distress at the space of air where the doorway had been.

Near her, Ashmodai laughed.

Serena gasped and scrambled back away from the demon. Ashmodai floated toward her, now free. She cringed as he leaned in so close to her, she could smell his foul breath. "The witch is in pain, fear. The Ashmodai enjoys," he purred. "It is like a fine wine to the Ashmodai's senses."

"Wha-what happened?" she whispered, more to herself than the demon. Then she pushed toward him in sudden fury. He floated backward and laughed. "What the hell did you do to him?" she demanded to know.

"The Ashmodai plays," he hissed. "The Cernunnos was easy to dupe. The witch was depressingly easy to fool. The Cernunnos and his human incarnation are gone now. In my dimension. No one left to hamper the Ashmodai here. The Ashmodai must now go find new playmates. Playing with the Cernunnos was fun. The Ashmodai is sorry it is over."

"Goddamn you," she screamed. "You bring him back!" her voice broke and cracked in her fury.

Ashmodai purred in the back of his throat. "Mmmm, the Ashmodai likes the Serena's pain and fear. The Ashmodai will leave the witch alive for now to savor it. But the Ashmodai will be back. The Serena should not expect to stay alive much longer.

Live in fear of the Ashmodai's return and what the Ashmodai will do to her then."

He disappeared.

Serena stared into the air for a few moments, then fell back into the grass, curled herself up into a ball and sobbed.

Cole was gone.

Cole was *in hell*.

No way was she going to let him stay there.

She slammed her palm against the earth and pushed up from the grass. Something, somewhere had gone terribly wrong. She thought she knew just *where*.

Serena ran back into the house, grabbed her purse and Cole's car keys. Another minute had her in Cole's SUV, racing to the university.

The tires squealed as she turned the corner into the parking ramp. She slowed, not wanting to draw the attention of any security guards. Man, she could use Morgan's invisibility spell right now.

She parked the car in the ramp, leapt out and hit the ground at a dead run. If any security personnel took issue with her being on campus at one in the morning, they'd have to catch her to make her aware of it.

The door to the ancient languages building was locked, of course. Her magick was greatly depleted from the summoning spell, but she had enough left to call up a spell to unlock it. The inside of the building was pitch-black and quiet as a morgue. She winced at that last thought, but the creepiness of her surroundings still didn't stop her from racing up the stairs and hitting the professor's office door at a run. Chest heaving from exertion, she turned the doorknob and entered.

A small light burned on a corner desk, near a row of crammed bookshelves. Glancing around, she determined that the office was empty. The computer was on. The light flickered blue, clashing with the soft white light from the corner lamp. Serena cautiously inched toward it. If what she suspected was true, she just had to hope the correct translation of the ancient text had been completed and was now stored somewhere on the professor's hard drive.

If it wasn't... She shook her head. No, she wouldn't let her mind go there.

She pulled the office chair back to sit down on it. A thick, sickening, sliding sound met her ears. She screamed as the professor's desiccated, sucked-dry and prematurely aged body slid off the office chair and collapsed on the floor with a sick-making thud.

Suddenly, there was a loud, high-pitched, *irritating* sound in the room and she realized it was her, still screaming. She slapped both hands over her mouth and backed away from the corpse, breathing hard in near hyperventilation.

God. It was *exactly* as she'd feared. When they'd gone to see the professor this morning, it had been Ashmodai in the professor's body. Ashmodai had given them a fake translation. The one the demon had given them had been designed to send *Cernunnos* to Ashmodai's dimension.

And they'd performed it, never even fucking suspecting *a thing*.

She pulled her hands away from her mouth. "God, I'm sorry, Professor," she whispered hoarsely. "I'm so sorry." She pushed him out of the way with her foot and there was a crackling sound of dried-out flesh. Serena screamed again and backed away.

"Okay, come on, Serena, girl," she talked to herself in a shaking voice. "Let's do this." Moving slowly and trying not to touch the body, she sank down into the computer chair and got to work.

Meticulously, she searched through his computer with a fine-tooth comb. It was no easy matter. The professor had a huge hard drive, filled with all kinds of texts just like the one she was looking for. For the first time in her life, she was beyond grateful for her geeky streak because she knew how to sift through all the files.

Time passed and the night wore on. The screen blurred in front of her and morning light lightened the sky. Panic started to fill her.

It wasn't here.

Goddamn it.

The file was nowhere on the professor's computer. Maybe he hadn't even completed the translation before Ashmodai had possessed him. Tears pricked her eyes.

What the hell was she going to do?

She ran both hands through her hair and fisted them at the top of her head. *Calm down. Think*, she told herself, squeezing her eyes shut. *If I were a file that the professor thought was something for a computer game, where would I be?*

Not a flicker of intuitive help came to the fore. She sighed and dropped her hands. "Professor…where'd you put it?" she wailed out loud.

The professor's voice entered her mind. *It's in the file drawer on your left.*

She opened her eyes and glanced around wildly. "Professor?" Over by a bookshelf an ethereal form wavered. It seemed caught somewhere between this world and the next.

You should have asked me sooner, he said. *You can talk with the dead, you know.* His tone was chastising.

She was being chastised by a ghost. Could this week get any stranger?

"I know. I-I just didn't even think about it," she confessed. She should've, but she hadn't. She frowned. The thought of finding the file had consumed all her thoughts. "Why are you even still here?"

His voice hardened. *I'd really like to see my murderer get what he deserves. Can you do that for me? When that's done, I'll move on.*

She opened the drawer and found a disk on top of the files. She snatched it up and stood. "That's the plan."

Go do it.

* * * * *

Serena slammed her fist against Alana's front door and fought the urge to scream obscenities. "Alana! Get up!" *You lazy bitch*, she finished in her mind.

The door opened to reveal a sleep-roughened Alana. Her tangled long blonde hair framed a face wearing a surly expression. Mascara smudges marked both sleepy eyes. She held a cup of coffee in one hand and a cigarette dangled by its tip from her mouth. "What the fuck, Serena," she said around the cigarette. "It's the crack of dawn."

She pushed past Alana and stood in the center of her living room.

Alana slammed the door closed, turned, and plucked the cigarette from her lips. "Sure, come on in," she shot at her sarcastically.

"You have to call your coven now, Alana. Gather every up every last member of the Three Ash. We've got to form a circle to gather enough power to do what we need to do."

"Now, why the hell would I do that? What the hell is it *exactly* that we have to do, anyway?"

Pacing the short length of Alana's living room, Serena told her why—the whole sordid story…minus the sex scenes. "I need your coven to do what it did before," she finished, "when you accidentally let Ashmodai into this reality. Only this time, I need you to bring Cole here."

"Why can't you do this on your own, Serena? You're a damned powerful witch. That's the reason you turned down membership in Three Ash," her voice turned petulant at the end.

That actually wasn't the whole reason why, but Serena wasn't about to say it was mostly because she didn't like Alana. Especially when she desperately needed the other witch's aid. "I'm drained. It took a lot of power to call the demon to me last night." She shook her head and her glasses slipped down her nose. She pushed them back up. "I need help."

Alana snubbed her cigarette out in a nearby ashtray. She'd sunk into a nearby chair and listened with rapt attention, letting the cigarette burn down to the filter, while Serena talked. "Fuck," she said.

"Call the coven, Alana."

She ran her hand over her face and licked her lips nervously. "Okay. Okay, I'll call them." She reached for the phone.

It took an hour for all the members of the Three Ash Coven to filter into Alana's home. By that time, Serena was near beside herself. What was happening to Cole right now? Where was he? A shudder went through her.

Was he even still alive?

In the hour that it had taken for the other witches to arrive, Serena had commandeered Alana's computer and had printed out a copy of the correct text translation. It varied by what they'd used the night before by only a little. Just a few little words had been omitted, and a couple substitutions had been made.

Tiny little changes had sent the man she loved to hell.

She stared at the women milling the room and tears clouded her vision. She *did* love Cole. God help her, she was head over heels in love with him. This world seemed dimmer, darker and a whole lot worse minus his presence.

Serena stood. "Let's do this," she said in a voice loud enough to carry over the giggling, talkative bunch. The room went silent. The women looked at her and then at Alana.

"You heard her. Come on ladies," Alana said. "Let's go." She clapped her hands and ushered them into another room.

They moved into the large room that the Three Ash used for spell casting and performing rituals. It was mostly bare, save for a profusion of already lighted candles, a corner shelf unit that contained some supplies and a long table lining one wall. The women instantly formed a circle and Serena went into the center, clutching the piece of paper with the translation on it.

The women clasped hands around the circle and Serena knelt in the middle. The instructions Alana gave them sounded muted to her ears as her power started to gather and pulse in the center of her stomach. She was exhausted, mentally, emotionally, and spiritually—but her will was strong. That strength of will was enough alone to trigger the remaining bit of power she had within her, to gather it and fold it, prepare it to release with the words of the spell.

They would get Cole back first.

Then they'd call Ashmodai forth.

Then they'd send his demon ass back to hell.

Serena squeezed her eyes shut even more. *She hoped.*

The coven around her began to chant. The power the women created together was instant and intense. Serena felt it trickle in from the witches around her. It greeted her magic, laughed with it, danced with it...then it fused.

Serena's back arched with a jolt of pure, sweet energy as it cavorted through her body. She opened her eyes. The women around her all had their heads tipped back as they chanted the words of the spell. They were like one being right now. One powerful magickal conduit.

A wind started in the room, making the candles first gutter and then blow out. Multicolored wisps of energy began to be visible. They flew around the room, buffeted by the wind. Slowly, they blended together in one big mass of blue. Within the blue was a spark of light.

The doorway was opening.

Serena closed her eyes and focused on that tiny little peek into the alternate dimension. The trick was bringing Cole back and not another demon. That was the danger here…and it was a big one.

In her mind's eye, she called up every image she had of Cole. Every smile she'd seen cross his face. Every look of lust in his eye. As she concentrated on the sliver of that alternate dimension, she called to mind his laugh, his groan of ecstasy as he released himself inside her, his voice as he said, "C'mere, beautiful." Everything about him that was burned into her memory she brought to the forefront.

Feeding the images and memories magick both from herself and the coven, she wove it all together in a beautiful pattern of love and intention. Then she sent the mixture out and through that doorway. Mentally, she trolled that huge, horrible dimension to find the one she wanted and draw him near.

Finally, she reached out and stuck her hand into that sliver of a doorway, grabbed onto the object she *hoped* she had called forth and pulled.

Chapter Eleven

❦

Cole figured he'd been wandering through this damn murky forest/bog for at least a couple hours. He'd been traveling aimlessly through the gloom and over the foreign terrain. Bog mud now covered every inch of him and he continually had to wipe it out of his eyes. He didn't know where he was, or why he'd been sucked into this place, but it really riled up the Cernunnos part of him.

Hell, it riled up the Cole part, too.

Even worse than being sucked into this alternate reality and landed ass deep in a disgusting, smelly bog was the fact that he didn't know if he'd pulled Ashmodai along with him.

Had Serena been left alone with a bloodthirsty, game-playing demon? If she had, what had the demon done to her? His stomach clenched tight at the possibilities.

He pushed a moss-covered branch aside and shied away from the massive black and red spider that hung from it. He was getting used to the spiders here. That was a *bad* sign.

He hadn't been able to get his mind off Serena since he'd "landed". Her smile haunted his mind. Her laughter, and memories of her moans of pleasure when he had her beneath him occupied his every breath and thought. Her smile and all those damn lip balms she had stuffed everywhere. He missed her laugh, her scent, and the feel of her corn silk hair between his fingers. Damn it. He loved her so much, and he could barely stand the thought of her being hurt.

God, he hoped she was all right. He could be trapped forever in this damned miserable place where it seemed to be perpetually dark and where spiders seemed to thrive, so long as she was all right. If given the option, he'd trade his life for hers. Too bad no one was giving him that option.

He reached into the pocket of his jeans and fingered the ring he'd made of some bog tree gum. If ever got back and if Serena was still alive, he was going to ask her marry him. It was rash. He knew that. It was silly since they'd known each other for such a short time. It was a completely crazy idea.

It was the only thing in the whole universe he wanted to do.

He shook his head. He was growing delirious. There was probably no way he'd be able to get back from this place. Not to mention, he was stupid. He was going to offer her a ring made in hell? Yeeeah…*not* ideal. Not exactly every woman's dream.

He'd only been in this place a couple hours and he was already losing his mind.

The only thing was, the thought of giving Serena this ring was the thought that kept him putting one foot in front of the other at this point. He held onto it like it was a magickal charm keeping him alive.

Cole stopped dead in his tracks, as a sliver of white light appeared right before him. *What the…?* A hand snaked in, grabbed the front of his shirt and pulled.

He tumbled for what seemed like forever and finally landed with a *whoof* on his back. Wind blew everywhere in this place, and there was a strange chanting all around him. He rolled to his feet and stood in battle stance, wondering if he was going to have to fight another of those damn green scaly things.

Feminine screams filled the air and Cole blinked. He couldn't see anything with this bog mud in his eyes.

"Wait!"

Serena's voice.

"Everyone, *wait*. It's okay. Calm down. It's Cole."

Serena? Hurriedly, he wiped the mud out of his eyes and the room came into view. The women of the Three Ash Coven, the ones who'd called Cernunnos forth, stood all around him. Cernunnos growled, enraged.

"No!" Serena's voice. "It's okay, Cole. It's okay!"

Serena.

The rage retreated at the sound of her voice. He found her and pulled her to him, his hands fisting in her hair and tears mixing with the mud in his eyes. He found her mouth and kissed her. "Serena, you're all right. You're okay," he said over and over.

Serena sobbed into his neck and fisted her hands in his shirt. "Oh, God, Cole. I thought I had lost you forever."

He pulled away and cupped her face in his hands. "You'll never lose me, baby. Never. I'm yours." He kissed her deep, tasting bog mud. He didn't care and it appeared neither did she.

Serena backed away. Tears tracked down her face. Her glasses were crooked on her face and she was covered with mud. Cole thought she'd never looked more beautiful.

He glanced around and saw the coven witches watching them. Some of them looked like they thought they were crazy. The rest appeared to think it was incredibly romantic. He blinked. Sunlight streamed in through the window.

"It's daylight already?" he asked.

"You were gone for almost twelve hours, Cole," said Serena.

"Really? It didn't seem that long at all."

"Time runs much slower there," said Alana. "And there are huge *canstin* spiders. Not very many nice playmates in that place."

Cole ripped his mud-covered shirt off and dropped it on the floor. He'd help them clean up after... What Alana had said finally registered. *Huh?* He looked up. "Hey, how did you know—"

Ashmodai separated himself from Alana, who collapsed to the floor. "The Cernunnos found a way back," he snarled as he rose above them. "The Ashmodai can't allow this."

The coven witches screamed.

"Serena, get back," Cole said.

"Reform the circle," called Serena. "Reform it, *now*! Build the power."

Most the witches did what Serena had ordered. A few ran out of the room. The chanting, though now done in very shaky voices, started again. Cole added his own rising Cernunnos power. The wind started up once more.

Behind him, Serena started chanting something else, a different spell. It took a moment for him to recognize it as the one they'd used last night, though this one was slightly different.

It was the correct translation of the ritual to send Ashmodai back.

He should've known Serena would find a way.

Ashmodai roared and made an enraged lunge for Serena. Cole thrust her behind him and bodychecked Ashmodai. They rolled together across the floor like they had at Millicent's the first time they'd summoned the demon.

But this time, Ashmodai wasn't playing around.

Cole felt claws rip his back open and hot blood welled. He yelled out in pain as both he and Ashmodai slammed hard against some invisible wall of power right in front of the coven witches. Pain exploded in just about every part of his body.

"Cole!" Serena cried.

He grabbed Ashmodai before he could scramble across the floor toward Serena and snap her neck. Serena was on the *wrong* side of that invisible barrier. "Keep chanting, baby. Keep chanting," he ground out.

Serena renewed her efforts with gusto and he felt her power reach out and touch him. Ashmodai felt it, too and roared in rage. They tussled on the floor. Cole punched Ashmodai hard in the cheek and thought he felt all the bones in his knuckles break. He hoped Serena had some success *soon*.

Ashmodai caught him under the eye in a mind-numbingly hard punch. Cole's head snapped back and the breath oofed out of him as he fell hard on his side. Pain exploded through his head.

But above him, a sliver of light glimmered.

The doorway.

Cole forced himself up and grabbed Ashmodai. Cernunnos rose within him, hard and hot. For the first time since the beginning of the entire ordeal, Cole let him take over. Ancient words poured from his mouth as he felt himself gain muscle and height as Cernunnos took over. Magick poured through him. He grabbed the demon by the upper arms and tossed him through the slit of light.

Ashmodai screamed as he was swallowed whole and the doorway snapped shut.

Cole went down on all fours, breathing hard. Slowly, Cernunnos retreated. Sated. Happy. For once, he wasn't gripped with the all-consuming need to drag his mate into the other room and fuck her until she couldn't see straight.

Well, okay. He *wanted* to, but he didn't *have* to with a capital "H".

With that thought, he collapsed straight to the floor and the world went dark.

Chapter Twelve

✄

"Serena?"

Serena laid a hand to Cole's cheek. "Shh, take it easy."

The coven had all pitched in and helped Serena get him to her house. It had taken pretty much all of them to lift him, but they'd managed it. Now he was lying in her bed. She'd gotten most the mud off him and dressed his wounds. Though he was still wearing the filthy pair of jeans he'd been trekking through the bog in.

Ashmodai had roughed him up pretty good. Besides the slash across his back, he had some cuts and bruises on his face.

Cole's eyes opened to slits. He smiled and then winced. "Serena," he breathed.

"Hey, baby."

"You did it," he rasped.

"*We* did it, yeah."

"You found the right translation."

Her smile faded. "Cole, I need to tell you something about the professor."

"Ashmodai killed him, didn't he?"

"I'm sorry. Reading the paper today makes me think he killed at least four people. There have been a rash of unexplained deaths by rapid aging around Newville. The medical community is stumped."

"That's horrible." He reached up, twined a hand to her nape and pulled her face down for a kiss. "But he's gone now."

She shivered. "Let's hope no one ever brings him back." She took a glass of water from the bedside table and pressed it into his hand. "Drink this. It'll help you sleep."

"I don't want to—"

"Drink. You need to sleep. Your body is healing really rapidly. Just the way you'd think a god would. Still, you need to rest. That drink is made with herbs to hasten the healing process."

He smelled it and grimaced.

"Yeah, I know. It tastes just as bad. Drink it anyway, okay?"

"Only if it'll get me back with you quicker." He grinned rapaciously at her and waggled his eyebrows.

She smiled. "Drink."

He held his nose and drank it down. Almost immediately, his eyelids started to droop. Soon, he was asleep. When she was satisfied he was in a deep healing sleep, she got up and headed to the oak grove.

She had a little unfinished business with the Elders.

Once there, she knelt on the rock and entered the Elders awareness, pushing through the layers of their trapped memories until she reached the heart of their collected consciousness.

An image of her mother floated in her mind's eye. *Mom? I don't understand*, Serena said. *I don't understand any of it. I mean, I'm not complaining, but it all happened so fast and—*

My daughter Serena, her mother said. *Always so logical. Always ruled by her head when her sister is always ruled by her heart. Cole is yours in the most fundamental of ways, Serena. Enjoy him and let your fears go. He loves you.*

Is that why you told Morgan I was supposed to keep him?

We knew that Cole had been your companion through many lifetimes. He needed you to defeat the demon, as you needed him to save you from your fears and doubts and memories of the past. Together, you two fit. You'll see this is true more and more as the years pass.

I can see it now.

Good, her mother replied in a warm, loving voice. *Go to him. Love him. Allow him to love you, Serena. Know we are always here.*

Her mother's image faded from her mind's eye, and Serena floated up from the depths of consciousness she'd reached and opened her eyes. Cole stood before her.

She got to her feet and brushed off her jeans. "I thought you were sleeping."

"I was, for a little while. But I wanted to find you because I have something to say, and I feel like if I don't say it now something bad will happen and I will never get to do it." He pushed a hand through his hand. "I'm babbling."

"What's wrong, Cole?"

He walked toward her and pulled something out of his pocket. She reached out and accepted a package of bubble gum flavored lip balm. "Been carrying that around with me for a while. It's been through hell and back, uh, *literally*. I bought it at the store a couple days ago and forgot to give it to you. I saw it and thought of you."

She examined the mud-smeared container of lip balm and laughed. "Thanks, Cole. But why do I have a feeling that's not really what you're so fidgety about right now?"

He dropped to one knee on the stone and reached into his other pocket. He held up a small...ring...it looked like, made from something brown. "I can't imagine life without you. I know this is fast. I know we haven't known each other very long. But I made a promise that if I ever got back from hell, I'd do this. Serena?"

She swallowed hard. "Yes?"

"Will you marry me?"

She took the ring. "You made this for me...in hell?"

Cole stood and paced away, pushing his hand through his hair. "I knew I should've waited and bought you a diamond. I just couldn't—"

She stalked to him, turned him around, went up on her tiptoes and pulled him down to kiss her. "Of course, I will," she said against his mouth. "God, Cole. I love you so much."

He gathered her into his arms and kissed her. "I love you, too, Serena. I promise, we'll get you a non-hell produced ring, okay? You can have anything you want. Anything. Your choice."

"Aw, baby. I already have what I want."

About the Author

෨

Anya Bast writes erotic fantasy and paranormal romance. Primarily, she writes happily-ever-afters with lots of steamy sex. After all, how can you have a happily-ever-after WITHOUT lots of sex?

Anya welcomes mail from readers. You can write to her c/o Ellora's Cave Publishing at 1056 Home Ave., Akron, Ohio 44310-3502.

Also by Anya Bast

❧

Blood of an Angel
Blood of the Raven
Blood of the Rose
Autumn Pleasures: The Union
Spring Pleasures: The Transformation
Summer Pleasures: The Capture
Winter Pleasures: The Training

COMING TO A BOOKSTORE NEAR YOU!

ELLORA'S CAVE

Bestselling Authors Tour

UPDATES AVAILABLE AT

WWW.EllorasCave.com

THE
☥ ELLORA'S CAVE ☥
LIBRARY

Stay up to date with Ellora's Cave Titles in
Print with our Quarterly Catalog.

TO RECIEVE A CATALOG,
SEND AN EMAIL WITH YOUR NAME
AND MAILING ADDRESS TO:

CATALOG@ELLORASCAVE.COM

OR SEND A LETTER OR POSTCARD
WITH YOUR MAILING ADDRESS TO:

CATALOG REQUEST
c/o ELLORA'S CAVE PUBLISHING, INC.
1056 HOME AVENUE
AKRON, OHIO 44310-3502

ELLORA'S
CAVEMEN
LEGENDARY TAILS

Try an e-book for your immediate
reading pleasure or order these titles in print from

WWW.ELLORASCAVE.COM

ELLORA'S CAVE
THE BEST IN TODAY'S ROMANTICA™

Make each day more *EXCITING* With our

ELLORA'S
CAVEMEN
CALENDAR

www.EllorasCave.com

Why an electronic book?

We live in the Information Age—an exciting time in the history of human civilization in which technology rules supreme and continues to progress in leaps and bounds every minute of every hour of every day. For a multitude of reasons, more and more avid literary fans are opting to purchase e-books instead of paperbacks. The question to those not yet initiated to the world of electronic reading is simply: *why?*

1. *Price.* An electronic title at Ellora's Cave Publishing and Cerridwen Press runs anywhere from 40-75% less than the cover price of the <u>exact same title</u> in paperback format. Why? Cold mathematics. It is less expensive to publish an e-book than it is to publish a paperback, so the savings are passed along to the consumer.

2. *Space.* Running out of room to house your paperback books? That is one worry you will never have with electronic novels. For a low one-time cost, you can purchase a handheld computer designed specifically for e-reading purposes. Many e-readers are larger than the average handheld, giving you plenty of screen room. Better yet, hundreds of titles can be stored within your new library—a single microchip. (Please note that Ellora's Cave and Cerridwen Press does not endorse any specific brands. You can check our website at www.ellorascave.com or

www.cerridwenpress.com for customer recommendations we make available to new consumers.)

3. *Mobility*. Because your new library now consists of only a microchip, your entire cache of books can be taken with you wherever you go.

4. *Personal preferences are accounted for*. Are the words you are currently reading too small? Too large? Too...**ANNOYING**? Paperback books cannot be modified according to personal preferences, but e-books can.

5. *Instant gratification*. Is it the middle of the night and all the bookstores are closed? Are you tired of waiting days—sometimes weeks—for online and offline bookstores to ship the novels you bought? Ellora's Cave Publishing sells instantaneous downloads 24 hours a day, 7 days a week, 365 days a year. Our e-book delivery system is 100% automated, meaning your order is filled as soon as you pay for it.

Those are a few of the top reasons why electronic novels are displacing paperbacks for many an avid reader. As always, Ellora's Cave and Cerridwen Press welcomes your questions and comments. We invite you to email us at service@ellorascave.com, service@cerridwenpress.com or write to us directly at: 1056 Home Ave. Akron OH 44310-3502.

Discover for yourself why readers can't get enough of the multiple award-winning publisher Ellora's Cave. Whether you prefer e-books or paperbacks, be sure to visit EC on the web at www.ellorascave.com for an erotic reading experience that will leave you breathless.

www.ellorascave.com